A Feast
in the
Garden

ALSO BY GEORGE KONRÁD

The Case Worker

The City Builder

*The Intellectuals on the Road
to Class Power* (with Ivan Szelényi)

The Loser

Antipolitics

George Konrád

A Feast in the Garden

TRANSLATED FROM
THE HUNGARIAN
BY IMRE GOLDSTEIN

A Helen and Kurt Wolff Book

Harcourt Brace Jovanovich, Publishers

New York   San Diego   London

Requests for permission to make copies of any part
of the work should be mailed to: Permissions Department,
Harcourt Brace Jovanovich, Publishers, 8th Floor,
Orlando, Florida 32887.

This is a translation of *Kerti mulatság*.
It has been made possible in part through a grant
from the Wheatland Foundation, New York.
Portions of this work appeared, in slightly different form,
in the *New Yorker*, the *Paris Review*, and *Harper's Magazine*.

Library of Congress Cataloging-in-Publication Data
Konrád, György.
[Kerti mulatság. English]
A feast in the garden/George Konrád;
translated from the Hungarian by Imre Goldstein.
p.   cm.
Translation of: Kerti mulatság.
"A Helen and Kurt Wolff book."
ISBN 0-15-130548-X
I. Title.
PH3281.K7558K4713   1992
894'.51133—dc20   91-42525

Printed in the United States of America
First edition   A B C D E

Chapters

1.

In which David Kobra is introduced

Calm Ecstasy

The house is on the side of the hill, the cemetery to the right, the mental hospital to the left. The three rooms, this clearing, and the area under the fruit trees provide ample space for guests. A hundred years old, the house is made of quarry stone at the bottom, of bricks at the top. It has a wine cellar and an attic. Usually I write at this tombstone table; sometimes, when I get tired of the table, I move to the boulder from the old winepress opposite the mighty walnut tree. There are sour-cherry and walnut trees here, just as in the garden of the house in which I was born. Under the rosebush, a hedgehog makes heavy puffing sounds.

Wearing a white shirt, I sit in the sun; I'm working off the time I still have left. Consciousness peeling. What you need at the age when you no longer have needs. Here, I am surrounded by the simplest things, and I don't have to accommodate anyone. I keep my manuscripts in one closet, my clothes in another. My books are on a plank laid across two tree stumps. Water I bring from the well. In the winter I stand naked in the snow, splashing cold water on myself from the washbowl on the tombstone table.

Thinking has its own definite location; you can sense where a thought comes from. In the house a world of memories breathes inside the walls, has been absorbed by the wooden ceiling. In the afternoon light the yellow walls are very yellow, the green leaves very green, the sour cherries very red, and the plums very blue. This sloping garden is the original stage on which my visions play. The paradise of my childhood disappears, then reappears. From spring to fall the days pass slowly. From a rocky peak a glider descends, drifts in circles around the town, then suddenly the wind yanks it higher. Sheer arbitrariness; calm ecstasy; the motionless journey of a human being. If someone were to ask what sort of celebration this was, I would smile but not reply.

3

The wind has driven the bees from the blooming rosebush; a rooster crows; a plane drones overhead. You can hear people hoeing, and pigeons are perched on the rectangular cross of the Greek Orthodox church. Behind me, a whitewashed wall; before me, a stretch of lawn. Below, people appear on the narrow paths between the rows of grapevines; they settle in wicker chairs in the arbor, on the swing, and on the low tree branches; they chat quietly. The whole town has gathered around the deathbed of a medieval peasant. The saints, too, are hovering in a corner of the ceiling, and the devil is slinking about, there, under the bed. Everyone the dying man has ever known is in that room.

A cat prowls in the green nettles, stepping delicately among the yellow flowers. A swallow comes in for a low dive. The cat hears my steps, turns, casts a questioning glance at me, and then, like a prim young lady, with undulating sensuous strides, she moves on. Three of my light-blue shirts flutter peacefully on the line. I'm expecting guests this afternoon; food is cooking in a large pot. A snail is glued to a tree trunk. Crimson plums and summer apples are sprawled in the depths of the garden; I gather a bowlful, the rest I leave lying among the weeds and nettles. Here, on the hill of Ófalu, I have found my observation post, my point of departure. The end-of-summer sun lies heavy on the red tile roofs. Among the branches, twittering birds and honeyed fruit. Vanishing swallows in the dry firmament. Growing shadows among the trees, the lake cooling off. At a time like this, you think of autumn tasks and long absences.

I am writing my most hazardous book. I have been sentenced to examine myself. To dissect myself in the morgue of my own conscience. To understand without resentment, without self-justification. To describe what hurts, even if that means going beyond the permissible. Writing is a never-ending transgression and border violation. No matter how far I venture, I am still too close. No matter how salty, I am still too sweet. The more preposterous literature is, the more relevant.

What has happened to me? What in my subterranean life can be brought to the surface? My biography, I see it groping. Like a lumbering animal it drags itself through the dust, trying to find its way

4

at the crossroads. Lord, give me the grace of veracity, and enlarge my memory. My philosophy can be found in what I did; it is written on my face. To the question What is the meaning of life? each man answers with his own.

It is a day obsessed, a day of the mind's explosion, a day of illumination. In our delirium we have received an advance of the freedom granted only to suicides. Whatever I can conceive exists; afterward, nothing will. In my mind I transport myself to other places, then quickly fly back here; the airlines of the imagination have their terminal, too. This tombstone table is an airport. All points on the map are temporary, less permanent than this garden. Viewed from here, nothing is serious; wars and revolutions are funny, flickering, turn-of-the-century film images. On the paper, words. Because of the noise made by the practicing fighter planes nearby, my neighbor suspects that World War III has been going on for some time. On the hillside a sheep's bell is heard. A dog runs about on this side of the flock; the shepherd stands on the other side. Whoever happens to pass by asks what time it is.

I have to go to the city, to see Resurrection Square and visit the Crown Hotel. I'm taking a long walk today, an unpredictable, re-velatory, farewell walk. The stories of the past slide with deathly ease into the ruthless present. Details swarm in the sunny drifts of the mind. I see and remember. Trees turn green, then yellow, and then they are bare. Secondary-school graduation. I am sitting in the garden, playing host to those dear to me. Come, friends, the quick and the dead, from overseas and from the cemeteries. And if we have already managed to gather here so nicely, let's have a feast in the garden to beat all feasts.

Opposite, deep in the garden, among the glowing roses, stands the cathedral; one need only walk through the gate of saints and sinners. In imaginary alleys I trudge after dark adventures. I rush past houses I used to live in. Deathly omissions. You cannot survive the deaths of others and remain innocent. There is no moral emergency exit. By the time I grow old, my knapsack will be heavy with mud and stones. This garden could be the main square of the city; and the house could be the hotel of sins and aberrations. My parents

5

could be sitting at the far end of the tombstone table, decked out for their golden anniversary. Two beautiful, worn-out faces watching the wall above my head. On parting, with grand nonchalance, my father invites me to have supper with his cousin Arnold at the Crown Hotel. The menu: consommé, asparagus in butter, roast veal with mushrooms, and drinks, of course. At my age, this much should suffice, my father says. I have no objection, he says with no particular emphasis, if you wish to consider this supper the last one. You have always liked a good time. Here, in this little bottle, we have some powerful red wine. He suggests I taste it. I accept. My father disappears.

The message of the Great Father is ambiguous. The Eternal One wants us both to suffer and to have a proper childhood. His Law is as murderous as it is provident. The Lord, like a child, undertakes many things simultaneously and loses interest in all of them. I wanted to write the story of the Last Supper, the eve of the final departure, when the man cries tears of blood because he realizes that there is no going farther. The son is alone now. He has spoken enough in parables, washed his companions' feet; now he is holding on to the earth, not wanting to go; he is afraid. What does he know, the man who refuses to run from the catchpoles? Is it possible, Lord, that only under your silent gaze do my contortions have meaning?

I'd rather be honest than virtuous. If virtue means the approval of my contemporaries for thinking what they think, I can do without virtue. Everyone is convinced that he is moral; at the center of the great hall of our consciousness, each of us sits in blossoming perfection.

A dying old man would not see trees smaller or skies lower than I see them. Past fifty, we ask ourselves: Have these twenty thousand days any enduring significance, inherent structure, unfolding explanation? Surely time has a shape! To lead an orderly existence is to feel its taut arch from the beginning to the end.

My first kiss occurred at the entrance to a cave. I had no idea what one was supposed to say on such an occasion. To fish for trout, for the first time, in a crystal creek; to ride a horse in the mountains for the first time; to kneel beside a wounded man for the first time;

6

to lie, for the first time, on top of a naked woman. To be interrogated for the first time. Are you an anarchist? Yes, sir, I am. Anarchist, loyalist, I am everything that's forbidden. Would the description "intellectual guerrilla" fit you? Yes, sir, it would. It would be rather flattering, in fact.

Reliving the past, that is the most fantastic adventure of all. The event, relived, grows more and more enigmatic, and richer and richer in meaning. Turning to the past, I reach the future, I recall people I never knew. In the time/space continuum of consciousness, Was and Will Be occupy the same point. The mind, too, is fortified, because we have dared the watchtowers and the watchdogs. Coming back from that journey, we find the police less terrifying.

I go for my customary walk after morning tea. Horse chestnuts are thudding to the ground, splitting open on contact. I pick up one and thumb the fuzzy brown body. To a man on foot, the world is paradise itself. The wind rocks a large spider as it sits at the center of its web. Like a curled-up yellow leaf, the spider is tossed in the wind, but the web does not break. The spider waits, knowing that a fly will come. I study the spider's use of time: It is no slave of time; time is working for it.

A novelist ought to take care of himself, as a pregnant woman does. Writing, obviously, is not harmful to me, and I cause no harm to anyone by sitting in this garden. Writing turns observation into physical action: moving the pen, hitting the typewriter key. It is a handicraft; the carpenter and the beekeeper are closer to me than the factory worker and the civil servant. And I get paid for writing, which is pleasant. From the very beginning of my office days, I tried, using all sorts of subterfuge, to retire. The offices I worked in were places of incessant chatter. I would sing my aria and quickly make my exit. I was a distinguished member of the international union of shirkers, always happiest when stepping out the door of a school or office.

My workday begins early in the morning, while I'm still in bed, and it does not end when I go to sleep. It's a workday for life. The majority wants promotion; the minority, to which I belong, wants more vacation time. In the eyes of serious jobholders, our kind is suspect.

But in my eyes, it is they, the serious jobholders, who are suspect. Whatever the job, whatever the obligation, they do their duty. Strange, how it does not matter, so long as a sense of duty is involved. I have no time for administrative problems, for drafting resolutions and reports. But I do have time, toward evening, for peeling potatoes, cutting up vegetables, and pouring wine for my guests. My favorite films are the ones about prison breaks. The fugitive, to me, stands for human observation, while human accomplishment is best represented by his pursuer, his investigator, his interrogator. I always side with the mouse; the cat I trip. Sooner or later, a man like me is asked to leave the office.

Writing, actually, is reading. We authors remember the sentences as they appear before us. We pull them out of some place where they have been lying and waiting for a long time. As we walk in the desert, our feet feel a path beneath the sand. We pave our own road of pilgrimage. This book is writing itself, accommodating no imagined plot or characters; the blueprint is revealed only in retrospect.

The hero of the following stories is born in these pages. He is an extension of the author; he is, in fact, the author's nightmare, drawing his life force from the author's blood. And since he knows he is dependent on the author, he tries, out of revenge, to get the upper hand at every opportunity. Thus he will be the innocent author's tempter. His name is David Kobra. With a name like that, he could be a detective in films, but he prefers to play the criminal. He is a star only with respect to his first name. The author now informs the reader that David Kobra has come into the world; he exists; in fact, he has already outlived several other characters. Barely having made his appearance, he has the audacity to claim that the author is merely the soil from which he, the hero, has sprung. The author is Monday through Friday; Kobra is the Sabbath. The author asks: Do you observe the Sabbath, then? I observe every day of the week, the hero answers haughtily. The author remarks: One born on paper has no history, at least not yet. Almost everything that could have happened has already happened to the author, Kobra replies disparagingly, while I, with great thirst for adventure, am all discovery, I exude freshness. Then he declares: As of today the author may speak only through me. In a sense, I will be destroying him. The dragoon digs his spurs into the side of the bear he rides. I will goad this sluggish creature, pulling from his brain what I please; out of his stuff will I compose myself.

I hereby absolve the author from being the recorder of facts, of reality, says our new creation. Reality is indescribable, and publicizing your private life is boring and improper. Writing about your relatives, who themselves do not write, is not nice. Whether the company you keep is good or bad, you are not the treasurer of the gossip concerning them. That gossip may wind up as a spy's report to the head of the central archives. And if you are the only subject of the narrative, which one of your days will you tell about? Why the twenty-thousandth day, of all possible days? Even if you start now, and put everything you have into it, you won't be done with your tale by tomorrow; you'll need a year to tell the story of an hour, and the hours will accrue with enormous compounded interest. Every moment is immeasurably greater than what it leaves behind. Bare facts are fiction.

And besides, who is interested in you? To whom do you bequeath yourself? People's interest in their ancestors extends only to a few anecdotes. If I wanted to learn everything about my ancestors, I would have no time left for anything else. Be content with the knowledge that literature is but the virgin honey of lies applied with a dropper. I am neither more nor less than this text. Our advice to the author is that he should calm down, stop arguing and showing off, be a lot less conspicuous, and write his sentences with more care. David Kobra expected to be carefully written by his author.

How am I better than this fly on the paper? Its character is at least as strong as mine. My task is to be uncertain (this may be true, but then again, that may be true). Slyly I bring my palm down. The fly takes off. It can escape in a number of directions; it has several alternatives, a frightening freedom of choice. It happens to us, too, that a giant hand tries to grab us. One must flee but at the same time, darting unpredictably, return to the honey.

Around fifty, death looks you in the eye. What would you call an infinitesimal being who believes himself to be infinite? I am looking at myself as I would at a desk drawer; there is no moral in this

9

observation. The thing to do is seize your pen and prolong the game a little. There is no activity more equivocal than writing: the mind portrays itself. My reflection stares me in the face. Can I slip offstage, in the middle of the show, without being noticed? The audience is watching intently, looking at me on the lighted, empty stage. I must play myself.

A novel, it is said, must have a plot, must have action. But this is only a manuscript, I said. It is a hostile act, said my interrogator. The knight acts; the peasant does not—he only works. The husband acts, the wife does not—she only takes care of the house and raises the children. Is the writer, then, a knight, a man of action? Meek men sing of jousting. I am looking at the TV screen: a constant explosion; every minute somebody gets knocked down, bumped off; the hero of this particular show has polished off his three hundredth body. Mainly stories of hot pursuit. We like to see a little blood with our report on the prevention of crime.

Men, because they don't give birth, are more afraid of death than women. That is why they are the hunters, the soldiers, the tyrants, and the killers of tyrants. Then epic time passes, and the champion, like an old rag, is kicked off the field. Let me clear out before all of us get kicked out. Retreat into the beaver den of inner emigration. Climb a long rope ladder into your ivory tower and thumb your nose as you look back. A rainbow is growing on the dark sky; an exit. I step into another city, I pull up the ladder and the drawbridge behind me.

A middle-aged man doesn't want to die or grow old. The knife of knowledge is in his heart. He tempts himself: Maybe I can designate the house when the unexpected visitor comes. I'll go meet him, so he won't have to drag me out from under the bed. If you can't kill someone else, at least kill yourself. A man is not free if he cannot kill himself, says a Russian colleague, whose name is also K. The murderer is simpleminded; the suicide, clear-sighted. The wiser and more powerful mankind is, the more suicidal it becomes. We need the protective darkness most when the light is brightest. Conscience, the assassin, lures you to the mountaintop, then hurls you into the abyss.

When the dead start visiting you, you can be sure you have been summoned. Leave-taking is preceded by celebration, the day of rest. A cicerone for my guests, I busy myself with the past. I decide on a character, I spin a yarn, I bring him to life. What I write today belongs only to today; tomorrow's writing is tomorrow's. Why should I be wiser today than I was yesterday? The baker bakes every day, the maid cleans every day. Distance and calligraphy; we move to another city. Its main square was once called Resurrection Square; today it's Liberation Square.

Death throes and bridal anticipation. I wait here, wait for inspiration.

Nature lovers understand the language of apples, grapes, mushrooms, coffee, hemp, and poppy. When they put me into the wooden box, I will have no technology with me. The purpose of life is ecstasy, not machines, not the automobile, not growth and speed, not the homeland and authority, not the family and the church, not sanctity and art, only simple existence and its pleasures. The ecstasy of the mind may be cultivated even in solitary confinement—be it a garden or a cell. But I do not wish to equate ecstasy—which in Greek means being put out of a place, moving away—with drunkenness. Ecstasy is not wild behavior. He who rejects anxiety chooses anxiety. In ecstasy, everything is real. On your bicycle, in a gloomy twilight you hurry over water-green flatlands. After work you walk home in the drizzling rain. The shaman wears the character of the academician like a light overcoat. He has a tweed jacket on and uses a fine aftershave. He is the first to wonder at anything. His knuckles have been rapped, his mouth bloodied. Still, the shaman is a born voluptuary. He knows that sometimes man is given birth, and sometimes he is hanged. At summer's end the wild grape is hollyhock-red. The emperor rides out of his fortified castle. The wind catches the sail.

Reception
at the Crown

Sometimes from the windows of my apartment, sometimes from those of the Crown café, I look out on Liberation Square. It's a portable space, this city square; I can take it with me anywhere. It is here, in the heart of Central Europe, that I bring everything I have coveted in other cities. Gingerly we collect pieces of reality, careful not to bruise them. I love this square. I am infected by it; its story and mine are nearly identical. Should a wall be erected down the middle of it, I would most certainly wind up hanging around its eastern, more neglected half. I would have lots of stories to tell about the difficulty of climbing across to the other side. There are parades here on red-letter days, when history parodies itself and the spirit of the place turns lewd. I look over at the cathedral. It is Easter eve; the candles pass from hand to hand, from soul to soul, following the temporary, liturgical death.

I step out of my home and traverse the forest of the streets. In my raincoat I roam the city like a ranger. I want to be familiar with every street name, every courtyard, every alley. In libraries I read old newspapers, muse over old photographs neatly collected in boxes and arranged by street. I chat with old people on the promenade, with cordial butchers, misanthropic anglers, and numerous old ladies gossiping over their coffee. Not even the mayor has knocked around these sooty, tough streets as much as I have. Through the winding promenade I reach the main square and run into acquaintances; encounters are frequent here. Six streets fan out from the elongated square, each with its own purpose. Agora and labyrinth.

For purely formalistic reasons, I need this urban background. It is better to stay within the proscenium arch of this stage, and not spread out too much, on avenues and boulevards, into shoreless spaces. Thoroughness demands limits, discipline. Let us remain on the square; on it I will change my scenery, my sets. There will be crowd scenes, popular uprisings, military occupations, and holiday festivities on the square. The fancy ball of the smart set; the plebeian carousal; the grunting swine, gaggling geese, and bellowing cows in the marketplace. A marching band, the drum major swinging high his baton and a donkey towing the drum. I look around. I feel at home in this city. With its rugged intimacy, limited traffic, passable wines, and shrill voices, it is a catalog of state-socialism suppressions, a dream-island country, a hiding place as well as a stage; it is my own portrait. Since this is to be an urban novel, I must be proficient in Budapest, I must revel in its gossip, its private and public insanities, its love life, underworld, and petty political mysteries. Let us treat each aspect of the city as if we had come across a new species of plant or discovered in our telescope a new star.

I frequent the red-brick courthouse as I do the theater; I like to ruminate over crime. I would love to eat my way through the entire penal code, as through the menu of a good restaurant. I am intrigued most by murder trials, with jealousy as the motive. The scandal is always stunning when ordinary lies unravel and the silent one, finally, speaks his mind, perhaps with a knife. I watch the noose tighten around the necks of my fellow defendants. In hospitals I stop by the intensive-care unit and suffer with the dying as they labor for their next breath.

I am sitting in the ground-floor café of the Crown Hotel, whose windows give on the square. I lean back on the overstuffed velvet couch by the window. There is a silver teapot on the pale-red marble table. Not wanting to greet anyone, I sit at my table pretending to be an abstracted madman. The more harmless they think me, the better. Before me, paper and pen, reckless calligraphy. Here I am, *écrivain public*, ready to be dictated to. The lighting is adequate, and my nook is fairly protected. I couldn't have asked for a better observation point than the café's window. In a profuse assortment, pedestrians strut about, splendid and sanguine targets passing in review. This is the most highly charged spot of the city. Celebrities often drop in—a glass of white wine, a lean veal cutlet, no dessert, just coffee—and practice the art of babbling over their business lunch. Out of woodbine arbors and abundant gardens, old men come into this buzzing café to smell cigar smoke. Some of the guests wave in my direction, signaling that they are here to see me off. They laugh and chatter supportively, wave amiably to one another. Rounds of handshakes. It is a September carnival, a vintage merrymaking, a farewell-to-summer celebration, the Feast of Tabernacles. All the outdoor restaurants are open, and in the roof garden the Ecstasy Bar is in full operation. The woman serving the coffee is an elderly baroness who has heard so many things in her life that for her the guests are like field flowers.

Kobra lives temporarily in his permanent residence, a transient guest in his own city. It is a remarkable experience to be an outsider here, inside the womb. He sits leisurely at his table, with no business to attend to. The greater the resignation, the greater the tranquillity. The guardian of common sense sits at his table and offers advice: Weigh carefully what you do. Give up dramatic gestures. You're on the right path now; you no longer laugh too hard, you've grown serious. Hem and haw politely, avoid giving yourself away, and don't sign petitions. Don't jeopardize your life's work by making unguarded statements. A comfortable retirement awaits you here. You can look forward to an uneventful old age, handsome prizes, and a fine eulogy delivered at your state funeral.

Kobra replies to this by saying: Noble friend, you are no voyeur and I am no exhibitionist. It is your prerogative to indict me, to give the table of contents of my sins of omission. Of the immeasurably larger part of the world I know nothing; my ignorance is to the nth power. The well-kept part of my garden is small; the part overgrown is enormous. By the time I am old, my entire conscience will be choked with weeds. Still, if occasionally I find a finely veined pebble in the sand, I will hold it up and show it to others: See what I have! True, that's foolish. Instead, I should put the pebble in my pocket and keep my mouth shut.

Complying with the guests' wishes, all the events that have ever taken place here are now summoned and gathered, because the past is no less real than the present. The curtains part, and on a lighted stage heads emerge from yesterday and pass slowly by my window. Even widows on their way to church have a voracious hunger for life. An ancient pair of lovers meet while tending the graves of their respective spouses. No matter the gray hair, no matter the wrinkles, still and forever, even beyond the grave, you are my one and only.

A hotel attendant leads you to the room reserved for you. It is a suite of rooms, really, with red plush curtains, a gilded night table, white angels at either side of a mirror so huge that it forms a canopy over the bed. The walnut wardrobe exudes lavender. In the bathroom you find an old-fashioned sunken tub and white marble floor tiles. Hot water gushes freely from the wide-throated brass faucet.

Since it is a ball you have come to, you may pick your seducer for the night. You don't yet know whom you will adore, but you will adore someone. Have no fear, though; at dawn you will return to your faithful spouse. In every year there is one night when everything is brand new. On the stage of the Ecstasy Bar our thoughts are made visible—holographically, not by magic, since we have burned all the witches and sorcerers. Guest, get to know your host. Make familiar use of his mind, take up residence in it. You are walking among the figures of an animated wax museum, soft as a shadow among them, who fill the square and the hotel. But here comes the manager to announce that as of now the café will be open twenty-four hours a day, just as it used to be, back in the halcyon times at the turn of the century. At these good tidings our esteemed guests want to share a glass of champagne with you. The band, mostly Jewish and Gypsy musicians, strikes up the anthem of the city's most illustrious hotel. Everyone stands, glasses clink, and in the crepuscular intoxication teardrop frost gathers on the glass of noble imaginations.

On this square I meet my friends. This is where we congregate whenever anything happens. National assemblies, revolutions, auto-da-fés. I can smell the odor of sinners sizzling at the stake. Dethronement and the proclamation of the republic are also memories worth probing. Passionate people fill the hotel rooms with their debates, carbines hang on the coatracks, and there is no time to change the sheets; the newcomer has to sleep on dried semen. The pavement here knows not only the caressing tread of rubber-wheeled carriages and elegant automobiles; it has also learned to creak under tanks, or to heat up when they burst into flame because a schoolboy threw a Molotov cocktail, using a brandy bottle, a wick, and a pierced cork to turn the soldiers inside into shrunken charcoal puppets.

I call on the statue of our national poet to come and recite for us a fiery, democratic, and patriotic poem. There sits the poet, pen in hand, recoiling from the vision of his nation in putrefaction, blood, and fire. Dramas of love and horror. Since I, too, have a penchant for the guignol and the baroque, I am afraid I might cram this novel too full of the square. Even if I sink back five hundred years, I would still be standing here and telling how the burghers of Buda cursed and denounced the pope. Or go further back in time and be a chronicler of our conquering ancestors, who loved the sun, the rivers, wild horses and women running in meadows, the speeding arrow and the tents. Poor, truculent ancestors, they did not understand why they should bend their knees before a dead man on a cross. The obtuse and the obstinate were broken on the wheel.

The square's most prominent structure is the cathedral. The courthouse ranks second, the theater third, and the hotel fourth. Traditionally, the cathedral and the courthouse disapprove of the theater and the hotel. Humility and state ideology stand together: Let the purveyors of ecstasy do penance. Whoever does not comply with history will pay dearly. The wise pagans, however, learned to disguise themselves. In the Middle Ages, Resurrection Square was the name of this place. In the baroque period, it was called Bomb Square. But, of course, in every age it was a marketplace, too. In Turkish times, it became the sultan's carpet, the square of the burning stake, the pillory, and the scaffold. Here hung the exemplary corpses, like fingers admonishing the city's populace, which was always prone to backsliding. On this spot, a half millennium ago, there stood a monastery in whose tavern monks served wine to transient knights, merchants, and inquisitors.

The local Jacobins were beheaded here, their bodies buried in great secrecy. The mass grave, however, was finally discovered. Most mass graves are. We look in and see the police spy cum leader of the conspiracy. We see him erect, at his full height, before he collapses and like a bundle of rags is dragged to the block. His long hair is pulled back, his impressive head, held by its beard, is raised and displayed. A neat little snip freed the head from its ballast, the heavy heart; a heart made ponderous by the great conspirator's gluttony and intemperance; a heart that had wanted to do so much with the king, for the king, and against the king.

I forgot to mention that the hotel also served as headquarters for the general staff of the occupying forces. Whenever friendly persuasion proved inadequate, the hotel could also be turned into a torture chamber. And at several different times friendly persuasion did prove to be inadequate. At one point the security police had its headquarters in the Crown Hotel. In the hall of mirrors, officers would listen to a thin little man repeat in a thin little voice: Hit, hit, you must hit! A fist is not a fist if it does not hit! But that was long ago, and maybe it wasn't even true. Those officers have since become well-mannered, pleasant old gentlemen. And we, too—do we not?—have the good sense to have learned this lesson from history: Get your house, your garden, your steak, and your brandy. We are busy building for ourselves, for our children, for our brothers, for our friends. No longer a nation of horsemen, but, rather, of bricklayers and nest builders, with mustaches, biceps, and potbellies.

Asceticism? All I need, in the end, is a white shirt and two flat stones for my eyelids. I will not keep this present shape long. Blow away my flesh, black wind, let my bones shine through. With visas and passports in my pocket, two packed suitcases waiting in the hallway, I have lowered the blinds in my room. On tomorrow morning's train I have reserved a seat. I close the door behind me.

But the unexpected, just as you would expect, happens. The rabble rises in revolt, the have-nots demonstrate, and so do factory workers and bearded professors. Three-year-olds pluck the bouquets from their mothers' hands and in the burning blue smoke of tear gas fashion flower crosses. Shields, clubs, white helmets, whistles blowing; brass-knuckled young men pluck a girl out of the crowd, then grab her boyfriend, too, and drag them both into a car. The square has emptied.

In the Crown café you must be cautious with those bejeweled, glittering women. They vie with one another in secrets, memories, letters, and lies. With good taste they wage war, lady against lady. The decades go by, and still they sit in their hats and silk scarves and eat chocolate cake with whipped cream. They have permanently reserved tables here. They went to school together, lured lovers away from one another, became widows, and buried their suicide sons. They have trouble with their digestion, gold teeth in their mouths, and a weatherbeaten, roguish wisdom in their eyes. Mornings, they do laps together in the swimming pool, body beside body, while reporting on the previous day's menu and discussing their diets. This one's cleaning woman is an absolute angel, that one's is a thieving beast. When a woman enters the café, she is subjected to a lightning scrutiny from her shoes to her gloves. Darling, wherever did you get that sweet (awful) blouse? It's pure silk, you say? There are some synthetic threads in it, I think. I have a new masseur; how do you like that? With hands like Franz Liszt. Under them, I am an old piano born anew. I dreamed about my dear departed. He kept calling me: This way, my sweet, to eternal bliss. But I told him: With that eternal bliss of yours, my own, you can wait for me a little longer. They tell outrageous lies, those sweet, fragrant, pastry-eating, youthful grandmothers.

On the brass-inlaid mahogany fireplace mantel, two mischievous bronze angels are holding up a globe. A half century ago I stood on a chair to stroke their cool thighs. They whispered to me: We'll hold this for a little while longer, then smash it to the ground. Now, I begged them, do it now! And then we'll roll it around the square. If we do, the angels whispered back, there will be no square. There will be nothing left but us angels without a load to carry. I put some crumpets before their feet to induce them to stay. They are still here, and so am I, and so are the Venetian chandeliers with their impenetrable branches and crystal pendants like glass skulls. And this table, too, with legs made of twin brass rods that terminate in cloven hoofs. If the table galloped off, it would take with it the almond crescents and the walnut buns belonging to the five gray-haired ladies, and they, in turn, would follow the table, their scented custom-made jackets light on their shoulders, out onto the main square. The ladies, with their hair cut boyishly short in the back, must have no difficulty with propriety. If you must go, well, you must go. The globe may roll out of the angels' hands and the table may gallop off, but they will stand erect, with gloved hands holding one another's elbows, and pretend not to notice, not even when they are rudely counted and led to the banks of the Danube and stripped and forced to stand barefoot at the edge until they are pushed into the water by a bullet in the back of the neck.

Stepping through the familiar main entrance, I notice on the second floor's indoor balcony the same fat woman who has been sweeping here since time immemorial. She knows everything that goes on in the building, even things that never happened. The dirty-green staircase is full of children's graffiti. A man, carrying a shopping bag, complains that the elevator has been making unpleasant noises for days. Lunch box in hand, a tall, retired engineer is on his way to the local soup kitchen, where food is cheaper and more substantial. On this subject he can talk at great length. The volunteer policeman, who long ago followed suspicious automobiles, is now widowed; he walks up and down the stairs, his mustache drooping, unable to find his place. On the third floor, the retired prison warden's grandchildren have come to visit him. They don't come every week, and when they don't, he stands on the balcony, not knowing what to do with himself. Several people have leaped over the railing of the seventh-floor rear balcony, to the concrete courtyard below. On such occasions the housekeeper is furious: Why must they come here to spatter their blood over everything, and after I mopped? On the fourth floor, the saxophonist leans out the window and sends a doleful note into the courtyard. The carpenter, who never bothered to use his ground-floor workshop, has now finally become extinct. His place has been taken over by a deaf-mute craftsman who makes Christmas decorations. The mysterious woman on the seventh floor lost her canary. And who else could have swallowed it if not the one-eyed watchmaker's tomcat, whose face is just as sly, cruel, and sensual as that of his master?

In this cavern of a building, surrounded by the memories of his buried family, Kobra looks at himself as if at a stranger or a figurine on a church-tower clock. He slips into strange rooms, he floats around the building, wanders from apartment to apartment, where beds smell of people, and bombings and occupations are no more than brief interruptions. The tanks are always followed by the milk carts and the garbage trucks: an oppressive permanence. This building digests everything—children, loneliness, marasmus. Women slink out of their apartments and into others. Lovemaking is better on deathbeds.

In the large apartment, the heavy furniture looks back at him with shabby dignity. As if the owner had gone away, and they, old butlers, were waiting for his return but could manage without him. The lines are emerging slowly on the white paper, the words tentative. Stand up! You will be questioned as a witness in your own case. Get out of your armchair. On the tapestry of the back of the chair, a hermit and an angel are conversing on the shore of a lake.

Who Is Expected?

In figure eights the lights are chasing around the roof of the hotel; weather vanes are spinning, the big bell is pealing. In the bar, a long-limbed, red-tailed devil plays the drums. On the screen of a video game, a motorist repeatedly crashes into exploding bursts of light. On the Day of Atonement, Regina darling, come to Resurrection Square.

Pigeons mark time on the red-basalt pavement; above the square, kites and Chinese lanterns flutter. A full moon hangs over the cathedral; dangerous feminine forces are on the rise. At sundown, grimacing enigmatically, the shamans murmur their incantations. Saturday night is approaching; a southern wind whips the Danube; right now we are at the pitch of lunacy; the hangover will start tomorrow.

Soft piano music, the drums brushed. Manly words buzzing around us, horsemen of the East seated on the barstools. Builders, realists, tough guys, closet sentimentalists. Do you see that delicate old gentleman? Would you have thought that he is a dealer in opium? I notice a bewitching female bottom as it slips onto one of the stools: alone, a mysterious silver pine in the corner of the snowy garden. When you first enter, the bar seems dreary, but after a while the arches and walls begin to glimmer with rosy hues.

The cathedral has a Gothic chapel and a Romanian crypt. Both were riddled with bullets, burned down, and rebuilt several times. In the sixties, a friend of mine did the renovation. He hated churches, was more interested in architectural utopias, but his hands and eyes did a fine job.

This morning the Rosicrucians, each holding a single rose, held a demonstration on the square. Would you like a Bloody Thursday? Then came the human-rights protesters, each holding a single lily of the valley. Some dandies, standing on the sidewalk, spat at them: Ah, leftists! This square lends itself extravagantly to revolutionary-romantic scenes. I have had occasion to run across it with a stretcher, toward friends cut down by machine-gun fire. I have seen prisoners led through it, a large column accompanied by a small number of armed guards. Those who have never been led away with only the shirts on their backs have much to learn. Like prisoners on leave, we keep returning to this square in Pestbuda.

The metalworkers are marching in neat formations on the square. From a side street, helmeted and masked troublemakers charge in with iron clubs and smash the windows of the well-insured department store.

Dark suits and evening gowns; an outdoor concert in the courtyard of the neoclassic house of law. In the purple sky above the music, a dreamy glass moon. Against red background lighting, the hanged man, upside down, appears and speaks in a voice of arrogance, rejection, and merciless truth. Meanwhile, the opposition is preparing a party in the art-nouveau building at the corner. At the gate, threatening leather-coated figures turn up their collars. Quickly I produce a wig from my breast pocket and, wearing my lunatic bird face, spin about, screeching: You may still leave, ladies and gentlemen. We'll return your admission fees. But you have only a few minutes to get away. So you won't move, eh? All right, then, we'll keep an eye on one another.

If you have no courage for a duel of the eyes, go see Aladár. He sits among his monkeys, munching on nuts and keeping his Afghan black and Lebanon red in the drawer of an ornamental chest. The place is as hot as a greenhouse. He will not fail to offer you a taste, through the long bamboo pipe, and let you inhale. But lo, here he comes, wearing pink glasses and a pointed hat. He has some stuff from Thailand. He apologizes for being late. Don't worry, Aladár, here you cannot be late; when it comes to waiting, I am a professional. You've come just in time; there'll be entertainment here tonight. We'll bury the devil in the pavement. At the end of the summer, we cling to our friends; maybe we can keep one another steady in the autumn winds.

For a meeting place, ladies and gentlemen, I can recommend nothing better than the Crown Hotel. We are roving Hungarians, wandering Jews in foreign cities, who with unflagging passion keep looking for the right place. Almost any place is suitable, but there is always a place more suitable. Ladies and gentlemen, you are standing here, on Liberation Square, in the full fallibility of your historical happenstance. Those about to check your papers are circling around you. You shut your eyes, not wanting to look, then open them again: The checkers are still circling, around and around.

The square has been a mock courtroom, too, for rehearsing mock trials, so the accused won't balk at regurgitating the memorized words of confession. Yes, he has learned by heart the ugly and unbelievable fabrications, because cake served on a plate is better than salt stuffed into his chops. But if something happens during the proceedings, if the flame of rebellion has not been utterly extinguished, and the accused departs from the script dictated to him, those sitting on the bench will break into laughter; and then you will wish that your mother had never brought you into this pestilential world. Only when you have puked your guts out will your soul be permitted to leave your body. Or perhaps you'll live, an esteemed and fun-loving guest, and find yourself in a hospital, where on short-legged beds the sick lie motionless, their mouths open. Yes, you recognize your former self lying on one of these beds. But you can fly from here, too, destination unknown. The plane lands at night, in the rain; there is no bus, no terminal, and there is no passport control or customs inspection. There is only the cold. The plane takes off, leaving you alone on the wet tarmac.

Crystal chandelier, crystal ashtray, Gobelin tapestry of black women squatting before a pith-helmeted guest, offering him coffee. I ask for vodka, coffee, and mineral water. As always, in this thrilling twilight, the same old couple sits at the next table. Over a bottle of wine they sit and smoke their cigarettes; they are taciturn and serious. The old-fashioned tunes reach our hearts. Look at the silver-haired pianist with the checked jacket: a large sharp nose, bitter chin, gray toothbrush eyebrows. We talk about—what else?—fornication. Last night I dreamed of a curly red-haired dancer. She brought me brandy and sliced tomatoes.

"Happiness is the natural state of life," declares the woman serving the coffee, the baroness Rosamunda. "Turn on all the chandeliers, sisters, in every room of the hotel. I have this message for the gentleman behind the column: Ahmed always smiles when he sees the caliph frown. And you, Master Kobra, a man of learning who has leaned on the bars of many a pub, give thought to the body, and body to the thought—that is my request for you. Do not neglect the body. We have tasted, haven't we, you and I, the difference between good and bad, man and woman? There was a time when you were all body and didn't need to be asked twice to stop up any orifice that offered itself to you in the rooms of this hotel. You went from one tryst to another, sniffing the female scent like a tireless hound. Now you commit your sins more in words than deeds, and this, coming from me, a buxom baroness importuned these days only by Father Time, is not praise."

"You ask me what I love, Baroness? I love orange blossoms, gotu cola, and Chinese ephedra. White brandy and barley whiskey, green tea and green tobacco, Burgundy and Riesling wines. But at the moment I'd like a good strong beef broth," Kobra answers evasively. "Tell me, Professor, what is the meaning of life beyond life?" asks the baroness Rosamunda, the coffee lady. "Madam, be content with the knowledge that God is not in the whole but only in the parts." "I've heard it differently, sir—that the devil is in the parts. What should I say to those short-necked gentlemen there, behind that column, who are inquiring about our guests? Should I tell them that the other day Mr. Gyula put away two bottles of champagne, and—horrors!—devoured thirteen pieces of chocolate cake? May his gall bladder ache! Should I reveal all this to the short-necked gentlemen? Or should I be a martyr, refusing to confess, saying instead: The moment I set eyes on you, Officer, I fell into a state of amnesia. Or tell them that Mr. Gyula flew out the window along with his armchair, in which he had just made an unforgettable pun, and over the Danube, hovering above the bridges, he read a German book about the latest philosophical implications of physics? I gave the short-necked one an aphorism, as a present: He who wants what is outside is an insider; he who wants what is inside is an outsider. Good, isn't it?" "Excellent," says Kobra. "Then he began to woo me, because breasts like these he sees maybe once every leap year. He couldn't take his eyes off them. But what about us, Professor; how long has it been since we shared a room? In the old, carefree days it was possible to exchange ideas in the bushes or on top of potato sacks. Now we make do with philosophy and have to listen to the speeches of charlatans. Either self-annihilation or ecstasy, here at the Ecstasy Bar! Would you like another glass, Professor? I see you've sold your soul to the devil. That writing has taken hold of you like a brain tumor. All you do now is bang on your typewriter during the day and drink in the evening here. What about that powerful third thing, sweetheart? What happened to fornication?"

Kobra makes excuses. In the afternoon, when he stops working, he is happy just to be alive. He and Regina eat something, if she is back from the library by then. Maybe they go for a walk; or Kobra goes by himself. Not cut out for anything that would further the common good, he spends his summers and winters dawdling. As Pascal says, the source of most problems is the fact that men cannot stay put at their own tables.

The pianist Zeno describes his relation to the Crown, saying he is so comfortable there that he will not leave it, except when he leaves for the cemetery. During the day he is a psychiatrist, at night a pianist in the bar. Nothing, he says, is more reliable than the old songs. Remember "On the Side Street"? And the words: "Each night I come to you, I do; on the side street, my dreams bring me to you." Zeno says, "I find, and maybe you do, too, that the ratio of strangers to acquaintances is just right. You can guess who the stranger is by noticing who he says hello to. In your room, Mr. Kobra, you are always alone, but here, in the Crown, there is that gentleman in the corner, for example, with his clipped mustache, two dark lines above his lips. How long a stretch do you think he did, and why?"

Kobra now astonishes Zeno: "Exactly ten years, for killing his wife." "Bull's-eye. So you know him? I helped Norbert Virág murder his wife—by taking pity on him, taking him under my wing when they hurt him. He was released by the authorities, and the very next day carved up his young wife. You can find corpses around the most humanitarian soul. Mr. Virág drinks only absinthe." Zeno stops playing the piano. "He's probably killed others, not just his wife, and will probably kill more. He wants to be evil, you see. He is not reckless or hotheaded; on the contrary, he is quite reasonable. At the moment he is confining himself to small crimes, but preparing for something big. When he dismembered his wife, I declared him insane; that's why they didn't hang him. The two of us, Mr. Kobra, you and I, with our bleeding hearts, are patrons not only of Norbert Virág but also of crime itself. Mr. Virág, too, is a human being. He fears death and in women hates to see the process of aging. Nowadays he seduces only young girls.

"But don't think," the psychiatrist-pianist continues, "that Mr. Virág is satisfied with necrophilia alone. He is also a professional stool pigeon who loves to ruin people. Betrayal is his greatest pleasure. If he had a mother, he would love nothing better than to inform on her. I don't know why he chopped his wife into exactly thirty-three pieces and put them into a suitcase, which he took up to Freedom Mountain and left in the snow. A little old couple were watching from the window of their quaint little house. On the third day, curiosity got the better of them, and they looked inside the suitcase, and the old woman went into hysterics.

"Mr. Virág's wife was nineteen. I asked him why he killed her. 'She was getting crow's-feet,' he said, 'and had bad breath. There was nothing interesting about her as a person, and she did not seem capable of further development.' 'But if you have such high standards, why did you lock those retarded schoolgirls in your attic?' I asked naïvely. Or why, for that matter, did he like to be urinated on while lying in a bathtub? 'You don't know much about love, do you?' he said, then knelt down on the rug and clasped his hands. 'Kick me in the face, kick my teeth out!' he shouted. I did not comply. 'Why are you clowning?' He said to me: 'Do you know what's so beautiful about a crime consciously committed? It's irredeemable.'

"Mr. Virág rarely reveals himself like that. He is good at dissembling. A cunning man, he would have no problem delivering a sermon in a church or sports arena. It would be a stirring sermon, and the audience would have no idea that he was a fiend. His curious odor is now wafting this way from the corner of the bar: devil's fart and muskrat. You, on the other hand, *lieber* Kobra, have lately been exuding lily-white virtues.

"I administered shock treatment three times today," the pianist goes on. "I know this bothers you. Man is like a transistor radio. It suddenly falls silent, you give it a good shake, and it works again. People need to be shaken up. That's why they long for old-fashioned wars. That's why they clobber each other wherever they can. That's why they get excited over mass disasters. Here, with these old tunes, I scratch their soft underbelly a little. Let their appetite for villainy grow. Without villainy there is no theater, there is only heaven, the home of absolute kindness. Angels are kind to the point of cruelty. What I'm trying to do with my patients is keep their souls in balance."

Regina and I are not ready to run to a bedroom and tear the clothes off each other. We are still splashing decorously about in the pool of civilization. We insist that the world be just as we know it to be. But the wish that it be different is already lurking within us; let it pounce on us like a tiger, let it snatch us up like a tornado.

Regina moves her right leg from side to side while flashing her coal-black eyes at me. She would appreciate a few compliments regarding her elegant caramel-colored calfskin shoes. She is aware that in this room absolutely nobody has legs of such splendid length and curvature. She is leaving now because she does not care for the smoke. Her swan neck is encircled by blue fox and by melancholy.

Yesterday I saw an accident. I was standing on the Buda side of the Danube on Dezső Szilágyi Square by that pseudo-Gothic Protestant church with its mosaic-tiled tower and brick walls. For no apparent reason, a car on the lower road suddenly changed lanes and crashed into an enormous orange garbage truck. There were two people in the car. The truck driver was unharmed, but the driver of the car, caught in its twisted frame, could not be pulled out. I stood above them, looking down as if watching a play. The passenger in the car was removed by ambulance, but there seemed to be no way to free the driver. I could see his chest; he was still breathing. Sirens, fire trucks, cranes, police stopping traffic, drizzling rain. Two firemen with an iron pipe ineptly tried to pry the victim free. Finally, the solution was raised to a higher technical level: two cranes pulling the wreck in opposite directions. The doors were ripped away. The man was still breathing when at last they put him on the stretcher. But the ambulance did not leave. A gentle rain washed the tire tracks as the body was put back on the pavement and covered with brown wrapping paper. Within minutes, black-clad undertakers arrived on the scene.

Since man knows he is mortal, he has every reason to hurry; and since he knows that his death is a certainty, he has no reason to hurry. In closets and on shelves, the sad mass of never-used objects is accumulating. I like books in which you can pause after every sentence. Speed reader: He's read the Bible in a week. At a certain point, reading and writing become an exercise in yoga. We withdraw from the city square, from the garden, into our room. Under yellow lamplight, a comprehensive survey is being prepared with the steadiness of breathing.

A block away, a young man has stolen a car. He would not stop when pursued; they shot him dead. They kill because they're in a hurry.

On his unicycle, a serene Chinese has been riding around the square for hours. A man my age now hangs his tape recorder on a tree and with graceful leisureliness and humor breaks into a roller-skating dance.

We have a date with a certain bejeweled, fur-coated woman. We'd like her to step out of a conservative British motorcar. She'll have two little lapdogs; her legs will be perfection. Every item of her attire will have been smilingly selected. She might be wearing glasses. But even without fur coat, jewels, car, and lapdogs, she is the one we are expecting.

A Soft Crystal

Introduction to inner space. Seven trellised arks surround the calf-faced idol. Its hands stretch forward, as if reaching for the gifts offered to it. For those sacrificing a bird, the first ark opens up, and the sacrifice must be placed inside it. The sacrifice of a lamb will unlock the second ark; a goat will open the third, a calf the fourth, a heifer the fifth, and a bull the sixth. But he who is willing to sacrifice his child will have all the arks open before him, and he may enter and kiss the idol. Then the idol is stoked until its hands glow white hot. The priests place the child in those hands, and drums beat with an earsplitting din to prevent people from hearing the screams of the father and the child. Wait, bring the bird, we don't have to start with the child. "Are you bringing the child?" the idol asks, his eyes closed. Never! You'll never get him. And I don't need an angel to stay my hand. You are getting enough as it is. I am neither pious nor rebellious. The Lord can do no worse to me than kill me. Everybody's time will come; everybody has his gate to pass through.

There are brief periods during which we see things clearly; these are the mystical hours. As many religions exist as individuals. Everyone can qualify and be initiated, the indolent as well as the alert. The shiftless, too, may be enlightened. Metaphysics must be preserved. In an age when total destruction is possible, neglecting the idea of God may result in total destruction. Carelessness in weltanschauung leads to extermination camps and mushroom clouds.

Being a citizen of a military alliance, I have hydrogen bombs. When others say WE, it is in my name. The WE-people everywhere speak to me about the common good. If I ask who the common good is good for, I am considered an evil mind, a serpent. The serpent hisses: a reign of error. Are you nodding? Are you silent? Even if you are silent, you are not innocent. You are responsible for what you say and for what you do not say. There is no such thing as silent power. Power talks. And talk is power. On the day we became capable of annihilating ourselves, foolish talk became extremely dangerous.

One kind of censorship is to separate, with a long face, art and science. The artist is chased to the playground of frivolity. They buy jokes from him, they smile at him, they put up with him. Knowledge that does not speak in the language of academies, politicians, and the church is not knowledge. Are you trying to be a good sport, according to their standards? It will not work; some part of you, either your imagination or your sense of humor, will slip out of the role of jester.

You may look at things without allowing for a hierarchy of heroes and deeds. We are all unique, all samples of humankind looking at each other in our failures.

I must make good decisions. With a bad decision I can destroy myself. I do not need a mediator to speak to God. A crowded subway car, too, can be a temple. I am trying not to do unto others what I don't want done to me. That is the essence of the Torah; the rest is commentary.

I discipline myself by walking and regulating my breathing. I try to reduce my cravings. Out of the repetitions of my notes, themes emerge. Communication in this book will remain in that borderland between reflex, fable, and testimony, where I myself am not certain what actually has happened or how. Perhaps I merely string the words together according to my whim. We cook our supper out of whatever is in the pantry. Sentences in a dancing, zigzagging relation to one another, yet also independent. The novel is a medium rather than a genre. You put into it whatever you wish; there are no regulations, only that it should not be boring. It is a long letter to my friends, but I will try to have it published. Words need the printer's ink; otherwise they stay with me, like children grown old. I'm no miser; to have the thing published I'm willing to part with a few sentences. What remains will grow together; you won't feel the gaps. In advance, I mourn my fallen sentences; hail to the survivors.

Table lamp, teacup, ashtray, fountain pen, documents, marbles,

29

pebbles, pipes, humidors, small containers. It is in my professional interest that the world should multiply. I delight in ambiguities. I can see God as law or ephemeral nullity; an injurious illusion or a cheerful absence. If I must choose between God and literature, I choose literature. Novel writing is a rebellion against God's oneness. I write against the eternal light, but I do not forget it. Mine is an atheism that goes beyond the flesh. A man capable of ecstasy can engage even a swine in conversation. You may touch another creature. The fierce spirit of the Jews has separated God from the world. They have understood that the more inhuman the Lord, the more divine he is.

The authors of the Holy Scriptures have assured themselves a book market. They claim that they wrote the Scriptures as a means to a great end, that the text was all dictated to them, but I suspect they were not entirely free of authorial vanity. They paid attention to the power and proportions of the words, correcting and rewriting to make their texts more attractive. Author paradigms: priest or artist. The priest says: This is the word of the Lord. The artist says: These are my words. He asks nothing of the reader. No prestige of any kind is involved here. Between two paper covers, and without canonical coercion, the Father and the swine will appear anyway, not to mention the blood dripping from the knife after the gelding. I am not a placid sacrificial beast.

I am writing a novel about a fictitious novel. Wending its way through labyrinths, the face regards itself in the mirror. Who can stand the sight of himself? The human element is a pollutant, a noise, a redundancy. I have stuffed the suicides into a sack out of which I now pull finely polished stories like an endless silk scarf.

The author demonstrates what he is doing right in front of the reader. In some scenes you can turn the spit over the barbecue yourself, or pick the sturgeon out of the fish tank. A biography is like a supper containing a large number of courses. Or like a farmyard: You look around and see so many things you could pick up. Everyone has had parents and many loves. There is more material than the imagination can grasp. This book is only the table of contents of another book. It is not a novel, essay, diary, or memoir. What is it, then? A sacrificial ritual, a theater of madmen performing on an island, watched by a sober audience from the shore of the lake. The priest dancing before the temple.

I am bored with literature. It is with aversion that I read Flaubert's letters about the sanctity of art. I am tired of invented characters and invented plots. Usually I do not manage to read a novel to the end. Isn't it strange that novelists seldom read novels? So many words, so few perceptions. I lift good books from the shelf and look into them. Good Lord, what verbosity! This one here takes such a long time to imagine himself to be somebody other than who he is. Why would you want to pretend to be somebody else? One author pretends to be the chronicler of actual events, another publishes a found manuscript, and the third merely passes on to us what he heard from a stranger, a fellow passenger on a train. You could also write about the thoughts you might have if you were a banker or a whaler. At least that would have more action than this tinkering with words. In every one of my novels I have woven adventures around me. But as the years pass, we begin to consider writing about the things that seemed unworthy before. The young writer is afraid that his own small bag of goods is not a subject for literature. Today I know that my friends are more interesting than the characters in my novels. My friends have created themselves with a finer ingenuity, and through the struggle of a lifetime.

I would not like to fall to my death from the wall of a half-built house. But I would not consider fate niggardly if it gave me time for only one more book. It is never foolish to write our last novel, to love our last love. Desire and nausea, dream and nightmare, that is what every biography is about. Every moment is the time for a final accounting. Don't put it off until total infirmity. I don't want to sneak out of this earthly dwelling as if nothing had happened. Let me, instead, complete this written survey before I cross the threshold of the house of secrets. The images of the dead, and the hereafter looming before my shiny brow, flow into each other.

The self, with its own unsurpassable truth, is king in only one place: in literature. Authorial thinking begins where public thinking leaves off. It is a sign language shared by attentive readers. The text unfolds in time; each reading of it is a unique case. Writing is an experiment in homecoming. The one who is writing is my freer self;

compared to him, I am a philistine. He sheds me like an outgrown garment. What I bend, he straightens out. He is more indulgent than I am. Tipping his hat from the heights of light sleep, he looks down sardonically at my dawdling.

Literature speaks of the possibilities of literature, just as painting does of painting and music does of music. What you see here is an endlessly teeming mind facing the finiteness of a book. Literature is not only words, but also the silence between them.

I would like to have written this book in one sitting, without once reaching back; to have written continuously; with one unrestrained gesture to have given the whole work its overarching structure; to have made a statement that would stand the test of time. But, in the end, that is not what I have done. I have been more interested in seeing how far apart two points of view can be, how the subject can be shifted, altered imperceptibly, from sentence to sentence. Let the reader get up and look out the window between sentences. Let each sentence stand on its own two feet without the support of the surrounding text. And let us not have the same person speak all the time. When one character speaks, the irony is in the voice; when several characters speak, the irony is in the structure, which is a mobile, a dancing architecture, a reiterative, rotating mechanism, a trance of yearning, an organic, soft, self-programming crystal. Magic must have structure. Without it, our attention is scattered, as the evening breeze sways the garden lamp hanging on a wire.

The Ram's Horn Is Sounded

As a young man I associated death with the image of villains trying to kill me. In 1944 a machine gun was pointed at me; in 1965 I slung one over my shoulder, preferring to be shot in an exchange of fire than by a firing squad. Fear teaches you about death. Paranoia can be a delusion; it can also be a source of wisdom. Out of two hundred of my schoolmates, only seven of us survived. One hundred and ninety-three were gassed by the Germans and their vassals of this region. My schoolmates were rounded up, put into the ghetto, and then packed into deportation trains by the Hungarian police. At the border of the Hungarian Kingdom and the German Empire they were turned over, in exchange for properly filled-out receipts, to the Waffen SS.

The old as well as the young had to go. Not one should escape. Nothing less than total extinction would do. And what did our Eternal Father have to say on the subject? If he had no part in this, then what did he have a part in? Was he looking at life as you look at a newsreel? Was he shaking his head, and then wondering whether the survivors still loved him? And what did Jesus do about Hitler, Himmler, and the Waffen SS? Turn the other cheek? And what did the pope do, and the Allies, and the Jews? God and man, old and young, wise and foolish, this race and that religion—who did not take part in this obscenity?

I live somewhat to the west of the Eastern self-renouncers. Around here we are not so ready to say that everything is fine the way it is. We do not leave the burden of thinking to the ruler. We are negligent in loyalty, slow to excommunicate those guilty of high treason. Still, we live according to the customs of the court: In a kingdom, we are republicans. In the East, the empire is important, for there is only one. People are as numerous as the leaves on a tree. We, however, are not so numerous. We know how to mourn one another. My experiences tell me that there is only one of each of us. There is no empire, no government, whose death I would mourn.

In the Western world of self-love, death is but a malfunction, not the conclusion of a story. The cemeteries are sensible and economical. But the more sensible the cemetery, the more senseless death. If I am alpha and omega, then how could I possibly end? But since it seems I will end, perhaps I am not alpha and omega, after all. In the Western world of self-love, the love of your fellow man is not sensible. It's enough to smile at your neighbor. Some people, throughout their lives, smile at everyone but love no one. I am neither

Easterner nor Westerner. Here, in the middle, I think, life is a drawn-out suicide. Some do it sooner, some later, some more timidly, some more daringly, but we are all suicides. Each morning I stare into my impending death as I do into my shaving mirror.

I see my old-man's mouth as I lie gasping on a hospital bed. My imagination has leafed through the picture books of natural and violent deaths. I am not quite there yet, I tell myself. The chess player still has a good position, but he knows the game cannot be won. Last night a restlessness came over me, and I looked into the closets, in front of which you always stand alone. I sat down, feeling dizzy. I held on to my desk; everything else was moving. My eyesight is getting worse, my back is stooped, calluses are growing on my right thumb. My literature teacher raised his hooked finger: Please do not obscure event with opinion.

They say that at the moment of our demise we project the movie of our life before the divine judge. Agony and the hereafter are for later; right now we need entertainment. The library of memories is neither the truth nor a pack of lies; it is a fable; the dance of unreliable fingers on a switchboard; a random walk. Metaphysics, ethics, and gallows humor do not help. There is no cheerful deliverance, and at the gate instruments of torture are waiting. The best place is here, the best time is now.

I don't know if I'm heading in the right direction, but I won't shift the blame to anyone else. Neither my mother nor my father can serve as an explanation for the choices I make. I do what I do. And you do what you do. Although there are a thousand determining factors, I alone meet my challenges. There is freedom of the will and personal responsibility even if no one keeps a record of them. I do not believe in regrets.

I have been condemned to review, from moment to moment, all my past deeds. Is it possible that my current life is my punishment? I look at myself, this phenomenon of light in the mirror, and wonder. The image grows hazy; I no longer see myself.

Dead friends visit me here, in this cozy, historical shapelessness. I am reading the book of my fate. The story of my mind is more daring than that of my body. I take notes. There is time yet; the printer's apprentice is not ringing my bell. This whole day may be but an exercise in penmanship.

I lift my eyes: I see a hill, a rock, and, farther, a steeple; everything is calm and enduring. I will not start anything new; I choose to consider the time remaining to me a bonus. I no longer have any vested interests, I am no longer trying to paste the mask of the future on the face of death. I am going back to where I no longer know anything about myself. How ludicrous, to be the bearer of the same name all these years. I hereby renounce ownership of this biography. The unhappy doubling of my self is over.

Sometimes, in my mind, I accompany myself to the cemetery, to my own funeral. As I look over the gathered crowd, I mourn with the mourners, but soon tire of the ceremony. I withdraw into the depths of the cemetery's abandoned paths, where ivy has long overrun the graves. The fresh burial mound rises above me with its many suffocating wreaths. I wriggle free and wonder whether I should sneak a look at those still lingering. But if I have had nothing to do with them before, why should I hang around them now? I have been betrayed by every event of my life; each has brought me closer to the end of the game. I turn away from the living and retreat to my den of divine light.

I have followed the swing of the pendulum between passion and surfeit, madness and wisdom. Wanting to know the difference between good and evil and man and woman, I disobeyed orders and broke taboos. Pounding the ground with my fists, I cursed original sin, willing to commit it over and over again. One, when split into two, falls into sin; the two would like to merge, to become one again. I have never believed that truth lies in the middle. Rather, I've always thought the pendulum is right to swing between extremes.

I am getting out of my past, my circumstances, my feeble and enigmatic intimacies. It is a smokelike drifting away, a convulsion-free displacement; the story of a separation. I am leaving. I lower the blinds and close the door. The accomplice, the loser, and the moralist I leave behind.

The harbor of light is approaching. Stretching from bed to bed, from dream to dream, I want this last day to be an illumination; a condensed phantom day in which everything that is significant may occur. The day of mercy and escape will come, like the last day of school. And, as predicted, the screw will turn and your ordeal will begin. The doors of the cattle cars slide back, the steel bars fold away, the iron gates crumble like bullet-riddled shirts. The guards no longer guard you, the German shepherds do not move, the state of siege is over. Day has come, a day that will be followed by an incalculably long night.

Everyone has left. I'll write one more letter, make one more long-distance call. There won't be any more alarming wedding nights or tender embraces in the morning. I make the bed. Lime-blossom tea. I read a few more pages of this book. Newspapers, reading glasses, a lamp, and a coffee cup by my bed. I don't have to talk to anyone. In my dream, somebody is looking at me, banging on the door, climbing up the wall to my window. I go out on the balcony and smoke a cigarette. On the sidewalk below a man is walking. Unable to sleep, I go down to the Danube, stop by a bar to have a drink. Cut loose, I let myself drift into the nocturnal bays of the city. You must keep going, while you can, on this harried path. By the time you grow tired, by the time you lie down, you, too, will agree that enough is enough. The soul shivers; it begs to return to its mother.

Give me some water, my love, prop up my pillow and hold my hand. How we used to cuddle in this room; now I am here by myself. The bed floats out of the room, the ship sails across blue sand. Those left behind are waving from farther and farther away. Yours was the last gaze that fell on me. This is a holiday, a wedding. The pearly ram's horn is sounded. Enter Death.

2.

In which David Kobra
returns to his
childhood home

THE MOVEMENTS:

An Autumn Trip
in the Yellow Lada

An autumn trip in the yellow Lada. I, a ghost, am returning to the scene of the crime. Always looking for the old, always finding the new. Above the dark-blue flatland, a starry vault. I feel the giddiness of the Alföld, the desert ecstasy. Nothing obstructs the view. We are swimming in the middle of an enormous open space, at the very center of the hemisphere. From here I can see equally far in any direction. The car cuts in half the neatly outlined moonlit plain.

We are approaching the village of my birth. I want my sister, father, and mother to be waiting for me in the living room of the old house. We should, the four of us, sit down at the table. The past is no more. I know but do not always accept this.

In the end, I go by train. The express does not stop at Újfalu anymore; only the local: Püspökladány, Báránd, Sáp, Újfalu. When the station comes into view, first the building is small, then I am small. A green iron railing, a yellow, glazed-tile platform, scarlet slag between the tracks, a tan one-story building. The railroad man, with his red cap and semaphore, is saluting. Behind him, the ting-a-ling of the telegraph room. The picture is as enduring and permanent as water buffalo at pasture.

Light red wine to go with the generous portion of fried meat. I am eating and watching strong, thickset men as they sing, their bodies grown heavy with drink. That corner table there used to be for the important men of the town; now policemen sit around it, because the county and local police stations moved into the nearby town hall in 1950, finding their old barracks too cramped. The chief sits at the head of the table; the men tell jokes. A good joke is one that the chief laughs at. There are no gentry or Jews now in this restaurant. What you see are well-fed, self-assured peasant faces, all from the same mold. They wear city-workers' outfits, dark jackets unbuttoned, white shirts, and rubber boots for the mud. Around the glasses, thick-fingered, large brown hands. They have taken over the restaurant that once belonged to small landowners and the burghers. They all know every member of the Gypsy band.

Sometime in the sixties, the soiled fabric was removed from the walls and replaced with black-and-white diamond-patterned plastic sheets that are now also soiled. Moderately prosperous people sit around me. They work their minds but never strain them. You can thrive by not talking much. But then, these people have never talked much. It is their slow-paced small talk, punctuated with frequent pauses and smiles, that I remember most vividly from childhood. And a woman's arm in the kitchen of this restaurant, an ample coffee-brown arm of the Alföld, the Great Hungarian Plain, greasy below the wrist, showing its strength as it carved up a roast.

I am lying down in a room of the Bihar Hotel, only a few steps away from the house in which I was born. Flies, white brandy, sweltering heat, the buzzing of the bus depot. Opposite is the cinema where Karcsi's mother used to hand out the tickets through the window of the box office, showing off her gold bracelets. The Gypsy children still make a noise when they kiss, just as they used to before the war. Today, in the cinema, spitting the shells of pumpkin and sun-flower seeds on the floor is strictly forbidden.

In my town the sky is bigger, the dragonflies more silvery, and the roads muddier. I last visited here ten years ago. This is the eastern edge of Hungary. Here, the clothes of old people have more patches. Before the war, too, this was where most of the country's poor lived. Old men in dark-blue burlap aprons stand at the main hotel entrance. The street pavement is spotted with dried lumps of mud. At the corner, an old tavern; whenever its doors swing open, huge puffs of steam escape into the street. Leaning against the railed-off counter, I am having a grape brandy. Soon I will switch to plum brandy. I am happy with both.

In the tavern a man stops in front of me. On his skin, women's names crawl like snakes in all directions. He wears a jacket over his naked, tanned, and tattooed torso. His head is shaved and shiny.

"I think I know you from somewhere. Do you know me?"

"No."

He tells me about his war experiences. One day, in a Russian POW camp, he stood behind a German prisoner at attention in the camp's parade ground. The prisoners had to have all their belongings with them, and standing at attention lasted for hours, just as it had in the German camps. But in the Russian camp, supervision was more relaxed. My man stood behind the German prisoner and with a razor blade slit open the German's knapsack while holding his own underneath it. When the German noticed this, he opened his mouth to yell, but my storyteller grabbed him by the throat and with his bare hands crushed his windpipe. He does have powerful hands. Even today he could crush a man's throat. He offers his hand for me to shake.

"Where do you think you know me from?" I ask.

"Would you believe that with these two hands I could wring the Communists' necks?"

"No, I wouldn't."

The bald man breaks into laughter. A thin, older man walks past us. The bald man, whose wrist is covered with a black leather band studded with iron nails—the style of a younger generation—pulls on the thin one's pants.

"Hey, Uncle Rezső, isn't Gyula the man to make mincemeat out of those Bolsheviks? Now Uncle Rezső here is a true Communist. He never drinks more than one wine-and-soda. If he wants another one, he goes home, rests up, then comes back for the second one. He lives right in that house next door. He's a joiner, and a damn good one, too. But these days he works his mouth more than his plane. Uncle Rezső always says what's on his mind. He inherited his workshop from his father. He's worked plenty. That's why his hands are so big. A little man with big hands. But mine are bigger. I could take little Uncle Rezső in my hands and crumble him like a dry leaf. And if I really got going, in ten minutes I could make blackberry jam out of all these respectable customers.

"But don't worry, Four-Eyes, I wouldn't hurt you. When I saw you last, you weren't wearing specs. You loved to sit next to me on the driver's seat of the wagon, and you were so proud when I let you

41

hold the whip. You wanted to have biceps like mine when you grew up. Used to check my arm with your two little fingers and yell: Make a muscle! Tighter! And you squealed when I did.

"I was the one who polished the linoleum in your room. Down on my knees, I would rub it with a waxed brush, then skate up and down on it with a cloth. I took care of the heating, too, so you wouldn't be cold when you went into the living room after your bath. I carried the firewood in. Juliska, the maid—or was it Piroska, or Vilma, or Irma?—anyway, she would fire up the boiler so that the young master would have hot water as soon as he opened his eyes. Your governess picked you up from the tub—which one was it, Annie, Hilda, Livia? I don't remember—and she bundled you in a large white towel. And I brought the firewood, me and Gyurka, the horse, and the water, too, in a water tank. I had to take it bucket by bucket from that slow artesian well in the park near the post office, behind the big flag. That water had a long way to go before it got to your tub, little master."

This Gyula with the strong hands, we used to call the "weekly" or the "yardboy." He was paid, not every two weeks, like my father's assistants, or monthly, like the bookkeeper, but once a week. In status and pay, only day laborers were below him. He had to go to the artesian well with the water cart and fill up the gray tank bucket by bucket, waiting for all the women to fill their cans and pitchers, and they each had at least two.

The water in ordinary wells was not potable. The district medical officer's instruction to drink only from the artesian well was announced, as was everything of importance, in the marketplace by the town crier, the announcement preceded and followed by the vigorous beating of a drum. The artesian water, trickling slowly up from a depth of twenty-six hundred feet, was lukewarm and fragrant with minerals. Gyurka pulled the tank home, and Gyula, through a rubber hose, led it out of the cart into a pit, from which it flowed down to the cellar and into another water tank, which was covered with a slab of concrete. From there the water had to be pumped to the attic. In this way our apartment, located over the shop, was supplied with artesian water. My mother had decided that we would take baths only in artesian water. We could have used the water from the well in our courtyard; it came from a depth of thirty feet and was clean enough, but my mother would not hear of it.

This system of water economy in 1933, the year in which I was born and our shop-apartment was built, depended on a muscular peasant boy's pulling and pushing the shiny arm of a pump. In return for a modest fee, the boy did his job in an orderly and disciplined manner, accepting his role in our bath-taking scheme, a rather one-sided role exhausted by the act of pumping. Gyula himself probably never had the experience of luxuriating in a tub. I doubt that he even washed himself from the waist down, certainly not every day. And also, for me to step into the tub, a maid had to light the fire and a governess had to set out my clothes.

In 1941 my father replaced the manual pump with an electric one. And in 1945 my mother (after returning from the concentration camp and no longer having any servants) resigned herself to using the water from our own well for bathing. Two revolutionary, democratic changes. Water lost its class role. Before, the lower-ranked well water from our courtyard was used by us only to flush the toilet. From the faucets in the bathroom of the masters, in which no maid could bathe before 1945, only artesian water flowed. There was a direct correspondence, therefore, between the fragrance I exuded, due not just to toilet soaps and baby lotions, and the fact that the maid had a maid's smell and the servants smelled like servants. One who bathes and changes underwear frequently is sensitive to the odor of those who do not. The servants bathed in the laundry room, using a galvanized iron tub, not a white enamel one, and they bathed only once a week.

Every object, every custom spoke of status. The maid would not only take her pay from my mother's hand, but also grasp the hand and kiss it. "Please, Piroska (Juliska, Mariska, and so on)," my mother would say, and try to withdraw the hand. She did not insist on this custom, and I think she even found it somewhat repugnant, because she would always wash her hand afterward. My father shook the hands of his employees only after giving them their pay envelopes.

I don't recall the "weekly" or the cook ever sitting down in any of our rooms. In the kitchen, yes. The weekly would sit there on a stool, spooning the thick soup the cook put in his bowl with an enamel ladle straight from the pot. This seemed strange to me, because the pot never found its way to our dining table; we saw only the translucent porcelain tureen, from which the soup was measured out with a silver ladle. Long hours were spent, in the afternoon, polishing the silverware.

Every bourgeois home had a parlor. This is where my father was supposed to sit, at the fancy carved desk decorated with lions. But I don't remember him ever sitting there. To me, as a child, the five-room house seemed to be the norm of living quarters; you could have more, but certainly not fewer, rooms. Anyone who had fewer was poor. I did not think of us as rich; we were comfortable. That's the word I learned from my father. Being comfortable meant having every-thing you needed.

My Father's House

In America, in completely unfamiliar surroundings, we rented a house. Husband, wife, two children, governess. The family gathered regularly around the dinner table: a restoration of the past. If the little boy was unruly, the father could be stern. I can see my father on the balcony as he lifts me into his arms. He was a lot younger then than I am now. There was an advantage to the infrequency of his appearances. He was no albatross around our necks. He had his territory, I had mine.

You can't go back. I will not sue for my father's house, even though I have every right to do so. Let those who took it return it, or offer another house in its stead, even a house at the edge of town or on a muddy side street. My mother, too, has a right to that house, which was built with her dowry. According to a law passed in 1950 allowing the nationalization of private property, you had no claim to your home if it contained more than five rooms. We had more, because the first floor was taken up by the spacious hardware store. But most people in Újfalu would resent my reclaiming the house. They have grown accustomed to my father's house belonging to the town, and to buying television sets in what used to be my room.

The house we have just moved into has eight rooms. Privacy requires space. Without some private space there is no human dignity; without quiet there can be no high-quality work. Besides these private spaces, we need a room to share activities. We cannot watch TV in the bedroom of another member of the family. We cannot receive guests where our papers are strewn around. This present arrangement and the old life of my father's time have now come together.

During the seventies I returned to Újfalu a few times, always taking a careful look at our house. I think I kept going back because I wanted to arrive at a decision. What decision? Perhaps to answer the question of whether or not I wanted to have anything more to do with this town. I'd ponder it while lying in a bed at the Bihar Hotel, which used to be the Lisztes'. If I were to go to Újfalu now, I would stay in Annus Lisztes' house on Martyrs Road, where the Jewish school and the synagogue once stood. Annus Lisztes sent me a copy of a monograph on the town's history, recently compiled by local teachers under the supervision of the Communist Party and the county council. A thick tome. My father is not mentioned in it. Nor are the other Jewish merchants of the town. Not a word about the fact that almost ten percent of the town's population was Jewish. And that the Jews are all gone. The process of making the town *Judenrein* has thus been completed.

The synagogue today is a hardware storehouse—not a historic sight, not even a theater or cultural center, as is the case with synagogues in many rural towns. Actually, it does not bother me that the synagogue is connected in that way to my father's business. In this synagogue, during the war, the wind blew the pages of the prayer books as the front lines passed through. Now it is rolled sheet steel, wrought iron, pine boxes fastened with metal bands, and stovepipes piled high before the Ark of the Covenant. A young man working in the storehouse claims that he has heard of my father. My father, he heard, was a good man. He also knows about Lajos Üveges, my father's assistant, who became the store's manager when it was nationalized. Üveges was a good man, too; he had the whole business at his fingertips. But he, too, has moved into the realm of fairy tales. Now Uncle Feri is the boss. Feri was once the errand boy, my contemporary, my classmate at school, a Lisztes grandchild. Having the skill and a thorough familiarity with the territory, he took my father's place. Feri is in the right place; so was Lajos, and so was my father. Only I am not. You know you're in the right place when you have the keys in your pocket and you open the store every morning. This young man in the storehouse-synagogue is also in the right place; with the help of his parents he is building a house. He is married already; the couple plans to have a child just as soon as they can move into their new house.

The rest of the surviving Újfalu Jews must also have felt that they were no longer in the right place. They came to this realization slowly, reluctantly. From a certain point of view the new regime began to resemble the old one: Independent merchants and independent craftsmen were suddenly ideologically tainted, and that meant, first of all, the Jewish merchants and craftsmen. People who had been members of the Arrow-Cross Party and abused the Jews now became Communists and continued to abuse the Jews.

One early summer day in 1949 the Jews all closed their stores and workshops and hung out their BACK SOON signs. At the edge of town they boarded a truck. By way of the Czechoslovak border it was still possible to reach the U.S. occupation zone in Austria, and from there the State of Israel. Most of them settled in the same town in Israel. For the rest of his life, Jankó Kertész, the cobbler, continued to gossip in Hungarian, sitting on his three-legged stool in that new little town on the coast of the Mediterranean, just as he used to do back in Újfalu. His customers were almost the same, and so were his friends: the people with whom he had gone to school and synagogue, served in the army, suffered through the labor camps, mourned wives and children. Today there is only one Jew left in town, a baker. It was not altogether unintentional, this consigning of the memory of the Jews of Újfalu to oblivion.

It was a sweltering afternoon, and I was lying on my soaked bed in the Bihar Hotel. I had roamed the main street, the marketplace, the soccer field; I had sat in the cinema; nobody came up to talk to me. At times I felt I was being observed, looked at curiously, but no more curiously than people look at someone they have never seen before. I was waiting for a sudden leap of my heart that would tell me: Yes! I talked to the president of the local council and to the Party secretary; the former used to be a peasant, the latter a shoemaker. The president boasted about the town's new prosperity. People building their houses tell the mason: Make it like the council president's house—only two feet longer. The Party secretary smoked his pipe sullenly. It was his thankless job to announce to the townspeople that anyone building on a newly apportioned lot would get permission only if he used one of the models provided by the Model Planning Institute. "It's not a bad design," I said, "but why should all the houses be the same?" "Why? So we'll have a uniform look on the street" was his answer. I could tell he was not crazy about the idea, but he must have received a telephone call from above on the subject. With significant smiles and telling glances, you can suggest that the higher-ups are crazy, but orders are orders. That same morning I inspected the new three-story apartment houses behind the Protestant church. Teachers, doctors, and lawyers were living in them. An old Gypsy happened by. "Who lives in these houses?" I asked him. "Secret police," the old man replied.

I lay in the increasingly hot, coffin-size room. Not another guest was on my floor. In the corridor a solitary Gypsy waiter was playing chess against himself. That evening, after closing, he sneaked down to the restaurant and played something resembling jazz on the piano. I gave him some money and asked for a bottle of red wine, assuring him that it did not matter if the bottle was not chilled. By the time I polished it off, it would be dark enough for me to start my shuttling between the Bihar Hotel and the Nylon and Kulacs bars, just like those two pitiful whores who followed the same triangular route in pursuit of clients.

I am such a stranger here that I feel at home only in the cemetery, which is both Jewish and Protestant. There, I am among people I know. The names on the stones and wooden grave markers are all

47

familiar. At the grave of my great-grandfather I sat on the grass, then lay down. I felt as if an old knot were coming undone inside me and slipping from my limbs into the ground. With my fingers I explored the Hebrew letters in the white marble. The gold had worn away, but the grooves of the letters remained. I traced the fingers of two hands clasped in prayer.

Near my place of work there was a small cemetery for the war dead. It's been liquidated since. I used to go there to get away from computerized sociostatistical data. Nothing worse than this can happen, you tell yourself while looking at the moist trail of a snail on a tombstone. My great-grandfather's bones cannot budge from here, but I can get up and go elsewhere. If the living can be conformist, why can't the dead also be conformist? It's like standing among ancient ruins and being surrounded by several hundred cats with burning eyes; if you don't turn into a cat, you'll be damned. What do these withered shadows want, approaching in their black and white shrouds? Bony index fingers, like arrows pointing from every direction: Renegade!

I could move here, find work, and in my free time do some gardening at the cemetery. Or maybe I'll take the afternoon train out and never set foot in this town again. In a noisy, stinking inn on a side street you can hear one another only by shouting. Those who like to sing start in energetically, then get bored, give up, and go to the window to look out.

There used to be a marketplace between the hotel and the Apollo Theater; it's a bus depot now. Dust and the exhaust of tourist buses rise from below. I can take the bus to Debrecen on the hour. In the old days I used to ride my bicycle or a hay wagon to Debrecen. Since I can leave here anytime, I will stay a little longer. I was at the new market today. You still have the babble of the women, the noise of geese and ducks, the drawn-out bellowing of oxen, the smell of fresh horse manure and strawberries and spring potatoes, and, in the rear, you still have the ever-new merry-go-round surrounded by vendors of cotton candy and penknives. You can also buy a small wooden rooster with a clapping tail. And yet it's very different. Now tractors and buses stir up the dust, youngsters fly by on motorcycles. The benches in front of the houses are empty; rarely does somebody sit on one of them and smoke a pipe.

As a child I felt that the town was an extension of my body. Lying in bed, I would pray for those close to me and then for all the locals. (If I got up now, threw my few things into my bag, I could still catch the afternoon express to Budapest at the Debrecen station.) In my bed in Pest, I used to dream that I held all the bridges of the Danube in my hand. It's eight in the evening. My parents have kissed me good-night and left the room. I hear measured breathing from the direction of my older sister. Through the bars of the curtained brass bed I peer into the darkness: What is happening outside the bed? In the moonlight the bedspread, draped over the back of a chair, turns into a lion. A burglar slips his fingers in through the slits of the shutters. He has a knife between his teeth and can climb walls. I turn over, lie on my stomach. By pressing the edges of my eyes, I create a magic lantern. I can see the African desert, and the Russian snowfields with slowly crawling tanks. In my film the Allies are in a better position than they are on the real battlefield. At Bizerte and in Tunis I tip the balance toward Montgomery's force over Rommel's. I manage to make my way into Hitler's banquet, and with a carving knife I slit his throat.

Early in the morning, throwing my leg over the brass rod, I crawl out of bed and through the keyhole in the bathroom peep into my parents' bedroom. Are they awake yet? Can I snuggle in with them? Can I jump from the dressing table onto the bed? They are still asleep. I go into the living room and then out on the balcony. Early spring. The storks are now arriving to nest by the Tables of the Covenant that are carved into the façade of the synagogue. Will there be a time when my parents will not be alive? Instead of a smile, will dirt fill my father's mouth? At such thoughts the eyes of a sensitive little boy well with tears. In the living room, the yellow breakfast service is brooding on the light-blue tablecloth. Logs are crackling in the cream-colored tile stove. I like to sit in front of the stove and follow the afterlife of the logs, the burned wood's moment of truth, when it is about to collapse for good. Softly the mauve edges of the logs sink deep into one another, grow white, then crumble into ashes. Mortality: the change from a glowing shape into formless ashes.

I wish my parents would wake up; lots of adventures are waiting for us. At the blacksmith's I watch horses being fitted with sizzling horseshoes. In the large iron stove of our store I heat a piece of steel wire, keep it in there until with a tong I can bend it into the shape of a bow. When the bow cools, I thread it with a violin string. I'd like to be a metallurgical engineer, to work with fire, to bridle it. When summer comes, I will again be able to drive the puffing little engine of Grandfather's mountain railroad through the woods. I will transport the cut logs from the mountain clearings down into the valley, to the train station. I gaze into the fiery belly of the engine and get lost in it. But all this is still far away; after breakfast I am alone on the garden swing, flying higher than the supporting frame. Later I stare at the sky from the walnut tree, then fly a kite from the courtyard of the synagogue. It stumbles upward, toward the sun.

Ever since I can remember, I have suspected adults of being childish. I learned how childish my father and mother were while eavesdropping on their early-morning talk in bed. They talked just like us, my sister, Éva, and me.

When they returned from the concentration camps, both of them scrawny and tattered, their backs bent, after we all had that one year of history behind us—from May 1944 to June 1945—we looked at them with adult condescension, as if we and not they were the parents.

That whole year, I'd felt their absence with my body. All summer I stood on the third-floor balcony of an apartment house on Hollán Street in Budapest, waiting to see them turn the corner, with knapsacks on their backs, or, better, wearing holiday clothes and carrying nothing. I waited for them even when there was no hope, judging by the turn of the international political situation, of seeing them again.

My familiarity with international politics began at the age of five, when Hilda, my Bavarian-born governess, became glued so enthusiastically to the radio, which made a racket, fuming and screeching, pronouncing the word *German* with adoration, the word *Jew* with loathing. Why did Hilda prefer that voice on the radio to me? "*Du bist lieb,*" she would say in the morning when, after my bath, we clung to each other. Who was this man whom she now loved more than she loved me? I climbed into my mother's lap and asked, "Who is Hitler?"

A Naïve Citizen

From the age of five I have been the same, I believe. Before stepping out of the bathroom, I glance at the mirror: Is everything in order? Am I presentable? Long blond hair curling on the sides, and dark-blue short pants with suspenders. When I'm older, I'll wear a belt instead of suspenders and have my hair cut short, like the rest of the boys of Újfalu. This image in the mirror is not bad, but it's a masquerade. Cocoa and sweet bread await me, and a pillow on my chair for elevation. I have to eat breakfast alone; my father is already at work in the store downstairs.

From the yellow façade of the synagogue across the street the early spring sun bounces into the living room off the railing of the balcony. Next to the carved Tables there is a rampartlike column whose concave top is just perfect for a family of storks to nest in. Our weather is good when the storks are back, across the way; chilly when they are resting on the banks of the Nile. This great distance fills the observer in Újfalu with mild sadness. But perhaps the storks do not have such a good time in Egypt. It was not for nothing, after all, that Moses led the Jews out of the valley of the Nile. With his hands clasped behind his back, the observer sees the male stork settling on the back of the female, his wings fluttering, his beak clapping. Then the female hatches the eggs while the male brings lunch. The mother distributes pieces of the frog into the gaping beaks of the little ones, and the father flies back into the azure, circles high above the river basin, looking for a snack. In midsummer the little storks learn to fly. In September they all leave, and return the following year around this time. But to this nest only the mother and father return; the young are building their nests elsewhere, with their new mates. "The stork is a faithful creature," my father said. And so was he. If my mother had not been with him, he would not have returned from the camps. In the cold, they huddled together under their coarse blanket.

But this picture is hidden in the distant future; we are still at our childhood observation post in the living room. Under the window we have a walnut tree and a sour-cherry tree. It is because of this duo that I fell in love, at the age of forty, with the sexton's house in Csobánka. Under a walnut tree and a sour-cherry tree I began to sketch the idylls of an endangered childhood.

This sexton's house, too, has seen a thorough search; even the ashes in the stove were sifted, and the searchers gathered every bit of paper that had the word *intellectuals* written on it. Afterward, in the inn, the Gypsies shook my hand warmly, patted my back, and told me I was a good boy. The schoolmistress next door smiled sympathetically. Father Zsigmond actually hugged me and kissed me. During the search—he was summoned, because the sexton's house belonged to his parish—he noticed that the creaking floorboards were distracting the man in charge. But Father Zsigmond had no choice; he had to keep moving, because the sexton's house was unheated on October 23, 1974. It was raining, too. He pulled galoshes over his thick socks and kept pacing back and forth, well aware which boards would creak loudest. The wise priest was particularly amused when the assistant searchers, in their great zeal, came upon their leader's briefcase in the kitchen and found inside it the most phenomenal piece of evidence: a revolver. They turned pale: Now they really had Mr. Kobra! They put the evidence in front of their leader, who recoiled. "And he calls himself an intellectual resister, eh?" He examined the revolver; he had one just like it. "Where did you find it?" he asked his men. "In a briefcase." "What briefcase? Idiots! That's mine." Father Zsigmond laughed and laughed. He got very red, and finally turned to the picture of a crucifix. In a silver-plated frame, the image of a wooden crucifix hung on the whitewashed wall above my bed. "Tell me, Father, does Mr. Kobra sleep under this picture?" "Why not? When Mr. Kobra gets sleepy, he sleeps. The picture doesn't bother him. If it did, he would have removed it."

After breakfast, I would descend into the masculine region of the house, into my father's hardware store on the ground floor. Surrounded by customers, assistants, and apprentices, my father—amiable and inaccessible—was exactly what he was supposed to be: boss, owner, and business successor. The prime taxpaying citizen of a not-so-small town. A year before my birth he built the first two-story house on the main street. Both the county supervisor and the town's mayor stopped by to watch the rapid rise of the new edifice. "Urbanization is catching up with us," they said, and shook my father's hand, thanking him for having taken so brave a step into the future.

Every morning at ten to eight, my father would hurry down the stairs, rattling his keys. His assistants were already waiting for him. In good weather they would sit on the bench in the garden; if it was too cold, they'd wait at the bottom of the stairwell. My father opened the steel door at the rear of the store, and the staff followed him into the iron-smelling dimness. The blinds were raised by the apprentices, who each afternoon would also lower the large brown roll shutters with hooked poles that could also be used for pole vaulting in the garden. In addition, these poles made excellent halberds, perfect for sticking into the bellies of enemies. In the increasing light, the apprentices drew figure eights with their watering cans on the oiled floor. They had all started here as apprentices, under my father or back during my grandfather's years. They spent their lives in this store, drawing figure eights in the morning, putting on their blue smocks, greeting customers in unison. They knew everyone by name. Outside, wagons rattled by; in short dark fur-lined coats, booted peasants came to stand at the counter.

Among the assistants, the second assistant, Lajos Üveges, was my friend. Bald, mustached, thin, and swarthy, he greeted everyone playfully, always saying something humorous. Out of cut tobacco kept in a tin box he could roll perfectly cylindrical cigarettes with his left hand; he could do this even without taking his right hand out of the pocket of his smock. His homemade lighter had a flame like a torch. He never failed to ask me: "How're things, young man?" Which was not easy to answer.

I accepted Lajos's superiority, because he was good at everything that had iron in it. He knew all about tools, scythes, rifles, engines, and bicycles. He would watch me fix my bike and help when I couldn't manage. Not only could he sell tools, but he also knew how to use them; he made a stand for our swing, built our seesaw and Ping-Pong table, and fixed the faucet and the lights. I consulted him on the construction of my first nonpaper airplane. I decided on wire and plywood as basic materials. The plane was much too heavy. "It won't fly like that," Lajos said. "That doesn't matter," I replied. "The important thing is that no bullets can pierce this plane." Lajos and I went upstairs, and from the balcony, standing on a table, I held the plane over the railing, then let it go. It crashed with a huge thud and on its way shattered the gilded glass top of a decorative trellis that supported the young rose bushes. The plane itself was intact. "It's well built," Lajos said proudly. "See how well it smashed that glass!" "If it had a strong enough engine in it, it could fly, too," I said, somewhat uncertain. "Oh, yes," Lajos agreed, "but then maybe it would fly away and you wouldn't be able to find it." The plane stayed there in the flower bed among the yellow tea roses; I never looked at it again. We went back to the store. Lajos made the customers laugh, and me, too, the designer of the town's heaviest airplane.

I sauntered from the store into the garden. Japonica, lilacs, fruit trees, flower beds, sandbox, swing. In the corner stood a tall pole, our radio antenna. The head of the swallow family living under our balcony was now perched atop that pole, bathing in the bright sunshine as well as in his own glorious rapture. Suddenly he took to the sky. I pumped the swing more vigorously; God's creatures strive upward.

Bars and a high railing prevented me from falling off the balcony. When nobody was looking, I would climb the railing and dangle my feet, enjoying the thrill of danger. Once, my father's favorite, Miklós Rácz, the first assistant, caught me. He was a dignified, taciturn man who hardly ever talked to me. When he saw me dangling over the railing, he came upstairs, walked out on the balcony, and without a word lifted me safely back in. He then informed me that he would tell my father, and he did. Another time, he discovered me in the attic. There was a concrete container inside a wooden crate, and in the container was some ammunition. Through the slats of the crate I was flipping lighted matches at the container, but it refused to explode.

Our attic was an exciting place; it early caught my imagination. From the top of the ladder, leaning against the window, you could look out on the meadow. After the steeple of the Protestant church, this attic was the highest point in town. I think I daydreamed a lot about highest points. In our part of the country, on the Great Hungarian Plain, there were no highest points. Expansion took place horizontally; the side streets of the village wound their way gloomily out into the fields, acacia trees lining the narrow sidewalks. Houses expanded inward, into the lots, like the teeth of a comb. Looking down from our second-story balcony, visitors often said they became dizzy. One of my classmates—I wanted him to be my friend because he was handsome and well mannered—once came in, shook my hand, then stood by the window speechless, overwhelmed by the opportunity to look down from such a height. In vain did my governess bring us ham sandwiches; my friend was unable to eat. I could understand his astonishment; I, too, was longing for a higher place, the steeple of the Protestant church. Later, when this wish came true and I walked around just below the belfry, I could see the edge of town at all four points of the compass. I felt I could stand there until the end of time, because I had never seen anything so beautiful.

A few years ago, when my children came home from Paris for their summer vacation, I took them to Újfalu. I showed them where we used to go sledding in front of the railroad station. There was a mild slope there, the only spot in the whole town good enough for sledding. All the wild youngsters of the town gathered there with their do-it-yourself, father-made, or store-bought sleds. With great bravado they would lie belly down on the sleds and plummet like tornadoes into the terrifying depths. The height of the slope was maybe ten feet. My children smiled at me compassionately.

As a young father living in Budapest, I often regretted that my children knew so little of the city: our home, the kindergarten, and

the swimming pool, that was about it. Whereas Újfalu was a whole
world. You could traverse its length and breadth; you could get to
know it just by being a customer in my father's store. "Who is that?"
I would ask, and my father would always give me a satisfactory answer.
He knew all the landowners, the army officers, the county supervisor,
the police chief of the county, the subprefect, the school principal,
the stationmaster, all the priests, the town crier, and all the small
tradesmen, railroad men, millers, journeymen, even the brick-making
Gypsies. In all probability he knew more people than I do now. The
people he knew had much in common because they came from a
society that could be grasped in its entirety. He knew them all, from
the richest to the poorest; from the village idiot, who could be made
fun of but had to be given money, to the county poet, our pride and
joy, whose volumes had to be ordered in advance of publication. It
was true of course that when the store was not too busy, customers
would linger at the cashier's and spice their business transactions
with a bit of gossip. You could talk with almost anyone about how
high the corn was now and how this little rain in May was worth its
weight in gold. Every day, about ten people and a few Gypsy children
came to beg. The craftier ones would enter twice, but were shown
the door the second time. Still, according to custom, they were allowed
in the next day.

Whenever the howls of professional mourners were heard, whenever a funeral passed through town, plumed black-maned stallions
of St. Michael drawing the fancy silver-adorned hearse, whose glass
walls let you read the writing on the coffin, my father always knew
who was going on his or her last journey. Piling out of the store,
boss, assistants, customers, and apprentices together would compose
the obituary of the deceased.

In my father's store you also overheard news passed on in whispers: secrets and sins. Who stabbed to death his father-in-law. Who
whipped his wife. Who was railing, just days before the fire, against
the thatched roof of a well-to-do farmer's corn loft. Who was on his
last legs in the TB institute, which we always passed with hastened
steps lest the resident germs leap over the fence and catch us. And
did the old doctor know that his wife took walks in Gacsa Garden
with the local printer?

My father was serious and affable; plain jesting would have been inappropriate in his position. He was a friendly man, always ready to smile, never obtrusive or supercilious. He was Csonka Bihar County's most respected Jewish citizen. He did not seek respect, he simply had it. Within the boundaries of his sphere, he did what he had to do always according to his best understanding. He kept his word, sold quality merchandise for which he'd paid cash, never got into debt or made undue profit, and never cheated the tax bureau. He obeyed the laws of religion as well as those of the state. He paid his employees well and was always generous with bonuses. As a wedding present he would give them a house to live in. As for the world upstairs: He was in love with my mother, whose mind and refinement he never ceased to admire with a child's enthusiasm. His visits to our room, when he looked in on me and my sister, were always pleasant. He showed interest in my various building projects, but before I threw myself back into the intricacies of assembling a crane from my Märklin erector set, he would tactfully withdraw, leaving the door slightly ajar, and sit down in the dining room to listen to Éva play the piano. For him, no one played the études of Chopin more beautifully than my sister. She was satisfied with her playing, too, except when it went awry, when it was spoiled by some treacherous elf who sometimes hid under the piano and at the height of the most heartrending passages wreaked havoc with the pedals.

Our misbehavior rarely brought parental interference. Father preferred to stay in the adult zone of the house. It pained him when he found me aiming my slingshot at my sister's oil portrait, in which she was smiling so sweetly and so blondly. Her hair was rolled up in curls, just like mine—only I wasn't smiling, I was sulking as I stood on the photographer's fancy podium and tried to extricate myself from the role of little boy. I loved Éva; we could get along peacefully for hours. She was a slow eater, a sound sleeper, and an excellent student; her bright blue eyes had a humorous look in them. But one has to irritate somebody, and she was at hand. Into whose bed, if not Éva's, should I put the green toad? Who else should I chase around the table, jumping over the chairs thrown in front of me? Look, she is pulling the door, and on the other side I am pressing down on the doorknob. We've already turned both our room and the living room upside down, and are now galloping around the dining-room table. She squeals; I am in silent pursuit, though I have no idea why—maybe because she made fun of me. There, I catch her; I wrestle her down, pin her shoulders to the floor. But nothing is that simple; flat on her back, she kicks and scratches, pedaling with her muscular legs, or—worse—she licks me! That disgusts me most. Being licked makes a self-respecting man shudder. The cold saliva on my face is just too embarrassing. When our mischief crossed a certain line, there was a chance that Father would spank our bottoms. He spanked me maybe three times. I was slapped in the face only once, for telling a lie.

Father wore his jacket, vest, and tie all day long. Only during meals were we all in the same room; otherwise we spent our time in the children's room and Father stayed in the living room, reading. He preferred newspapers to books. Sometimes Mother gave him novels to read. Whenever we ate together, he sat at the head of the table, and she served him first. He would wait until she finished serving everybody; our signal to start was when he picked up his spoon. Sometimes, when he didn't pick up his spoon because of some political discussion he wanted to conclude, we would rattle our glasses.

Sitting in a high chair that was also my potty, or, later, propped up with pillows in a regular chair, I could not stay put, and proceeded very inventively to tease my sister. At first, Father pretended not to notice, but when he felt that enough was enough, he would give me a look. His eyes were very blue, childlike, with a guileless light, but at times like this they darkened and filled with rebuke. I could not endure that look; I would return it without blinking until suddenly my tears welled and my throat constricted.

We listened to the BBC after lunch. All through the war, Father listened to the Hungarian broadcasts from London and Moscow, and I was always there, curled up beside him on the sofa. When I was seven or eight, I made an exact drawing of the front lines on the map, and checked the exaggerated German military reports as they appeared in the Hungarian papers. The broadcasts were jammed; the radio crackled. My mother and sister were bored with the reports from the battlefield; politics was the men's domain. We kept the windows closed, because listening to the enemy radio was forbidden. I liked the idea that my father and I were lawbreakers together.

He used his time well; he was never in a hurry. I don't think he ever missed a train. He showed interest when talking to his customers or fellow passengers, and mulled leisurely over what he was told. He did not try to be more than he was. Although he had a membership in the local gentry's club, he never crossed its threshold. Collectors for charitable institutions would come to Father first, and he always knew what the other donors expected him to pledge. In the store, with obstinately bargaining customers, his was the last word. For an enamel saucepan, peasant women would reach into the hem of their skirts and produce their carefully saved money tied in a handkerchief. If the money was still not enough, Father would advance credit until harvesttime. His debtors did not avoid him.

He had neat handwriting, could do sums beautifully in his head, was a fair chess player. He did not speak much, and not brilliantly, but did so with a certain flavor of the Bihar region and in complete sentences. Whatever he said made sense, and it often had charm. In his life everything had been decided and arranged from his childhood on. He attended the business college of Kezmarok to study German, and there could go ice skating, even on summer afternoons, in the grotto of Dobsina; or he roamed the walls of the local castle, or taught chess to the blond, braided, and somewhat dull-witted daughter of his landlord and math teacher. But mostly he spent his time brooding over his textbooks, longing to be away from the High Tatra Mountains and back on the black soil of the Bihar plains. With appropriate self-effacement, he listened to the conversations of the adults of his large family; he went to the synagogue and did his military service. He had a dozen suits and several dozen embroidered and monogrammed shirts, as well as starched collars, bamboo walking sticks, and spats.

After the death of his beloved and honored parents, he married a girl, not from his own town, but from Nagyvárad, the former county seat, the daughter of a well-to-do Jewish family, about whom my father's sisters had inquired and known everything before the two were even introduced to each other. The honeymoon was in Semering.

He had the old house pulled down and replaced with a new, prouder one. In this house he maintained a staff and, with his beloved wife, Rózsika, and a German governess, raised a son and a daughter. He did all this to fulfill his civic duty, which he inherited from his father, and which he would have liked to pass on to me, but God did not want it that way; although why he didn't is a mystery. Years later, Father would spend much time pondering this puzzle.

That he and his family could move, could escape from dusty Újfalu, because the noose was tightening, never occurred to him. Here is where he increased the wealth and respect he had inherited from his father. He knew most of the townspeople, and they had known him since his childhood. He was expected not to disgrace the family name. The family graves, too, were here. First his mother's, on whose stone his father had had inscribed: "You were our pride and happiness." Then his father's and his favorite younger sister's. He wanted to be buried here, too; that would be in the order of things. And his plan would have been feasible if, in the year of my birth, Germany, manufacturer of splendid steel products, had not fallen under the sway of "the scoundrel who squeals like a stuck pig." Father could not understand how decent people could take that blustering windbag seriously. He hoped for the victory of the English-speaking democracies. "After the war I'll stock only British steel products. I'll have them flown here by plane." "Here, into our garden?" Mother smiled. "Could you also tell me when this is going to happen?" "Soon, by the summer for sure," my father answered, and kissed my skeptical mother's hand.

A Child's Train Trip to Budapest

Can you imagine what it is like for a child from Újfalu to roll into the glass-covered terminal of Budapest West? We are from the region of Sárrét, where after a rain the mud is so deep that wagons bog down, horses and all, and you need high boots just to cross the street. The mud is not only a slushy slop, but also fertile, black, shiny, resilient, dense.

From the West comes the steel plow, from the East come the cereal crops. The son takes part in this trade; he pulls down the brick-walled house left to him by his father and erects new, thick, two-story-high walls. My father's innovation was exhausted by this rise from the ground-floor bedroom to the bedroom on the second floor. The house is on the very same spot where my grandfather's house stood on the main street with its back to the synagogue. In Sárrét, wood and stone are expensive building materials, brought from afar. That is why the poor build with brick, and the poorer plaster their walls with plain mud; their floors are nothing but beaten black earth. Only the well-off can afford to build with wood. Putting another house on top of an existing single-story structure is clearly a departure from tradition. Having these high aspirations may also be conceived as laudable civic progress that lends an occasional vertical articulation to the flat panorama of our modest town. Here on the Great Hungarian Plain, although situated horizontally, we are still above or below each other.

We boys tackle and wrestle one another to determine who is the strongest, who alone can nail both shoulders of every other boy to the oily classroom floor. Zoltán and I have pinned them all; equally strong, we share the winner's platform. This is friendship: for me to admit that you are as good as I am. But friendship is also to be in love with your friend's otherness. Zoltán's otherness was his brooding intellectualism, his discipline, his chaste coolness in the stickier realms of the emotions. He tried to avoid wrestling and, in general, all bodily contact. When a fight was inevitable, he proved who was strongest, but if he had a choice, he would walk away from an insolent remark. I was a fairly quarrelsome child, not shy of touching other bodies, and as a result I frequently wound up lying on top of someone, dirtying my hands and knees—but never my back—on the oily floor. Yes, we also proved to be the victors in that other test of strength, the one concerning our Jewish classmates, the test of survival. By the age of twelve, Zoltán and I were alive; our classmates were not.

We are coming to Budapest from a place where heights are unusual and ambitions provocations. Not only the stork but also the tiny swallow flies upward, and higher than the roof of a two-story house. Higher even than the massive three-story Calvinist brick clock tower that was built in 1812. Better have a seat here on this bench. Made of a split acacia trunk laid across supports also made of acacia, dug deep into the ground, this bench will hold you well enough. And so will the earth. As for the heights, they tend, as everybody knows, to be uncertain. For that matter, you are more secure on all fours than on two feet. A careful look around will reveal that here in Újfalu we are surrounded by quadrupeds.

The tall buildings you see as the train rolls into Budapest West are all instances of getting up on two feet, of ambition and risk-taking. Is it possible to live like this, so close to one another, on top of one another? I see a window open on the second floor, on the third, and on the fourth, too, and figures resembling women leaning out of them. And there is a boy, much like me, peeking out. What magnificent vistas he can choose from! He can look at trains leaving and arriving all day long. We country folk used to take a walk to the station at five in the afternoon just to watch the Budapest express go by. These people here can see a train any time they feel like it.

For me, beginning with the first yellow streetcar and blue bus, Budapest became one big amusement park. Defying gravity, the city rose higher and higher. The boy who glued his nose to the window to see out of the train, who from Csonka Tower in Újfalu arrived in this enchanted forest of towers where roller coasters speed dangerously in all directions, felt that a more wonderful thing could not happen to a human being.

Following the bellboy, we stepped out on the balcony of our hotel room overlooking the Danube. The weather was nice: silvery September. Before me, the Castle of Buda, on Gellért Mountain, towers and towers; behind me, my mother, unpacking. I was not yet of school age. There are those who during their earthly career—in fact, at the very beginning of their earthly career—arrive in paradise. One starts in the east, travels west about one hundred forty miles by train, and reaches Budapest. On the fourth-floor balcony of the Crown Hotel he feels what any country boy reaching an elevated spot in the capital feels. And now it's my turn! Here I am, a little dot in this great teeming maze. I pick myself up and dart across the Citadel. Witches whiz by me, the wind blows. Using the wings of my tartan coat I swoop down to the city, flit among the streetcar wires, peek into lighted rooms. I am amazed, like a mouse in a granary. I think I will stay here for a while. The slow-witted inhabitants of Újfalu, who love to walk with their hands behind their backs, must take such a giant step to reach Budapest that going farther west is not to be imagined.

To the child in us, the center of the universe is where we stand. And the child is right; there is no correlation between the space of our minds and the space of the map. The mind can hop at random on the surface of the earth, yet its journey is continuous. On this city square before me, the dead are strutting about cheerfully. Father comes over to sit with us at our table. Among the guests at the Crown we recognize the people in our dreams, the ones who sit on our chest, the obstinate characters we live with under our closed lids. Those who were hanged now extricate their necks from the noose. The fatal blood clot removes itself and the heart resumes its regular beat.

I have many acquaintances on Liberation Square. A whole cityful, a whole cattle-carful. Our dead live in this square, which is sometimes a garden, or a balcony, or a café. The scene is constantly shifting. The guests take seats at the table. For a fleeting moment we seem to understand one another. We are familiar with the many ways in which body and soul, friendship and memory dissolve. We raise our glasses to this city that has brought us together. To the judges in the other world we will show the list of our friends.

Berettyó

As the snow melted, my sister, cousins, and our governesses were standing on the bridge over the rising Berettyó. In the summer the Berettyó meanders narrowly in its flat, grassy bed, pretending to be

63

harmless. Still, in every swimming season, hidden whirlpools drag somebody down and later cough up the lifeless body. Now, in the spring, the river was pushing wildly, taking with it goats, hay wagons, rabbits perched on rooftops, uprooted trees, and carrion. It hurdled the dams and flooded the Jewish cemetery and the low-lying outskirts of the town. Kneading troughs and pastry boards were being rescued by men lying on flat, hastily constructed rafts.

Nothing is safe, I thought, holding the hand of Livia, my new governess. To the left stood Csonka Tower; danger lurked there, too. The turret of a former fortress, it was cool even in the summer, and in its musty darkness bats whirred. The fortress itself was demolished, although several hundred years ago it gave shelter to the whole town. This has always been wild country, with armies constantly passing through and people hiding in the marshes. Foreign soldiers, marauders, Haiduk, and catchpoles riding freely on the Great Plain.

In the afternoons, the returning herds would take up the entire width of the main street; cows turned left and right into side streets. Each cow knew her own address. The cowherd cracked his fancy whip louder than thunder, not to scare the animals but to let people know that he was coming through.

Conversation in the town was slow, sleepy. The men took their time cutting thick crumbly cubes of bread to go with their thinly sliced salted bacon. "A bit of bacon, lots of bread," they taught their sons. Lovers would sit silently on the seats of farm wagons. The blue-aproned peasants had a way of looking into each other's eyes and understanding everything. The police were not brutes; a slap in the face did not have to be followed by a rifle butt.

The last of the outlaws was sitting in the corner of my great-grandfather's tavern, holding on to his gun. Great-grandfather was behind the bar. The tavern was surrounded by the police. The outlaw's sweetheart, at whose place he had hoped to hide, had betrayed the poor man. He was now having his last drink. "To your health," my great-grandfather said, and they both laughed. The outlaw fired a bullet into the face of a policeman looking through the window. "I won't be able to pay for that window," he said. "Pour yourself another," said my great-grandfather. The outlaw poured with his left hand, lifted the glass to his lips, but had no time to drink. He had not shot a policeman, but only hit a policeman's hat lifted on a broomstick, and now from another window a rifle took careful aim at the outlaw's temple.

My great-grandfather was a tall, muscular man. He would not tolerate foul language, and unruly guests found themselves flat on their backs outside the tavern. "Put that knife down, you ruffian of Bihar!" Every customer carried a wood-handled knife in his boot. Cutting in on a dancing couple on Saturday night was often followed by a stabbing. Some men would not hesitate to stamp the face of their floored rivals with the iron heels of their boots. A big-bellied woman once took an ax and cleft in two the skull of her faithless husband. Among older couples the jealous used the well; you threw your spouse in or else jumped in yourself.

At seventy-eight, my great-grandfather remarried. The woman was less than half his age. A customer once touched her skirt, and the old man heaved him out by his ears into the snow. "You want me to knock you dead, old man?" said the customer. The old man grabbed a pitchfork. "There is another one by the stable door," he said. A pitchfork duel ensued. Punctured in the side, the customer collapsed, but didn't die. My great-grandfather was acquitted. The other white marble stones with Hebrew letters have all tipped over and are lying facedown in the neglected cemetery, but my great-grandfather's still stands. He had a fierce-looking, forked beard, and his face was bony and brown, his eyes scornful. Whenever I look at his picture, he looks right back at me. He knows something.

My father, the eagerly awaited male child, was privileged to visit the tavern of his grandfather in a four-wheel carriage. The tavern was on the outskirts of town and had a large vineyard. The red Othello grapes stung my father's mouth. His stepgrandmother baked crescents out of flaky pastry dough and filled them with apricot jam. That was my favorite, too. My father was a very gentle boy; he never learned that you must be strong, never learned how to knock the knife out of the hand of your opponent, to throw your cap down on the ground next to his and fight until noses bleed and lips split, to avenge an insult. "My dear daughter, why are you bringing this boy in white stockings here?"

My grandmother had not wanted my father rolling around the

65

pasture with the boys from Szentmárton. She made him take violin lessons and protected her little Józsi from every draft. He should study, graduate from high school, and become a gentleman. The violin teacher had long hair and long jackets. His bow often landed on my father's ear for playing off-key.

"Climb up in the hayloft," my great-grandfather whispered to my father. To please the old man, Józsi climbed up into the hayloft and watched the birds in the sky. Later, when I was around, it would happen that during lunchtime, after coffee, my father would recline in a deck chair on the balcony. The disquieting newspaper would drop to his lap, and his eyes would search the sky for birds of prey. He smiled silently, smiled without even moving his lips.

Everybody agreed that little Józsi was behaving himself properly. At thirteen, in the synagogue for his bar mitzvah, celebrating his coming into manhood, he recited beautifully his explication of the Torah passage. And later, he looked very handsome in the uniform my grandmother had ordered for him at the local tailor, because her recently graduated son was going to the Romanian front in World War I. On the advice of all the other Jewish mothers, and through some connections, my father became an artilleryman. Grandmother didn't allow him to join the hussars; that would have taken him too close to the enemy. And a hussar could be thrown by his horse, and during charges he would have to wave his sword above his head while galloping and lop off other men's heads. An artilleryman, on the other hand, was a great distance from the thick of things, firing away without knowing who or what was the target. "If possible, don't fire at people," Grandmother said to him. "There is so much room in the world where there are no people. That's where you should aim. Don't harm anyone, my precious flower, and the Lord will protect you, and then, if he is willing, no one will harm you either." My father was the baby of the family, younger than the daughter of his oldest sister. The Lord had blessed my grandmother with great fecundity. She was ashamed about having become pregnant when she was past forty. But my serious and gaunt grandfather, with the ruddy complexion, was not ashamed. He kept impregnating that plump little body as often as he could.

In the entire county, my father had the only license to sell hunting weapons and ammunition. This was a considerable privilege, demanding civic and commercial trustworthiness. All the finely chased hunting rifles were kept in glass-covered showcases under lock and key. Looking into the barrels of these rifles, I saw a radiant infinity through which death arrived. Men in fur-lined, fur-trimmed short jackets would crack the barrel, peer inside, then put the rifle over their shoulders to see if the stock lay well in the hollow of their necks. Serious customers could try out the weapons in the courtyard. Father himself took no joy in weapons. It would never occur to him to go hunting. He didn't even swat flies with an intent to kill, he only shooed them away.

But I was very interested in weapons. My slingshot was everything to me. I made it myself, out of a forked cherry-tree branch, rubber thongs, and a piece of leather. I didn't shoot birds with it, however. I watched the swallow father come home to the nest under our balcony, bringing a worm, and the little swallows strain and stretch for it. How could I shoot their father? Shooting was fun, but not at living things. I fit a slender arrow to the string of my bow. The arrow was tipped with a nail, which gave it weight and carried it farther. With it I could fell even that goat in the synagogue's courtyard. It was a she-goat; I watched her heavy udders swing as she moved among her kids. On her forehead, between her horns, there was a tuft of white hair. I tickled it; she hung her head. I tried to push her back by her horns; she shoved me away. I fell on my bottom; she walked away, bleating in triumph.

I was also crazy about knives, switchblades, and daggers. I loved to finger their edges, to draw them from their scabbards, to make the switchblades pop out of their handles. Buckling a hunting knife to my belt, I looked at my manly, rugged self in the mirror. I grasped my father's Browning as if it were a royal scepter. This Browning was locked in the drawer of the dressing table in my parents' bedroom. Above the dressing table two naked angels held a mirror. The upper right drawer was locked, but I got hold of the key. There was something next to the revolver, which I learned to identify later: contraceptives.

My grandfather's name was Ignác Kohn. After graduating from

high school, my father Hungarianized the name to Konrád. He had an uncle by that name in Debrecen, a Talmudic scholar and owner of a bookstore, who would sit up in the mezzanine of the store and read and not come down even when someone rang the bell below.

We were not only Kohns, we were Cohanites. Father explained what that meant: As descendants of Aaron, we were not to set foot in a cemetery, were allowed to marry only virgins, and in the synagogue we were the only ones who could hold the Torah scrolls. The religious community kept this priestly nobility of ours well in mind. Although the privilege was not transmitted through the female line, my grandfather on my mother's side was also a Cohanite, and this, too, was known in the town. "And it's nothing to sneeze at," my father said. "Two thousand years ago your ancestors were scholarly priests, the caretakers of the Temple and the Holy Ark. Though, true, this does not amount to a family coat of arms," he added pensively. From our window I used to watch the black hats of the Jews as they walked to the synagogue, their shoulders stooped. On holidays I stood next to my father in his box behind the brown pew that faced the Ark. He covered me with his prayer shawl, white silk with black and gold stripes.

This is what was written on the façade of my father's new house, and on the printed stationery of the business: HARDWARE STORE OF JÓZSEF KONRÁD, SUCCESSOR OF IGNÁC KOHN. ESTABLISHED 1878. Several times he attempted the literary task of integrating my name into this sequence, so that I would appear as the next successor. When I grew a little older, I regretted that my father was not stronger, a man on a grander scale. But today I am grateful to him for not exercising strength over me. He gave me love, breathing space, and he taught me by example. I respected him. And it's better that he was a hardware merchant and not a poet. "You know, son, hardware may not be as easy as the clothing or perfume business, but it is more serious. Here you will not see restless women who don't know what they look good in. What we get are farm managers, peasants, and craftsmen who know exactly what they need. The hardware merchant does not flatter or fawn; his merchandise speaks for him."

I was a powerful, thickset little master, kind to everybody. The owner's son should be friendly. My father, appointed to his post at birth, was an heir, and so was I. I, too, would have an heir, because when I grew up I would start an airplane factory in Újfalu, and my son would have to carry on with it. I would enlarge the pool/ice-skating rink, which was nothing more than a duck pond now, and as a personal gift I would have a set of bleachers added for patrons and visitors. My favorite pipe dream was a scheme, after I came in to a bundle of money, to beautify Újfalu. One thing was certain: On the banks of Káló creek the mechanical organ of the merry-go-round would play continuously, and the circus monkey would never stop beating the cymbals.

I was my father's heir in many ways. In my ability to make myself understood. And I listened to people with interest. I asked questions, sometimes to the point of absurdity. "Tell me, please"—that's how I began my sentences when I was younger, and perhaps I'm still doing it, because the phrase has become a joke among my friends.

For my father, the store was not only a place of business transactions but also a kind of club for good conversation, like the taverns, the mill, and the smithy. Part of his eight hours spent downstairs was devoted to chatting with people from Szentmárton, Furta, Csökmő, Bagamér, Zsáka, Darvas, Bakonszeg, and Derecske, but most of all with the people of Berettyóújfalu, who were the residents of the county seat, the center of the world.

He felt that the important things of the world were to be found in Újfalu, and I felt that way, too. Újfalu was the only place worth living in. All other places were too far, as remote as the stars around our sun. Father was the king in this house, and I the heir apparent, the future master of the dozen people who worked for us, and of this solid building. Grandfather's education had ended in secondary school; my father graduated from a business college, and he wanted to send me to a university, to Oxford. His plan was that I would not only maintain the hardware store but also build a factory in Újfalu.

But in my teens I thought that the truly interesting people were elsewhere, not in our family. There had to be worlds more exciting than the one I knew. The milieu I came from—provincial, Jewish, bourgeois—was so thoroughly criticized, even its very right to exist, by the intellectual circles of Budapest, that I came to doubt my own right to exist. Why couldn't my father have been an illegal Communist ironworker before the war, or possibly a destitute day laborer? But he couldn't be that in the "social origin" rubric of the questionnaires—in those days you had to fill out countless questionnaires—so I always entered "middle class." In the official lists, the rubric under my name was "Class: alien" (which does not differ much from the former regime's "Nationality: alien").

Or, if Father did not come from below, if he was not the child of simple folk, why couldn't he have come from higher up? Why couldn't he have been a leading banker? And why didn't we live in Budapest, in a great big villa on the green hills of Buda or in a grand apartment on the bank of the Danube? After my father's house, store, and entire existence were nationalized—that is to say, seized—why did we have to live in such cramped quarters that I had no real room of my own, unless you called a former servant's cubbyhole a room? If my father couldn't be the child of simple folk, why wasn't he a great scientist or a nightclub star or an eccentric country landowner? And why was he so good and kindly; why wasn't he wilder, more wicked?

Today I am grateful to him for allowing me to grow at my own pace, for not forcing me to fight him. I felt neither resentment nor rebellion toward him. His authority was a benevolent authority. He never stepped over the lawful boundaries of his life. My life, on the other hand, has been a series of border violations. As a headstrong young man, I soon found myself in conflict with higher authorities. I was more vain, curious, and restless than my father. I used to call him the principal, because sometimes he would speak with such solemnity it was as if he were addressing a graduating class. Whenever he did that, I lowered my eyes and with some jest or witticism tried to lighten the mood. Now, I think, I would listen to him with more attention. I miss those Sunday dinners that in my younger days I would rather have skipped.

There was something of ritual in those Sunday dinners, with my Mother's three-course masterpieces: vegetable soup with liver dumplings, fried meat or a roast, and the always reliable chocolate cake, or thick rolled pancakes, all full of Mother's provincial but wonderful flavors. Sometimes my mind would wander, and silence would fall on the table. I would pat the retired merchant's hand, full of thoughts I could not discuss with him because they were too personal.

When my first novel appeared, Father took aside Julia, my wife at the time, and asked: "Tell me, dear, what is bothering my son? He has a nice family, a regular job, a pleasant home. Why does he write about such sad and awful things?" Julia was unable to give him a satisfactory answer. He sat meditating by my son's crib. My mother had chosen our daughter, Dorka, as her favorite, and Father chose Miklós. He never tired of him. For hours he would watch the tiny hands poking at the equally tiny nose and ears, perhaps in search of the mouth. If Miklós started to cry, and the crying worked up to a more dramatic sobbing, Father would tolerate it for a while, then pick up the boy and pacify him. Opening the door, we would see the two of them, Miklós in my father's arms, looking out the window.

Since then, Miklós has acquired a respectable twenty-year-old biography of his own. He lives in Paris, studies history and Hungarian literature at the Sorbonne. He has been playing the drums for eight years and wants to be a rock star. He is alternately scintillating and pusillanimous. We see him only at vacation times, just as we do Dorka, who will soon finish her medical studies in Paris. A shame that my children could not see their grandfather in his house and store in Újfalu, his true and natural environment.

In May 1944, my father and mother were arrested, placed in a detention camp, and then deported to Austria. Having survived the concentration camps, they both came back. Meanwhile, my sister Éva and I had moved to Budapest and kept alive. We have been an exceptionally lucky family. Most parents did not return to Újfalu, and to have surviving children was almost a miracle. Every Jewish family had a missing spouse or child, and although they wished us well, it must have been painful for them to see our family intact. Father still considered leaving the Berettyóújfalu area inconceivable, and started over again. But in 1950 his store was nationalized. He asked to be allowed to continue work as an employee—after all, hardware was his trade, that was the only thing he knew. The new government firm did not want my father's services, however, only his house. The result: a repetition of what had happened six years earlier—he was left with nothing, a houseless snail. My father moved to Budapest and became the manager of a government-owned hardware store. Our bourgeois existence had come to an end.

He was forty-seven in 1944, when he first suffered the humiliation of being at the mercy of others. I was eleven at the time. It is possible that this is the reason I am so prepared for life's calamities. I grew up with them; they have kept me on my toes. I know that there may be a knock on my door at any time. My father's sister and most of his friends and relatives were killed. Those who survived soon emigrated to the West or to Israel. A few Jews from Újfalu have come only as far as Budapest. Of these, some joined the Communist Party and landed fairly good jobs in state-owned companies, usually in their own lines. They had been timber merchants, haberdashers, and grocers, and that is what they continued to be. My father's friends knew nothing about politics, made no speeches at assemblies; even in the capital they remained country folk, hardly seeing anybody outside their own circle. Leading this new/old life, they have slowly passed on. Only one of them is left now, eighty-seven-year-old Uncle Marci, my father's cousin, who has so beautifully recited the Kaddish over the others' graves. But I know of no Jew from Újfalu, here in Budapest, who will be able to do the same for him.

Father did not understand how taking everything away from him could be called progressive. "Those two scoundrels have robbed me of everything," he declared. In our circle of friends and family there was no doubt as to which two famous scoundrels of twentieth-century history he meant. It was baffling to him that the state, whose law-abiding citizen he had always been, was suddenly doing things no decent person would have thought of doing. In the later part of his life, during the twenty-two years he spent in Budapest, in this not-truly-real life, he became a forgotten little man afraid of Communist Party seminars and of the possibility that at the compulsory demonstrations somebody might stick a flag into his hands. On Sundays he went on hikes with my mother into the hills of Buda, if for no other reason than to avoid the visits of agitprop workers whose duty it was to report on people's moods, carefully jotting down whatever incorrect views they heard and the names of those who had expressed them.

Father was glad that his children were good students, but his eyes grew moist when he spoke of his murdered sisters. He was repeatedly amazed that he had survived the war. He did not want to emigrate anywhere, and brooded over his daughter, Éva, my sister, who in 1956 left the country because she could get no work as a research biologist. Father would go over her letters many times, read aloud to me the passages that could be construed as optimistic.

Of the merchandise in the state-owned store, he spoke with embarrassment. "My boy, I would never have carried such inferior things in my store." During shortages he had never allowed his assistants to put items aside and then sell them at higher prices to their friends. The assistants denounced my father as a reactionary, and so fellow-worker Konrád was transferred to the firm's headquarters, as an accounting supervisor. And then he retired. At home he did the vacuuming, the shopping; he chatted with the concierge, with the fishwives in the large indoor marketplace, and with the butcher. He was happy to get a part-time job as assistant salesman in a department store. He read, but often dozed off over his book, and he still listened to the Hungarian broadcast of the BBC. Most of all, he liked to play horsey with Miklós.

Reminiscing, we talked about the winter mornings when his assistants used to stand in front of the hot stove, its colored windows aglow, rubbing their cold hands as they looked out on the street, listened to the sound of bells around the horses' necks, and watched the snow-covered wagons slide by on their runners. In those days people got everywhere on time, and bought only what they needed: enamel pots, nails, wire, scythes, axletrees, hunting rifles, fishing rods, pocketknives, bicycles, stoves—so many useful and durable objects of reliable quality. There was nothing synthetic then; even aluminum was suspect compared with cast and wrought iron, or with steel. The enamel did not chip off the pots, bicycles lasted a lifetime, and even horseshoes, plows, and zinc-plated buckets were made so that no one returned them with complaints.

Father's heart attack came in the afternoon, and he was dead by dawn of the following day. He was seventy-two then; I was thirty-six. Around midnight, he took hold of my hand, as if about to say something significant, and smiled. "You see, my little boy, a man's life is nothing." Apologetically, he turned to the wall. He didn't speak again; his body was in a cold sweat, his face white. The last thing he did was ask my mother for a glass of water. By the time she returned from the kitchen, he was no longer alive.

Above her bed hangs his picture: a long, smooth, confident face. In the black-and-white photograph you cannot see the innocent blue of his eyes. I don't believe it ever occurred to him to be unfaithful to my mother. He answered annoyance and irritation with humor. Raised voices and shouting bothered him. When I went to report his death and make funeral arrangements at the offices of the Jewish Congregation of Budapest, the elderly clerk raised his head from the enormous, copper-clasped tome. "József Konrád? Berettyóújfalu? I know the name. It was a good firm, of fine reputation." When I last saw my father, in the mortuary of the Rákoskeresztur Jewish cemetery in Budapest in December 1969, he was wrapped in a white shroud, a flat pebble on each eyelid. Ten old Jewish men from Újfalu prayed at his grave. With his hat on my head, I repeated after uncles Imre and Marci, hesitantly, the prayer for the dead.

Grandfather

My grandfather on my mother's side lived in Nagyvárad and did not take his business too seriously. Around nine in the morning he would walk into his office, and by noon he would be back home. Before lunch he had a shot of brandy; after lunch he took a nap in the easy chair, not wanting to lie down. He would finish his coffee, put his pince-nez on his nose, pick up the newspaper, lean back, and fall asleep. This postprandial routine lasted for decades, its details unchanged; and nobody ever thought of making fun of him for it. Whenever he visited us, I sat opposite him in a high-backed overstuffed chair in the living room. I was given lumps of sugar dipped in coffee, which made me very lively and more curious than ever.

Grandfather was very mysterious. On his night table there were scholarly volumes in German about the Crusades and the Jews of Venice. My father never read books like that. Grandfather was in the lumber business, and with his son he ventured into other industries, opening several factories, some of which worked out and some of which didn't. Uncle Ernő provided the enterprise, Grandfather the dignity. I wanted Grandfather to talk, because he knew so many things. Even now (with pince-nez on his nose, his Franz Josef beard and bow tie below) he is probably dreaming of higher things, and has visions that reach far beyond the horizon of Újfalu.

But no one could accuse him of being talkative. He would start telling me a story, then lose interest in it. "Should I leave the room?" I would ask. His answer was slow in coming. "Stay," he would say. "But you are reading." He couldn't tell me to pick up a book and read, too, because I didn't yet know how. "Think," he said. Ever since then, I have been thinking. I think even in my sleep. When my mother leaned over my canopied bed and asked if I had slept well, I would correct her, saying that I hadn't been asleep, only thinking with my eyes closed.

Even today, my mother blushes when she tells me of the great and much-envied honor of being asked to go for an early-afternoon walk with Grandfather. After his siesta, the old gentleman would select one of his children to accompany him on a somewhat indirect route to his favorite café. "No need to take the shortest road," the old gentleman used to say, and he would add all sorts of detours to his itinerary. He wanted to see if a certain row of linden trees was coming into bloom, or to say hello to another gentleman, many years his senior, who was also taking his constitutional, his cane tapping the sidewalk under the worrisome gaze of his daughter, who was leaning out a window. "Where are you going, Uncle Zsiga?" Grandfather asked. "To see the pretty girls, my boy," the old man would say, then add, "You gallop on ahead. I'll meet you there." Of course Uncle Zsiga was only joking. But he knew what he knew. Even

Rózsika suspected that the venerable gentleman was not altogether indifferent to the fair sex.

Curious, puny little Rózsika was Grandfather's youngest daughter. He preferred to take her, and not Gizella, on his walks, because Gizu was given to temper tantrums in public. To me, all three of my mother's sisters were more or less the same: slightly slanted eyes, large noses and lips; and plump, as aunts generally are. Their kisses were always more smackingly thoroughgoing than their bashful, reluctant nephew liked. As soon as these aunts lay their eyes on us, when we were still in the foyer, joy would erupt in huge waves. We hid behind Mother's skirt. But there was no such threat from Grandfather. He would put his large, handsome brown hand with the signet ring on our heads. Nothing more, nothing less; that gesture sufficed.

My mother recalls how she used to walk with her father hand in hand—he with his fur collar, his white mustache twirled into the shape of a treble clef, his short, parted beard, pince-nez, bowler hat, and ivory-handled walking stick—and how people made a point of saying hello to him. He held himself aloof, merely returning salutations. On these walks he would talk to my mother about the old days; he liked to describe human folly in humorous, colorful terms. When they reached the café, which was full of ornate chandeliers and columns, he hesitated: Should he take the little girl into this less-than-pure place? There, poet-journalists, music-hall starlets, and cavalry officers often had one too many, even in the early afternoon, and created scenes whose rapid and smooth suppression required the offices of tall Mr. Poldi. But the early afternoon was also the time when the café's pastry case was refilled, and not inviting Rózsika for a piece of chocolate cake would have been sheer heartlessness. Grandfather solved the problem by having the waiter telephone home, after the cake, and ask the governess to come and fetch my mother. Returning home in the evening, he would withdraw into his separate, man's, quarters, to be alone with his books.

When they were in their teens, my mother and Gizu, the two youngest sisters, played the piano and studied French. They spent their afternoons taking walks and sitting in the confectioner's shop, where they would meet their girlfriends. In the evening they went to the theater; they had their own box. The local company changed its fare often, and my mother and sister went to everything—operas, operettas, folk plays, comedies, social dramas, and tragedies. Mother was a vigorous piano player, and Gizu sang bravely in her alto.

One day, a potential groom appeared on the scene, sending enormous bouquets of red roses every morning to Aunt Gizu. Who would have guessed that he bought all those flowers on credit, and that eventually the dowry would be used to pay off his debts? The day of the wedding arrived. At the birth of each of his children, Grandfather had bought a barrel of wine and put it in his cellar. Only at the child's wedding would the barrel be tapped. Now, out of tumblers, the guests were drinking the thick wine. Heady fragrance everywhere, a happy daze. The pleasant and as yet unsuspected son-in-law was co-owner of a bank; on bended knee he asked Grandfather to transfer all his money to that bank. How would people regard him in town if his own father-in-law did not have faith in him? So Grandfather entrusted everything he had to his son-in-law. But even that was not enough to avoid bankruptcy. The scandal broke a week later. It was not easy, even with the concerted effort of the whole family, to save the son-in-law from prison. From that time on, Grandfather was no longer a rich man, and he would not acknowledge the existence of his son-in-law. Once, at a family gathering, I saw Grandfather look right through him. This was equivalent to a death warrant. "A man who lies is no man," he once remarked.

I was already in secondary school, and Grandfather long dead, when on the Number 6 streetcar on the Great Boulevard in Budapest, he came to life with such vividness as to bring tears to my eyes. A few paces from me stood an elderly gentleman holding on to the hanging leather strap. His mustache, like Grandfather's, curled up, though he had no thick, round-trimmed, precision-parted white beard. He used the same mustache cream Grandfather used. It was the smell that had summoned Grandfather. It was snowing. I got off the streetcar and turned down a side street. Grandfather also liked to walk in the snow; he would walk wrapped in thought, tipping his hat like someone not interested in conversation but simply out for a walk and quite content with his own company. People sensed this; they would smile at him and move on, joining him only when they had something important to discuss.

After one of these walks, with a particularly absorbed look on his face, Grandfather produced from his briefcase a leather-bound Bible. The reflection of my mother's Friday-night candles in his pince-nez made my heart beat faster. Even before his arrival I had been in a festive frame of mind, because of the slow jingle of the sleds, the soft hoofbeats in the snow, the murmuring voices of Jews passing our house on their way to the synagogue. My emotions reached a peak as the old man put his hand on my head. He wrote in the Karoli Bible: "To my favorite grandson." We were standing by the window, looking down at the street. In the steady snowfall, the Jews pulled in their necks, but continued to gesticulate as they talked. "A strange people," said my grandfather, who had never acquired the habit of speaking with his hands.

Grandfather Is Gone

My family had lived mostly in the towns of Bihar County and in Nagyvárad, once the county seat, which was also an episcopal see. Nagyvárad was a teeming and vibrant town on the bank of the Sebes Körös, where the Great Hungarian Plain meets the mountains of Transylvania; where the commerce of the entire plain and highland region was organized by quick-witted Jews (one third of the population), and where actors and journalists who wanted to revel all night were served by a sleepless citizenry. "We've got everything," people of Bihar used to say. The northwestern part of the county was a dark plain, yielding good wheat; the mountainous area in the southeast was rich in ores and minerals. Nagyvárad the locals compared to Paris.

My family can be traced back to the eighteenth century, to Hungarian-speaking Jews, most of whom married and remained in the same county, Bihar. Among them you can find innkeepers and peasants, sellers of hardware, wine, textiles, and perfume, booksellers, pharmacists, restaurateurs, tinsmiths, printers, owners of furniture and hosiery factories, publishers, and occasionally a respected physician or lawyer. They rose slowly within the hierarchy of the emerging middle class; they wanted their children to attend universities.

The first great shock experienced by my family was the peace treaty of Trianon in 1920. As a result of that treaty, the country was split in half. Part of the plain became Csonka Bihar or Truncated Bihar County, and the new county seat was Berettyóújfalu, a "frontier metropolis," as a radio reporter broadcasting from the national fair once called it, a name the townspeople adopted with a smile. The other half of the plain, and the highlands, went to Romania. Nagyvárad also ended up on the other side of the border. Overnight most of our family became Hungarian-speaking Romanians. They continued to consider themselves Hungarians.

In the spring of 1939, having been a widower for six years, my grandfather, at the age of eighty, married for the second time. The new wife was thirty-eight, a hairdresser. She had been sent by her employer to take care of the elderly gentleman's white hair, mustache, and beard. Fastening a white damask kerchief around Grandfather's neck, over his tobacco-colored dressing gown, the woman set to work. It is likely that, since her dress was not a long one, Grandfather's hand may have brushed the hairdresser's thighs. The touch was not rebuffed. His two sons and four daughters did not attend the wedding. Nor did they visit him later. They were glad to see him when he visited them, but they would not pay their respects to *that* woman.

As a grandchild, I was allowed to stay with him in Nagyvárad. In that long single-story house crammed full of heavy furniture, not only was I not bothered by *that* woman, but, on the contrary, I found her pretty and amiable. For the first time I saw Grandfather wearing only his shirt and vest. Before, he would never be seen without a jacket. His heavy, musical pocket watch was still running; when he held it to my ear, I felt like crying.

In our house all the table linen had to be of damask, including the napkins, which right after dinner we would roll up and put into silver napkin rings. We each had our own ring, with our names engraved in fancy lettering, so we wouldn't wipe our mouths on someone else's napkin. My sister and I competed to see whose napkin was more colorful after a meal. Grandfather's napkin ring, in our home in Újfalu, at 9 Miklós Horthy Road (now György Dózsa), used to wait for its owner for months at a time, in the upper drawer of the dining-room cupboard. We all wanted him to come, to take the train and a hansom and be with us; we wanted him to sit at the head of the table, put his hands above the candlesticks, and lead the ceremony. My father would sit on Grandfather's left, my mother on his right. Being the smallest, I sat at the far end of the table, opposite him. When I took several gulps of the seder wine, as the ritual required, when I munched on the mixture of bits of walnut and grated apple (I wouldn't touch the horseradish), I received great smiles from the head of the table. I duly recited the Four Questions, but then asked my own as well. "You certainly will not be like this one," said Grandfather, pointing to the last of the four sons in the parable, the simpleton who is unable to inquire.

It was considered an event whenever Grandfather visited one of his forests, lumbermills, or houses at the foot of the high mountains, the favorite vacation spot of his grandchildren. Even in summer, the tops of these mountains were aglitter with white expanses and silver brooks in blue meadows. He entrusted the management of his business to his energetic son-in-law and his taciturn son. Ernő, my uncle, was in charge of the lumberyard. He was good at hunting, trout fishing, and getting along with the workers, but he was not good at management. Nearby was an abundant, swift, and very cool brook. With his pants rolled up, my uncle loved to stand in it and feel the stones at the bottom.

Grandfather arrived in his own little train, in a small parlor car behind the lumber-carrying flatcars. On top of the pointed cupola of the log cabin, a weather vane creaked mournfully. He sat on the veranda overlooking a large clearing where goats grazed. In the early-afternoon heat, when either the air or my eyes were shimmering with rainbows, the charcoal-burning Gypsies emerged from the forest bringing their taunting, curious children. They sold wild strawberries in glazed mugs. I was a little afraid of them, because the men's hair and beards reached down to their belts. One of the girls could roll her eyes inside with her two fingers; she said she was looking inward and could see a snake on a flat stone. I'll never forget her white eyeballs. In the evening, meat was roasted by the brook that ran through the clearing, near a little waterfall. Clinging to the rock wall, you could cross from one side of the brook to the other without getting wet behind the dense curtain of water. Grandfather also came to sit with us. He'd gaze into the fire and listen to the rumble of the cascading water. On the spit: chicken legs, onions, and tomatoes. In the old man's presence, pork and bacon were out of the question. To me, he seemed unaccountably sad; if addressed, he nodded distantly.

Grandfather did not trust Uncle Imre with anything. Uncle Imre loved a good time and a good hunt. In the café, he would take the fiddle from the Gypsy and play some strange song on it. At night he was a croupier in a casino. He showed up unexpectedly at our fire with his actress girlfriend in tow. I had never in my life seen so many varieties of red on a woman: Her hair and large mouth were one red, her large face was another, and her nails were yet another. Uncle Imre's little mustache was already turning gray. Because he was a highly decorated officer in World War I, in World War II he was allowed to wear, in spite of being a Jew, a white armband instead of a yellow one, which granted him special privileges. In 1944 Hungarian Nazis shot him dead in the street, paying no attention to his special privileges. The Cross of Valor on the velvet cushion became the victim of a firebomb. Uncle Imre's small bachelor apartment, along with its roof terrace and all his curious keepsakes, simply disappeared. Nothing is left of him.

When the Hungarian army was permitted by the Germans to march into northern Transylvania in 1940, half of Grandfather's house in Nagyvárad was taken over by Hungarian officers. They lived there for a whole year before being ordered to the Ukrainian front. They were polite and got along well with Grandfather and his wife, occasionally dropping in for coffee. Then came one little officer, still wet behind the ears, who made a nuisance of himself. He could not get over the age difference between my grandfather and his wife. When he made an impertinent remark to her, she replied: "When you are led by my house as a prisoner and I give you a piece of bread, remember this foolish remark." She was sent to an internment camp for predicting, with this one sentence, the defeat of the Axis powers.

Grandfather sought help, turning to one of the town's well-known right-wing lawyers. First the drawers of the cupboard were emptied, then the cupboard itself disappeared. It was followed by the musical clocks off the walls and, finally, his gold pocket watch. He gave everything he had to the lawyer, expecting no money from his children on behalf of his new wife. In the end he went to the camp, so he could at least see her.

"Grandfather is gone," my father said, his elbows resting on his knees. Yes, "gone" suited him better than "dead." Death does come to all men, but one whose collar is so fresh and pince-nez so clean every day, one who goes walking in the snow the way Grandfather did, a man like that does not die; rather, he departs, unwilling to acknowledge certain things, letting the snowflakes close in behind him.

It was snowing hard in 1941 when Grandfather circled the barbed-wire fence for hours, hoping to get a glimpse of his wife. The prisoners did not leave the barracks, and the guards watching the old man from their tower wondered how long he would keep this up. The camp commandant refused to let him in. Wearing his bowler hat, Grandfather walked around and around the fence in the deep snow. Perhaps somebody leaving the barracks would see him and let his wife know that he was there. But the snow kept coming down; it covered his hat and astrakhan-collared coat so thoroughly that his figure became indistinguishable from the white field. Then one of the guards yelled down at him that enough was enough and the old man should go away.

Nearly frozen, Grandfather got on the train at ten in the evening. By the time he reached Nagyvárad, he was running a fever. He had pneumonia. Shortly afterward he lost consciousness. For a while he kept repeating the names of both his wives, then called only for his mother. Before his death, the fever subsided; his mind cleared for an hour, and he looked around cheerfully. "Comb my hair," he said.

"You've been good daughters. You got married. Some of your husbands are decent men. There is that scoundrel, too. You married him because of your weakness. But you could not overlook my weakness. I asked your mother for permission to marry a second time, and received it, but I did not tell you. May the Eternal One keep you all. Regards to my sons who are so far away. The management of my business affairs I leave to Ernő. Imre should play the violin at my wake, and I don't care if he dances on the table. Let him rend his finest jacket as a sign of mourning. Only Ernő is authorized to read my letters and other personal papers." Grandfather asked for a glass of water. Somebody gave it to him. Then he sent everyone out of the room. "Turn off the lights, girls," he called after them. His daughters pulled the double doors shut, but not all the way. Grandfather, looking at the ceiling, threw his head back a number of times. The upper lip wanted to part from the lower lip but could not, and by the time it did get unstuck, the sound escaping from his throat no longer resembled words. He tilted his head toward the opening in the double doors. His eyes were still searching for his daughters when he grew rigid. It was easy to readjust his head on the pillow, and he had clasped his hands himself, as if expecting a photographer.

"Whether we say that Grandfather is gone or died, he did it just in time," my father said years later, leaning back in the same overstuffed chair Grandfather used to sit in. In 1945, using a handcart, we rescued this overstuffed chair from the town's poverty row; its back had been upholstered with some other material. It is still in my room. So many people who sat in it are gone. Father, too, has long ceased to analyze the political situation. When his time came, he turned to the wall, surprised that it was happening. In this chair he often wondered at how fast time flew. But I agreed with him about Grandfather's leaving us in time. A stylish life required a stylish death. In the ghetto, in the cattle cars, and in that certain shower room with hundreds of other people, all naked—no, that would not have been going in style.

The hairdresser, Grandfather's second wife, survived the concentration camp. She was a kapo; she beat other inmates. Liberated by the Americans, she did not bother to come home, afraid of her fellow survivors. She went to São Paulo, then to Sydney, where she married, but was soon widowed again. I've heard she owns a number of beauty and massage parlors, wears heavy gold bracelets, has become a passionate bridge player, and swims daily. She takes trips with one of her parlor managers.

My Uncles

Except for my uncles Pali and Miki, all our relatives obeyed the orders and regulations of the authorities. Law-abiding Jewish fathers led their families by the hand into the gas chambers. Pali was a handsome boy and a big rascal. For his university studies he was sent to England, but instead of attending classes he played cards and tennis, and was busy turning the heads of pretty girls. The family disgrace was recalled; he married a beautiful but poor Jewish girl, and they had a daughter named Judit. No one in the family would trust Pali with any serious undertaking; he was always in debt. His debts accumulated at the card table. When Judit was four, she and her mother were gassed. In 1944 Pali escaped from the forced-labor service and organized a Partisan unit in the alps of Máramaros, near one of Grandfather's sawmills, an area he knew well. He had several hundred men, armed mostly with axes instead of rifles. These were labor-camp fugitives, soldiers, Jews, Hungarians, Romanians, and Ukrainians brought together by my uncle not so much to fight as to get away and survive, though surviving involved some shooting.

After the war, Uncle Pali went to England to see his brother, who in the meantime had become a reputable architect, an expert in light-concrete structures, and also a Communist. He had married a large woman, a red-haired Labour MP. The men of our family seem to have a penchant for unearthing the magic of redheads. Pali smuggled weapons from England for the Jews in Palestine. When Israel was declared a state, he went back to reliable and liberal England, where, so I hear, he owns and runs a small hotel in the north. He is married. The couple lives in harmony and laughs a lot.

My other ideal was Uncle Miki. He could hardly wait to join the labor battalions in Yugoslavia. He let me in on his secret: Once in the mountains, he would go over to the Partisans. To me, at the age of eleven, the Partisans were heroes out of a fairy tale. Miki did what he said he would; he fought with the Partisans and survived. Coming home, he learned that his parents had been murdered. He could not settle down. "How many did you kill?" I asked him. He did not answer. I pestered him some more. "Seven," he said, and added, "That should be enough for you." He began smuggling contraband goods across the Hungarian-Romanian border. In the spring of 1945 you could still move freely between Nagyvárad and Újfalu without going through checkpoints, but by the end of that year smuggling had to be done with weapons. Miki and his partners would speed across the border in a truck. If the mounted border guards fired on them, they would return the fire. Miki said they only fired in the air, to scare the guards, but I didn't believe him.

In his thick-soled shoes and leather coat, carrying his Leica—as if he were a photojournalist—he came to see us in Újfalu to say good-bye. He was leaving for Israel; there was nothing more for him to do here. He wanted adventure, risk. Miki sailed for Haifa and joined the Irgun. He worked with explosives, fought the British and the Arabs, smuggled illegal immigrants from sea to shore, and fell in battle. God rest his soul.

In 1940, following the Axis powers' decision in Vienna, Transylvania was again partitioned. Nagyvárad, as part of North Transylvania, was returned to Hungary. South Transylvania remained Romanian. The Romanian-Hungarian border was now about six miles south of Nagyvárad. My family had some business interest very close to the border, at a place called Mezőtelegd.

My favorite aunt, Ilonka, lived in Mezőtelegd. She was a phenomenal cook and even harder to ruffle than my mother. Her husband, Pista, was a violent, large, not-too-bright man. Whatever he tried his hand at was sure to end in failure. He let people steal from him, and preferred picking strawberries to keeping his books. He also enjoyed roaming in the mountains, hunting, and simply feeding pigs. They would come charging out of their pen to the trough, jostling and grunting and squealing while he kicked them in the rear and laughed uproariously. At his table Uncle Pista, the son of an impoverished Jewish cantor, mocked the Jews, especially the ones with earlocks, the Talmudists. He was always teasing me, too, asking if I had been a good little boy at heder.

I didn't attend heder, and that was quite a problem, because my classmates did and considered me an apostate for staying away. Every afternoon at three they went to heder, a room in the whitewashed little house next to the synagogue, and until six in the evening they listened to the old rabbi holding forth, trying to lead them into the world of the Talmud. All these boys were pale and had very little time to play and grow strong.

One afternoon I was standing in the courtyard of the synagogue when a brick from the direction of the heder flew over the fence and hit me in the head. Bleeding profusely, I ran upstairs. Mother washed the wound, and Father took me to the doctor. We did not pursue the matter, aware that the Jewish community was not pleased with us. Father kept his store open on Saturdays, and Mother did not keep a kosher home. We did not always wear hats, and I had no fringed zizith under my shirt. Occasionally the rabbi would come to school and inspect us, to make sure that all the boys were wearing their zizith. We were supposed to pull the soft little fringes out from beneath our shirts and show them to the rabbi. I kept a fringe in my pocket and during inspection held it in my hand. "Pull it out all the way!" the rabbi shouted one day, and was horrified at my perfidy, dangling in his hand, the useless fringe not attached to any garment.

If my assimilation was civil and moderate, Uncle Pista's was vengeful. Out of spite he would eat bacon and ham on Yom Kippur. He took pleasure in sacrilege. A worshiper of nature, he loved mushrooms and venison, was an old hand at flaying and gutting deer. At the annual pig-killing he let no one else work the knife, and kept the women away from the sticking of the pig, the singeing off of the bristles, and the skiving of the hide. When in charge of roasting the cutlets, he would whittle all the spits himself, lay them out in neat rows, then pierce the evenly sliced chunks of pork, poult, tomatoes, and onions. He picked just the right wine from the many barrels in the cellar, and also gave his fiddle a good workout, humming along with the music. He did everything with such enthusiasm and gusto, the evening was always a success.

Sometimes, for no reason, Uncle Pista would pick a quarrel with his wife. Her good nature irritated him. He kept insulting her until he worked himself into a fury. When I was at their house, he made me a target, too, usually at lunchtime. He would say things about my father, about his being so meek, a merchant, a man who sold guns but never fired one. Now, take Uncle Pista, for instance! He cut the throats of chickens himself. Grabbing them by their feet, he twirled them above his head, then lay them on a tree stump and decapitated them with a single blow of the ax. A blue-trimmed white enamel bowl was always handy to catch the blood. He cooked the blood, mixed with onions, and offered it to me, saying that blood made one strong.

His own son was an embarrassment to him. Gyuri was a handsome boy, mild-mannered and gentle to a fault. (He survived Bergen-Belsen, was liberated, but typhoid fever carried him off while he was still in the camp.) Uncle Pista had no use for gentle souls. He loved to see me get angry. I may have been nine years old at the time, but I tried to hold my own, arguing with him as best I could, my face growing redder and redder with the effort. "Well, now, a bit of fight in you, at last," he'd say, rolling up his sleeves.

The two things that irked him most were the Jewish religion and capitalism. Personally, he took care of capitalism, brilliant at turning a profit into a loss. When he inveighed against Jewish tradition, merchant mentality, and gutlessness, he became so heated that his head turned an alarming purple, at which point Aunt Ilonka, without a word, would bring in a jar with a dozen leeches writhing in it. Uncle Pista straddled his chair, took off his shirt, and she decorated her husband's broad back with the sticky bloodsuckers.

On one occasion this obstinate man kept on spewing out his words of bile during and after his abundant lunch, even while he drank his coffee. The smell of roast goose and steamed cabbage still lingered in the air, and my cheese turnover was still on my plate. Above the table, on the honey-colored strip of flypaper, a new victim buzzed. Only one of its legs was stuck, but in the course of its struggle more legs became glued to the fatal, vertical road that the fly had found so inviting. I imagined that I, too, was walking on such a road. My leg gets stuck; I try to free it; I squat down, and now my hand is caught. I wave with my free hand, but nobody comes to the rescue. All around me, nothing but corpses. Uncle Pista noticed the look on my face and smiled. His anger subsided. One after the other the leeches, having drunk their fill, dropped to the floor. "We ate ourselves to the limit, but for that, animals had to die. I slit the goose's neck so you could eat greaves and liver with fried onions, and that special delicacy, its kidney. If every grown man killed one or two pigs a year, there would be no wars. Only people who can't stand the sight of blood want war," he said, and waved his hand, indicating that I wouldn't understand. But I did.

After a short nap, Uncle Pista went about his business. The plant in his charge was near the small railroad station. The firm's bitumen barrels were neatly lined up in the large storage area, just like the stacks of wood in the lumberyard. The blue mountains and white houses to the south of the plant now belonged to Romania. You could take a leisurely walk to the barriers, and if you did not follow the road, you might wander across the border. Uncle Pista, his family, and all his relatives could easily have escaped across the yard into Romania, where in the early summer of 1944 Jews were not being forced behind ghetto walls or into cattle cars. But no one thought of escaping. Uncle Pista was happy to be on Hungarian soil again and not have to take orders anymore from porridge-eating Transylvanians. When the orders came, he obediently rode into the ghetto of Nagy-várad, taking his wife and son with him. They all went to Auschwitz. Their son, Gyuri, was assigned to a work detail, whereas Aunt Ilonka and Uncle Pista, exhausted from the long journey, went to take a shower in the gas chamber.

Zoltán: 1

Zoltán and I were cousins twice over. His mother was my father's younger sister, and his father and mine were also cousins. His parents' marriage, this joining of first cousins, did not turn out to be such a splendid arrangement. An alliance of wealth with a sizable dowry; a great age difference; an ardent male and a cool, unresponsive woman. She was sallow first, then deathly pale.

They lived in a spacious house behind ours, owned a large ground-floor store that sold clothes, fabrics, and shoes. Zoltán paid little attention to his father's store, hardly ever set foot in it. He did not like the role of his father's son and being told how much he had grown. After perfunctory greetings, he would withdraw into the private zone of the house. Zoltán hated to part with a single word that was unnecessary; you could see on his face that small talk caused him physical pain. Conversations with his father had clarified for him the general theories of commerce; the details were of no interest to him. Zoltán was a month younger than I; he was a Taurus, I an Aries. We came into the world in the same delivery room. He was handsome, swarthy, and of a calm disposition, whereas I was ruddy, bald, and haggard. We lay in the same playpen while our mothers chatted. We got along well, played and grew up together. Facing each other under the cherry trees in Zoltán's garden, we learned together how to kick a soccer ball.

In school we sat behind the same desk, on the same bench. I talked with him more than with anyone. Because of our uncontrollable chatter, they tried to separate us, but then decided to leave us alone—not out of mercy, I think, but because there was something impressive in our incessant and deeply involved dialogues. Arms on each other's shoulders, we would walk around the schoolyard. From

89

time to time Zoltán would ask, "Do you understand what I'm saying?"
I always understood him.

On my first day of school, my governess, Livia, had to sit next
to me in the classroom; every time she got up to leave, I would
scream. On the fourth day, however, she tore herself away from me.
When the other children began to jeer, I got angry and proceeded,
one by one, to beat them up. At home I insisted that I did not want
to go to school. I insisted until my parents finally relented. I became
a private pupil, and so did Zoltán. The teacher would come to our
house in the afternoon. With homework quickly done, there was plenty
of time left for playing with Zoltán and his younger brother, Marci.
In the brook below their garden we captured frogs and skipped stones.
That autumn, in the garden, the carpet of fallen leaves under our
feet stimulated our conversation. I found everything interesting, but
Zoltán often appeared to be bored, distant. His Yes or No, no matter
what the subject, was much more forceful and effective than mine.
Cautiously I followed his logic. I liked drawing final conclusions from
his observations. With my own opinions I took fewer risks, not quite
trusting myself, because the next day I might think otherwise. The
Zoltán in me is a man of unequivocal gestures, not the one to ensure
the continuity of human endeavors.

Zoltán's mother died when he was five; at eleven he lost his father.
He was left with the aunts and uncles, the bourgeois family he viewed
so sardonically, and for models to emulate he had middle-class boys
with their Marxist-Leninist abnegation of the self and their rebirth as
Communist intellectuals.

Whenever his mother would let him, Zoltán would go into the
bathroom and watch her in the bathtub; he would also touch and
smell her clothes and perfumes. His governess, Nene, would shout
through the door for Zoltán to come out immediately and not bother
his mother. Nene's sense of decorum was unshakable. But he kept
looking at his mother and would not budge. Through his befogged
glasses he watched her turn her shapely legs. Who knows, Naomi,
his mother, may have spent all her life preparing for something that
never happened. She liked to dress beautifully, expensively, and
originally. With my mother, she often traveled to Budapest to have

dresses made. They wènt to the theater every night. For provincial middle-class women a trip to the capital was an event. They bought books, too; modern literature for themselves, novels about Indians for their sons.

Reading these adventure stories, I was baffled by the shootings; I had not yet seen a wounded man. When I finally did, and lots of them, at age eleven, I looked at them long and with amazement. In my reading, I tried to imagine the stench of Dakota Indian corpses after the vultures got through with them. Today in Újfalu they call Dakotas those Gypsies who wear red pantaloons, talk in loud voices, and dance an unbelievable gyrating dance, not to music, but to the rhythmic beat they produce by clicking their tongues.

When we were older, Zoltán and I admitted to each other that we had been mortified, as little boys, having to parade through the main street of the town with our governesses behind us. Mine was the pretty Hilda; Zoltán's, the haughty Nene. We wore trench coats and funny little hats, and had to ask permission to take off our gloves or unbutton the top buttons of our coats. Peasant boys, in their down-at-heel shoes and shabby clothes, stared at us, these walking exhibits of Jewish capitalism.

My hair is long, and I am prattling away in German. The natural wave of my hair below my ears has been teased, then crimped with the help of a curling iron. I have the impression that my mother wants to turn me into a girl. Every month I make the barber promise that he will give me a boy's haircut. Mr. Szatmári makes house calls, his leather bag is just like a doctor's, and he cuts my hair in our bathroom. The drawback of this procedure is that only he can see what he is doing; I cannot see myself. The mirror is above the sink, and I can reach it only by standing on a chair. I can stand on the chair only after Mr. Szatmári is finished and on his way out. That is when I invariably find that there has been no change: I am still a girl. Under my shirt I wear batiste vests, mostly pink ones, my sister's hand-me-downs. Once, my younger cousin Vera arrived early to play and, while waiting in the living room, she saw me, through the door left ajar, standing on a chair, being dressed. She broke into a gleeful cry: "Girl's vest, ha ha ha! Under his clothes, a girl's vest!"

We were planning a war against the girls, on the soccer field. Boys at one end of the field, girls at the other. One boy for each girl. We, the boys, prepared the ground by digging small trenches in the grass. The idea was to lure the girls over to our side, and whoever fell into one of these traps would be a prisoner. The boy or girl nearest would have the right to jump on the prisoner and mount him or her like a horse.

I hoped to mount Baba Blau. She had beautiful, heavy brown thighs, a brown mouth, and thick braids. She sat in front of me in the classroom. She'd tilt her head back, I'd grab her hair, and she'd laugh a deep laugh. But one day she turned me in for pulling her hair. I had to take my wooden pencil case to the teacher. With it, the teacher hit my palm several times. When I returned to my seat, Baba grabbed my hand. "Show me your palm." It was red. She blew into it. It didn't seem to matter that I was beaten on her account. She looked up at the ceiling, her large mouth in a mocking twist, and her hair again on my desk. "Get your hair out of here!" "Should I?" she asked slowly, lazily, pretending to be stupid. We exchanged sandwiches. She took a bite out of mine and offered me hers. The rule was that both of us had to eat both sandwiches, taking turns. If I offered her mine without taking a bite of it first, she'd get very angry. Baba Blau, too, was gassed and cremated.

I offer Zoltán a seat on the far side of my tombstone table. I ask him if he is allowed to drink. Being an archangel in charge of sailing to the shores beyond, he is in charge of departures. This responsibility, I hope, does not prohibit the occasional consumption of alcohol. While he was still at home, he did not drink. After 1956, however, at Oxford he drank manfully, until March 1960, when he killed himself. Excuse my rustic way of thinking, but I cannot imagine that the problem of what is permissible and what is not ceases to exist over there, on the other side. Why should rules be less strict there than here? A strapping angel like you saluting all day, and not imbibing intoxicating beverages? Zoltán motions for me to desist. "If we were completely free, the other world would be only a white void. It isn't. It is an exceptionally rich world, and therefore has a variety of rules." "If that's the case," I object, "then why have another world at all? If it's variety you want, this world has plenty of variety!" Zoltán says that just as I have accepted the existence of other planets, I should accept the existence of other universes, universes not of objects but of ideas. "You are not looking," he says, "in the direction you ought to." I am not happy about the existence of other universes. I like it where I am, and I like to be left alone. But one cannot defend oneself against unexpected visitors. "What is your business here, anyway, dear friend? Visitors always want something." Zoltán admits that he's come to call me to account. It is out of consideration for me that he, and not somebody else, has come. Quite a few, both from here and from there, offered to play the role of my interrogator. He was only twenty-three when we last saw each other, in October 1956, but in outward appearance he has kindly matched his age to mine. For them to slide up thirty years or down is child's play. Zoltán hints that the hereafter is monochromatic, coherent, amplified imagination. He has a multicambered brow and a voracious jaw.

"Are you listening, David? Do you understand?" Zoltán wants to be sure that I follow closely what he has to say. In the schoolyard, arm in arm, we contemplated and pondered the world. In our respective homes, away from each other for only a short hour, we each felt the need to share the accumulating ideas in our heads. We would crank the arm of the old telephone; the operator would come on the line, saying, "Switchboard." "Number eleven, please," I'd say. "Number sixty, please," Zoltán would say. When we called each other for the third time on the same afternoon, the operator would ask, "Why don't you just go across the street?" "Please, connect us," we said coolly. As early as the age of seven we were calling each other on the telephone, though our fathers still held on to our shoulders before letting us cross the street. When one of us visited the other, the host would wear a jacket. We'd shake hands, offer a seat to each other, and get down to the burning issues at hand.

Zoltán: 2

Until the end of the war, in February 1945, Zoltán and I were constantly together, always in close proximity. But when we met again, in August 1946, at the age of thirteen, our relationship seemed different. He called from the border station of Biharkeresztes, asking me to come and fetch him and his younger brother, Marci. Two orphans on their way from their aunt in Cluj to their uncle in Újfalu. My parents happened to be vacationing in Hajdúszoboszló. My father had left me in charge of the store.

Standing by the cash register, I took my job very seriously. I had planned to revive the store after our liberation, while the war was still going on elsewhere, and repair our house, even if my parents were no longer alive. I would hasten down the stairs, just as my father used to, and all the assistants would be waiting for me, lined up in their proper order. I would greet them amiably; we'd file into the iron-smelling, dim space, roll up the shutters, and wait for customers. Come, dear customers, bring us our lawful, commercial profit, and not only in tire irons and bicycles; there is profit, too, in a pound of nails or in plain wire. I'd look at the receipts, check and double-check them, take the money, make change. Bourgeois wisdom: succession.

In 1944 Uncle Kálmán, Zoltán's father, had moved heaven and earth to get on the train of the wealthy Jews, which in return for huge sums of money would take a few hundred people to safety in Switzerland. He wanted to buy his family's life from the Gestapo. Life must have a price. He traveled to Nagyvárad, to his wealthier older cousin, in whose house the ceiling could be rolled open for the family to celebrate Sukkoth under the open sky and still be inside their comfortable dining room. "For that you don't have enough money, Kálmán," his cousin told him, but did not offer to make up the difference. Although Kálmán lived long enough to be liberated in Mauthausen, his body was destroyed. When the liberating soldiers, well meaning but innocent, made regular, solid food available to the former prisoners, my uncle, unable to control himself, ate without restraint. Dysentery finished him off.

Zoltán's call from Biharkeresztes made me very happy and excited. I went to see a drayman I knew. He said he was too tired to go anywhere that day, but his team of horses and wagon were available if I would do the driving. This was a shocking offer then, comparable to letting a thirteen-year-old today operate a car. Until then I had been allowed to hold the reins only if the driver sat next to me on the seat. The drayman hitched up the horses; I got into the wagon, took hold of the reins, and felt like a man. I could have taken the old road, but I chose the new one so I could drive through the entire town. Sunshine had left the wheat fields, the countryside was cooling off, and by the time I reached Biharkeresztes, everything was dark blue and starry.

I would have loved to embrace Zoltán, but he only offered me his hand. We were standing by the wagon, and I mumbled something about the horses. He was coming from an uncle's villa in Cluj, which was a kind of watering hole for the cream of Hungarian intellectuals in Transylvania. Suddenly all the interesting things I had to tell Zoltán shriveled into insignificance. I could think of nothing but provincial anecdotes. "How is stabilization affecting this area?" Zoltán asked, taking us to a topic more universal than Újfalu. He was referring to the recent monetary reform. I was proud to be able to answer him. Unfortunately, the long ride home in the wagon did not interest him at all. "It's slow and bumpy," he said. I could not argue with that statement. At the draw-well I watered the horses. Zoltán barely paid attention to what I was doing. I asked him if he had had his bar mitzvah. Of course not. He was through with Judaism; it was all gone with history. In Újfalu, I told him, the synagogue was full of rubble, all the windows were broken, torn pages of prayer books swirled in the constant draft. Both the Germans and the Russians had kept their horses there.

Zoltán became irritated when I mentioned Uncle Kálmán. I had my parents; Zoltán was an orphan. With his parents dead, he had no reason to continue to love bourgeois reality. He didn't mind having been born a bourgeois; it gave him an opportunity to understand the morals and ethics of wealth. "I'm glad my father is dead," he said. "If he were alive, we'd be enemies." "Why shouldn't one born a bourgeois stay a bourgeois?" I asked. "I am not what I used to be," he replied. He had already read *The Questions of Leninism* several times, and was just starting on *Das Kapital*. At that time I was nowhere on that particular track; I was still reading Plato, delighting in Socrates. Ten years later, Zoltán wrote bitterly from England that the bourgeoisie had won, having outlasted the romanticism of the extremists.

Back then, in 1946, Zoltán wanted revolutionary change in Újfalu. I was not fired by such ideas. I decided that people could never be entirely different from their former selves. The adroit shoemaker was now a fumbling party secretary; the irritable blacksmith with the large hands was becoming a laughingstock in his role as the leading figure in town. Nor could I grasp what historical progress there was in Uncle Kálmán's most scatterbrained assistant's being appointed police superintendent. Zoltán was soon busy distributing fliers and putting up posters for the Communists. I put up no posters. I went to the meetings of all the parties, glad that there were many, but found them all more comic than serious. I liked the Communists because they were communists, just as I liked the Small Landowners because they were small landowners. And in 1956, too, I was more an observer than a participant in events. Since 1945 I have been unable to pick an enemy for myself.

At the age of thirteen Zoltán Kobra joined the Hungarian Communist Party. At fifteen he was a professional Party functionary, a paid instructor in Marxism; he explained *Das Kapital* to adults. As a steadfast Communist, then as a steadfast liberal, Zoltán was always more political than I was. He had a more theoretical mind; his ethics were more finicky and more consistent. Had I been as consistent as he, I would not be alive today.

I have always been skeptical about making life decisions based on ideologies. I put off those decisions: I did not join the Party, yet even after 1956 I did not feel that I had to leave the country. I was always an eclectic, who liked views diametrically opposed to each other, particularly if they were well expressed. In conversation I said all sorts of things, whatever came to mind, not concerned about maintaining the appearance of a pure Communist or a pure anti-Communist. Recklessness and caution alternate in me; I let my paradoxes ripen. Zoltán didn't like my jumping from paradigm to paradigm. Everything he said was according to a lucid outline. If he approved of one of my efforts, he would click his tongue: Elegant deduction. He spoke inwardly, as if meditating aloud, formulating solutions to problems. When we were teenagers, I thought his ambition was to be something other than he was: a radical hero, a saint, a genius! Or maybe just a scholar, combining all three. His class origin and the fate of his father, murdered in a concentration camp, impressed him no more than did the English tweed suit he wore.

The three distinct chapters of his life were his childhood, Communism, and his role during the emigration after the 1956 revolution. "This revolution," he said to me at the end of October 1956, as we were leaning against the cab of a truck, machine guns over our shoulders, "is directed not only against Stalin. It doesn't want Lenin either. Lenin, remember, had no qualms about putting Kronstadt down." But Zoltán did not find our postrevolutionary situation palatable, namely, that Communism grew a little less communist and a little more bourgeois. He thought that if the country could no longer be consistently communist, because that would have meant the loss of many more lives, then it ought to be consistently bourgeois, like England. In his room at Trinity College, a valet attended to his needs. In a letter to me he described the place as a soundproofed sanatorium.

I was in Újfalu in 1948, and again in the seventies. In the interim there were letters from the local party secretary to the universities I attended, claiming that my father was not a member of the lower middle-class but of the upper middle-class, which made me a class alien, thus an enemy of the people, and they, the people of Újfalu, did not approve of my attending the university. Disciplinary action followed: I was expelled. But the people of Újfalu exaggerated; my father was middle middle-class, and so was Zoltán's father. They were plain, provincial, Hungarian-Jewish middle-class citizens. I think that if Zoltán were here now, he would agree with this definition of our origins.

In the seventies I went back to Újfalu several times, once with my children and Marci's son, Tony, from America. Tony was Zoltán's nephew as well as mine. Among the high weeds we made our way to the family graves. "Jesus Christ, I'm standing on my grandmother!" Tony cried. He was standing on the white marble stone of Naomi. My daughter was bored with the graves; she wanted to go swimming. We took a dip in the Berettyó, but the water smelled of pig shit. A nearby collective farm pumps the refuse of its pigsty into the river. As we climbed out of the river, we were attacked by mosquitoes. My son, who hadn't gone into the water, laughed as we dodged the mosquitoes and waited for the foul-smelling water to dry on us.

We took a walk through the town. The flower beds had disappeared from the sidewalks; there were lots of cars, trucks, tractors. The single-story houses were still standing, gray and seedy. Farther on, apartment buildings were under construction. Our house was now a hardware department store. The manager, Feri, recognized me; he used to be one of my father's apprentices. He showed me the storehouse; behind bales of wire mesh, the finely carved Holy Ark still stood. Twenty-two people worked in this department store, which had been enlarged by the addition of our living quarters. The store had a substantial inventory, but customers were often told, "Sorry, we're out of it."

If Feri needs his passport, all he has to do is go to police headquarters—"Come on, fellows, stop joking, give it to me"— because they are all his friends. He is on good terms with everyone in town. He asked me what kind of car I had. He couldn't understand why I didn't have a car. He also wanted to know why he had never seen me on TV. He advised me to write to suit the spirit of the times. I should also write his story. His house, he told me, was larger than that of the president of the local council. The only thing he lacked was a child. That was the great sorrow of their lives, his and his wife's.

We went to the railroad station. I had a brandy at the station inn.

Everything was exactly the way it had been forty years earlier. Except that the hansoms were absent; the railings were broken; the restaurant was now an inn. On the train an old Gypsy was slapping a young one because the latter had accused him of stealing his money. A father slapping a much stronger son. The son didn't resist; he simply cried that he would kill the old man. "I can't lift a hand against my own father, but I can put a knife into his throat!" A knife? More slaps followed. A policeman turned up, with a German shepherd on a leash and carrying a rubber truncheon. Just for show, he hit the son once on the arm. "Why don't you respect your father, you son of a bitch? I'll take that knife! You'll get it back in Budapest. You're not sticking people on my train. Save that for the big city!" And the dog growled authoritatively. The rest of the Gypsies from Újfalu, who filled the car to capacity, continued to play cards, suckle their young, and squabble among themselves. "It's so real!" Tony said rapturously. "This *would* be the car where Father feels right at home," my son, Miklós, remarked, somewhat bitterly.

Zoltán liked to make distinctions, connections, between events. We reminisced about the good old days. In the fall of 1943, of all the Jewish children only the two of us were accepted for secondary school. But we were not allowed to take the course on civil defense. We were not recruited into the town's paramilitary youth organization; we could not train even with small-bore rifles. It was out of deference to our fathers that we were not given toilet brushes in the place of rifles, which was done with other Jewish boys.

I touch this tombstone in front of me; the sun has made it warm. Perhaps I do attribute too much significance to earthly existence. After all, I know nothing of other universes. Zoltán says that a radical is not he who causes his own death but he who kills himself. My view is that either is insane. "We, the dead, are coming, but not in spaceships," Zoltán says. "The interior invasion is far simpler. We teleport ourselves into the living. We observe. The one possessed senses our presence. I terminated myself. You read about it in the *Esti Hírlap*, a small news item."

Zoltán has remained young in my memory. Yet on this current visit he appears as worn out as I am. We are walking together in the marketplace of Újfalu. In small groups of three or four, wearing black boots, short fur-lined jackets, and hats, men are talking calmly but intensely while waiting for their women to come out of church. Then, in the afternoon, in the tavern, we drink brandy with our beer. Maybe someone will flatten his best friend. Rage bursting suddenly from tranquillity. It seems that the old knowledge is still alive, of which insult requires the pulling of the knife out of your boot. In the hotel there is no hot water. The toilet door cannot be locked; sitting on the toilet, you have to hold on to the knob.

3.

In which Melinda Kadron introduces herself

Melinda

I am Melinda. It is my turn now to speak. I have the stage, and all the spotlights are on me. The spotlights are you, dear readers, as you sit around me on your garden chairs under birch, plane, and walnut trees. You are leaning against the trees and looking about curiously. Well, this is my house, my balcony, and my garden. The humming of cars barely reaches us here.

The woman you see before you is thirty-eight years old, a mother of two. She still has her own teeth. There are bags under her eyes. Her hair, which reaches her waist when let down, is sprinkled with the silver of experience. I am, like my mother, a broad-shouldered, slim-waisted woman with strong thighs; neither small-breasted nor flat-bottomed. Dark-brown eyes, deep voice, no mustache. I am five feet nine inches tall and weigh one hundred thirty-two pounds. My shoe size: eight and a half.

In this living room or on this balcony or in this garden, guests are always offered something; the pastry tray and the wine bottles are seldom empty. Here I can find the light switch with my eyes closed. My old familiar shops and repairmen are close at hand. If I had a say in where the demon of birth would drop me, I'd let it be here in Buda, on Leander Street, with my family. Wherever they feel good, that is where I feel good, and vice versa. István, my boy, is all boy; Ninon, my girl, is all girl. They are both beautiful, well-turned-out children. They can stand on their own two feet already. The time we spend together is brief but stormy.

Ninon, eleven, sits on the living-room sofa, elbows on her knees, and says she'll never have a baby. She doesn't want anyone kicking, twisting and turning, and growing in her belly. She doesn't want morning sickness either. And the skin and muscles don't regain their original freshness after two births, and one child is not enough. Besides, she can easily imagine a man cheating on his pregnant wife.

No, not for her; Ninon is determined. A child, she feels, should be in the shape of a flower, floating on a lake. A stork circles by, plucks the flower out of the water, and, flying through the window, drops it between a man and a woman. There the flower lies, and if the two so wish, it turns into a child. The way children are made is too disgusting. At this juncture I cannot refrain from remarking that it is also disgusting for a girl to drip cherry jam all over the place.

I have a husband and a lover: silent Antal and long-winded János. They're both good looking. Antal and János were classmates. I lassoed them both. With the two of them, I expand my life. For almost eighteen years I have been living with Antal Tombor in lawful matrimony. He makes movies, sometimes sculpts, while I busy myself with the children. I have a part-time job in the Budapest Museum. I also like to take pictures of houses, courtyards, homes. I arrange my photographs in boxes, by street. They are not artistic, but create a mood of nostalgia. I've been doing this for over ten years. I have no ambition to get higher on any ladder; I stay away from office squabbles.

My father used to translate foreign-language books into Hungarian. Sometimes, when he was tired or a deadline was dangerously near, I would help him. Once he let me translate an entire book, then had it published with my name on it. I was very proud. I am tenacious, long-suffering, and friendly. I like stability, am suspicious of change.

In this thick notebook I will try to draw the portraits of my heroes, the men I love and the men I may have to bury. In this garden I am the one who has put down the deepest roots. Who will leave this house only for the cemetery? Not János or Antal, not even David Kobra, but the only daughter of Jeremiah Kadron: I, Melinda. But maybe this old hag will still be knocking around in the twenty-first century, dragging herself along between two graybeards. Panting, palsied, they fall to their knees before me in our old-fashioned intimacy while the walls become covered with moss and the radio goes on playing Viennese waltzes.

Since our wedding day, Antal has had a succession of mistresses, whereas János Dragomán is my first and only lover. I am not willing to give up either man. I know it's not easy. They want things that are not to my liking. They want autonomy. Of course, I always manage to nip rebellion in the bud, each time with a different stratagem. Here we are, sitting on the balcony of my father's house, tempest-tossed but cheerful. In every house there must be somebody who wants to hold the house together. Otherwise everything falls apart.

To join the outer circle of our friends is not difficult; to join the inner circle is very difficult. I expose myself gradually to the unfamiliar; I don't like to eat things I haven't eaten before, and think twice about sitting next to somebody my instincts tell me I should stay away from. Like a horse, I don't drink out of a dirty bucket.

The pair of deer in my garden have grown sleepy. A reconnaissance helicopter is buzzing in the dusky sky. This afternoon, using the clippers, I pruned the hazelnut bushes and sawed the cut-off branches into the right size for kindling. The deer, those masters of silent speech, followed me; we're not afraid of each other. But with my son, István, the deer have a mystic understanding.

David arrives with his wife, Regina, eighteen-month-old Zsiga, and five-day-old Döme. We're having a reasonably good conversation. I put Döme on the armrest of the easy chair. He sits there pleasantly, studying the edge of the wardrobe. Once in a while he squeals; to clicking sounds he replies with a smile. He pulls the red knit hat off the stuffed penguin's head. He is capable of piercing cries of joy, hooting, and burbling. When he gets hold of my hair, he yanks it with fingers of steel.

Surrounded by a quarry-stone wall, the garden is partitioned by hazelnut bushes. Until very recently my father cut the lawn and tended the walnut and fig trees. Since he's gone, a well-preserved pensioner from the neighborhood has been doing the gardening. He also fixes things around the house, using tricky, not always successful, methods. We have deck chairs, of course, a hammock, and a swing. Quiet conversations on the balcony. Antal is whittling. János, the old fool, is dancing with me; we're doing something that in the fifties was called the tango. Christmas is already in my end-of-summer thoughts. I am ready to make stuffed cabbage, fried fish, aspic. I know how to set the table for both Easter Monday and the Passover seder. We amuse ourselves until dawn. It's getting light outside, but we stay here in this artificial light, in this candlelit cave. Dawn, guttering torches, cowbells of pestilence, drunkenness, and fairy tales. In this house I am Scheherazade.

Of course this story will also be made into a movie by Antal, even if I have to push him a little. He'll get up, brush off his pants, and make a prizewinning film. After an awful day, I complain to him about the rudeness of people—although, as I have said, I am no delicate flower. More than once I have had to slap a man in the face. In Budapest, you are exposed to coarseness now and then. Coarseness, too, has its piquancy. So I work the insults I have suffered into appetizing little anecdotes, and Antal gapes at me incredulously. He is sorry that he has no share in such atrocities, because for him it's Dear Director, Our Honored Artist, et cetera, everywhere he goes. He is well known from television. The people he deals with are all important. They tell him about their families and their nightmares. And love stories, which to him are vulgar, stupid, and pornographic, like a piece of headcheese. Sometimes I feel sorry for my husband, who is beginning to take up too much space. Now that he has reached and passed his zenith, there are plenty of those who would love to knock him from the saddle. Your death, my only one, will open great vistas for your followers. They are stamping impatiently, the young ones, in line behind you. They circle the house, closer and closer. When you fall, it will be of interest to many: Who will move into the museum? Who will gain the widow's hand?

I now make the two opposing principles of life burning in Antal and János confront each other. I can do this, because they are both in me. Once, they both wanted to beat me. Then they stopped dead in their tracks. János launched into a tirade; Antal made some movements with his hands. We are bubbles in an aquarium. A triangle, a ravaged trinity, an intersection under a streetlight. According to the day of my birth, I am a Scorpio; according to the hour, a Cancer. I therefore should long to be away; I am a traveler by temperament. Yet the men around me are such scoundrels that I have no choice but to put down roots. Let everyone take his place at my table. There is a barrel of Újfalu wine in the cellar. Friends from the farthest points of the globe coming home to roost gather around my ancient green table. This living room, with its balcony, is a recurring scene in our common mythology. To my left and right, my father, my husband, my lover. May the house remain protected, as well as the friends of the house, and of course the institution of marriage. A two-pound Gruyère cheese full of holes rests happily next to the large basket full of Jonathan apples.

Behold, our suspicious beloved approaches: Master János, the dark-skinned pirate. I can hear the deep-sea boom of conches around him. His long lashes hide eyes of rich white fields at whose centers anthracite windows open and close as if obeying a royal whim. Due to the use of stimulants, more and more red capillaries are encroaching on the white expanse. In this notebook I'll catch and trap János. I'll use his voice, make him speak, tear off his masks. But I probably won't reach the real face; other masks will block my way.

I am drinking a dry white wine. In the garden a great horned owl is flying among the trees. There is no presence here now save for this lonely sound. Shivering with cold, wrapped in shawls, a woman casts anxious looks toward the garden gate. She looks out the window, amuses herself by trying on prematurely old frames of mind, strokes a cat by the fireplace. Walking softly in her ski socks, she gives names to every corner of the room. My major accomplishment is this hospitable house. I know where every book, every button belongs. For a long time I consider the photograph of somebody in knicker-bockers, but I don't remember who it is.

Our house in Leander Street is located on the side of a mountain; we can see the city from here. This old family villa, built by my grandfather, is always in need of repair: the drains, the plumbing, the wiring, the parquet floors. Tomorrow I'll clip the front hedge; on the other hand, I may just let it grow wild, grow as it likes. The place where we have been put, with all its petty little problems, is our gift—and also our cross to bear.

I called my father, but he hasn't come. I have no idea where he is in this great wide world. I also called my mother. She will definitely come, unless something crops up, like having to take an ailing old actor to the hospital or find a home for a crippled dog. The children are on a school outing to a mountain lake, taking a miniature train ride through the woods. Antal is working in Ófalu, carving away at the local rocks; he should be back before midnight, on the eve of my birthday. David called in the afternoon to say that he and Regina might be a little late. They have a baby-sitter, but unexpected guests dropped in on them. They may bring those people along, too.

On the other hand, Antal may stay in Ófalu because of Franciska, and have a good time with that large-bodied scatterbrain. What does he see in that woman? Why Franciska; why of all people did it have to be Franciska? Is it because she is always there, always available? Is it because when she jumps into the pool, she displaces more water than a whale? Maybe Antal won't come home for Christmas, either; he is angry because I didn't do what he asked me to do. Men are treacherous, like crocodiles. Where is that old bright confidence that says: Wait, wait, my little sheep, you'll all be grazing in my garden yet. But maybe they won't. I should start with the premise, nightmarish but well founded, that no one will visit me on my birthday. Could it be that János has kept his word and really left? Why doesn't he phone from Vienna, then? Or from San Francisco? Where is our strong husband, and where our stout lover? I fear that this house, homey and overripe, is so unbearably my own that suddenly everyone wishes to flee from it.

But, alone, I can look back with gratitude, even on the painful hours. I have friends who did not betray me, friends who were kind when I was weak. The room fills with acquaintances. We are like cards just dealt; we haven't yet taken a good close look at one another. Yet we did so many good and awful things to one another. Now, as friendly kisses are administered, lips find lips, and there they linger awhile. In the snowy arbor of the garden new lovers embrace.

Jeremiah: 1

Whenever we have company, here in our living room, people look to my father. They seek him out. He, however, keeps to himself. His smile says, "I'm sure you're very nice, but I am not yet convinced. Later, maybe." Father has always been an object of envy. He looks good, for instance, no matter what he wears. He sleeps little but very soundly, and is not troubled by dreams. He can read a book in the woods, his back against a tree. He knows all about tools; he learned to use them by watching various craftsmen. He rises at five every morning, goes for a walk on the mountain, then a visit to the pool, and by ten he is at his desk. He translates and writes until three in the afternoon without looking up from his large brown spiral note-books. In his advanced years he puts his work aside and devotes more and more of his time to eccentricities. After lunch he usually visits friends, including girlfriends, and inevitably he drops by the Crown. In the evening he reads, taking notes, then descends from his haunted castle to join us. His life has a regular routine, but he hates old men who brag about how they keep to their routines. That's all they have left, routines.

During the past few weeks, my father has spent a lot of time with his old friend Arnold Kobra. The two of them talk in loud voices out on the balcony. "You honor me with your visit, Arnold. What brings you here? I am, as you can see, on my way out. I mean, I am not so soft in the head as to plan my one-hundredth birthday party in your beloved Crown. I've been a pensioner long enough; time to be a grasshopper. My chauffeur will put my steamer trunk into my little Austin, I'll put my checkered cap on my head, and then I'm off, out of this country. I'll travel around the world. In strange bars I'll order strange drinks from barmaids with painted eyelids. I'll sniff African pubic hairs. But no syphilis for me, thank you. This harpy of mine, Melinda, thinks I don't need women anymore. We'll see who laughs last. Arnold, you have no idea how hysterical she can get. Women are nothing but trouble. Mother, wife, daughter—eventually the witch surfaces in all of them. The poison is part of their system, and sooner or later they sting you. Melinda, more coffee, please! She brings me my coffee, and in return I cater to her whims. Well, let's drop it; it's not worth talking about. I just want to say one more thing: Your Zsuzsa was a queen.

"Look around, look at my grouch of a daughter, and that dolt son-in-law of mine, and look at your own nephew David, carrying the weight of the world. Just look at them all. I'm surrounded by morose stick-in-the-muds. I miss happy faces. This old graybeard would like to bask in the light of a few big smiles. Thanks for the flask, dear Arnold. In the thirties and during the war I drank plenty from that silver flask, always plum brandy, so it would have a nice smell to it. Just holding it makes my heart beat faster. The last time I drank from it was on Christmas Eve, in '44, right before your violent death."

My father knew how to adjust to new situations. When he had to leave the capital because of his bourgeois background and because the publishers would no longer hire him, he bought two horses in Ófalu and made a living hauling coal, firewood, and construction material. He was allowed to stay in his own house, but the house was officially allocated to a certain Aunt Sarolta. He often fell asleep on the driver's seat—he may have been drinking too much—yet the horses always found their way. He would stop in the woods to pick mushrooms, wild strawberries, and mulberries. He always brought me mulberries in that tin mess kit he still had from the war. He occupied himself by whitewashing his house, which stood at the edge of town, between the forest and the cemetery. He smoked Munkás, the cheapest cigarettes. In the taverns he drank rum, because rum was not watered, and chased it down with beer. There were always people around him, because he was a good storyteller, and also because he had a knack for making people tell their own stories. His chair was at the corner table by the wall. He learned the art of pigsticking, and also how to use all the parts of the pig. His eyes would light up when he spoke of gammoning bacon and smoking sausages.

After his relocation from the capital, my father decided to talk only about practical matters. He had various odd jobs. He made money by taking care of graves for people who couldn't visit their dead often. When they came, he would ask them about their departed ones; this made his work more interesting. He let the fruit, fallen from his numerous trees, ripen on the ground, and then, in the teeth of the state monopoly of alcohol, he distilled them into liquor. He bought good wine directly from the growers and kept it in barrels. He hardly ever drank water.

Obeying different laws at different times didn't seem to bother him. Periodically he was seen with small packages tied to his bicycle as he rode to the post office. He was sending choice tidbits of country food to his friends in the capital: honey, plum jam, cherry brandy, and dried salami. In town he wore his old hunting outfit. The buckskin suit with knickers was just wonderful, he would say, impossible to wear out. The local tailor made him very happy when he said, "Take it from me, Mr. Kadron, that buckskin suit is a real gem." From the way my father used to chat with that woman running the post office, I suspected he wouldn't come home at night. He claimed he couldn't sleep and took a walk. Of course he couldn't sleep, frolicking with the postal woman. "One should never give up having a good time," he said, and sent me out to play. He told me to go visit the pious Toths or the alcoholic Galabar family.

And now lately, too, Father acts as if he's having dates. He puts on cologne, leaves the house, then returns two or three hours later beaming like a tomcat licking his whiskers. I suspect that he goes only as far as the Dream, the nearest espresso-bar, sits there for a while by himself, maybe exchanges a few words with the new, long-mustached owner, and keeps glancing at his watch to check when he can go home and rest on the chaise longue reserved just for him in the corner of the living room. I suspect he goes through this whole charade for my benefit, so I won't worry about his declining powers. He thinks I fuss too much about his health, making him cover himself up, wrapping shawls around his neck and knees. Perhaps this irritates him, because secretly he still believes that he can live as long as he wants to.

His widow girlfriend, Magda, thought that he was only pretending to woo her, that he was too old, tired, worn out. She learned otherwise. When they met, my father was close to seventy, and Magda was forty-five, a quarter of a century's difference. The flu took her away when she was sixty-five. "Once you've buried me, old man, you can follow me, you can rest, too." I had the feeling she died out of courtesy, not wishing, by her continued presence, to keep my father any longer from the death he desired. He buried her, but was not ready to follow her.

Jeremiah: 2

"I'm not saying au revoir, my little girl, because you won't see me again. You won't be closing my eyes for me. Last night I slept long and well, and this morning I'm all spruced up. I want you to remember me as I'm standing before you now. Take a few farewell pictures." The other departure Father would carry out more discreetly. Let the body washer be a stranger.

He was seventeen when World War I broke out. Then followed the rest: revolution, counterrevolution, restoration, prefascism, fascism, a little democracy, then the long winter of Communism, some days more bitter than others. In each reign the rhetoric was different, but they were all alien to him. He watched the marching crowds from the sidewalk, always content to watch. What he wanted above all was to be left in peace. He wasn't famous, but enough people recognized him on the street; trouble catches up with you even if you don't provoke it with fame. His way of thinking was not in tune with Budapest. It probably would not have been in tune anywhere. He did derive some enjoyment from the different fashionable, shallow jargons of propaganda. He would use that language when talking to Oliver, the parakeet. There was a professional informer in our neighborhood. My father loved to talk to him. "An interesting character," he would say. "The man is driven not only by personal gain but also by envy and malice. He loves to lie in bed contemplating his future denunciations. Somebody should keep a record of the vileness of obscure people, too, because the newspapers of the world do not report that, and it doesn't get into the history books; though, true, neither does the heroism of obscure people."

My father was Jewish to the extent that his mother was Jewish, so we may be sure at least of fifty percent. But it is not out of the question—although it has not been proved—that he was also half Gypsy. Grandmother had my father circumcised without telling her husband. By Jewish law, therefore, my father was completely Jewish. But Grandfather, when he saw the loss of the foreskin, not to be outdone, took my father to the Catholic church to be baptized. He said that the Lord Jesus was a good Christian in spite of the fact that he, too, as a sign of the Covenant, as a babe in arms, was deprived of his foreskin. Thus both the rabbi and the priest were tricked.

My father did not consider bad the mixture of Jewish and Hungarian in him; for him, they were compatible, complementary elements. By themselves, and in concentrated doses, the Jews were too gloomy. They couldn't get past the paradox of a universal God and their being his chosen people. Your neighbor, whom you were supposed to love, didn't have to be Jewish. That, at least, was my mother's opinion. My father was given to catnaps and daydreaming; she would fire various questions at him, try to animate him, challenge him. She was convinced that with these prods she was prolonging his life. The hardiest nation, my mother believed, was one that made love, both in thought and in bed, to other nations—but without becoming assimilated, without losing its own identity.

"One should not be famous," my father once said, "because it damages one's ability to think. Being famous leads to an inflated ego, which interferes with clear-sightedness. A celebrity becomes a chatterbox, because so many people want to hear his views. He repeats himself, mouths banalities, and expects people to buy whatever he has to sell. And they do buy. The cheaper the material, the more people buy it. In this way, you experience your death while you're still alive." My father was spared the plotting envy of the young. He was not turned into an entry in some encyclopedia. Few people insulted him behind his back. He did not play the pitiful role of an old man dominating a conversation. The most awful thing in the world is retrospective whining, a litany of persecutions suffered, a miserable childhood, poverty, neglect, and being ignored. My father would listen to such talk for a while, then gently ease the speaker over to the flowery field of vainglory, pride, and boasting.

Thanks to his clever camouflage, Father avoided being put into any role. He was grateful to the dictatorship of the proletariat for having fortified him in the discipline of inner emigration. When all his friends were onstage, in the sycophantic limelight, he remained in the wings, a good translator. And this left him time for his own pleasures. Jeremiah shuffled about the mountain, went swimming, rode the buses, took walks in the city, looked out the window. He made good use of the pensioners' discount season ticket on all public transportation.

In times past, words would pour out of him. Gradually he spoke less and less. He mostly hinted at things. As if it were impossible to be too laconic. Can it be that now, in a place unknown to me, he's again a lively raconteur? Here, in company, rubbing his favorite pebble, he would doze off. Waking with a start, and as if by chance, he would drop a sentence that made one think even the next day.

Notes in the margin, by a freethinker in a land deprived of freedom. If you don't fit into any box, and still want to have a long life on this earth, be careful. In the Danube basin especially, you'd better go incognito. A man's life is not separate from his creative work. My father's chronicle kept him alive; he was a secret agent for children not yet born. If you want to know how others live, live like them. The chronicler is a monk. The holy order of chroniclers has its own unwritten rules. You must know, for example, that combatants want to be portrayed as men of honor who are forced to fight. Don't try to talk them out of fighting, don't poke at their conscience, just describe them. Where communal pathos rules, truth flees. Father told me not to visit him in the cemetery. In return, he wouldn't come and bother me.

"I am not happy, my boy," he said to a no-longer-young David Kobra, "that you have become the hero of political scandals." (He used the formal *you*. It was that way from the very beginning; formality was flattering to a secondary-school boy.) "In politics, one must be very careful, not only with one's enemies but also with one's friends. I can see, however, that you are a member in good standing of the opposition. Now they will count on you to support every one of their ideas. And you keep coming back. So you have chosen this country, along with its regime, whatever that regime may be. In that case, my

dear sir, why so sour? And what else would you expose? Here everything is already as exposed as a plucked chicken's bottom. Also,
some of those public pronouncements of yours are a bit vulgar. There
are things that more refined people leave unsaid. Retract your claws.
And do not use so many abstract nouns in your writing. Also, instead
of being in control of your plots, you blunder from scene to scene,
from predicament to predicament. They'll make you a spokesman.
You'll be forced to share the hopes and fears of the public. With his
head down, the soldier hugs his wife and goes where duty calls him.
That's the young for you. Though some confirmed bachelors act the
same way; under the influence of books, I suppose. Wouldn't it be
more interesting to try to get inside the head of the enemy? That way
you might really influence. Though influence, too, is a very questionable goal."

Father received quite a few guests in this living room; often his
guests and mine were the same people. Even in a bore he would find
something interesting. He seldom criticized, having learned that in
our highly charged environment the driest statement of fact may be
taken as insult, slander, or sedition. Touchiness is rampant in our
city. The adventurous journalist must dissemble, must appear inef-
fectual. An ignorant peasant and not a feudal lord.

He had many different pens, fountain pens, ballpoint pens, felt-
tip pens, and he wrote beautifully with all of them, but none was the
pen he really wanted. I did not peek into his notebooks. How could
I have stooped to such a thing? We were always bashful with each
other. We never shared our medical problems, either.

Now, using a word processor, I daily copy my father's notes, not
in chronological order but as they come to hand. Sometimes I have
the feeling that he really wrote all this for me. Or that these are
chapters of a book that even he was unaware of. I always liked to
see him in a jacket and bow tie. Sometimes I put a flower in his
lapel. I liked it, too, when he dressed up as a hiker in the woods.
But his most becoming outfit was that of a beekeeper, a dark blue
coverall. In his diary, my father is not naked, but he is not completely
dressed, either. It is not pleasant to see one's parents exposed.

János and I have tried to put Father's effects into some sort of order. Father assigned this man to me so we would keep an eye on each other. There is no doubt that of all our friends János is the most unemotional. It is his duty, therefore, to say: "No, Melinda, we'll leave this item out. This is not a scholarly edition; it's meant for the average reader, and I'm sure Jeremiah wouldn't want to bore him." Father had no idea how to edit. He didn't write a book, he wrote several thousand pages of fragments. Perhaps his sole purpose was to collect fragments. But what shall I select from this mountain of material? How shall I put these sentences together to make a book that will interest a publisher? There are many repetitions, so many passages that run parallel to each other, it is frightening. Somehow, János and I take pieces and fit them together. This requires courage.

Before his disappearance, Father had become weary. Sometimes I slam shut the heavy door of his safe, then turn the key twice in the lock of the door that separates his quarters from the rest of the house. I am angry with him. His departure was a challenge thrown at me. I, the careful little editor, am supposed to make order while he plays the free spirit. He has treated me like a radio one turns on and off. Sometimes listening, sometimes withdrawing, and when he withdrew, the very sky darkened. Unbearable that it should be more important for him to think than to listen to me. And the things I said were merely a springboard for his own ideas. Everything reminded him of something else. He is ninety years old, for God's sake! But does that mean anything to him? No, nothing. Well, it's a damn good thing you left, old man. You've spoiled the air in this house long enough.

My father likes to think of Budapest as the world. He has been a cosmopolitan by not leaving the city. This house, too, this garden is also the world, and he has placed the story of our lives in it. I lock myself in his room and sit at his typewriter. János sits in the easy chair we use for reading. I am getting nowhere, I am stuck. I compare documents and discover that this diary, too, is a fiction, a cunning use of mirrors. Luckily for us, there were some months when Father wrote nothing.

Where in God's name is the old impostor now? Come, dear Papa! He may show up this very evening, if all the twin phenomena I have seen today are any indication. I saw twin cucumbers, twin strawberries, even twin matchsticks. He'll show up because he is in fact my twin. I found a snake in the garden, wrapped it around my brown fist. An incantation. And behold, Father is here, beside me. He's never looked healthier; he is sunburned and his hearing is keen. How was it all alone in the big world? He says, "Not as good as here with you." In my excitement I confess to the old geezer that I might be pregnant. He is pleased. "By whom?" I'm not sure. This doesn't bother him either. Because of his experiences with Klára, Father is familiar with this kind of uncertainty. But how dare he compare me with Klára? You see, he's just arrived and already we've managed to get into a fight.

It's a pleasure to fight with him. Sometimes I hurt him, and then he clams up detestably. I respond by going at him relentlessly, like a fury. I keep it up until he, too, explodes. And then we throw a great many unforgivable things at each other, all direct hits. Then, tired of fighting, we have a good laugh at ourselves and follow the laugh with a drink. Father is already opening a bottle of red wine. Why is the table set for so many? Who is expected?

János Dragomán

János Dragomán turned up here one day in March, during a week of fatigue due to depression and vitamin deficiency. At seven in the morning on that day, I went to the pool. Stretching in the water, my limbs waking up, I began to take control of my body. I am pleased when young and old gentlemen, following my progress through their goggles, remark: "When a behind is nice, it's even nicer in the water." As a young girl, I swam in competitions. In a race I leave my two men behind, leaping past them like a dolphin. I feel the water all around me; it is the physics of freedom, the liberation from all usual obstacles. The bottom of the pool falls away, and we can swim downward all the way to that other world. Faces look up at me from the depths; the blue tiles lift like a stage curtain, and water lilies appear. Figures move among the coral; streets become visible down there. The walls of the underwater houses glow with heat, become transparent. I see a multitude of naked people; some sort of celebration is in progress. The bloodless but bloodthirsty creatures are roving, restless; with their large fangs they fall on one another, kneading, biting, pommeling, testing the strength of the flesh, trying to be rid of an unaccountable wrath. In the showers I watch silver-haired, bone-dry matrons attempt to cure their circulatory problems by standing under jets of water, now hot, now cold. Everybody is trying to stave off death. I, too. With the perseverance of a nun.

I had a lot of work that day. Around six in the evening, when I stepped into my living room and found János sitting at the piano, I recognized him immediately, though it had been twenty years. He was playing nothing in particular, just warming up. His long hands swept over the keys. Then he was ready for requests; he embellished tunes, made them sparkle; his head thrown back, he hummed nonsense words to go with the music. Antal was there, playing his saxophone, and David was drumming on the table. This is not the sort of thing that usually happens here. The three of them had been classmates. Apparently they once formed a trio. "When we played this piece," David said, "János had a black leather jacket and smoked a cigarette. Trying to prove that women didn't interest him anymore. We were not even sixteen then."

Whenever the Kobras come to our house, my children get out their large old playpen for Döme. When I entered on this later evening, Döme was lying on his stomach in the playpen set up in the middle of the living room. He was surrounded by animals. Rhythmically wriggling his bottom, he greeted the zebra with a smile of recognition. Zsiga was playing *bucco* with János, which is to say they were butting their heads together. "The more human your eminence becomes, the more treacherous your heart will grow." Zsiga loves to repeat interesting words. *Treacherous. Your eminence.*

Not long before, when I visited the Kobras, Regina was sitting in her easy chair, inspecting baby clothes on her shelf. Her belly was enormous; the baby was taking its time. Regina had swollen feet, kidney problems, and difficulty breathing. How wearisome, to shift your stomach from one uncomfortable position to another. It is not only the eating of the cake that is intriguing. What about the process of baking it?

By the time I got around to addressing János, Zsiga was in my lap, and we were nibbling at each other, an activity Regina looked upon with mild jealousy and János with great interest.

Two weeks ago, János Dragomán was sitting by the Damascus Gate in the Old City of Jerusalem. "A pipe smoker likes to have several pipes at home," he said, "because he may like the feel and the smoke of one pipe one day, and another pipe the next day. If you like to smoke through a hookah, then you're bound to cheat on your home hookah with another when you're on the road. Of course, one is not always traveling. Between trips, the smoker returns to his original, lawful hookah. What I'm saying is that even a rogue like me will remain faithful to his wife.

"A real woman is the one you always return to. I know from experience that the aging adventurer loves to return. Past the prime of his manhood, he no longer craves the taste of strange women, who according to the Bible are only temporarily sweeter than lawful wives. Unkempt, unshaved, and with a sore throat, he dreams of a gentle hand placing a glass of rose-hip tea with honey and lemon on the night table, smoothing the blanket, taking the book from his hands, and stroking his head, as if to say: You'll be better tomorrow.

"The man sitting opposite you, my friend, is not ashamed to rub himself with ointments or massage the soles of his own feet. If you accuse me of narcissism, madam, I cannot deny it. When I am exhausted or ill, or, I should say, when I am in a state of reduced capacity, I long for a rocking chair, just like this one you so kindly offered me, and I also wrap several silk scarves around my neck. And whether you believe it or not, I put a white, tasseled nightcap on my head. If I were so fortunate as to have a splendid spouse like you, dear lady, I would not hesitate to keep her informed of the minutest changes in the state of my health," János finally concluded. "How exciting," I said dryly.

From the far side of the green table, he watched me crack open

119

and munch walnuts. I felt him following the walnuts' paths between my teeth, and he was with the walnuts, sliding down my esophagus, looking into my stomach, touching my organs, and finally settling in my womb. Wait, you just wait. This wizard seemed to know his way around inside me as if it were the playground of his childhood.

He got up and walked to the window. He withdrew his eyes from me so suddenly that I felt a chill. Tall and slender, he stood nonchalantly by the window, looking boyish. His upper body broadened gradually from his waist to his bow tie. I wanted to measure our guest's chest with both my hands under his poplin shirt. I wanted to crawl up and down his body. I am a carnivorous plant, and my palms have become suction cups. Lowering my eyes, with my left hand I cracked open another walnut. Then I smiled. This man will cuddle up with me and then disappear; he will have his pleasure and then return me to my good husband. When János looked at me again, I had the sensation of being wrapped in a warm coat on a cold night.

"In one sense, sir, what you are saying is far removed from us; in another sense, it is very familiar to us. Our husbands are rugged heroes. It's not just that you won't hear them boast about their pains and weaknesses; but our men don't even admit to having such things. I would welcome, and I think Regina would, too, being served a cup of rose-hip tea once in a while, or receiving a little attention. But even when we do get some attention, our husbands remain workaholics, dependent on work. As for me, I will not deny that now, with the children a little older, my nurturing powers have again increased. Every night, in every bedroom of my house lovable beings slumber, expecting me to wake them in the morning and serve them breakfast."

"The young mistress strengthens my impression," said János, "that an asylumlike air of homeyness pervades her abode. It puts this widower, vagabond, and good-for-nothing hypochondriac into a curious frame of mind. After a long absence he has returned to the city of his birth, bringing with him an urn and numerous vials of vitamins, to visit his former classmate and bosom friend, who—unlike me, frivolous *Luftmensch* that I am—loves the soil, loves to dig it, stamp it, mold it. And who takes mud baths after his drinking binges, and follows his periods of continence by gorging on rye bread and ham, headcheese and crackling, which he washes down with a soothing stream of beer before taking an equally soothing nap. The traveler is reminded of his hookah, and his wife, when he looks at his friend's wife, who also happens to be the daughter of the traveler's teacher. The last time he saw her, she was a teenager.

"Yes, in my self-solicitous and fashion-conscious decadence I have brought with me a variety of pills, miracle-working plant extracts, and all sorts of macrobiotic abominations from the civilized world to this barbaric land. Already I have inquired about the availability of a masseuse who makes house calls. No, I don't mean one of those barrel-shaped down-home females; what I have in mind is a discus-throwing champion in her thirties, with the therapeutic massage techniques of both East and West at her fingertips, a sophisticated woman who likes broccoli, asparagus, and bicycle trips. I have reliable information regarding swimming establishments and the level of bacteria in each pool. It is the colder, so-called men's pool at Lukács Baths that is least polluted. I'll be going there every morning, starting tomorrow."

I mentioned that I had been there myself that very morning— and the next day I met János at the pool, and the day after that, and the day after that. These morning meetings have turned into a habit. If we miss each other, he comes up to see me in the educational counseling office, or at least calls me there. My female co-workers are exceptionally tactful; they assist not only in our communicating but also in the creation of smoke screens. I return the favor when my co-workers are in a similar situation.

Even on that first evening I felt that our visitor wanted to grab my buttocks while I straddled him like a bridge. But it took months before that came to pass, before I began slipping into his apartment nearly every day, before he took my old nipples into his mouth and had a chance to witness, from his supine position, the fitful dance of Melinda's thighs and pudenda. I would spend an hour or two with him, then go home, righteous and beautiful, as the mother of my children and the wife of my husband. Once, I had to call Antal to tell him what to buy for dinner, because we were expecting guests. I made the call with the telephone resting on János's stomach and me propped between his legs. I like having this secret.

Last Will
and Testament

What sort of man is János Dragomán? In his Calvin Klein shirts and Yves Saint-Laurent pants, he is a genuine lady-killer, which is somewhat of a rarity nowadays, a vanishing breed. Passions are so disappointing. What he does with women is exactly what they expect him to do. When he wants to annoy me—and his current woman is very pretty—he brings her around, and the two of them spend time closeted right here, above my head. I never had to put up with such noises while my father lived in that room. All this, I know, is a strategy on János's part; I am the target of it. I have been his target ever since we set eyes on each other. When they're finished, János calls a taxi and accompanies the lady to the garden gate. He takes no woman to his apartment on Klauzál Square. I wonder why. Returning from the garden, he greets me with insolent adoration. Lately, the ladies have been replacing one another in quick succession.

Between János and the world, the attraction is fierce, the friction passionate. Talking to him is a function's downward curve, on which we women slide into an abyss. He touches the lady, rests his hand on her thigh, and she goes limp; her thoughts are already one with those of the gentleman. Stepping on the brakes only delays the moment when undressing begins. I clamp my thighs closed; he pries them open to get between them. But I will not fall into the trap; with dignity, and of my own free will, I will yield when the time comes. I am at an advantage here; I'm on my home turf, where he is not his real self. After showering and getting dressed over coffee, he leads the conversation to neutral ground. My face burns as I come downstairs. Up there, madness resides, an anonymous ghost who has come not to strengthen boundaries but to weaken them.

"János will carry on the tradition. He must continue the chronicle," my father had said, and entrusted the whole thing to this international vagabond and scoundrel because his mind was brighter, his critical skills sharper. Antal and David, in my father's eyes, were too ponderous. And he knew that I would censor him. My father was the one who encouraged János to get away from the pressures of Budapest, use his brain, and not become angry and bitter. What does it mean to carry on a tradition? It means faithfully seeing to the manuscript. János was given my father's room upstairs along with the key to the safe. Out of my father's papers found in that safe, he was to create a book. He would be given a savings account; it would provide him with an income for three years. He was to complete the editing of the papers during that period, but would have enough time to himself so he wouldn't get tired of the project. János Dragomán was named executor on the eve of his arrival, here on the balcony. My father was waiting for him. János arrived with David Kobra. The two of us, Antal and I, did not know he was coming. Antal was overjoyed to see his former classmate; I scrutinized the unexpected guest, my heart in my throat. János was stunned by my father's proposal. But he did not refuse. "Here we are," Father said, and handed János the keys to his room and his safe.

No sooner did János arrive than Father left. Father had set in motion something whose consequences he did not care to witness. At one in the morning a handsome, dark-suited driver called for him. Father kissed all of us, then followed the driver, who, picking up the two travel bags, hurriedly walked ahead.

There is a sadistic streak in my father. He didn't even ask János if he was interested in the project, but simply called him to our home, as if knowing that he would accept. My father thus condemned not only János, but me, too, his daughter, to a different life. Bringing in this man to be over me. Conciliatory, János said that although he would be working here, sorting and editing the papers, he would live in his own apartment on Klauzál Square. That was an acceptable arrangement. But there was no mention of the females trooping through my garden. Why did my father want to punish my husband? He was all in favor of my marrying Antal, because Antal was a man of such prodigious strength.

Antal, David, and János had been my father's students. When I was two, I used to ride on their shoulders. That was the year of their graduation. I was demanding, I wanted them to pay attention to me. Later, growing up, I secretly hoped that they were all in love with me. I preferred to be detested, in those days, than to be ignored. I thought that any man who was not like my father ought to be like those three young men. Antal and David are perhaps too serious, too heavy in some ways, but this János, this graying tough guy with his partly man-of-the-world, partly childish-cruel sarcasm—he should be Father's successor?

Sitting at my father's desk, he has become the prisoner of the large brown spiral notebooks. The first thing he did, in his imprisonment, was to desecrate my father's sofa. Then suddenly he left off with his women and spent the afternoons pacing up and down in the room like a master of peripatetic meditation. His need for human contact seemed to decrease. He shortened our trysts, took obvious pleasure in being alone. Now I don't know where this seductive impostor is, and it makes me uneasy. A little while ago I closed my eyes and saw him climbing a fence. After nightfall, under thick November clouds, tramping along an unlighted highway. Staggering.

If things were as they should be, my father would be sitting at the head of the corner table among his cronies in the tavern of Csillagvölgy. His thumb would almost cover his shot glass. The old man refused to let us install gas heating here; in his own glazed-tile stove he fed the fire himself, using the wood he cut with great expertise. He did not mow the lawn, but cut it with a scythe. For fear of blunting it, my father allowed only Antal to use the scythe. His stories sent the listener's mind careering through the twentieth century. On the New Year's Eve of this century, my father was brandishing a hussar's sword while astride his hobbyhorse, and probably drinking champagne. In the tavern, after the third glass, he puts out his foul cigar, which I have forbidden him to smoke in the house.

Antal, János, and I could all live under the same roof. The

children would be no worse for it; they would lack nothing. If I swore to give up either my husband or my lover, it would be only playacting. The age of matriarchy has come. The strong one makes the rules, gets what she wants. If I were weaker, I would let my lover go but prevent Antal from having serious love affairs. If I were weaker still, he would have a mistress and I nobody. And if I were weaker still, I could keep neither husband nor lover. Occasionally, goodness tries to shine through this dark astronomy. Sitting cross-legged, rocking back and forth, I concentrate on my desires.

Maybe the garden gate will now creak open, and Father, slowly, tapping with his stick as he used to, will plod up the path. With small cries I'll embrace him. I don't know where he has been. Half a year ago, on the telephone, he said that where he was, stones were real stones, orange trees real orange trees, and blood real blood. "When are you coming home?" I asked. "Home? I'm enjoying myself here!" he had the nerve to say. "Then enjoy yourself!" I said, and slammed down the receiver. Once, my father went to Korcula, in Yugoslavia, and sent me a lot of postcards as well as a snapshot of himself by a cathedral: having a good laugh in the company of some women who were no longer young but still merry. He called to say that he was staying another month. I was shattered. But five minutes later he was huffing and puffing up the pebble path, carrying his travel bags. He had played his little joke from the corner phone booth.

"You are my eyes, Melinda. You can always find my glasses when they hide from me." He acted as if he were more helpless than he was, so he could lean on me. He would sit here on the balcony turning the dial of his shortwave Sony radio. "Idiots! What idiots! What do you say to all this, Oliver?" The more ridiculous a phrase, the more he would repeat it to the parakeet. Then the parakeet would ruffle its flaming red hackle, extend its green front tuft, and screech happily: "Idiots! What idiots!" In his old age Jeremiah made sure that the practical matters of his life would not interfere with his pastimes. He paid them the minimum amount of attention. He did everything I asked him to do, but I had to repeat myself several times, because he chose to be forgetful. Perhaps he encouraged me to marry Antal because he wanted a chauffeur, a gardener, and a jack-of-all-trades to move into the house. Moreover, Antal was a man people liked to do favors for; an ideal son-in-law. The two of them enjoyed sitting side by side on the balcony.

Gradually I took control. I could always run things better than men, could always see them in their proper proportions. Men are best at creating confusion. If they argue with me, they usually have to admit in the end that I was right. Then they fawn, show gratitude, and I let them continue playing the little games that are so important to them. What is it that a woman knows and a man doesn't?

I am one of the preservers of the mythology of Budapest; I keep a record of who is whose divorced husband, jilted lover, or fourth child born of a third marriage. It is important that we have a large family, crisscrossing relations by blood and by soul. We care for one another; those whom we accept will never be abandoned. In this home we live, we work, we gather more cheaply than we can in a restaurant. Here you don't have to see people you don't wish to see. Here you can get up, leave your chair, move around during the conversation. This house is a locus of strength, and I am the mistress of it.

Sarah

I have always admired my mother for her ability to be by herself. All my life I lived with other people, my father, my husband, my children, always needing someone to touch, to move, to part with, to say good night to. My mother stays home and makes phone calls. People see her enough on the stage. Besides our daily phone conversations, we sometimes write letters to each other. In these letters we complain about each other's lack of understanding. We conduct negotiations, like the foreign secretaries of two superpowers. We mutually agreed, several times, that Father should live under my jurisdiction—but those two old conspirators may in reality be united against me. I have noticed the delight my mother takes in my failures, and in my health problems. She commiserates with me brilliantly when I am ill, just as she weeps convincingly after burials of fellow actresses.

My mother lived with my father, thirty-one years her senior, for only a short while. Then she let him have me, let him raise me while she returned to Budapest to study acting. She was twenty-one at the time and interested in other things. I was all right at my father's place. I felt protected in his large hands. He took me to school and brought me home. He adjusted his life to mine. Old enough to be my grandfather, he was sillier than I was. We both looked forward to Mother's visits. We'd put out the beautiful tea service, cakes on a silver tray. Cheerfully she helped herself to the cakes as she sat under a plane tree, the leaves casting shadows over her eyes. During these visits dear Mama was not concerned about her dress or her appearance; she let me cling to her, let me burrow into her, wrestle her down on the sofa, roll over her head, squealing happily. Then I would sit quietly on the floor by her beautiful legs and beautiful shoes and hold on to her, never wanting to let her go.

Father and I were Mother's stronghold, the castle from which to sally forth and then return, a youthful poet or a tiny jockey between her teeth. Father and I could chew on one small experience for three days, but she needed lots of experiences; she was a grand consumer, devouring ten times as many impressions as we did. Lately, though, she has taken to reading in bed, preferring adventure books. But, with her, you never know. Mother has her own metamorphoses and molting seasons. She looks into your heart and plays the character you secretly want her to play. She can be suddenly disloyal, not only to others, but to herself as well, to her own performance of the day before. Was she too refined yesterday, too horrified by vulgarity? Well, today she is so loud and obscene that my head hurts and I can't wait for her to leave. My mother, when she is nervous, can set the entire house on edge, my father, my husband, my children, even the cat and the parakeet. In her presence everybody feels an unaccountable, intense anticipation, as if something was going to happen. Good or bad, it doesn't matter; only let it happen! But perhaps this aura is generated not by her but by the local soil, the local weather.

"Farewell, my dears, an era has come to an end. Jeremiah is gone, and, from what I hear, Papa Kádár is also retiring. The theater is full of new boys. I can't promise you that they are nice or upright or even wonderfully talented, but they are new. They have a different tale to tell. The story we have been living belongs to years past. Our characters are outdated. Let youth be enthusiastic; it is time for us to mourn the old order—and our old waistlines. János, too, like a dog with his nose to the ground, anticipates the approaching earthquake. But instead of running from it, he rushes toward it. He sniffs the nervous air, his heart racing. Do you feel some restlessness, Melinda my girl? Is your heart, too, full of premonitions? Do you see cracks forming in the wall?"

To this theatrical inquiry of my mother's I make only this reply: "Father went on a trip around the world. When he is through, he will come home." "But what if he should die there, somewhere in a strange land? Maybe he left because he'd had enough of us. I can imagine that by the time one reaches ninety, one becomes quite sick of one's family." My strong conviction in her Jeremiah's return usually reassures my mother. I kindle in her the hope that once again she will have a chance to throw a hysterical fit in her husband's presence. Her calmness is good for me, too, because then everybody wants to be around her. She serves cocoa and pound cake at six in the evening, and I can sit and talk to her. Sometimes she understands me, knows me down to my innermost organs. Her eyes sparkle so poetically then, with happiness that her daughter is sitting with her in her living room, near the shore of the Danube, opposite the Tabán section of the city, at the foot of Gellért Mountain.

She is five years older than János. They are old friends; at various times in the past they were lovers. Suddenly they would be together, clinging to each other, then just as suddenly they would part and go their separate ways. Together from afternoon until dawn, then no contact at all for a week. Well, now my mother is closely following my story with János, wondering why it isn't more intermittent. "A woman is a woman as long as men desire her," she says. Men still desire her. She exercises every day, goes swimming, applies her creams, and her clothes are all first-class. She looks even younger from behind. Looking at her behind, men still get ideas. Sarah and János were moderately jealous of each other; one would step in only when the other seemed to be getting too serious about a third party. The premise was quite simple: He/she does not belong to me, but he/she shouldn't belong to anyone else, either. In their game it was permissible to show up at the most compromising moment, and rant and rave until the third party was utterly crushed. Theirs was the fidelity of two unfaithful people who tried to protect each other while constantly fleeing each other. But this, too, belongs to an era that has come to an end.

For a long time I felt that every man in Budapest was a visitor to my mother's boudoir. With inexhaustible cheerfulness, she does not allow any of her visitors to stay. A man can sleep with her until dawn, but then she wakes him up and sends him away on the first streetcar. For some she'll call a taxi, and slip a bill into their pocket. She'll do anything to avoid having a snore and wheeze on the pillow next to her. Some men take umbrage at such treatment. No matter; there are always plenty who accept Sarah's conditions. She likes to wake up alone in her wide bed, around eight in the morning. She changes the sheets every day.

Mother is well known for her loose tongue; nothing is sacred to her. One well-placed barb of hers can sweep a new and popular star right off the stage. When she sees genuine talent, however, she can be graciously and inventively tactful.

Mother was a poor girl from the outskirts of the city. She wanted to be rich and famous, with enough money to eat to her heart's content in a good restaurant and not have to look at the prices on the menu. To have a seamstress constantly at her side while she preened herself in the mirror. And, of course, she would order several dresses at a time. That's exactly how it turned out. She needed an apartment? Through Father's connections she got one. In return, she left me in Father's care, thereby forever putting him in her debt.

They met through János, who invited my father to see the graduation production of the Academy of Performing Arts, in which my mother played the shrew. Here on Leander Street, things were very busy at the time: a publishing firm, run by a few friends and with its editorial offices as well as its warehouse located in our home, was about to expire. Mother was offered the attic if she didn't mind the attic's doubling as a storeroom for books. János did not make my mother chastely avoid the owner of the house. I was born in the summer of forty-nine, at the time of the great Stalinist World Youth Festival. My mother's ideal at the time was a French Communist count, the leader of the world's progressive youth, with whom she had no trouble making herself understood, possessing a vocabulary of three hundred French words. Taking me under one arm, my baby accessories packed in an old mailbag under the other, she dragged me around, and gave me her breast in various offices, on bleachers, buses, and in hotel rooms.

In 1951 my father was relocated by the government. Through connections it was somehow arranged that he could take me and move to Ófalu, his officially designated and mandatory residence. My mother had first worked for the State Touring Theater, then in the theater of Pécs, but soon she was getting parts in films in Budapest, and became a permanent member of the Vig Theater, where she has been ever since. It was natural that she did not go with us to Ófalu, just as it was natural that she visited us whenever she could. Father and I busied ourselves in the kitchen and in the other parts of the large peasant house. When he bought the house during the war, he'd thought of it as a possible haven for his friends from the bombings in the capital. Over the years the house has been enlarged. Out of the stable, with its quarry-stone walls, Antal made a glass-walled studio for himself; it could be heated in the winter. He wanted a place where he could escape from my harmful influence. Days in the country are long, and Father had time to fuss over me when I came home from kindergarten. I grew up under his wrinkled smile. The garden was large, full of fruit trees; at one end of it there was a bubbling brook, on whose banks pheasants strutted. Each morning, with a great fluttering of wings, a flock of geese, both wild and domesticated, would fly over the stone wall on their way to the open fields. From my window I could see the mountains and, from the left corner of the balcony, the lake. In that corner, each evening, my father would sit in his wicker chair.

We moved back into the house on Leander Street in the spring of 1956. Father was given permission by the current occupant, a Communist journalist, to move into the basement, which used to be the caretaker's apartment. The journalist liked the new arrangement, because the former caretaker had been in the pay of the security police, and the journalist meanwhile was becoming critical of the regime. He spoke out in favor of some badly needed reforms. Pacing back and forth on the balcony, he took apart the government. When his bottle was empty, he would call for more and, putting his arm around Father's shoulder, praise socialist humanism as the solution to all their problems. Father introduced him to our Ófalu wine, and the journalist quickly grew addicted to it. Drunk, he would go on and on in the first person plural, chiding and castigating himself. "We have been cheated," he'd say, and grow increasingly sad. Father would nod and open another bottle.

Father saw to the duties of caretaker and gardener. He was re-establishing a foothold again in his own house, determined, with my help, to reclaim it inch by inch, this crazy house with its bastion-shaped library, and then bequeath it to his daughter and grandchildren, because it is a good place to live in. With a few interruptions, Jeremiah has lived in this house for all of the twentieth century. The journalist, installed here by the authorities during our absence, left the country in November 1956, and my father retook possession. I went to school from this house, and so did my children, and I hope my grandchildren will, too.

Mother has a sixth-floor penthouse on Petöfi Square, on the bank of the Danube. Beneath her is the Paradiso Bar, in whose windows green fish swim among orange water plants. She used to frequent the Paradiso, and the Poppy Bar on Aranykéz Street. The women bartenders were her friends, and so were the girls just sitting around on the barstools, not bothering to hide their thighs. The pianist and the drummer would brighten when my mother took the microphone and sang a few songs. The pianist was Dragomán Senior, János's father. Sarah and the elder Dragomán would exchange information, within the bounds of propriety, about the younger Dragomán. Some patrons were passionate about my mother. The Swedish consul sent her a whole case of Absolut vodka. A hulking American farmer, wearing a loud red jacket, found himself dancing alone with her, because all the other couples had withdrawn from the dance floor. The dance he did had no name; it was something meant for just the two of them, but its message was clear: The farmer, no longer young, wanted to marry her.

For her one-night cavaliers my mother does not always open her door a second time; some have beaten her. But she seems to have a need to get into impossible situations. For example, she loves it when her men run into one another, especially those who shouldn't, the ones she'd like to keep for a while. She takes no interest in their family entanglements, or how they make their living. She is not inquisitive about the obstacles to their careers. A day is enough to assess most men's vanities. A friend is a different matter. In a friend, my mother is interested day after day. She is careless about her sleeping partners, particular about her friends.

Out of her overflowing box of photographs strange figures emerge. My mother shakes her head: "And this one. I know I have no talent for making the right choices, but how can one tell in advance what will happen? Sometimes the surprises are pleasant, sometimes they are unpleasant." She is a squanderer. She enjoys excess, and that applies to her weight. It is as if she and János were twins in their appetite for love, in their aplomb and unpredictability, which to me is dreadful. They cannot be humiliated; they laugh when they are caught. They are predators, looters. It was inevitable that they would meet, and just as inevitable that they would not stay together.

My mother opens and closes like an anemone. She sometimes suffers from depression. She might call in the evening and tell me that she has not left the house all day. She seems to be more absorbed in herself now, less in need of company, although she is still effusive, loud, and domineering. "Lucky for you, my dear, that you haven't heard my cries of pleasure. I can wail a whole concerto for organ, not only at the peak, but also all along the winding path that leads to it." This I can easily believe, because I know how much my mother

132

values her voice. After lovemaking, she is as hungry as a wolf. "You shouldn't let a man leave your bed unsatisfied," she says. Nowadays her voice sounds strange when she calls at night. Maybe she calls me just after a man has left and she is on her balcony looking in our direction across the shimmering garland of light that is the river.

Antal Tombor

Antal: large white teeth, lots of black hair, a growling, bearlike basso profundo. He is taller than anyone around him, and more strapping. Women are drawn to his heat; dogs rub against his legs. The cat throws herself on her back in front of him, hoping for a good scratch; she blinks up at him, flicks her tail, and purrs. Three-year-old girls flirt with him, sit beside him. Like a good-natured horse, he has a soothing effect on people. One likes to pat Antal. He puts me on his shoulders, and we gallop around the garden, to the great delight of the children. When we go on a trip, he carries four large suitcases, while we take only our handbags.

There are hardly any lines on his palm, but the triangle of good fortune is there, all right: the conjunction of life, talent, and success. There is nothing disturbing in this palm. When he speaks, his voice seems to come from his stomach and not his throat, which gives greater weight to his words. Let's say that people gather to discuss or debate a question; for a long time he says nothing, then he utters something terse, and there you are—that is the point, that is what they can all go home with, that is what the whole evening has been about. He handles life's delicate situations with ease. That splendid rejoinder, which occurs to most of us only halfway down the stairs, if then, issues immediately from his mouth, when it is most effective. He is a defensive player, the kind who waits for the right moment, when a small hit counts more than a big one. Though lumbering, he makes lightning-fast moves on several different game boards.

On any team he joins, my husband is the captain. In his youth he was the one who took the girl home after the other boy—say, János—courted her all day. He is the true center of any group, the one whom his peers elect president without even thinking of another candidate. People try to be his friend, but some, because of his provocative size, challenge him. He usually steps aside, but when someone goes too far, Antal offers his hand, which the other takes instinctively. And then Antal grinds the knuckles of that hand until the man is writhing on the ground. I can punch his stomach with all my might, and he just smiles. He asks me to stand barefoot on his back; the best massage for him is when the entire family is walking on Dainty Daddy. That's the name with which our son, István, swept Antal off his feet. There is something inhuman and irritating in his strength. There were times when in a fury I punched him all over his body, wherever I could land a blow. He would take it very calmly. I could beat him until I was exhausted. He didn't even raise his hand and say, "Enough." "You rotten sadist bastard!" I would yell, kicking him.

Antal makes no false moves. He can grab the walnut-tree branch that is below the balcony, swing across the railing, and slide down the trunk. He can nail a board into place perfectly by hitting each nail only three times, not missing once. When David or János has to deal with a machine, you can expect trouble. Machines play tricks on them. But for Antal, machines are like tamed animals; even with his eyes closed, he always reaches for the right place. When the children throw something at him, he catches it without looking, as if pulling it out of the air, as if doing the flying object a favor. If, in Ófalu, he chops the firewood, you can be sure that not one stick will be too thick or too thin. Once, on the road, an oncoming army truck crossed the solid line and came at us. The driver, bald and round-headed, must have fallen asleep at the wheel. Antal honked his horn and in a beautiful arc swerved around the truck to the left. Then he got out of the car, walked back to the ditch, and reassuringly patted the head of the bug-eyed driver.

For quite some time our son was especially proud of his father's ability to hit a tree trunk at fourteen feet with a well-aimed blob of spittle. Antal also has a guardian angel. Picture this: We are meeting in front of a certain store; I am coming from the other side of the street when suddenly Antal starts, jumps back, and hugs the store window. From the building's façade the head of a plaster king comes crashing down right at his feet. And he had not even looked up. In the company of my husband, hotheads cool off; at a single word from him, they sit down, not sure why they are sitting down, and lean toward him, as if to touch his hand. It's good to hear him eat, to sit silently next to him. And when he puts his hand on your shoulder, you know that the hand resting on your shoulder is a hand to be reckoned with.

Not once has he let the bathtub overflow because he was thinking about something else. His self-absorption does not blunt his politeness; I ask him for a glass of water, and he promptly brings me the alarm clock. But when he pays attention, he misses nothing. Then it's impossible to surround his men in a game of Go, which is unpleasant, because I feel trapped. No matter what I try, he surrounds me; he seems to be able, all by himself, to stand on every side of me. I can feel his whole weight, even though it is he who lifts me onto his shoulders. Antal was a frequent visitor in our house when I was a little girl. I would ride him, always wanting to control him, to be above him. Ever since then, I have been an imp of a little female next to him. He says that he does not think of our relationship this way. "I'd be crippled if you left me," he told me on our tenth anniversary. He had waited that long to deliver this compliment. Perhaps I've known from childhood that Antal is mine, and that all the other men in my life are only temporary. I think he knows it, too.

Twenty years ago today, in 1967, I pounced on him, and have been trying to define him ever since. He doesn't like it when I talk about him. "Let's talk about more interesting things; I am not really here." And he really isn't here. Having packed a sizable snack in his shoulder bag, he spends the afternoon roaming the woods with his handbook for identifying plants. He pours for everybody, but his own glass he puts on the floor next to his stool, in the corner, as he whittles, doodles, or peels an apple. He must keep his hands busy —he's even learned basket weaving—because he simply cannot think when his hands are idle. When editing one of his films, he paces the room, passes me, his hands drawing in the air, trying out various solutions. Once he has the answer, he cheers up and puts his hand on me. He prefers to let others do the talking, but remembers well what they've said, returning phrases to them on appropriate occasions. He is not one for repartee; if you ask him something, he answers only after having thought, and his reply may carry more than one meaning.

There are always wicked witches who love to remind Antal, in company, of some tender little interlude involving them. Seven women could be sitting in the room, with their respective husbands or boy-friends, and each of the seven would talk to my Antal with intimate innuendos, as if she were his true wife. On the other hand, I have never heard my husband brag about his conquests; he does not talk about women. In his films there are female characters who make women instantly jealous and set men fantasizing. But you will also find in his films a dry awareness of human loneliness and images, inexplicably nightmarish, of everyday life. Whatever they do, the women in Antal's films are redeemed. But the women of flesh and blood who are infatuated with him turn into witches under his influence—like me.

I have put the chain into his nose ring, and here he is, dancing before me. I call him using the familiar *you*, but he addresses me formally: "I will deceive you with a dozen easy females." "Don't trouble yourself, Dainty Daddy, you don't impress me with your easy females." Once, while he was working in the country, I dropped in on him, hoping to give him a sweet surprise. Opening the door of the hotel room, I found a situation that admitted of only one inter-pretation. Even then I expected him to deny everything. And he did, fuming. In the end I let him believe that it was worth making a show of himself in front of me. To his women he does not deny my existence; to me he denies theirs.

Antal's love children visit us sometimes; we're on good terms. At Christmas, the fecund father rushes around the country, on icy roads, to deliver his gifts. The love children gather here from time to time, around the richly set table; interrupting one another, they regale their father with their stories. It is amusing, the resemblance between them, as if they had no mothers. They ply me with questions about Antal. In our families, even the grandfathers of our grandfathers behaved the way Antal is behaving now, yet their marriages were dissolved only by death.

Once I made him really angry. I was becoming very knowledgeable about lookout points in the Buda mountains. He found it surprising that I was going on hikes by myself, because ordinarily, when I went with Ninon, we first baked a cake, packed it in a tin box, and took along a thermos of lemon tea; with all our equipment and supplies, we would stop in a clearing not far from the edge of the woods and not far from the car. But with a hiker for a father and a hiker for a husband, I could hardly be expected to walk in the city, inhaling the exhausts of buses and hurting my ankles on the hard asphalt. The walking I did was different from that of the men, it was not as controlled or linear; it might best be described as circular zigzagging. At any rate, Antal had every reason to be suspicious of my familiarity with lookout points. There was a young actor in his film crew who adored him but adored me more. Learning of my fondness for the outdoors, the actor invited me to the mountains. I went along with this fledgling because he had such a beautiful mouth and his eyes were always in a tearful haze. Why that should appeal to me, only my psychiatrist could tell you, if I had one. Nothing happened, or at least not very much. Such adoration deserved *some* reward. During the shooting of the film, it somehow came to light that this youngster, too, was an expert on lookout points. Antal came home one day, bent over, put his hands on his knees, and proceeded to huff and wheeze, taking very long breaths. I realized that it was only this huffing and wheezing that kept him from knocking me dead. After a while he looked up at me calmly; he no longer wanted to hit me. The heroes of his films are blundering little men whose wives desert them.

Whenever I return from a trip, Antal is at the airport, on time, with a bouquet of flowers, and he won't let me carry anything but the bouquet and my handbag. In restaurants, doormen and waiters busy themselves attentively around him; he acknowledges their efforts, and in return they purr happily. If one of his co-workers—say, a certain Béla—utters some terrible stupidity, Antal smiles at him and says: "What an ass you are, Béla!" This does not mean that he has locked Béla out of his heart, but, rather, that he values Béla for qualities other than his mind. "Stupid people are the hardest to portray," he once told David, whose books are full of clever characters. Now that János is here, the three of them have looked up old classmates; they've all become excited, sad, and drunk. Antal rolls his camera, preserving all these ugly people on film and putting them away in metal boxes, where they will become beautiful after their deaths.

My husband has read *Anna Karenina* seven times. "If Tolstoy could rewrite it seven times, then I can read it seven times." Slowly, scene by scene, he plowed through it, learning the musical structure of the novel. Antal, a master of time, is especially interested in rhythm. He remembers the most asinine stories of the city, knows exactly what tools are in the toolshed. If we park somewhere in a strange town, he always finds his way back to the car without difficulty. If you are looking for a nice outdoor restaurant, trust yourself to Antal. Effortlessly, as if on a platter, he hands you the most amazing undiscovered charms of the city. When he had his gallstones removed, gallstone removal was all the rage; when he talks about his army service, everyone wants to go to basic-training camp.

His father was an officer in the regular army. While the regiment he commanded was stationed on the left bank of the Vistula, in the Prague section of Warsaw, Antal's father came to terms with the rebels, the officers of the Home Army. They agreed not to fire at each other; in fact, he even supplied them with weapons. Then he led his regiment home, without combat or defeat. In reward for this success, he was taken into the new army in 1945, but there he was made first hunting master, the officer in charge of hunting and culinary events arranged for generals and guests. He saw to the decorum of those social situations. But since the Polish Home Army had connections with the Polish government-in-exile in London, the comrades in Budapest began to suspect that Antal Tombor Senior had been recruited as a spy by British intelligence. In 1950, then a colonel in the Hungarian People's Army, he was arrested. They didn't have a chance to execute him, however, because during his detention he died of a heart attack. Unless—which is more probable—he was beaten to death, because he was a man who always returned a blow. Very stubborn and rather obtuse, he lived by this principle: If someone hits you, hit him back. It was a question of honor with him. A plainclothesman rang the Tombor bell and told Antal's mother that no matter what people might say about her husband, he was a real man. "I've seen it; I know. That's all I wanted to tell you." He wouldn't say anything more, turned on his heel, and left. Antal followed him. He did not have far to go. The family lived on Damjanich Street, and the stranger lived on Murányi Street, by the marketplace. The man went into a tenement. With careful inquiries, it took Antal two days to locate the right apartment. But by then it was too late. The man was an officer in the State Security force, and later on the same day he had visited the Tombors he shot himself with his service revolver.

For a long time I was unaware that Antal was religious. He is no saint, to be sure, nor does he ever put on sanctimonious airs. He does not like to talk about faith or divine matters. He is a Calvinist and feels that religion is like a garden: It needs cultivating. "I am Moses, I am Jesus, I am Calvin, I am Tombor, I am drunk." I think that is the longest statement I ever heard Antal make on the subject of religion. Four hundred years ago, one of his ancestors, a preacher, was chained to a galley navigating the Danube. The man managed to jump into the river and reach shore. While still on his knees and panting, he broke his chains with a stone and gave thanks to the Lord for his newly gained freedom. Acknowledging his debt to God, he made a vow in his own name and in the name of his male descendants for generations to come: Every Tombor would marry a Catholic girl, but the children were to be Calvinists. Let the sinful multitude of papists decrease, at least by this modest number; and may the souls thus saved gain admission into heaven.

Antal speaks no foreign language but has found, in his own way, a language in which to speak to me. The first time I took him hostage, physically, I wanted to live under the same roof with him. The baby fit his hands well, but he did not like watching me nurse our children. He would put the baby on my knees and as soon as the tiny creature began to function as a milking machine, he always found some excuse to slip out of the room. He left the raising of the children to me, and took on extra jobs as a cameraman so I could have a cook and a nursemaid. Toward evening he would spend an hour in the children's room. He did not want more time with them than that. Antal presents himself as less than he is worth, as simpler than he is, but his films show that he is mysterious, that he is the kind of field in which excavation unearths an underground city.

Brief Survey

Leaving the Hilton, János Dragomán was careful not to take anything with him, not even a toothbrush, lest he be tempted to stay over at his mother's orphaned apartment. The walls of her building are still pockmarked with bullet holes. The offices of the same company with the long name are still there on the ground floor. On the wall of the living room is a colored photograph of his bar-pianist father. A copy of this photograph was burned in the fire that destroyed János's house in America. Döme Dragomán, wearing a dark-blue suit, is standing beside a bird-faced drummer, looking lost, leaning on the piano. On the ring finger of his restless hand, an onyx signet ring.

János did settle into this dilapidated apartment. He is enjoying the house and the neighborhood; everything is rather provincial, but nice. He frequents the Tango, another bar where his father used to play. Sometimes, when the mood hits him, he plays, too. The more he gets used to being here, the more he thinks about staying for good. János's residence permit is renewed monthly by the police. He reads old newspapers in the National Library. In the Castle of Buda he meets Melinda for lunch. He goes home, takes a nap, then goes down to the Tango. He wonders whether he should order his wine one glass at a time or ask for a whole bottle. Morality holds the scales of Ecstasy and Sobriety. Stained-glass windows, Swedish tourists, a couple arguing in subdued tones—all familiar to him from the cobwebbed recesses of the past.

Before he left New York, János had a long discussion with the bank official handling his account. The official was a young black man with a crisp voice who liked to pronounce the name Mr. Dragomán. The money from the university and his literary agents would be coming to this bank. János asked for three thousand dollars to be sent to him each month. He would notify the bank by wire of all his address changes. Never more than three thousand. Not even if he sent a letter, even two letters, asking for more. Only if he wrote a third letter. Should three letters arrive, on three consecutive days, then he was to be sent another three thousand, not a penny more. And if he still asked for more, the official should tell him that he could get it only in person. And in case Mr. Dragomán found himself in a real emergency, then he should be sent a nontransferable plane ticket. And—oh, yes—pay no attention to the handwritten dates on the letters, only to the dates of the postmarks. He'd be gone a year; he was on sabbatical. Maybe he'd write a book, but more likely he'd just be roaming, taking notes.

He took a lot of photographs in 1956 and managed to get them out of the country. He walked around the city like an investigative reporter. He interviewed the rebels, telling them that he was writing a book about the revolution. When they wanted to put a submachine gun in his hands, he thanked them but refused. "I am not a revolutionary, only a chronicler of the revolution." For two years he was treated to the healthy exercise of peasant labor on a state prison farm. He left the country in '66. In May 1968 he was in Paris; he went to South Vietnam, Chile, Portugal, Iran, wherever things were happening.

In his usual fashion, János teases David, his host: "Is it really true that you write with a fountain pen, then make a clean copy on the typewriter? Fascinating! And you receive letters of invitation, I bet, from all over the world. You shuttle between summer and winter, from glaciers to palm trees, and the money pours in, I bet, and you get to wrap your spouse in the finest. But what if, my dear Kobra, a heart attack comes dancing through the balcony door? What if you get bitten by a rabid dog? What if torture and interrogation ring your

141

doorbell? And what's your excuse, by the way, for not answering my letters?"

"I probably would have run into you sooner or later," says David. "It's good that you're here now. Welcome. In this town we talk every day from five in the afternoon until the wee hours. We talk a lot more than we should, and therefore there is no time for writing letters. But let me disconnect the phone. When I'm alone, imagining that I'm talking to you, you always sit in that overstuffed chair." János drinks, stretches, looks around, and smiles.

There is a framed old photograph on Kobra's wall: It's the picture of his great-grandfather, may he rest in peace, Samuel Gottfried, Hungarian peasant—Jew. Sharply carved face, sharp gaze, sharp nose, sharp wrinkles. His graying beard, whose every hair seems bent on spreading as wide as it can, hides a scornful smile. He is neatly dressed in a buttoned-up white shirt, a short fur-lined jacket, a black hat with the rim turned up all around. His earlocks are combed behind his ears. The face of a lady-killer: This one knows what to say to a woman. He remarried at eighty, taking a thirty-eight-year-old woman. A man who sees through all illusions. Words won't convince him; he knows too much. He is the host to every guest: tavern owner, restaurateur, vintner. He serves his own wine, makes his own brandy out of whole fruit. In his deep stone cellar, slivovitz matures and mellows for seven years. Samuel knows how to rule his servants and maids; he also knows all the horse dealers and thieves—everybody on the wintry road who longs for a bowl of hot soup and a glass of good wine. From his garden you can see far: warm brown fields, bare trees, not a house anywhere, the lowlands. The old man let his eyes rove over the landscape.

"My house burned down, and Laura killed herself. I got money from the insurance company and from my publisher, and came here for the wake. And to keep you, early-to-bed person, up until dawn. And to pick up a woman to match my mood, a woman to go to mediocre theaters and restaurants with. Here, even mediocrity is an achievement. One of your problems, Mr. Kobra, is and always has been that you're still a country yokel of the Great Plain. Though slow wit, true, will win the race. I came to tell you that I am staging an international witches' Sabbath in this city. Where in this place? Right here. I

142

invited a hundred madmen to your place. And you, too, are welcome.
The child in me, the letters you didn't write, and Jeremiah's phone
call brought me back to Budapest. The city is becoming fashionable.
Nostalgia for the revolutionary. I like the cozy chaos of your room.
Let's reconnect, friend, with our memories.

"I got an advance on a book. Funny, a few years ago I wouldn't
have thought that my Hungarian background was a marketable item.
I have a contract to write a guide to Budapest, in my own style. Soon
I'll be throwing a party at the Crown, complete with dwarfs and a
female snake charmer. To celebrate my arrival. It was very moving
to find myself in the dimly lit stairwell in front of your door. My heart
was actually pounding, the way it used to when we stood before each
other's doors as children. We were such competitors. I would insult
you in school; you wouldn't return the insult right away but plan it
carefully; and the thing escalated. On the way here I was wondering
if you'd become bald and fat, if you were preoccupied with your
prostate and hemorrhoids, if you suffered occasional attacks of hy-
pochondria, angst, and what does it all mean. Or if, instead, you
were still blissfully inane.

"So I came home to blow this little insurance money. I'll look
around awhile, and then it's back to Jamaica. I like the climate there,
the marijuana is first class, and everything else is dirt cheap. I met
a woman there, Cheryl. I won her with my drumming. In an outdoor
restaurant I took the sticks, did some tricky twirling, then an Art
Blakey—like solo. Cheryl was tiny; she could be twirled too, but she
did the twirling, bless her. There is a tavern on the hill there, a
terraced structure on wooden posts, with a tile roof. Clay pipes, white
wine, and seaweed served in garlic sauce. In that tavern with its
ocean view, the black witches take their places on the barstools. I
buy them drinks but ask the waitress not to send them over. Because
once a black witch did come and sit in my lap, and three days later
I had stinging when I urinated.

"I am looking at this brand-new Melinda, watching her play with
the rings on her brown fingers, and the way she bites her white wine
as if she were dying of thirst. I feel that you, Melinda, and you, too,
David, would not mind if I stayed, but would sigh with relief if I left.
I talk too much, I know. And now, with your permission, I will hold

forth on the problem of wandering. True, I am in a state of mild inebriation and may not be saying what I really mean. My mind is out of shape. There are indeed moments when I see life as bright and cloudless, but I keep this a secret, not wanting to be put away. You probably would like me to slow down a little. David, you look gray. Do you want to blend completely into the colors of the land? I am not large or confidence-inspiring, like Antal, or respectable, like you. All three of us should surrender to Melinda. I say this, now that I'm getting older, with a Mona Lisa smile.

"No matter where you go, there is some sort of authority, and every authority is limiting. I keep moving in order not to have to deal too much with any one authority. It is so easy to get entangled in the weeds of some local stupidity. I like change; I keep putting off the time of being serious. I have no permanent address; everything I own fits into two suitcases. When I finish a book, I give it to somebody, if I liked it. If I didn't, I throw it away. I roam the world with a laptop word processor. I can take it out anywhere, and send my small electronic reflections by telephone to the magazines that create tomorrow's styles. I am not yet bald. I take care of myself; I don't go to doctors, because I've discovered that they are even crazier than I am. At airports and railroad stations a wandering Jew like me is more interested in departures than arrivals.

"At their best, I find governments laughable. At their worst, they are horrible. I have contempt for the issuers of passports, and consider all imperialists to be mentally ill. I can fly from place to place without readjusting borders. Borders are made to be crossed. I am a professional emigrant, with an aversion to administrators, organizers, to all constructive, useful people. Line up, all you bricks, and form a wall! But enough of that. I'll play the piano for you awhile. You could call the Tango ugly, but it's not so bad. And actually I enjoyed being relocated, and the forced labor, and the revolution. I walk the city now: 'Excuse me, ma'am, may I take your picture?' 'Mine, a picture of this ugly old hag?' 'I think you're beautiful.'

"On my way here I met two of your fellow writers. They send you their regards. They don't know what you're working on—as if they never heard of underground publications. When I pressed them, they became tense. Like honest citizens who run into each other in a whorehouse. A rather crude form of editing; it deletes not sentences but whole authors. You are forced to console yourself, my friend, with the art of resignation. You postpone your hopes, try to make peace with your situation, and curl up as small as possible, to be as little dependent as possible on the outside world. And, indeed, why do you need another family, another house, another city or country, to be happy? Why cling, like one possessed, to your desires, and feverishly accumulate junk you don't need? Every day you give up something that you can do without, so that the lust for possessions will not force your proud soul into humiliating circumstances. Freedom is self-discipline.

"I, on the other hand, like a child, love my clever new gadgets, and become very sad if they are taken away from me. In the West, the enjoyment of consumer goods does not clash with one's loyalty to the powers that be. It is best to be positive. You can't win races by being melancholy or self-critical. Honor the existing institutions and the prejudices of those around you. Keep your dissenting opinions to yourself. I appreciate your strategy of unassuming asceticism, which may be emptiness by another name, but I am not the unassuming type. I am too conspicuous. Several policemen have told me that I could get a few years in jail just for my physiognomy.

"Of course, you can dismiss him, wave him aside, saying: Oh, yes, János Dragomán, the monologuist, the peripatetic philosopher, the boozer and drug user; we know him. What shall we smoke, what shall we drink? Have I mentioned that the age of hedonism is approaching? The simple warriors will be cleared off the stage. Our next act is Don Juan's seduction aria—or, in a more Eastern fashion, a book in short paragraphs, a pocket edition distributed in esoteric bookstores on Broadway: The Sayings of Dragomán, collected by Kobra. But I am bored with the role of haruspex, of Cassandra. Today everyone predicts catastrophes, bankruptcies, doom. The truth is that people don't want to hear that we're in big trouble. We are, of course, in big trouble.

"But, believe me, my friend, the only real problem in life is that one has to die. The rest is not so bad. Whether the state or a private insurance company pays the bills for your final stay in the hospital is not the supremely important question. Politics is only a word. If

145

I want to, I listen to it; if I don't want to, I don't. I have learned in the West that politics belongs to the politicians. Every domestic and international drama is their meat. The cameras are focused on them as they labor to improve their chances for reelection by a percentage point or two. How does the poet put it: Hair grows differently on their heads. Their business is different; they are a different breed. They must always be in action, blowing things up out of proportion when public attention flags. A juicy little scandal here, a new public opinion poll there.

"I've been to a few parties since I came home. Your topics are boring. I hear a lot about politicians: This one is better, that one is worse. The system should be a little more nationalistic, a little more democratic, a little more liberal, a little more ecological. I applaud this patriotic desire for reform, and take pleasure in these theoretical skirmishes conducted on the telephone or face to face and which usually end in some compromise. Are you supporting this big shot, you, the deviant thinker? All right, you'll be the spice in his casserole. I've met many generous people, people with a sense of humor and a sharp mind. I would have to be blind not to see and feel the magic of Budapest. On the dirty gray walls, which haven't been painted since the war, I see the lighter spots left by the bullets fired thirty, forty years ago. Even with the pestilential stink of traffic, I cannot get enough of the intimacy of the streets of Budapest."

János apologizes for the pathos in his words. You should always be ready to move on, he says, to leave everything behind. He has in his pocket an American passport and an American Express card, allowing him to depart immediately. He may have to leave in great haste the side of an African dictator, say, whom he photographed while the dictator was carrying out executions with his own hands, or when the great man dashed against the Holy Rock—a historic moment—bottles filled with the blood of rebellious students. János would have continued his journey around the globe, dragging himself from continent to continent, if he hadn't come across me, Melinda.

If my world is constantly shifting under me, then at least let my daily routine have permanence and regularity: my morning swim, for the benefit of my body. When János appears each morning under the plane trees of Lukács Baths, a sense of satisfaction courses through him; he is doing what he has to do. Ever since his house in Princeton burned down, and with it all his possessions, ever since he began roaming the world with two bags, he has understood how incidental possessions are. With the worship of our cherished and familiar objects, we confuse, even paralyze, our children. We bury them in our legacy.

It was here in his suicide mother's bed that János realized I, Melinda, am the one. That's what he told me, as we held each other after we made love. In other words, I am not just a "good piece," though I am that, too, but she who comes but once in a lifetime, she compared to whom every woman before her is a shadow. Which was flattering if a bit high-flown. Antal never said anything to me like that. But János, I suspect, has used it more than once. He certainly does repeat himself: He falls in love with a city, then runs from it; falls in love with a woman, then walks out on her in nothing but his pajamas. He has no destination, only the feeling that he should not deprive of his presence those places he has never been. By now he would be far from here, too, if it were not for this new story of his, in which I also am involved.

I have a photograph of him: He is sixteen, the collar of his leather jacket is turned up, and he is smoking a cigarette. Existentialists, in their black leather jackets, smoked black Munkás cigarettes. He had just announced to his classmates that he was no longer interested in women; from now on he would sit aloof on the shore of nothingness, wanting no part of that sentimental cannibalism. At five or six in the afternoon, he shows up in my garden. There is a hammock and wicker chairs. The visitor knows that a roast lamb and pastry horns are being prepared in the kitchen.

There is a temporarily blown fuse in the brains of János, the guest, and Antal, the host, but not in mine. In this garden I receive strength-giving vibrations from the deeper layers of the soil. I am a cat loyal to the house and the garden. These two married pupils may swagger, but with one sudden upward sweep of his eyebrows Father could knock them both to the ground. The bear does not strike you dead with its paw; it only gives you a little slap on the side of your head, so that you learn your lesson. In my father's absence I represent his spirit. The two come to life again after a hiatus of zero brain activity. They ran into each other head-on, collided hard. After this, they'll be more careful playing king of the hill.

In the blue heat below sea level, a strange intoxication lures János to the Sea of Galilee. Looking through his goggles at the layered sand on the bottom of the lake, at the haloed shadows of the fleecy clouds, he has the notion that he can make it. If he can't, he'll die trying, he'll decompose and return to the rocky soil, and olive trees and date palms will grow above him. Take deep breaths and go for a stroll on the surface of the lake, as if the sunbeams were a golden sidewalk beneath your feet.

Who's entering my house? There is no one here, only my own whispering voice on the balcony. Candlelight, a set table, and no one but me. The food is on the warmer, on an earthenware tray. Shall I eat alone? I invited my father—today is his ninetieth birthday— but he hasn't shown up. I invited my husband with the children, but they're at Ófalu, sailing on Lake Balaton, getting tipsy at a wine festival, or taking a horse-and-buggy ride with bells through the countryside. They're having a wonderful time, they won't leave Ófalu. And David will probably call soon to tell me they can't make it after all: too many guests there.

From under the earth, from out of the mental hospital I summon János Dragomán, I call him back into Hungary, back from the border, to be here, in my house. And suddenly he is here, but strange, about to blow up the house. He must have taken something; I don't know what. He may have wanted to boil water for his tea, and turned on the gas, but forgot to light it. He has the match in one hand, the matchbox in the other, but the two hands do not come together. The kitchen is filled with gas; I can smell it. János is thinking about something, abstracted. Then, remembering, he strikes the match. The kitchen and the attic above it explode. János stays alive; his body does. He is unconscious, hospitalized for three months with terrible burns. His eyes are open and bright, radiating from a shiny limbo. God, why must I see such things? God, if only he would call.

148

4.

In which David Kobra
recalls a few episodes of
the war's last year

THE MOVEMENTS:

It Came to Pass

And Then One Morning They Came

*Authorized Departure on the Day
  before the Last Day*

The Discipline of the Cardplayer

The High Priest of Frivolity

Arnold's Legacy

We Have Survived

The End of Winter

Homecoming

The Strange Month of March

The Garbage Speaks

It Came to Pass

On March 19, 1944, when the Germans marched into Hungary, I was eleven years old. What we had been talking about fearfully at the family table now came to pass. The privileged island was no more. Now something else was about to begin. How simply it all happened! And how laughable everything preceding it suddenly became! I had listened many nights to the dinner-table strategies of the men. The English would come via Italy and Greece, spearheading the invasion from the west. This would give Horthy more room in which to maneuver, and a chance, perhaps, to pull out of the war altogether. Hungary, following a new political evolution, would develop into a neutral, Anglo-Saxon type of democracy. Until that happened, our fathers would carry on as usual in their shops and doctor's and lawyer's offices. Until the arrival of the liberating British, little Jewish children could keep attending the single-story school that had two classrooms and a dusty courtyard, and the teacher would not humiliate them just because they were Jews. On Friday nights, feet shuffled in the street near our house: dark-clad men with wide-brimmed black hats on their way to prayers, and with them my classmates with earlocks and large eyes, sons in peaked caps holding their fathers' hands as they went to the synagogue.

On the day of the occupation I was sitting with my father in front of the radio in the bedroom. We were listening to London and Moscow. There was no news of resistance; the Hungarian forces put up none. The regent, the government, the whole country lay prone before the Germans.

I did not trust Horthy; I had already given up on him. When I was younger, I had a toy soldier that represented him. Around him stood his officers, mounted troops, and foot soldiers, all in green uniforms; only Horthy bloomed, in a rear admiral's garish cornflower-blue jacket with gold epaulets. I also had a cannon, and I could fire tiny clay cannonballs a distance of three feet. The large linoleum floor was the battlefield. I divided the men and the equipment into two. In the beginning, at the end of the 1930s, it was always the side led by His Serene Highness, our regent, that won. All the troops were knocked down by cannonballs, but he was unharmed. Later, when we entered the war, a clay cannonball knocked His Serene Highness off his feet, and after that, on the linoleum, the losing army was always the one led by Horthy. I took aim at him with my cannon, I hit him, and he fell. As time went on, I preferred to read instead, or build model planes or play soccer with players made of buttons; I had outgrown toy soldiers.

That evening, my uncles and cousins were sitting around the table as usual. There was a rumor that the commander of one of the army's local units objected to the Germans' invasion of Hungary, and soon I found myself hoping that it would be the unit in Újfalu, under the command of Lieutenant Colonel Egyed, that would stop the Germans. There was, after all, a big garrison full of big soldiers at the edge of town, and they had big cannons pulled by huge artillery horses. If the regent called for a war of liberation, what better place for him to make his stand than here in Bihar County? "Our regent? Here?" Zoltán's smile was more than sarcastic. Yes—why not?—the colonel was a decent man, no lover of Germans. By now we children were very experienced in political matters. For years I had been murmuring political prayers after lights-out. In the state-run school I talked politics with Zoltán, but only in the corridors during recess, always making sure to be out of earshot of the others. We'd learned about our pariah status very early. In school we dreamed of a democratic European union. When London reported that the glorious Red Army troops were continuing their advance, I truly believed that they were glorious. But that evening we had to acknowledge the fact that not just Horthy but even the commander of Újfalu had failed to put up any resistance.

The following morning, German tanks stood in front of the town hall and the Protestant church. Soldiers in field-gray uniforms were sitting on them, watching the activities of the small marketplace. Civilians avoided contact with the soldiers; some did not even look at them. Soon, on our own main street, to blustering martial music, in ranks so densely packed that they nearly touched one another, the Germans gave us a demonstration of how to march in perfect precision—not like Hungarian sloppiness. Patrols were sent out in all directions, to requisition houses, which included my uncle's. My cousins had to move in with us. Relatives and friends came to see my parents, to exchange news and information, to share their perplexity and their helplessness. With his eyes closed, my father sat in the sun on the balcony. He had been forced to shut his store, was not allowed to set foot in it; the steel door was sealed. And all our valuables had to be turned in, including the radio. My mother had her hands full, cooking for so many people.

New decrees were published daily. One thing we learned quickly: Tomorrow things would be worse. Three of us boys slept in the living room, or pretended to sleep; we turned on a small lamp and raided the cupboard for the homemade walnut brandy that would keep us awake so we could continue our political discussions. We'd played Ping-Pong until dark. It was nice not having to part at the end of the day. Having no patience for board games, we spent all our time talking. Zoltán figured that the Russians would reach us first, and Hungary would become Communist. We didn't know much about Communism. Those who had come back from the Ukraine told of poverty in the countryside, of cows kept inside houses, while in the cities several families shared a single apartment. Sitting in our high-backed overstuffed chairs, we decided that poverty was bearable as long as there was justice in the world. And besides, it was more fun to have ten people instead of five around the dinner table.

The Jews of Újfalu have dark memories of the Ukraine. In 1942 the younger men were taken away and put in a labor battalion. They had to run naked up and down the corridor of a Ukrainian school whose floor was strewn with tacks. Soldiers standing against the walls struck the running men with rifle butts at random. Drunk on rum, they worked themselves into a frenzy. Finally let out of the school and into the snow, the Jews of Újfalu were allowed to dress, but not before an inspection of their belongings. They had to turn over their watches, rings, anything of value. Whoever tried to keep something was sent back to dance in the corridor. When the inspection was over, the men were lined up and marched westward, because the army was in retreat. The sick were dropped off at the hospital. Sick meant anyone who could not walk and had to be carried. Later, when night fell, great tongues of flame rose in the sky behind the marchers: the soldiers had first poured gasoline over, then set fire to the hospital. In the thick snow Bandi Svéd began to run toward the flames; he thought he saw his brother, who had been left in the hospital. Some of the men ran after Bandi and brought him back before the guards had a chance to shoot him down. Those who stayed alive were mustered out in 1943, came back to Újfalu, and resumed their lives. Everything seemed to return to normal, but these men grew silent.

Whenever the soldiers sang, on the main street, "Jew, Jew, stinking Jew," my father pretended not to hear. Our classmates were not particularly hostile to us; instead, they were hesitant, indifferent. They mostly looked at the tanks and said nothing. "Now you're going to get it," jeered a puny little boy, the worst student in our class. His father had joined the Arrow-Cross to get a job as a construction worker. There were only two Jews in the school now, Zoltán and I; the poorer Jewish children were not accepted. Zoltán liked to state bitter truths, the kind of truths you didn't know what to do with. "In our class we are not only the smartest but also the richest students. Little wonder they don't like us. There are very few people in the world who are not envious. But the Jews in general, rich or poor, are not liked. It's all right with most people if the Jews are allowed to live, and if they aren't, well, that's all right, too."

We were still heating the living room; the atmosphere at home was still cozy. My mother sewed the yellow Stars of David on everybody's jacket and coat. There had been homemade, clumsy stars, but private industry quickly responded to the need. It was a matter of public concern that there be regulation stars: canary yellow, machine-finished, six-by-six centimeters. The mass-produced stars had to be sewn on our outer garments with stitches close enough so that a pencil point could not be put between them. Because those wily Jews were capable of anything; they might wear the badge, and then, whenever the mood hit them, remove it. The Jewish newspaper urged people to comply promptly and fully with the new regulation. One day Zoltán and I decided not to be ashamed of the yellow star, to walk through town wearing it. It was spring, the school year had ended in April, and we had plenty of time on our hands. Wearing boots, we deliberately jumped into the mud puddles of the long, unpaved side streets. From the doorsteps of white-columned, thatch-roofed houses, women gazed at us with wide eyes.

It would have been impossible for us to go on living like lords, I thought. It was absurd that when I press a button, a hired person comes from the kitchen to ask what the young master wishes, and I say, "Ilona, please bring me a glass of water." And Ilona says, "Right away, sir." She leaves, returns with a glass of water, I thank her, she puts it down, I drink, and she comes back later to take the empty glass. It would be easier for me, when I'm thirsty, to go to the kitchen and pour myself a glass of water. Now I was going to the artesian well myself, the one by the post office, wearing my good suit and shoes, giving those around the well the chance to sneer at me. But even with my yellow star I managed to make new friends. Some women greeted me kindly on the street. Indeed, we had nice little chats while waiting on line at the well. The town idiot—once, on a bet, he ate a whole pail of boiled beans—asked me for my yellow star. And everyone laughed.

And Then One Morning They Came

And then one morning they came. Loud knocking on the garden gate. I looked down from the balcony and saw five German soldiers and as many Hungarian, and that funny policeman, Csontos, who was always threatening to denounce people but was willing, for a few pengö, to change his mind. The flat-topped black service caps I saw were those of the Gestapo, but we did not know that at the time.

Father put on his English tweed jacket with the regulation yellow star and went downstairs to open the gate. The Gestapo officer told him, in German, that a report had reached them that said my father was a British spy and kept a secret radio transmitter in his attic. The house would be thoroughly searched. I knew there was no transmitter, but it made me feel good that my father should be suspected of such a thing. I needed to be proud of him. I would have been even prouder if he was suspected of hiding guns.

My father was a timid man, afraid of physical pain; my mother had always protected him; she was the stronger one. It was she who showed the Germans and the policeman around. Walking through the house with them, unusually calm, she answered all their questions. They seized a number of things—money, jewelry, our camera—but found nothing important. When the search was over, they seemed dissatisfied, and ordered my father and my uncle to accompany them to the police station. There, my father and my uncle were to reveal, not only where the transmitter was kept, but also what else was hidden and where. Did they really mean to say that they were hiding nothing? My parents looked at them with innocent faces. We went to the balcony over the street and looked down at the men. The Gestapo men were in front, followed by a pair of Hungarian hats with cock feathers, then my father and my uncle; the rest of the Hungarians walked behind them, and the funny policeman, Csontos, brought up the rear.

The rear was always brought up by something funny. When the military band marched in a parade, the drum major with his colorful, carved baton was in the lead, and in the rear was the large drum, drawn by a donkey and beaten by a short, bowlegged, flat-footed private. And behind him Gypsy children hopped and skipped, hoping to touch the donkey; they marched, too, to the music of the brass band, as if they were all kings and field marshals.

On that day, May 15, everything was as usual. Horse droppings lay drying in three-ball clumps on the warm pavement, and the light was yellow on the thick steeple of the Protestant church and on the rows of acacia that lined the indifferent street. Father looked neither to the right nor to the left. Nobody greeted him. Looking at the faces of your acquaintances while being led by armed guards can be edifying. Father knew everyone he saw in the street, but he had nothing to say to them; he walked as if in a scene being filmed. The scene was not upsetting, perhaps not even sad; only unusual. The faces at first showed puzzlement, then the features were rearranged: Ah, yes, this is what's happening now; they're taking away the Jews.

Only my mother and the children remained in the house. She felt she had to do something. How was it possible for her husband to be taken away, just like that, at the order of a few black-uniformed Germans? What about the leaders of the local government? Had those gentlemen, all acquaintances of the family, agreed to this absurdity? Mother dressed and went to the police chief. Two hours later, she was arrested, too. Do you want me to lock you up next to your husband? Mother nodded. They did her the favor of putting her in the same jail with her husband, but in a separate cell. The soldiers rounded up several Jews, the wealthier ones, as hostages. The wives of the others remained at home; only my mother was with her husband. And that is what saved our lives.

I learned later that my father had been denounced by a pastry cook, a member of the Arrow-Cross. I bless his name, because I owe that man my life. Possibly he resented the fact that we did not patronize his shop, despite its fancy front. Two polar bears, plywood cutouts painted in oil, licking strawberry and vanilla ice-cream cones, flanked the doors of the shop, but the ice cream sold inside was not as good as at Petrik's. At Petrik's, with its friendly beige tile walls, two bird-faced spinsters, their gray hair in buns, served the always reliable napoleons and ice cream. They did not skimp on eggs, sugar, vanilla, or anything that made for excellent pastry. They baked tried-and-true cakes, which never disappointed; they didn't experiment with confectionery innovations. Churchgoers, they were not Nazis. On Sunday morning, arm in arm, dressed in white silk blouses and wearing dark-gray hats with veils, they went to church, and opened their shop only after Mass. Smiling, the fragrance of the church still on them, they would sell the warm napoleons they had baked at dawn.

But these women were not the players to determine the course of history. Fate had put the hand of a loudmouth fraud on the switch, a man who used all kinds of artificial ingredients and instead of quality provided painted icebergs and seals in the August heat. It was given to him to decide my fate. Following the inspiration of his soul, the expression of which inspiration took the form of a letter of denunciation, he secured a place for my parents in the detention camp of the Gestapo, and thus my family was spared the common fate of the Jews of Újfalu: Auschwitz.

The four children—my sister, two cousins, and I—were left in the house with Ibi, my cousins' Jewish governess, who, in those days of fear and uncertainty, had an unpleasant odor. A clumsy, soft girl, she did not do too well with the cooking or the housekeeping. The meals she prepared were tasteless, and the house was dirty. A whole way of life was coming painfully apart. Our constant anxiety and not having our parents with us were bad enough, but the disgust at seeing this daily deterioration was worse. Zoltán and I came to the conclusion that it was all our parents' fault. We should have left everything behind and got away while there was still time; now we were losing the house and garden anyway.

It was a warm, beautiful early summer; the storks were at their customary place by the Table of the Covenant. With abandon we threw ourselves into Ping-Pong. Monday was still market day; a fair was still held every Thursday; and on Friday afternoons, yellow stars on their jackets and prayer shawls under their arms, Jews passed our house on their way to the synagogue. We obeyed the blackout regulations; every evening our windows were fitted with construction paper stretched over wooden frames.

The swimming pool was now off limits to us. Wearing our yellow stars, we would stroll by and peek at it through the fence. The boys inside were imitating Stukas, the German dive-bombers, screeching and hurling themselves headfirst into the pool, which was eighty-five feet long and fed quietly by artesian water. It was drained on Sundays and refilled on Wednesdays. The year before, Zoltán and I were doing our fifty laps and had enough pocket money to eat chicken paprika with macaroni at the pool's restaurant. Now we went instead to Gacsa Garden, but it was becoming increasingly unpleasant to be seen with our yellow stars. The faces we encountered seemed to say, Now you're getting what's coming to you, aren't you? Or, more indifferently, Ah, so this is how things will be from now on. And that emphatic, wordless look and the quickening of steps: a passing fellow sufferer. We preferred to stay home, in the garden.

I would sit on the swing, flying back and forth for hours, until I reached a state of total vertigo. Late in the morning, silvery British and U.S. bombers would streak by overhead. They dropped nothing on us; they only sparkled in the bright light on their way to bomb the Debrecen railroad station. The church bells rang, sounding the alarm; a siren wailed; the police checked to see if people were taking shelter in the cellars. But we did not hide; throwing our heads back, we searched the skies. Good; at least the Allies ruled the air. A postcard arrived from our parents, from Debrecen, saying that they were all right; nothing more.

There was no radio transmitter in the house, but there were other things that had to be kept secret. An unauthorized sack of flour and a few good pieces of bacon were hidden in the cellar, in a very devious place that the architect (Mr. Berger, with whom my parents wound up in the same train and camp) had shown my father in 1933, saying that it might come in handy someday. Behind the concrete water tank under the steps there was a dark alcove that only a sharp eye could detect, a sharper eye than the searchers had. There was also money hidden behind the drawer of my father's desk: three batches of hundreds, thirty thousand pengö in all, the price of a good-size house. But the most serious violation was buried in the storehouse adjacent to the courtyard: gold jewelry in two small iron chests. Over the years, little by little, Father had converted a certain percentage of his stock into gold. One chest was buried in the corner; it was later discovered. But the other one wasn't, because it was buried in the middle of the asymmetrical room, directly under the gray enamel pot suspended by wires from the ceiling, which held the oats for the Angora rabbits.

In those days we kept a dozen rabbits in the garden. At the side of the two upper cages of the rabbitry, two separate wooden boxes were placed for the new litters. A door connected them to the cage, for the use of the mother rabbit. Baby rabbits are hairless and pink after birth, and they huddle, quivering, under their mother's belly. I wanted so much to touch them, at least with the tips of my fingers, but I was told that the mother could smell the touch of humans, and she would reject or even eat the touched baby. We were allowed to pat the young ones only when their fur began to sprout. Then, in the mornings, we could put the snow-white little creatures on a sheet and play with them.

It was also nice to spin the freshly cut fluffy wool into yarn on the spinning wheel. The thread broke easily, but if I did it carefully, the wheel, which was a bicycle wheel and operated by a foot pedal, would spin for quite a while without tearing the yarn. It would delicately twine onto the shuttle the thread emerging from the batch of wool I held in my left hand. I regulated the thickness of the thread with my right thumb and index finger. On winter afternoons, with the tile stove giving out plenty of heat, we would roll the yarn into skeins as we listened to the war news on the radio. Or I would just sit reading a novel about Indians while Mother knit warm hats and sweaters with Norwegian motifs for us.

As for that pot in the storehouse, it hung on wires to keep mice out of the rabbits' oats. But the mice still managed to get to the oats. Scurrying up to the master beam, they would drop into their promised land, which also proved to be their doom, because their tiny claws could find no purchase on the slippery enamel inside surface. They kept scrambling and circling helplessly, and became dehydrated in the midst of infinite plenty, until a horrible hand grabbed them by the tail and knocked them against a stone.

Before this, my mother had shown me what she and my father had hidden, and where, in the course of many nights. "Someday, my little one, we may be separated, we may never even see one another again. The two of you should know what we have. If we still have it." My sister and I noted the precise location of everything we were shown. We said not a word to anyone; children, too, can keep secrets. Only in April 1945 did we tell our uncle László, who was to be trusted. Mother also sewed a few thin gold chains into our coats. No matter where we wound up, we could always use gold. We were preparing for our dispersion. As I remember, the tone of this conversation was very matter-of-fact.

Authorized Departure on the Day
before the Last Day

In May 1944 it was decided that the Jewry of the Hungarian countryside, young and old, would be deported to labor camps in the territories of what once was Poland. Towns had been built for them in forests and around lakes. The Jews had to be separated from the local population; they could no longer live with Christians. The authorities needed our consent. Yes, of course, it was only natural, we wouldn't think of living with the Christians. The newspaper for Hungarian Jews urged us to comply with the law to the letter. If now, in this dark hour, in this time of trial, we showed that we were good Magyars, then we could hope for leniency.

A fine idea, this national unity on the matter of separation, but for it to be achieved what a lot of organizational and administrative difficulties had to be overcome! How many officials of the Interior Ministry, how many executives and their subordinates had to burn the midnight oil, apologizing to their wives! This deportation was indeed a troublesome business. Every government branch, from the police to the State Commission on Abandoned Property, had to show its mettle. Special commendation should be given to the workers of the national railroad for their exemplary conduct in the face of heavy enemy bombing. In only a few short weeks the Jews were rolled smoothly out of the country. To have put six hundred thousand of them in fenced-in quarters, under armed guard, and then to have shipped them all off in cattle cars, that was something to be proud of. With joyful sighs of relief the provincial newspapers reported that the air had been purified, the countryside made *Judenrein.*

Having received a letter of invitation from relatives in Budapest, we had to decide quickly whether to stay where we were or go to the capital. Jews were no longer allowed to ride the trains; there were constant checks on every line, and reporting Jews was mandatory.

161

To go to Budapest legally, we needed permission from the police, a special waiving of the rules. But why go at all? Why not stay here with the rest of our family? We had aunts, uncles, and cousins in town. Maybe, in our own house, we wouldn't be touched. Maybe some higher authorities would intercede.

I was rocking myself on the swing. I was every inch a boy of Újfalu; it was here that I had to live and die. But what if they took me away? It would be harder for them to do that in Budapest. In Budapest I could hide, I would be a needle in a haystack. I tried to weave a magic spell, so that there would be a knock at the garden gate. I'd open it, and there they would be, my parents, standing before me and smiling. Thinking I heard a knock, I jumped off the swing, ran to the gate, and opened it, but there was nobody there. On the street, German soldiers were strolling with local girls on their arms.

I made up my mind: We'd leave. I went and checked to see if the thirty thousand pengö were still in their secret place. Then I went across the street to a Christian lawyer. He was a good customer of my father's, right-wing but not too anti-Semitic. I asked him to get us a travel permit. It would cost a lot, he said. Did we have the money? Yes, I said. How much? I told him. That would do. I should give him half in advance. I went home, came back, and gave him fifteen thousand. He said he would let us know the next day what he could arrange. The matter should be kept between us, and not a word to anyone about the money.

At home we talked things over. I insisted that we go; the others were reluctant. It was understandable: None of us wanted to be a burden on other people, even if they were relatives. Here we could still curl up in our own easy chairs. Maybe it wouldn't be necessary to leave. Maybe they were taking people only from Várad, not from Újfalu. What had happened to the Jews of Poland could not—in the very center of a New Europe of national socialism—happen to us. Yet even now, at the order of the town clerk, Jews were being listed by street and house number. The Jewish community was in charge of compiling the list, which later would make it easier for the police to go from house to house and herd us all out onto the streets at the crack of dawn. I said that there was nobody in town who would have the courage to hide us. It would be harder to deport the Jews of Budapest because there were more of them. They would probably be the last to go. We would at least gain a little time.

The next day, the lawyer came and told me to give him the other fifteen thousand and get the necessary papers. First, I was to go to the school and see the principal, Mr. Somody, who was a very good man and thought highly of my academic achievements. I was to thank him for having helped persuade the other leading men of the town to approve of our request. I went to the principal, clicked my heels, and thanked him. He smiled, patted my head, and said that I should continue to study hard and stay a good Hungarian child. Then I had to go to the police station, where I would obtain our travel permit. At the police station a sergeant with large fingers filled out the permit, letter by letter, on a typewriter. It took a while to match the information on the residency register with the information on the birth certificates, and include it all in the permit. In the corner of the room, rifles were stacked in their stand, and a line of black hats with cock feathers hung on a rack on the wall. On the desk were a green table lamp and stamp pads. The whole room smelled of boots. The separate permits for the four of us required eight bangs of the stamp. At another desk, a corporal was eating bacon. He looked over at me: "So, you kids are leaving." "Yes." The sergeant handed me the four pieces of paper; he had worked hard on them and now looked very pleased with himself, and with me, too, because I smiled at him approvingly. "Have a good trip." I thanked him. The papers fit into the inner pocket of my jacket.

On the street, I realized that I possessed something the other Jews of Újfalu did not. The leaders of the town, giving their blessing to our departure, had let us four children slip out of the trap that was closing on us. Their decision was, perhaps, prompted by pity; after all, we had been left without parents. One of my aunts, the mother of little Vera, asked me how it felt to abandon the family. Aunt Ilonka was not a cheerful woman. She had a limp and was fat, but she played the violin beautifully. As a girl she had dreamed of a life in the arts. Providence granted her two beautiful daughters, but only after the birth of a retarded son. Never satisfied, cold, easily offended, Aunt Ilonka was a woman acutely aware of the world's predicaments.

Laló Kádár came and offered to take us to our relatives in Budapest. We were very glad. By now Christians would not set foot in our house; the separation of Christians and Jews was nearly complete. Laló, an assistant in my uncle's drapery store, was a tall, elegant young man who played center forward on the town soccer team. His younger sister, Katalin, was my sister's classmate and had been to our house often. We had all played together. Katalin had black braids, very white teeth, and large brown eyes. I loved looking at her. Whenever Kati came in or was about to leave, I made sure to kiss her on the cheek. She was three years older, taller than I, and now she, too, came to say good-bye. We were silent. Cousin Vera, my age, also came. Will you write? We didn't know what would happen to us. At that time it was not clear who should feel sorry for whom. At dusk, on June 5, 1944, I kissed both Kati and Vera on the cheek.

Left alone, we began packing our belongings. We faced overflowing closets. So much stuff, and for what? We couldn't take everything. There was an official weight limit for luggage per person. But, more important, from now on we should have only as much as we could carry. The next morning we got up at four-thirty. I took a cold shower and looked at myself in the mirror: I must have grown some. I was eleven, my parents were who knows where, and the stork couple stood motionless by the Table of the Covenant. The ancestral home was closing its door to us. Let whoever wanted take what was left in it. Laló Kádár, wearing a light-gray suit, came to get us at five. We took a hansom to the station; there were few people in the street. Those who saw us looked at us impassively and said nothing.

At the station we had to wait for the Budapest express coming from Nagyvárad. We leaned against the green railing of the platform, which was warming up in the early-morning sun. People stared at the yellow stars on our chests. Some must have wondered how it was possible for us to be at the station. I was glad when the train pulled in. Standing in the crowded corridor and looking back, I saw only the steam mill and the steeple of the Protestant church, and then nothing. Something had come to an end. Today I would say: my childhood.

The next day, one day after we left, the rest of our people were taken away. Under local military guard, the Jews of Újfalu struggled with their suitcases while the townspeople watched them from the sidewalks. Some said good day, some shouted insults, but most just watched in silence. The Jews were transported in cattle cars to the ghetto in Nagyvárad, and from there, not much later, to Auschwitz.

We stood at the window, looking out, not saying a word. German military trains; cannons on flatcars; the sound of a harmonica; gray uniforms, rubber raincoats. People were working in the fields. The wheat stood high, here and there turning yellow, a good crop that year. At the Szolnok station, bombed the previous day, burned freight cars and uprooted semaphores greeted us. The overpass for pedestrians had also been hit. Our train stopped for a long time; we had to give the right-of-way to a German military transport. Another train passed. Cattle cars. Behind the narrow openings covered with barbed wire, female eyes, the eyes of Jewish women. On the platform, people looking grave, frightened. The train stood for hours. Everything was very slow, very matter-of-fact. Several times we heard the phrase "rail repair."

Twice during the trip, security police came to check identification papers. First, the ruddy-faced, mustached chief, who wore a round felt hat with upturned brim and a decorative feather. He snapped at Laló, "If you're a real Hungarian, why get mixed up in the affairs of Jews? Why are you escorting these Jewish brats?" Laló did not answer; he turned pale. Our papers were in order, but I had the feeling that this round-hatted policeman could easily have pulled us off the train if he wanted to. He looked at us, making up his mind. We looked back at him, not smiling, with a serious expression. We were the children of a higher class of people, a class he did not belong to; this much was obvious, but I wasn't sure whether it would be an argument in our favor. He moved on finally, leaving us in peace. After this little incident, and with the yellow stars on our chests, we became conspicuous and undesirable passengers in the spacious car. The other passengers did not talk to us, and nobody talked to Laló, either. The second check was more businesslike and went more smoothly. The papers were in order; the police looked at them and nodded coolly.

I was in awe of Budapest. The year before, we had been there with Mother for a week's vacation. In the glass-covered terminal of Budapest West we entrusted ourselves to a pink-capped porter, a taxi took us to the Hungarian Hotel, and a bellboy opened the doors for us, and drew aside the batiste lace curtain so that I could step out onto the small French balcony and take in the Danube sparkling in full daylight, and the bridges, and the row of chestnut trees on the far bank, and the Castle. A year ago, it had been a happiness that made my throat tighten. I grew weak at the sight of the city, as when the curtain goes up at the opera and a fantastic ballroom emerges from the dark. Then, my mother stood behind me, but now, perhaps, she stood in that train that had just passed us.

The terminal was still beautiful; it had not been bombed. We had to carry our own suitcases now in the hubbub and bustle. Newsboys were shouting: "Invasion!" "Allies land in Normandy!" People crowded around them, but the newsboys knew no more than what was in the headlines. We put our bags down. Zoltán and I shook hands. We watched the people around us. They were just like the people in Újfalu: The news stares them in the face, but they go about their business as if nothing has happened.

At the front door of our relatives', with a sinking heart, I said good-bye to Laló Kádár. He was a familiar face, a face from Újfalu. I would have loved to go back home with him, but it was not possible. I waved to him from the balcony. And I kept standing on that balcony throughout the summer, waiting for our parents to come and get us.

The Discipline
of the Cardplayer

I owe my life to a series of fortunate coincidences. It is remarkable, too, that an eleven-year-old can realize the cold fact that he can be killed at any time, and yet not falter. In the winter of 1944—

45 I thought of death almost the way one thinks of firewood: There was nothing special about it. It was a thing beyond my control, and there was no point in fearing it, for it had as much probability, no more, no less, as drawing a bad card and losing.

There were certain apartment buildings designated as protected houses; in these the wealthier, more secular Jews lived, those who had managed to establish contact with the embassy of some neutral country. The less well off—and the Orthodox Jews, with their black hats and beards—ended up in the ghetto, along with their wives, their *peyis*-wearing sons, and their large-eyed daughters. Their place was there, near the rabbinate and where most of the synagogues were also located. They must have felt that this arrangement was proper —as did, no doubt, the diplomats of the neutral countries. Arrow-Cross men venturing into the ghetto through the wooden fence found a free hunting ground within. Their bullets spared only those they didn't feel like shooting. Immediately after the liberation of the city, I looked into a café at the corner of Klauzál Square. It was piled to the ceiling with corpses. To dig the mass graves, it was not easy to break the icy ground.

The building in which Zsuzsa had her studio, on Pozsonyi Road, came under Swiss protection. Our relatives could have moved to the adjacent building, which was under Swedish protection, and rumor had it that Swedish protection was more effective than Swiss, but they decided to stay in their own apartment, which was a nice apartment although eighty people were living in it now. Every evening, all the furniture that could not be slept on was piled in one corner. There were not enough beds or mattresses to go around, but at least everyone had a rug under him. Sleeping was done in close proximity; it was a continuous pajama party, and there was always somebody to talk to. We were allowed to leave the house for two hours every morning. On the front entrance hung a yellow star and a sign that said the house was protected by the Swiss government. While Communists, members of the Resistance, and braver souls in general were hiding in all parts of the city, constantly on the move and carrying false papers, the more resigned and perhaps more timid middle class hoped to ride out the worst in these protected apartment houses.

In our apartment, beautiful long-legged young women in ski boots, pants, and heavy sweaters with Norwegian motifs, their abundant hair combed flat, stood around and smoked cigarettes. They laughed at things I did not understand—but Klára understood. Not at all like their small-town counterparts, these women were cynical, enigmatic, radical, and refined. They spoke of French surrealists, German expressionists, and Russian abstractionists as old friends. Being modern dancers, they could stretch their bodies. For us, the children, they sang the "Internationale" and other Russian revolutionary songs. I was in love with all of them, but especially with Zsuzsa—or, more precisely, Aunt Zsuzsa, who was not yet thirty then. I would have loved to do something heroic for her. She'd call to me in a drawl: "Would you come and escort me, my cavalier?" I would have escorted her to hell itself. I turned fiery red when Zsuzsa walked into the bathroom once and saw me naked. For her sake I was willing to eat with a thick novel clamped under each arm: to learn to stop sticking out my elbows.

Half the occupants of the apartment soon had been shot and thrown into the Danube. There was more room. Those who were frightened moved down to the cellar, but Zsuzsa was unable to separate human dignity from hygiene. It was out of the question for her to hide from incendiary bombs, cannonballs, and artillery shells in the gloom and stench of the cellar, the cramped confusion of people who hadn't washed themselves recently. Human dignity was worth more than safety, she would say. Not wanting to get lice, we didn't go down to the cellar even when the siren sounded. One Jew marched around in a funny helmet; he was our air-raid warden. Wearing several arm bands, he would bravely venture out into the lobby of the building. Once I went downstairs just to watch him. Back in the apartment, I imitated him, the way he pointed his chirping-blinking flashlight in all directions, the way he tried to calm people down, and how occasionally he would bring news, such as: "The bathhouse across the street is burning" or "The mill was hit."

The most sensible place turned out to be the roof terrace, where every morning the sun was bright, even in the January cold of twenty degrees below zero centigrade. With a few pails of water we created a splendid ice-skating rink. With the metal taps on the heels of our shoes, we could slide grandly across the shiny surface. We stared at the sky when the bombers came, and watched their bellies open, and followed the fall of the bombs to see where they hit. Only the plumes of dust or flame would indicate whether they were explosive or incendiary bombs. Then we watched the smoke rise. On the street below, Germans shouted. The Russians were already near, but, in the neighborhood, the Arrow-Cross men were still carrying on their massacre of Jews and Christian deserters. The word *massacre* appeared in every notice posted. Its meaning was clear: to be shot on sight and left lying where you fell. All through this period, intermittent rifle shots were heard in the streets.

Identification papers no longer meant anything; one's fate was determined only by drunkenness, fear, a moment of empathy or antipathy. People were still being shot, but the arm-banded shooters sensed that they would not be able to finish off every Jew. Perhaps, too, they could not work themselves into a manhunting mood every day. To fill the rolling Danube with the wounded bodies of old women and little girls proved to lack effectiveness as decorative art. And even these helpless people, of whom the Hungarian Nazis were permitted to kill as many as they liked, voiced, if only by the look in their eyes, a protest, a protest repeated and strengthened by the gaze of witnesses, who watched with some compassion as silent Jews in winter coats were escorted to the lower wharves of the Danube. It must have occurred to the Hungarian Nazis that if the Russians reached the outskirts of Budapest—and the constant booming of artillery indicated that they were on their way—then it was not likely that they would stop and not enter the city. And if the Russians entered the city, then many things would be in store for the Hungarian Nazis, things that did not include decorations. An unpleasant thought. The lust to kill alternately left them and flared up in them. To fire at the Russians was dangerous; to shoot the Jews was safe, like shooting clay pigeons.

Life is good luck, death is bad luck. People in the apartment were taken away last night; by chance they were taken from the adjacent room, not from ours. In the bright January morning I am skating on the roof. From a machine gun of a Russian fighter plane overhead, bullets crackle on the ice. A streetcar rattles by, carrying ammunition to the front, which is only five blocks away. I watch the Germans: military fuss, boyish activity around the weapons. Do they really believe they can repel the Russians? The Germans are intelligent, but don't see what is obvious. And these Arrow-Cross men, these Hungarian Nazis—they are the trash, the ones who flunk school, who are talented only in torturing cats. A child grows up and learns how childish adults are. Learns that mass murderers are not evil, but only rotten kids with runny noses; rotten kids, even if they are fifty years old.

An armed fourteen-year-old takes unarmed grown-ups to the bank of the Danube. And they, instead of disarming him, do what he tells them. Most victims consider inevitable what ought to be fought. The attitude of a gardener to the hail falling on his flowers. Just as a farm animal grows accustomed to the slaughter of its mates, man grows accustomed to the slaughter of his fellow human beings. You cannot be shocked every half hour.

As we were standing on the roof terrace, the sound of rifle shots came from several places in the neighboring streets. A man was checking another man's papers; one armed checking one unarmed. The one armed did not like the face of the one unarmed, so he made him stand against the wall and shot him. And the people taken to the Danube had to line up in a row facing the river. Then came the round of fire, from behind. Yet even all this violent death could not eclipse the icy beauty of that bright winter morning. In the shadow of our doom, bread was more like bread, jam was more like jam, and I took pleasure in making firewood out of furniture. Venturing out to the docks and using an ax, we knocked apart a small wharf made of nice dry pine. The wood, with its white oil paint, burned wonderfully.

On the roof Klára often arranged her braids, tying and untying them. I would pull them sometimes. Klára had beautiful brown earlobes, a small birthmark at the root of her nostrils, and a freckle on the tip of her nose. I was given permission to plant a quick kiss on the freckle. A long kiss was forbidden. Klára liked to speak of the parts of her body as independent beings. "The nose has had enough of this," she would say. We wrestled a lot. It wasn't at all easy to get Klára to the floor. We would roll over and under each other. Sometimes I'd manage to pin her shoulders to the horsehair mattress on the floor and lie on her stomach, but then she would bite my wrists so hard that for a long time I'd carry her tooth marks on them. "I dare you to put your hand over the candle," Klára said. I did, and promptly got a small burn on my palm. Klára kissed it. I tucked my fist into my pocket carefully, as if holding a tiny bird.

Klára could not stand being cooped up all day in the protected house; the curfew of the Jews couldn't possibly apply to her, too. I tried to make her stay inside. I was afraid for her, but did not watch her all the time. Klára would wander out into the neighborhood, then brag about the things she had seen. But once, when she was stopped by a roving patrol, she had no ready answers. She was taken to the Danube with a group of Jews, and recognized among them one of her aunts. Klára managed to get next to her. They all had to empty their pockets. As they were standing with their hands up, looking at the trees of Margaret Island and the solitary piers of blown-up Margaret Bridge, the aunt was hit and fell into the river. But Klára was unharmed. "Lucky for you I ran out of bullets," said one of the men with submachine guns, an older man, his tone friendly. "Get out of here. Go home and be a good girl!" With this advice he sent Klára on her way. I opened the boarded-over front door for her, recognizing the sound of her footsteps. Klára said, "Let's just stand here, and you hold my hand. Don't let me go out tomorrow. Stay with me all day. Don't tell Mother what happened. They shot Aunt Magda to death, right next to me."

The following morning, I was squatting in the courtyard in front of a fireplace made of three bricks and an iron grill; on it, at a painfully slow pace, bean soup was cooking. My job was to stir the soup occasionally, to test the beans for softness, and also to feed, one by one, cut-off chair legs into the embers. Klára was standing behind me, telling me about her first two years in school, when she didn't dare open her mouth. She'd do her homework, but never say a word. She would have liked to say hello, at least, to the other children, but just couldn't. Interested in the progress of the soup, I

took off the lid and stuck the wooden spoon inside. A Russian Rata
zoomed by. Klára ran to the wall and yelled "Come here!" with such
anger that I turned around, puzzled, to see what was wrong. With its
machine gun the plane sprayed thoroughly all the courtyards on the
block. No one was hit. Klára said later that what made her angry
was that I was always playing the hero, which was an exaggeration.
Then a sizzling sound came from the fire. I looked closer: through a
small hole at the bottom of the large red enamel pot, soup was running.
If I hadn't turned when she yelled at me, I would have had a hole
in my head, too, as I bent forward to taste the beans. It was not easy
finding another pot.

Standing on the roof, Klára and I listened to the voice of the most
popular actress-singer of the time, Katalin Karády. The voice, coming
from a Russian army loudspeaker, boomed, and the song had an
added, more threatening depth. With this song the Russians meant
to plant fear in the dispirited hearts of the Hungarian soldiers still
defending themselves on the side of the Germans. "In vain you run,
in vain. You cannot escape your fate." The Russians were in the
outskirts of the city and already held the suburb of Angyalföld. The
loudspeaker was operated from only a few blocks away. A Stalin flare
howled into the sky and lit up the roofs. We stood there, holding
hands, blinking in the sudden brightness. "Beautiful," Klára whispered. We laughed: Why was she whispering?

The High Priest
of Frivolity

On Christmas Day, 1944, my uncle Arnold Kobra was sitting in
his easy chair, wearing his winter coat, smoking his pipe, and looking
very lean and sarcastic. He was taking great pleasure in the movements of his young wife, Zsuzsa, while he entertained us with interesting stories. He kept looking at the tip of his thick shoes and at

the crows on the windowsill. He was the most spectacular figure in the family: the grand master of spectacles, a Freemason, and Jeremiah Kadron's friend. Picture a sixty-year-old gentleman with barely graying hair. If he were to enter now and approach our table, he would probably be wearing a cashmere topcoat, his felt hat in his hand, without scarf or tie, the collar of his white shirt open. But in that Bauhaus-style building on Pozsonyi Road, with the seventy-nine, then fewer fellow tenants and the broken windows, Arnold wrapped a wool scarf around himself over the cashmere coat. The corner of the room had been hit by a bomb, but it would have been beneath Arnold to attribute any special importance to a gaping hole. Rather, he gathered the children around him, to tell them about the round-the-world adventures of a cabaret dancer, and about the Middle East and the Far East. "She must have been his mistress, too," whispered Klára, whose remarks were not always noticed by her father. "Papa was quite debauched," Klára said. "Tell me, Papa, why did you have to have so many women?" "You know, my dear, when we get undressed, everything is discovered. Maybe that's what we want, discovery." Klára gave him a dark look. "And what is this everything that gets discovered? You men have one thing sticking out below, and we women have two things sticking out on top. That's not terribly interesting." Uncle Arnold disagreed: "Man seeks moments of truth, and sometimes finds them in bed with a stranger who turns out to be not such a stranger after all. The Bible also tells you to love they neighbor as thyself. This is best done in bed." "And what about fornication?" Klára demanded. "When you cheat on Mama, that's called fornication, isn't it? Did you cheat on her?" "No." "Never?" "Never." "Why not?" "Because." "What about your other wives? Did you cheat on them?" "Yes." "Why?" "Because I felt like it." "And you didn't feel like cheating on Mama?" "No, I didn't." "Why, dear Papa?" "Because it was with Mama that I was unfaithful to all the other women."

Would you, Regina, like to see your grandfather Arnold? Here, take a look: an elderly gentleman lying on muddy light-pink marble, and in a steady stream blood flows from his forehead into the sockets of his eyes. If he were sitting here now at our tombstone table, this is what he would say: "My dear nephew, I haven't had an opportunity to thank you for what you did for me. It was your display of resistance, you know, that made that young man shoot me in the head. I also see some connection between your slamming the door in the face of that Arrow-Cross man and the fact that Zsuzsa later threw herself from the balcony, from the same balcony where I last kissed her, when she felt that she had done her duty, when you and Klára were already sleeping together.

"What had happened up to January 1945 was quite enough for me. When it's clear I'm not wanted, I don't cling to the doorknob. I thought I was a hospitable citizen. My innkeeper ancestors, too, leaned on the respective counters of their establishments, waiting to see whether the cops or the robbers would come in. Let them all come in; everybody has to eat, drink, rest, and have a little fun. A good inn is a valuable thing. But they called me a harmful Jewish capitalist. They? It's hard to describe them. The ones who have hated my kind from the start, and now invented some humbug theory to go with their hatred. Some of them hate the Jew in me more than the capitalist, and some vice versa. I am harmful, too, because I corrupted people's morals. Besides my hotel, the Crown, I maintained a music hall and a reputable private meeting place for couples in the city. I worked on the premise that people need food, lodging, entertainment, and sex. And with a verve characteristic of Budapest and my own kindly misanthropy, I set about providing all this at reasonable prices.

"Why, you ask, was I a hotelier in Budapest? Why not a fur trader in China or a shaman in Senegal? What does a people who depend so much on personal hospitality have to do with the industry of hospitality? Perhaps I wanted to encourage hospitality in our fellow citizens by providing them with a blue saloon, a cabaret, and a winter garden. A hotel is civilization itself, don't you think? Meanwhile, in increasingly unfriendly tones, I was given to understand that I was no more than a guest myself, a guest whose presence was becoming more and more intolerable. To stand one's ground or to flee, that was the question. I realized, too late, that to flee meant to stand one's ground. Our business is to stay alive, along with our family.

"My life was not in danger; I would just keep on doing what I had been doing. Thus did I fool myself, too lazy and too proud to run away or to help you run away. I didn't even go out to do the shopping; I only sat in my armchair and loathed mankind. It's a comic sort of end, isn't it, that one can be shot down like a stray dog. I was not prepared. Since then I have had time to wonder what would have happened if that young man hadn't got so angry with me, if he had spared me my declining years. Even old age has its sweet moments.

"We should have got out in time. My instinct was always to make myself scarce when tempers rose and melodramas brewed. In 1939 I called Zsuzsa from Paris and asked her and Klára to join me. I wanted to go into the entertainment industry in Rio. But Zsuzsa said I had better come home, Paris was no safer than Budapest. We had a beautiful autumn that year; we took walks in the hills of Buda. On all of Mount Hármashatár there wasn't a man more in love than I.

"I suppose I disappeared from Zsuzsa's life at the best possible time. I had never known anyone more beautiful. She had an ironic, yet warm countenance. The jet-black wavy hair above her high forehead was made more interesting by the few strands of gray. Her manner was distant, somewhat capricious. Good taste surrounded her from head to toe. Zsuzsa did have other loves after me. What she received from them must have been different from what I gave her. Far better, and more elegant, to abandon Zsuzsa as a sixty-year-old, still-trim gentleman than to remain by her side and turn into a toothless, potbellied fool."

"Here everything will be exactly as you wish it," said Arnold to Zsuzsa when he carried her into this studio apartment with the roof terrace. He got down on his knees and kissed her foot, begging forgiveness in advance for all the sins he was going to commit. Zsuzsa decorated the studio in her own way, with shiny black reflecting surfaces and large lamps in the shape of metal bowls that scattered the light across the ceiling. And, of course, there were chrome tube chairs with raw-leather strap seats. In her bedroom, ascetic sharp angles and geometrical abstractions awaited Arnold's art-nouveau virility.

She wore knee socks and tartan skirts, read books on psychology and sociology, was interested in the architecture of apartment build-

175

ings and in the history of clothes. She had her hair clipped short, was friendly with leftist poets who thought that Arnold, thirty years her senior, was a peculiar sort of prehistoric creature. But they were glad to see him whenever he joined them, and even gladder when he invited everyone to his place. His own apartment was located on the fourth floor of the building behind the hotel. Arnold surrounded himself with old objects, all lovingly made, most of which sent shivers down Zsuzsa's spine. He would sit in the living room, by the tile stove, in his rocking chair, his feet on an upholstered stool as he designed unprecedented lighting effects for his next show. He had started many things; he had failed at many things.

When he was cheerful, he needed the cabaret and the sound of clinking glasses. Passing through the several halls of his hotel, he would disperse his little jokes. In the bar, the dancer would put her head on the lapel of his shiny tuxedo, and he would sink his fingers into the girl's curly hair. Arnold liked to watch women come through the revolving door, survey the place while fluttering the wings of their coats, and then move to the bar. The fragrant newcomer is already awaited by a carefully trimmed mustache. With a barely audible clicking of the heels, the gentleman rises, kisses the lady's hand, and takes her coat to the cloakroom. Arnold nods with sympathy. It will not be easy for the gentleman with the mustache to listen to the lady's chatter in a public place like the Crown while holding her hand. The lady must be a recent divorcée now looking for a witty companion who will boldly ring her bell, take her to dinner after the theater, and know how to make a good appearance anywhere. The gentleman with the mustache knows how to make a good appearance, but senses, with trepidation, that he will be unable to leave the lady's apartment, full of china and antique weapons, before three in the morning. His wife will not say a word. With slightly trembling shoulders she will cry in the kitchen while making coffee. The husband, leaning against the doorjamb, will watch his wife's wrinkled elbows. He, too, will have a lump in his throat. Arnold nods; he knows all this in advance.

What Arnold liked best in life was to play with his hotel and nightclub. For this he needed a lot of free time from Zsuzsa, but didn't want her to be unfaithful to him. In his music hall, women fell on the table with laughter, and army officers couldn't hold back the tears behind their monocles. The Crown was the city's most popular spot. Once Zsuzsa burst out, "For you, the worst trash is permitted if it provides a laugh!" She lowered her eyes when he addressed the maid, "Please bring me my cigar box." It contained cash. Through Zsuzsa he made handsome donations to the glee clubs of the workers' movement. If they used the money for secret activities instead, that was their business. He was more interested in eccentrics than in benevolent causes, in luxury and inspired madness, but with his left hand he also gave the more enduring forms of culture their due.

Having grown up during the time of the most extensive construction in Budapest, when suddenly this obscure Central European city emerged as a metropolis, Arnold knew the old names of the streets, and the people who used to live in the single-story neoclassical commercial buildings that were torn down at the end of the last century to make room for six-story luxury apartments. He liked to talk about the auto races he saw at the beginning of the century, and about eight-oared boats, in one of which he had been coxswain. He was a conscientious citizen, secure in his status, equal before and protected by the law of the land. It was not race but achievement that counted. It was who had contributed what to the city.

Above her bed, Zsuzsa had a photograph of her husband: the young Arnold among country people at the time of the wine festivals. Wearing white pants, sitting with crossed legs, he is dreamily holding his glass. People appear to be talking to him, but it's not certain that he hears them. Sometimes Zsuzsa would pour out her complaints in sharp words. He would nod, nod, then sigh: "Instead of this hard-to-please queen of the night, I could have picked a meek housewife and talked, at her side, whatever nonsense I chose." Bareheaded, wearing a black coat, he drank champagne on his wife's roof terrace covered with soft snow. "The whole city is frivolous and rotten," said Zsuzsa, "and you are one of the high priests of frivolity." And she rested her head against her husband's chest.

The café was Arnold's natural ambience. He lent his name and style to the place. But when he felt depressed, he would take to the hills. Wearing hiking boots, a leather jacket, and carrying a knapsack, he would go off by himself, unable to bear the company of anyone. And when the scene around him became too familiar, and he could tell what was in the head of every author sitting in his café, he would put on his brown jacket, his checkered light coat, and his thick-soled shoes, and step out of the revolving door of his hotel, his destination Málaga, where in paved courtyards beside beautiful fountains he would enjoy himself with Spanish women of questionable character. He loved many a woman precisely because her character was questionable. "A woman without deceit and designs is like a lily of the valley without its fragrance." He would come back slightly thinner but looking better, and in a more accommodating mood.

Arnold's Legacy

Arnold spent his last days sitting in his armchair and talking like one whose train was about to leave. He had escaped the brick factory, in whose enormous drying hall he and hundreds of other men were made to stand in mud. He had come home to his wife, was now holding her hand, and David, Zoltán, and Klára were standing around him, listening to his words. The high priest of frivolity, during his last days, grew somber. That was the time of rumors about the gassing of those who had been deported, the time when the word *Auschwitz* began to appear in conversation.

David looked around the room, in which only one memorial candle was burning. Was there a deeper meaning to the evil that had befallen them? Later in his life, many times, he would feel that there was, out of either weakness or fear, but then, at that time, he found no deeper meaning. Those who had murdered half the people in the apartment had had no reason except stupidity. They went about shouting and shooting, showing off. David tried to imagine the Russian soldiers. They would come, running from house to house, always covering themselves. He would go downstairs to meet them. One of the soldiers would pick the yellow star off his chest. Why should he wait? Why not remove the star now? The moment he asked himself this question, he made up his mind. With a fingernail clipper he cut the stars from both his jacket and his coat. First he thought of burning them, then decided to put them into the Bible his grandfather gave him. "I'm not wearing it anymore," he said to Arnold. "You know what you're doing," Arnold replied.

"You ask me why I don't fight them?" Arnold said. "Should I make them shoot me sooner just so I have the chance to shoot someone, too?" He looked out the window as if enlisting the support of the cloudy sky. "The people around us have become accustomed to the idea that we should not be alive. One can return the fire, yes. But I would find it difficult to shoot a man who could be mad or simply an imbecile. You can say, of course, that it makes no difference. I don't believe in the existence of monsters; there are only imbeciles, and private imbeciles can easily become public imbeciles. They ape every stupidity they hear. They are malleable, like wax. Their heads are full of advertising slogans, propaganda, lies. They are drugged with pills of hate; they are addicted and feel lost if there is nothing to hate. Or to worship. And both are deceptive emotions. A person who worships something does not know what love is, and a person who hates has no conception of anger. The difference between hate and anger is that hate does not see the human being in the enemy, whereas anger does. But some of my contemporaries have swallowed so many hate pills they'll be able to calm down only when dirt fills their skulls.

"And this Hitler, with his folk community! The Germans are incapable of loving themselves, so they try hysterically to love themselves by hating others. And here, right on our main square, we have the statue of a janitor with a machine gun. This figure will stay with you, children. The little people, the men of the street, don't consider their acts to be crimes. It is these little people that the big scoundrels appeal to. The little ones are now allowed to shoot any Jew on the street. Just as they were allowed to shoot sparrows with their slingshots when they were children. And you throw in the possibility of a little looting, and if you can see this whole package as a kind of victory or hunting trophy, or make the killing and robbing a patriotic deed for them, then in some private calendars these days will be red-letter days, and will be always remembered as such. So the little remaining time should be taken advantage of. You can still kill that Jew on the street corner with impunity. If his coat is better than yours, well, take it. Jew coats are good coats. First he hands it over, then you shoot him. Come spring, these arm-banded little people will be the same nobodies they were originally.

"But don't you give up, my boy. Don't live the way I did. Don't own a hotel, don't own anything except paper and pen. Write about my hotel someday, about the hotel of experiences. Don't be a scientist about it; just write the kinds of things you have written in this checkered notebook. Let your mind dance, and make use of every trick found in the freedom of madmen. It won't be easy for Hungary. To all indications our small nation is not strong enough to be independent. It has belonged to the Germans until now; the Russians will have it soon. The Allies are too far away. The Russians, not the English, got here first. As for me, politically I'm more an Anglophile. The Russians I prefer only when it comes to literature. But what can you do, they got here first. Even in World War I the tsarist generals wanted to come here. And now, with a slight delay, the Red Army has finally made it. Don't think they've come such a long way just to turn around and leave.

"For the Germans I was a Jew, for the Russians I'll be a bourgeois. There was plenty of laughter in the house where I welcomed my guests, who came to eat, sleep, and make merry. But my entertainments were too pungent to be tolerated. For both Germans and Russians I am too cynical. And you, too, will be called a corrupter of decent people. You are already wicked. This whole section in your checkered notebook is very wicked and very funny. But this page here is stupid, because it is pure. Avoid being stupid and boring; the rest doesn't matter. Don't worry about money and success; you'll have enough of both. Never worry about anything that can be taken away from you. You see, my whole capitalist life is already unreal, a fairy tale."

"I should be a revolutionary," David said to his uncle. "My father was a good citizen, and where is he now? Why do we all have to be so helpless?" "If you become a revolutionary, you'll be able to shoot people," Arnold replied, "first one, then another, and maybe a third. And, because you are a revolutionary, you'll have to applaud those shootings. Revolutionaries of all stripes feel entitled to execute their enemies. Nationalist and Communist revolutionaries have learned from each other; for example, that it is permissible to shoot civilians. Where civilians have to fear organized, armed people, there is no civilization. It doesn't matter what the man with the weapon says; the main thing is that he should not be able to shoot at will. Around here, soldiers have always had too much liberty. Among Jewish capitalists you may find corruption, but never terror. It is not healthy for a Jew to be in a country where at the head of a united people stands a leader who cannot lawfully be removed.

"I've always thought of politics as a circus," Arnold went on to say. "In the ring the clowns kick one another in the rear, brawl and quarrel, and throw things at one another while we munch on pretzels and drink raspberry juice. Then we go home and don't think about the circus for a long time. But the situation changes when the circus gates are locked, the cages are opened, and the lion is set free to run into the audience. Then the tamer with his whip is truly the grand master. Someone from the audience protests: 'Let us out of here!' The lion tamer cracks his whip, and the lion mauls the protester to death. When I find myself in such close quarters with politics, the laughter freezes on my lips.

"Life will be good here only when you don't have to think about politics because it cannot harm you, physically or otherwise. If the premier doesn't interfere with me, I won't interfere with him. If he doesn't like my jokes, let him make some of his own. In my nightclub I offered the kind of shows my audience and I liked. Then one day I was summoned to the information center of the premier's office. The devil got into me, and I said: 'Gentlemen, I confess I read about your jockeying for political position the way I read the race results in the newspaper. And I wouldn't mind betting on politicians, too, if there were a great horse like My Treasure among your excellencies.

Why don't you treat my shows the same way, like horse racing? If you think that my jugglers, dancers, and comedians are winners, please come, pay your admission, have a bite, have something to drink. If you like what you see, come again. And if you don't, well, no harm done. The worst that can happen is that we won't see each other again.' A young man who seemed pleasant enough throughout the interview asked me if my words contained a veiled insult to His Excellency the Premier. 'What I said was only a parable, not intended as an insult to the dignity of His Excellency,' I replied, looking into the air.

"Just before World War I, my dears, things began to look up; life had great variety to it. But the generals didn't want that life. They put us in uniforms and said: 'This isn't a whorehouse, Mr. Volunteer; this is a trench.' And I was supposed to fire at Russians, Romanians, and Serbians, all of them our neighbors. What an idiot that Franz Joseph was! Why would anyone in his right mind go around shooting his neighbors? And what was this Mr. Volunteer business? Volunteer, my foot. If Mr. Volunteer doesn't march into the machine-gun fire and be a hero, we blindfold him and stand him before a firing squad. The world is all right when around the café table you can say the most impudent things; when the neighboring tables can exchange witty broadsides, but sweet peace reigns; and when the great ballerina sweeps by the guests and only the woman at the cash register turns green with envy.

"I tried to enliven our capital city with a little humor. Without the poems written at my marble tables, Hungarian poetry would have been poorer. I gave to the blind and orphans in general, and to the Jewish blind and orphans in particular. That's what a bourgeois citizen is for: to give what he can, and to the causes he likes. I even gave to poets and painters when they had the talent but not two coins to rub together. Yes, some hated me—those who had neither money nor talent. By giving them nothing, I insulted them. Unfortunately, the bad poets were in the majority, and they took their revenge. They became journalists, and at their papers' expense came to see my shows, and then in their reviews denounced me publicly. They loved my girls and the way they danced almost completely naked, lit from below on the revolving glass stage, but in the papers I was accused of pornography. The reviewers roared at my jokes, then declared them offensive to the regent of the country."

Arnold Kobra got out of his chair and went to the window. He pointed. "That's where my hotel was. Now it is a house of torture. What can you do when such idiots are turned loose? Our words are given a background of machine-gun fire from below. There is no connection whatever between our behavior and our being shot and pushed into the Danube. They shoot those who resist, and those who don't." "Mostly those who don't," David put in. This was already the viewpoint of his generation. It is refreshing for a child to realize that obedience offers no more security than defiance. That in fact, in such times as these, obedience is a moral error. The young nephew learned this maxim so thoroughly then that he carries it with him to this day.

"You can learn something from all this, and the next chapter will be yours. I wonder what you will do with your dual status as Jew and citizen. Will you try to scratch the Jewishness off like a scab? Will you try to be one or the other, or neither? The God of our fathers has now shown us his other face. He gives us life, but he gives us death, too. At times he does this in the right proportion, bringing death to old people. But when he brings it indiscriminately, wholesale, to children, well, I can't go along with that. While remaining a God-fearing man, I still say that God wasn't paying attention.

"The battle of taking apart and putting together again," Arnold said, "that is the Jewish drama. Abraham the shepherd, with the sun above and his flock around him, is alone when the Lord addresses him. All the greatness and misery of the Jewish way of thinking originate in prophetic thinking. It is at once metaphysics and business as usual, gospel and lampoon. We tell our jokes with straight faces. But every man possesses the possibility of a new start—that is the essence of Jewish spiritual democracy. With the birth of each baby, human history begins anew. Nobody can speak in my name; I have no representative before the Lord; I must pray to him myself.

"A Jew who refuses to believe that his parents have left him a legacy, which may be a time bomb or a death sentence made out in his name, is a fool. But others think this fool of a Jew is cunning,

183

fiendishly clever. The meek majority occasionally feels like burning the houses of this fiendish minority. Maybe you are not more intelligent than other people, but because you are a half-outsider, because you do not completely swallow the local prejudices, you may know something that the insiders don't. But in World War I a lot of Jewish boys were not that bright as soldiers. When medals were being handed out, they reported for duty, raised their hands, and, screaming, charged with fixed bayonets other stupid boys in uniform.

"Jews have been more predisposed to international, portable knowledge—to the universal languages of finance and science, art and revolution—than to thought tied to the soil. This has been their greatest aptitude: international information-gathering, the building of networks. Jews conspiring, rebelling, preparing to overthrow tyranny. How many groups have there been since the Maccabees? And the prophets of dark utopias? And what about the men of letters ready to blow the established order to smithereens? They know no limits; they must be put behind barbed wire."

We Have Survived

We had an unexpected visitor in the protected house: Nene. She brought a small oval-shaped medallion on a chain. It was the figure of Mary. Nene asked us to wear it. We should convert to Catholicism, she said. If we did that, or at least declared our intention to do that, she would take us to a convent where converted Jewish children were being hidden. We thanked Nene for her offer but declined. To remember her friendship, however, we did accept the medallion of Mary, even though we wouldn't wear it.

We decided, conferring, that if we were taken away with a group of other people from the building, which would mean they would shoot us on the banks of the Danube, then at the edge of the park nearby we would throw down our backpacks and run, each in a different direction. Even if they fired at us, some of us would get away. The guards would not leave the column of hundreds of Jews to pursue a few children. The following day we almost had the chance to put our plan into action. At dawn five Arrow-Cross men and a policeman broke into our room, yelling at us to get dressed, turn over all our weapons, including kitchen and pocketknives, and everything of value, then line up on the sidewalk in front of the building. There was a rabbi with them. He urged us to obey, said that that was the wisest thing to do, that we should surrender all our valuables, our necklaces, heirlooms, even wedding rings. Pulling on my socks slowly, I could see Rebenyák's red cap downstairs, already out front. Rebenyák was the bad boy of the building; he had wanted to join our group, but we wouldn't accept him. We looked at one another, wondering whether the time had come to carry out our plan, and whether to let Rebenyák in on it. Just then, two men arrived. One was wearing the uniform of a police officer, the other that of a German officer. They, too, yelled, but not at us—at the Arrow-Cross men and the policeman escorting us. They ordered everyone back inside. Perhaps they were Communists in disguise, or two Jewish actors. In any case, they played their role far better than the "rabbi" had played his. There we were again, upstairs in our room, sitting in our coats, confused by the turn of events.

The lobby was our clubhouse. There was a great deal of sliding down the banisters of the lower marble stairs. Rebenyák showed up, too, in his red cap. He may have been as old as fourteen, and was constantly pestering David about his stamps. David had brought his stamp album with him from Újfalu, and now and then exchanged his smaller but more valuable stamps for Rebenyák's larger, prettier ones. It was hard to understand Rebenyák sometimes, because his language was full of strange expressions. Instead of pissing, he'd say wetting down the weeds. He punctuated his monologues with the foulest words. "He's just showing off," Klára said, and also said that her shoelaces had more brains than you would be able to find under Rebenyák's red cap. Sometimes Rebenyák would tilt his head wearily to one side and say that he was so exhausted, he couldn't look at another piece of ass, in other words, women, who were all hot for him down in the cellar. Klára looked at David's transactions and checked the value of the stamps in a catalog. "He's cheating you. Don't you care?" David didn't care. In the end he gave the whole album to Rebenyák for a piece of bacon, which, when fried with onions and served on top of strained peas, gave the whole apartment cause for celebration. Rebenyák took the bacon out from underneath his mother's bed in the cellar, and returned there with his new acquisition, moving like a weasel. He slept in the same bed as his mother, a malodorous, plump woman with whiskers on her chin.

Decades later, David met Rebenyák, who now had a limp and made his home in a basement. He had left three apartments to three wives, each of whom had brought home a lover more muscular than he and told him that from now on he would have to sleep elsewhere. In his basement apartment Rebenyák collected girls who had fled from the home for the retarded. He bought and sold them, hired them out to wealthy tourists, and trained them to steal their passports. He reveled in the possibilities: Should he be Swedish, Brazilian, Australian? He also collected photographs. His walls were covered with naked women, corpses. At the time of David's visit, he was working as a coroner's assistant, and would get drunk on ether. He gave David a present: a blackened forefinger tied with a pink ribbon.

His musty closet was full of letters. He perforated, tied together, filed, and every day read these letters like volumes of poetry. He insisted on reading aloud some of his personal ads: his published work. He was looking for a woman to sail with blissfully on the Aegean Sea. For a physical-education and voice teacher to go skiing with him in the Alps. He signed himself "Jaguar." Some of his ads drew as many as three hundred replies. For example: "I claw the walls in my loneliness. My sweet, eternal mate, free me from this dusty hole, where only vodka and madness await me." Or, from the manager of a hairdressing and cosmetics salon in a small frontier town: "I'll cook for you, delicacies like stuffed goose neck and chestnut crescents made of rich, larded dough." One woman apologized that she could not offer her virginity to Rebenyák, because once, in the company of an actor from the capital, she had lowered her guard. She promised that until their long-awaited meeting there would be no more lowering of her guard. But none of the women had a chance to lose their virginity to Rebenyák, because the busy author of personal ads confined his activity to writing letters. On his typewriter he wrote several each day, with carbon copies, now telling about his St. Bernard, now saying he had traveled to Hong Kong. "My theory, in these letters, is that not one word should be true," he said. To the hot-blooded women he wrote of the sublime joy of self-denial; to the pious ones, of the torments of lust.

In the protected building, despite his mother's warning—she told him that the higher floors were more vulnerable to bombs—Rebenyák ventured upstairs to visit Klára's family. He was attracted to the sophisticated atmosphere of that apartment. Longingly he would examine the Rosenthal china, the fine soup bowls out of which we ate beans at the long black table. Holding them up to the light, he was amazed to see that they were translucent. He stole one of them. "Why are you hoarding everything? You could be shot tomorrow," David said. Rebenyák, superstitious, snarled. "You're the one they're going to shoot tomorrow, you dickless Újfalu shithead!" Klára grabbed Rebenyák and twisted his arm. "You take that back!" she said, because she, too, was superstitious. "Suck my dick, cunt!" Rebenyák cursed as he writhed in pain, but he finally took it back. A shell hit nearby, and the boiled beans in the Rosenthal bowl became inedible, since they were now mixed with slivers of glass. The iron stove, whose pipe went out the window, doubled over like a man kicked in the stomach. Machine-gun bullets spattered the wall outside.

Klára was returning to her early childhood: She would sit under the table and arrange a fancy wedding between a clay sheep and a wooden mouse. David produced a gold necklace with a Star of David and cautiously offered it to her. She put it around her neck. "Why are you wearing that?" Rebenyák asked. "I got it from him." Klára pointed to her cousin, looking at David proudly, as one might look at a prizewinning hog. "Are you in love with that idiot? He doesn't even know what an allegory is." "What's an allegory?" David asked, suspicious. Rebenyák kept picking up and putting down the pot with the bullet hole in it. "Listen, forget that idiot and be in love with me instead," he told Klára. "All right," said Klára, "if you give me your whole stamp and pen collections and bring me your cap full of lump sugar." Rebenyák turned red, but did not reach for his cap, whose cornflower-blue tassel dangled before David's eyes from morning till night.

One other thing happened that evening. A young man named Mario, who lived in the next room, came back from the Danube. The bullet that was meant for him had hit him only in the arm, and he was able to swim ashore. His only difficulty was freeing himself from his father. Father and son were tied together. The father was shot in the chest. After they both fell into the water, the father held the son for a while, then slowly released his grip. The son, hanging on to an ice floe, drifted downstream under the bridges. Near the Elizabeth Bridge, where the bank has steps, he managed to get out of the water and, just as he was, soaked and bleeding, made his way home. He was stopped once. In a dull voice he said: "Shoot me again if you want to, and throw me back in the Danube." "The Jew is like a cat, always lands on his feet," said an older Arrow-Cross man. It was this feline ability that made the Jew so dangerous. Turn your back for a second, and the Jew climbs out of the river and becomes impertinent. The next thing you know, he'll be in the driver's seat again. "Weren't you our guest before?" Yes, he was, along with his father. The father had been interrogated about his younger brother, whom the Hungarian Nazis suspected of smuggling weapons. The father knew nothing. He was given a choice: Either tell them where his brother was hiding, or they'd kill his son, Mario. The father gave them a false address. The Arrow-Cross men came back furious; they had shot the wrong person, not the younger brother. With the heels of their boots they kicked Mario's testicles to a pulp.

Ten years later, Mario became Laura's lover, and since Laura and David were lovers for a short while at the university, he also became David's rival. In those days Laura wore round glasses. In class she would hiss at David as he pawed her thighs. "Don't touch me; you're driving me wild; let go of me!" But she would also say, "Leave Klára; move in with me." David had long hair then, and wore a tattered leather jacket; people said he looked like a youthful Lenin. In class, he divided his time between *Being and Nothingness* and

Laura's thighs. They made love in a confessional, in the mountains, in an open snowy arbor of a garden. He liked to go with her when she had her hair done. He sold some of his books so they could drink champagne.

Mario, with his crushed testicles, was capable of erection and intercourse but not of procreation, and thus proved to be a safe partner during the time of strict abortion laws. He had a job with the security police. Sometimes he would follow David and Laura in his official car. Once, on Költö Street, he suddenly appeared behind them. The couple was sitting quietly on a bench; the whole city was bathed in turquoise light. Mario kept his hand in his coat pocket. "You want me to shoot you?" he asked David. "You have no right to Laura. Go back to Klára. I need Laura more than you do. I can do more for her than you can. And tell your friend János that he'd better stop hanging around Laura, too. I've got a pile of written denunciations against you, turned in by your philosophy friends. You won't be smiling if those get into the wrong hands."

In the street, a barricade of cobblestones was growing higher. Along with other old Jewish men, Arnold was ordered outside to carry the stones. The younger men had long since been taken away. Rows of cobblestones, six deep: an impenetrable wall. The T-34s that had come all the way from Stalingrad would surely be stopped by these few stones. From the entrance to their building the children watched the old men as they labored with hammers and fire irons, bent over in the freezing cold, to separate the stones that were stuck together with pitch, and then carry them and add them to the puny obstruction in the middle of the street. Young men in hunting boots, black pants, and green shirts supervised the work, pressed the old men to move faster. One of the youngsters had a fancy whip, like that of a hansom driver. With it he would hit the old Jews in the neck. There was no denying that they could have worked faster. It must have been the young man with the whip who outraged an elderly gentleman from the building next door, where Christians lived. It does happen that the old side with the old, even across religious barriers. The elderly gentleman produced a shotgun, fired, and wounded the young man. The Arrow-Cross men thought it was a Jew who did this. What else

189

could they have thought? They began to shoot wildly in all directions. The twenty barricade builders scattered, ran for cover, and Arnold left, too, but walked, didn't run, so as not to draw attention to himself.

At the main entrance to the building only David still stood; the other children and the adult doorkeeper on duty, a very old Jew, had run upstairs at the first sound of gunfire. David opened the heavy boarded-up door, and Arnold jumped inside. David tried to shut and lock the door before the tall young man with the arm band, who had been following Arnold, could force open the door. Two pushed from the inside, an eleven-year-old and a sixty-year-old, but the young man won, sticking the tip of his boot in the crack of the door. He stood before them, his pistol drawn. He was taller than Arnold, and his lips were quivering from injured dignity. These Jews would slam the door in his face, just like that? A faint smile from Arnold, the smile of the loser. The young man put his pistol to Arnold's temple and pulled the trigger. Arnold fell, and the blood from his head flowed across the dirty, pink fake-marble stone of the lobby.

The man now took aim at the child. David did not understand. Would this, then, be death? More in wonder than in fear, he stared into the tall man's face. The man's anger subsided; he lowered his pistol. After all, it was only a child. Magnanimity got the better of him. He left. Which was a mistake. Two weeks later, Klára stabbed the man in the back with a kitchen knife. Silently she came up behind him, entering an apartment whose door he had shut but did not lock. The Arrow-Cross man fell to his knees, looking for the pistol in his jacket pocket. With the second stab she found the man's jugular vein. There were a woman's limbs inside the tile stove. Next to the body, a volume (Ita to Lor) of the *Encyclopaedia Britannica* with hundred-dollar bills between its pages. When David came through the open door to rescue Klára, she had already finished the job.

On the night of January 17, 1945, we watched one tank and then another roll over the barricade the old men had built. The German soldiers, who had been lying behind the barricade clutching their machine guns, fled to the park. That night we slept, not on the floor of the living room, but in the hallway, farther from the fighting, but we kept sneaking to the window to peek out. In the light of the

Katyushas we saw a few newsreel scenes, but this time close up and without the customary frame of the cinema screen. And once again we sang the "Internationale." Aunt Marta, a Communist, had taught us the song, and told us that we should be Communists, too, because that was the only party that had been outlawed; all the rest, simply by being legal, collaborated in some degree with the authorities. "Learn Russian, children; you'll need it." Later, in 1949, in the same ski boots she had worn through the winter of the city's siege, Aunt Marta tried to flee across the border. The border guards fired a few warning shots, one of which hit her. She died in the hospital. But on that night in 1945 we did not fall asleep until four in the morning. We drifted off with the idea that we would wake up liberated.

The End of Winter

The next day, January 18, at ten in the morning, I stepped out the front door of 49 Pozsonyi Road. Two Soviet soldiers were standing on the sidewalk. Wearing torn quilted parkas, they seemed more indifferent and exhausted than friendly. People spoke to them, but they did not understand, they only nodded. It was obvious that they were not interested in us. The two soldiers asked if Hitler was there, inside the house. Hitler was not living with us Jews on Pozsonyi Road, in a house protected by the Swiss. Then they asked about Szálasi, the leader of the Arrow-Cross Party. He did not live with us, either. Slowly we began to understand that by Hitler they meant Germans, and by Szálasi, all Arrow-Cross men. These Russians were simple souls. With their machine guns at the ready, they went down into the cellar. They made everybody stand up and, using their flashlights, looked into every corner. There were a few deserters in the cellar, all in civilian clothes; they were left alone.

There was one man there who spoke Slovak and seemed to understand a little of what the Russians were saying. Immediately he appointed himself interpreter, and when the Russians moved on to the cellar of the adjacent house by breaking down the fire wall between the two cellars, the Slovak-speaking Jew spoke as the newly elected leader of these people wrapped in blankets, who were about to be liberated. After a short hesitation he said good-bye to his family and ran after the Russians. On the ground floor, the soldiers broke into a perfumery and drank a large bottle of Chat-Noir eau de cologne. They went straight for this brand, as if familiar with it. It must have been the most drinkable cologne. In their wake, we poured into the store, all of us, Jews, Christians, civilians. Some enterprising people brought their knapsacks with them. I stole a harmonica, which I later exchanged for a bag of lump sugar.

So we were liberated. Liberated from the shooting and the bombing. We could come up from the cellars. There were still occasional shots. A burst of flame hit our street. I learned how flat I could make myself by pressing close to walls and sidewalks. In the morning we walked around our neighborhood. Some apartments were still on fire, flames shooting out the windows. On the street we came across dead men and dead horses. The survivors, hurrying along with bundles on their backs, left the dead men alone but carved meat from the horses, leaving skeletons. This was the first time that I left the house as a free person. Some buildings already had Cyrillic writing on them. The yellow star was taken off our entrance and thrown on a heap of snow in front.

Because the studio apartment had been hit by a bomb, and because there were about thirty people living in it besides us, and because Arnold had been killed in the lobby of this building, Zsuzsa and all of us children suddenly felt a great urge to break free of this Jewish house, this seven-story ghetto in which we had been herded together. Mrs. Arnold Kobra, with a team of five young children behind her, set out for Liberation Square to reclaim her husband's downtown apartment as well as all the personal belongings it contained.

We walked out of the protected apartment house. On the sidewalk the snow had hardened into ice. Each of us had a knapsack, and we also carried rolled-up quilts, and pulled the rest of our possessions on a sled. A fine, powdery snow was being blown by the wind. It was much below freezing, and we had no gloves; our fingers were reddish purple. In the gathering twilight we passed burning houses. Through blackened windows, dying flames painted the ceilings rusty red. A brass chandelier still held on. We stopped to look at a house split in half, a cross section stripped naked and exposed. The façade was gone. A bathtub balanced itself precariously, but the sink stood firmly in place. A heavy mahogany cupboard against an intact wall. A dining table fallen three stories. The indecent and malicious humor of destruction. And everywhere people, tired but showing more and more signs of life, were carrying their belongings here, there. They were going home, or looking for their loved ones, or just walking around for the joy of being able to walk around. And, who knows, someone might be baking bread somewhere. The bundles of our bedding kept spilling open; desperately we hugged the thick eiderdown.

I was anxious to win Zsuzsa's praise. Once she had called me "my little cavalier." That was a great honor. But there was a fly in this ointment: She had also called me, once, "my little hypocrite," for fawning over her. In my enchantment with her I had courted her beyond what was proper, and that was the way the sweet lady, slightly embarrassed, had warded me off. But what did it mean to be a hypocrite? I looked it up in a dictionary. Even today I feel a dark ache at the memory of reading the definition of that mysterious word. Did she really believe that my compliments were motivated by selfishness, by an ulterior motive? Didn't she realize that in her I saw perfection itself—no less, though differently, than I did in her daughter, Klára? The coolness that so characterizes the flirtatious sarcasm of this branch of females in our family was there again in Zsuzsa's gaze as she watched me wrestle the big bundle of bedding that was threatening to overwhelm us.

Miraculously, Liberation Square was intact. Every building was pockmarked, but the holes could all be patched up. The Crown Hotel was undamaged, and so was the elegant old apartment house behind it. From the amphoralike pitcher held by a stone-buttocked nymph at the top of the fountain in the courtyard, icicles hung. Arnold Kobra's brass nameplate had been removed from the front door of

Apartment One on the fourth floor. Zsuzsa's key did not fit the lock, and the bell did not work, so we had to knock. In the long dark hallway we saw a light flicker, as if from a candle. As the barred window of the front door slowly opened, a gray-haired woman stared at us, her gaze coldly inquisitive.

Zsuzsa said, "Good morning, madam. I am Dr. Zsuzsa Tárnok, Mrs. Arnold Kobra, the owner of this apartment and everything that's in it." From behind the door, the gray-haired woman replied, "I am Dr. Kázmér Dravida's wife, the lawfully authorized tenant of this apartment. Your apartment, if indeed it is yours, madam, was allocated to us, Transylvanian refugees, by the authorities." Now Zsuzsa: "Madam, several aspects of your lawful authorization are questionable." Mrs. Dravida's turn: "I hope, madam, that you don't intend to question our honor or our patriotism." Zsuzsa: "On both grounds, madam, you will let us in." Mrs. Dravida: "Madam, the general situation—one that we did not desire but followed with civility—has taken such a turn that I am obliged to let you people in, although I see you have removed from your coat the mark of discrimination, in the hope, I suppose, that that discrimination is over. Well, madam, I will not discriminate either, and will turn over two of my five rooms for your use." Zsuzsa: "Madam, I would have preferred to have found my apartment empty, but where would you go in the dead of winter? What can I say but make yourself at home in my rooms, among the furniture that belongs to my husband, who was killed three days ago. Let decency dictate the length of your stay."

With astonishment we watched these two old people, Dr. Kázmér Dravida and his wife, rush about with the speed of a whirlwind to remove their food from the pantry and stash it somewhere in their bedroom, in fear of the invading troops, of us, who might loot their precious stock. There were several sacks of potatoes, beans, and flour; some sausages; sugar in large paper bags; lard in a red enamel pot; and cracklings in large pickle jars. Only when everything was safely tucked away did they ask us, still panting with exertion, whether we had brought with us anything to eat. No, we had nothing to bring worth mentioning. Charity then got the better of the Dravida couple, and for supper they gave us some potatoes, a bit of flour, and a few slices of bacon. We made the gift last two days. On the third day they gave us nothing, but told us that in the basement of Zrinyi Secondary School, only a few buildings away, there was a German food depository. Although the stock had been nearly depleted by the people in the neighborhood, there was still something left. With our knapsacks, we, the boys, set out to explore. A machine gun sputtered somewhere; the sound came from the direction of the Danube. It would be awful if the Germans returned. The Dravidas would have us taken away, and never again could we cross that once-brass-plated threshold. Somebody told us that the shooting came from the Buda side of the Danube. On the Pest shore, the Germans were either prisoners or dead.

From the school's lobby a beaten path led across the courtyard to the rear stairwell, which went down to the basement. Under the snow lay German corpses, with narrow paths winding around them, paths made by many feet. I had thought that the dead made faces, but these Germans all had calm, relaxed expressions, including the one who lay on top of a wooden crate next to the quickly disappearing lima beans. This soldier seemed to be in a very uncomfortable position, his head hanging in the air. Perhaps it had been supported by another crate, which was later removed. We filled our knapsacks with beans, peas, wheat, and dried onions, but the crate under the German intrigued us. He was a tall, handsome young man with prominent brows and large deep-set eyes. There was a light stubble on his drawn face; he seemed to be looking at us reproachfully. "Forgive us," we said to him as we tried to roll him off the crate. "I won't forgive you," the soldier said. Then he went on: "I have no idea why I had to die on this crate. Apparently I was shot and dragged myself here. I don't even know how I wound up in this basement in the first place. You'll find good-quality sausages in this crate. They may have turned white, and some will call them moldy, but if you scrape off the white, they're perfectly fine. You'll take this crate from under me, and slink away with your booty, while I have to remain here in the dark, in this cellar of death, until some volunteer undertakers remove me and put me in an even darker place. No, I will not forgive you."

To this statement from the dead soldier we replied in the following manner: "Unknown German soldier, if it were a matter only of disturbing your mortal remains, however uncomfortably they are positioned, we'd grant you the right to be offended. But it should be pointed out that although you may be here in this cellar, so far from your home, not of your own free will but at the command of others, you are certainly not here at our invitation. It is likely, too, that before stopping that fatal bullet you were engaged in activities highly unpleasant to us. You may have been ordered to kill us, but personally, orders or not, you had no great objection to doing so. Also, you have lost your youth and innocence, but we are still innocent— if understandably cynical—boys. As we pick up this crate on our way out and shine our flashlight into your face, we are keenly disappointed by the lightness of the box. And when we scrape the white off the ten sausages, what is left will not last long when cut up and mixed with the beans cooking on the utility stove." We did not deceive the soldier; two short weeks later, we had nothing but a little wheat, which we ground and then cooked for hours to soften. While we stood around waiting for it to be ready, we ate dried onions dipped in mustard, to fool our hunger.

Wearing a fur cap and wrapped in a blanket up to his waist, Mr. Dravida sat in Arnold's chair, pumping a tennis ball in each hand. "Physical exertion, very soothing, very beneficial to thinking." He wore a fur-trimmed overcoat, and leggings over his hiking boots. His thin, sharply drawn lips, topped by an equally thin mustache, were bent in a bitter curve of sarcasm. From Arnold's high-backed chair Mr. Dravida cast occasional glances at us. "You don't have to peek and spy on us just because you have won, you don't have to peek and spy." His old dog sat beside him, wagging its tail left and right. Sometimes Mr. Dravida would touch the dog's head with one of his tennis balls. "There are too many of you, and you are too noisy, and you eat my dog's potato. Don't stand in the doorway. In or out. What's your problem? You ate garlicked sausage, I can tell. You do all right for yourselves; you always do all right for yourselves."

It was true that we ate the dog's potato and stole garlic from the Dravidas' kitchen cabinet. We were hungry. Munching on a clove, we could pretend that we were really eating something. Machine-gun fire in the street. We looked at one another, then at Mr. Dravida, who seemed slightly encouraged. "The game is not over yet," he said. "When the wheel turns and our troops come back, you will need my protection. Maybe I will protect you. It depends. If you behave, nice and quiet, and don't eat Bella's food, I will put in a good word for you, even though you are nothing but a bother to me. The bathroom door is always locked. You must be eating too much if you have to sit on the toilet all the time, you little locusts."

The four of us lay side by side on the double sofa. In the dark, I fantasized. I saw myself in our town, at home with my parents, as if nothing had changed. I was ashamed to talk about it, but wondered what the others were seeing. It was cold in the large apartment, because the fire always went out early; we slept with our socks on. Once, Russian soldiers came to check our papers, and they looked at Zsuzsa and my sister the way a cat looks at cream. My sister, who was in bed, quickly pulled her clothes under the cover and got dressed. Zsuzsa went into the bathroom. One of the soldiers followed her, but returned a moment later, walking on tiptoe, as if to show that he was a man of delicacy. Then they shone their flashlights on us, and saw the faces of four children watching eagerly what was going on. They praised Zsuzsa for taking care of so many children. "Good mama, pretty mama, lots of children, very good!" They snarled at us to be quiet, even though we weren't making any noise. They put a can of meat and three eggs on the table. "It's cold," they said, and lit the fire in the stove. They took out a bottle of brandy and ate whole red onions, lard, and bread. We each got a piece of bread, too. They were hosting themselves. Then they left, after shaking everybody's hand. I put my hand on the round magazine of a machine gun. "And what would you want with that?" The soldier stuck his fur cap on my head, then put it back on his own. They took nothing, and left a warm smell of onions and boots behind them.

Homecoming

I was standing in line at the bakery, if only for the smell that came from it. More determined people had lined up at dawn, even though the sale of bread would not start until ten o'clock. I seldom managed to get there early enough; usually I was among those turned away empty-handed. At least we no longer had to cling to the walls for fear of bullets. The fighting had ceased in Buda, too. Hawkers were shouting the name of a newspaper: *Freedom!* I read every word of it. There were rumors about SS soldiers still hiding in the bowels of Buda's Castle Mountain, inside secret tunnels. The parks were full of makeshift graves; people came and went, asking one another about missing relatives.

I went with Zsuzsa to the ghetto hospital on Wesselényi Street, where we found her mother, who was still alive. A bullet had entered the right side of her skull and come out under her left ear. A slight, middle-aged woman, she was able to smile at the sight of her daughter. We could bring her only a few lumps of sugar, but neither of us dared to put one in her mouth. This ghetto hospital had been a school. Now, forty-two years later, it is a school once more. But in January 1945, I looked out on the schoolyard and saw a mound of corpses that almost reached the second floor. Zsuzsa sat beside her mother, and they held hands. Neither asked what had happened to the other during the past months. The next day I accompanied Zsuzsa again; by then her mother was on her way to the mound in the courtyard. Zsuzsa sent me home while she tried to make arrangements for her mother to be taken out of the mass grave.

I didn't feel much like wandering around Budapest; the city seemed unfriendly. I longed for familiar sights, for our house in Újfalu. It was not fun coming back from the bakery without bread, or stirring and stirring the wheat in the pot with the fire almost out.

The bright sunshine you saw from your bedroom window was not cheering while you blew clouds on your hands and waited for nothing in particular. There was nothing left to steal. The sight of well-dressed gentlemen in their galoshes, who three weeks earlier at this same corner were straddling dead horses in the snow, receded into a comic memory. (The frozen flesh did not get blood on them. Wearing gloves and using pocketknives, they had hacked bits of meat off the horses' ribs.) I began to feel that my sister and I were only a burden, two extra mouths to feed, no longer in need of protection, and that the smartest thing we could do was go home. Besides, there was sure to be food in the countryside. So Éva and I decided to leave and wait for our parents in Újfalu.

To take the train we needed tickets. Rumor had it, in the line at the bakery, and the Dravidas confirmed it, that tickets could be bought only at the Rákoskeresztur station, which was a walk of several hours, along Baross Street, from downtown Budapest. Russian and Romanian soldiers were everywhere. I was a little nervous. My sister could not come with me, the city being considered too dangerous for young girls. Having no gloves, I tried—God knows why—to keep my hands warm with a hair net. But on this long walk, there were plenty of interesting things to see.

The soldiers on the street were now those of the second line; the front line had moved out of Budapest in the direction of Vienna. Some of them, standing in a truck, had collected all kinds of clothes. Some had pulled skirts over their pants to keep warm, and some wore women's turbans. They were like wild children, yelling at people from the truck, laughing hard. Now they were pissing over the side of the truck, enjoying the sight of women averting their eyes, and this spurred the soldiers on to wave their members all the more vigorously. One of them jumped off the truck to offer a square loaf of black bread to a woman. When she tried to avoid him, he insisted, shoving the bread into her pocket. The woman trembled. I couldn't help but admire these bullet-headed fellows, their joking, their parading of newly acquired rags, also their sudden bursts of temper. Everything about them was natural, if a little strange. They were watching some Romanian officers, who wore lipstick, white gloves, and brandished their cameras in all directions; the Russians roared with laughter, holding their hands to their mouths like country girls at the sight of a fancy city lady. Some of them, submachine guns slung over their shoulders, led civilian men to do a little work in the next street, the next city, country, continent, beyond the Ural Mountains, *davay, davay*. They promised *bumazhkas*, identity cards, and grown men obediently marched out of the city, all the way to the Tisza River, continuing from there by train to work camps in remote frozen lands, where they would finally get what they would not have needed so much if they had stayed at home: a stamped identity card. From the work camps the percentage of fugitives among both Jews and Christians was very low. Many more could have escaped than did; many more could have stayed alive. Is it possible that this suicidal obedience was related to the traditional Eastern European sense of honor?

These newly arrived Russian soldiers could also be indifferent and cruel. They were not as well groomed or as disciplined as the Germans. The Germans did little raping, but the Russians were quick to unbutton their flies. On the other hand, they did not kill out of principle. No matter how morosely they would be eating out of their mess kits, they were ready to smile at you, free of charge. You could tell what they wanted: a warm room, a hot meal, and a woman. Give them that, and they would roll the moon out of the sky for you. *Davay*, little moon, *davay*.

The station at Rákosrendező was one heap of ruins. A long line of people wound its way toward a makeshift ticket booth. So all these people must have had the same information: This was where you came for tickets. The word was that the window, still closed, would soon be opened. Hours went by. It was getting dark when a railroad man showed up and told us that there would be no tickets, that in fact there was no need to buy tickets at all. If you could get on the train, you'd travel; if you couldn't, you wouldn't. The following day, at two in the afternoon, an eastbound train would be leaving Budapest West.

By noon the next day my sister and I were at the station, amazed at the crowd. We let the human current carry us back and forth alongside the train, which seemed very long. It was impossible for us to get on. People were sitting even on the roofs of the cars, and some had climbed up on the couplings. Inside the cars we could see people crammed into the luggage racks. There was no chance to get a foothold even on the first step; we weren't strong enough to deal with such a crowd. A hopeless situation.

But, lo and behold, wearing a fur-lined coat and a Russian-style fur cap, there stood before us none other than Frici Nagy, Újfalu's photographer, who had been taking pictures of me and my family since the day I came into this world. As a three-month-old with hardly any hair on my head, I lay naked, on my stomach, looking around with anger, my wrists ringed with rolls of fat. And then, maybe three years later, I was wearing a sailor blouse and sitting on my father's knees. On my mother's lap sat my sister, her head thrown back coquettishly. From that black oilcloth funnel, pleated like an accordion, into one end of which Frici Nagy had stuck his head—was it still attached to his neck?—we waited for the promised bird, hoping for a canary to take wing, but only heard a click. No bird appeared. Frici Nagy withdrew his head from the dewlap of his glass-eyed box, like one who expects applause after a great performance.

The same Frici Nagy was now on the platform, hugging us both, overjoyed that we were alive. "Wonderful! Let's travel together!" He was there with his wife and two children. We should join them. I was glad that Frici Nagy was so kind to us, but I also remembered that, only a year before, he was a member of the Arrow-Cross Party and an ardent supporter of the Germans. He was theatrical and wore his hair long; a man of excesses. His younger brother was eccentric, too, but in a different way: a Jehovah's Witness, with hair very short, a meticulous man given to proselytizing, a father of many children, honest in business, a tyrant in his own home. For Frici Nagy and his family, the escape from Újfalu to Budapest and being caught in the siege of the city was enough; they did not want to continue west. Like us, they longed to be back in their own home. My sister and I knew that our parents wouldn't be home, but perhaps the house would still be there, and in it we could start our new lives.

What I only vaguely sensed then was later confirmed: Frici Nagy figured that by helping us get home he would be rehabilitating his reputation. And so it was. A veil was cast over his Nazi past, and he continued to be the most popular photographer in town. We were now allies of Frici Nagy, and not without results. We managed to push my sister through the window of a compartment and straight into a luggage rack. Then it was my turn. Frici Nagy squeezed me into a freight car, where people were pressed so close together that an older man said to me, "Stand on one foot, boy. You're young, you can take it. No room for both feet. Keep switching them."

That was my first great journey. It lasted a week. Not away from home, but homeward; not a flight from, but a return to. A return to an unfaithful paradise. A house is always unfaithful; it either falls into ruins before you do, or, surviving you, is ready to shelter others. Who was living in that house now, I wondered, who had the keys? I did not dare hope that we would find everything as we had left it. Maybe the furniture would be rearranged, maybe our clothes would be missing, maybe the house would be empty.

And how was Éva taking it in the luggage rack? And how long would the strained peas last in the small aluminum pot, or the two small unsweetened cakes we had bought from a young man sitting amid broken glass in an empty store window? What if the journey lasted a long time? Would Frici Nagy provide food for us? Would he be able to, would he want to? Word had it that the Russians had taken our engine but would soon give us another. The train still stood in Budapest West. But I was more comfortable now, with both feet on the floor, because somebody got off. Through the small window I could see the moon shining between the glassless girders of the terminal. Jumping on and off the train, people passed along rumors: The train would leave at one in the morning; at five; at ten. I pushed my way off, urinated between the wheels, and the yellow urine froze immediately. People were still sitting back to back on top of the train, but not as many now; some had given up and gone away. If the journey is not that important, you get fed up sitting on the outside. I could now squat down next to a fat old woman. Although we hadn't got an inch closer to our destination, it was good to know that a long night on the train was behind us.

And then the train moved. It was a journey of stop and start. The tracks needed repair; military trains had priority; engines were changed. Now we could sit together on the benches inside the car. Frici Nagy gave us some bread and bacon, not enough to fill us but enough for us to know that there was something in our stomachs. And then, as the train stopped in the middle of nowhere, we heard machine-gun fire. Some said that soldiers were going from car to car looking for women. With lumps of coal—who knows where they got them?—and with the help of pocket mirrors, the women proceeded to blacken their faces to make themselves ugly. Even the old women rubbed coal into their faces. I positioned myself in front of my sister; I would not let her out of this corner. The women pulled their kerchiefs over their faces and huddled like hunchbacks. Then the soldiers arrived, five or six of them. One spat on his finger and rubbed a woman's cheek. The coal came off. Angry, he spat in the woman's face, and the soldiers got off the train.

An improvised bridge led across the Tisza. The old bridge had been hit by the Allies, and the Germans blew up what was left of it. The temporary structure, erected between the old pillars with the help of piles, could not support the train, but the passengers could walk across it to a waiting train on the other side. We were on the move again, but not for long. The new train stopped in the dead center of the Great Hungarian Plain, in a February snowstorm, in the middle of the night. On this train we could find room only on the snow-covered coal heap in the open car behind the engine. The powerful wind of the plain whipped us mercilessly. Our hands were numb, our eyelashes crusted with ice. We decided to get off the train, find a road, any road, and follow it to the first farm and ask for shelter. Dragging our bulky luggage, we were nearly knocked down by the wind. At last we saw a faint light flickering on the bluish-white horizon. I was numb and purple by the time my feet got me there. Gratefully I collapsed on the straw spread out on the earth floor. But it wasn't until a young servant girl lay down beside me and told me to cuddle up to her that a little warmth began to course through me. She took my frozen hands and put them on her belly. No longer shivering, I curled behind her, around her, as close as I could, my face burrowed into her neck, and we were one. That was the first time I felt that it was possible to love a person whose face I had never seen; that a stranger could be experienced as one's closest relative. I clung to this young woman as if she were my true love, chosen out of all the girls of my childhood long ago. In the morning, bowing, I thanked my hosts and my bedmate for the shelter and their kindness.

The following day, when our train was forced to stop again, I went to explore the area around the station. In a clump of grass not far from fresh horse droppings, I found in a tire track a flat black square object. On closer inspection I saw it was a loaf of Russian bread, frozen solid. If it was bread, then no matter how frozen it was, the lukewarm water that trickled from the bronze pipe of the artesian well would soak it and thaw it into edible softness. As I chewed my soaked geological find, a woman came by, scattering goat manure as if sowing it in the snow. Taking the dung from her breadbasket, she pitched it left and right. She saw me, looked at me, then held out her basket. "Have a little meat, too. You can listen to the bleating in your belly." She broke into clear, gay laughter. "Where am I?" "You are in Törökszentmiklós," she answered. "What should I do with this bread?" "Leave it here for the birds."

The Strange Month of March

We arrived at Újfalu's station on February 28, 1945. The scene had changed little during the year we were away; there seemed to have been no serious battles around the station. Dragging our bundles, we clambered off the end car. The last leg of our trip, starting at Püspökladány, had been in a proper passenger train. No one commented. Everything was just as it used to be. We could almost have expected Father to be waiting for us, and for the three of us, my mother, sister, and me, after the happy reunion, to tell him that, just imagine, we went ice skating on the lake in the city park, fed apples to the baboons in the smelly monkey house, and in an operetta saw the great comic Latyi Matyi, who could hardly get a word in edgewise because the children laughed so hard. And that we touched the rope the regent touches when he walks around the Castle, and that there was an air raid, too, which caught us in the Castle quarter, and we went down to a shelter dug in the rocks, a cave, where a professor, standing next to us, told us that deep inside the mountain there was a lake on which you could go rowing. But Father was not waiting for us on the platform. Nobody was, except a woman who hugged Frici Nagy, which did not make Mrs. Nagy happy.

Suddenly Sándor Kreisler was standing before us, my former teacher from elementary school, a short, mustached, spunky man. This was almost as incredible as if my own father had appeared. Kreisler had been a good teacher, kind, firm, and just. He tutored Zoltán and me in our living room, from three to four in the afternoon. Sometimes he would come down to the garden with us and kick the ball, but did not get involved in our game. He was careful about his reputation. His father, a good tinsmith and an excellent politician, was my father's friend and a daily visitor in our store. The two of them would stand by the stove, talking and joking.

In 1945 Mr. Kreisler returned from his forced-labor battalion to find that his parents, brothers, and sisters had been taken to Auschwitz. As far as he knew, all his pupils had perished as well. So he was all the more surprised and pleased to see us. He hugged and kissed me, something he had never done before. He listened to Frici Nagy's story, thanked him for helping us come home, and promised to bear witness to this good deed should the occasion arise. Eight months before, it was politically dangerous to escort us to Budapest. Escorting us now was praiseworthy.

Mr. Kreisler's career after the war was not spectacular, but he was progressing. First he worked as a teacher in Debrecen, married there, and was promoted to school inspector. He retired in that capacity, first to the life of a pensioner and then to heaven.

The second familiar face we came across was that of a broad-shouldered young man wearing a leather coat and high boots and carrying a revolver. He was the son of the aloof, white-bearded, tall watchmaker who always wore a yarmulke. To Mr. Kreisler he said, "Let's raise these kids to be good Communists, Sanyi," and slapped our teacher on the back. He slapped me on the back, too, but spared my sister. Decades later, I saw him again, on television. In a well-cut, slightly old-fashioned suit, his hair now gray, he was analyzing the news. But Mr. Kreisler was thinking about more practical matters, such as where we would live and what we would eat. Nodding good-bye to the man of the new era, he picked up our bundles. He had no news of our parents. When I told him that I wanted to go straight to our house, he said that we would do that later.

On the main street we turned in to a store where three people welcomed us: Imre Székely, Márton Glück, and András Svéd. The first two were my father's cousins. They had come back together from labor camps. Each had lost a wife and two children. Pooling their resources, they opened a small general store, which had everything in it from brown sugar to black kerchiefs. They brought the merchandise by hay wagon from Várad and Debrecen, and in exchange took flour, smoked salami, and wine to those towns. Now, as we entered the store, there was great rejoicing. Then all three moved away, each to a different corner, and wept. When they turned back to face us, they did their best to smile.

They took us to our house. Only the walls were standing. On the floor, knee-deep rubbish, trampled books and photographs, the bath-tub full of dried excrement, and in my parents' bedroom we found a naked store mannequin, its body riddled with bullets. Only a large white three-door wardrobe decorated with rococo cherubs was left untouched, including its mirrors. It must have been too heavy to carry away. In front of me on the floor was one of my compositions from elementary school, about a young pine tree that becomes the mast of a ship at sea and talks to the wind, an old friend from the days back on the mountain. Torn pages of a dirty photo album with many faces, ours among them. I turned around; the three men were standing behind me. "Well, let's go to my house," Uncle Imre said. His housekeeper cut huge slices of round bread, spread butter on them, salted them, and set them before us.

206

Out of Újfalu's prewar population of twelve thousand, one thousand were Jews. Of these, perhaps two hundred survived, mostly the younger men, who were inmates of a labor camp whose commander happened to be the former manager of a large estate in the area. He used to shop in their stores, used to have things repaired in their workshops. During the war, all he wanted to do was return to the days of peace, to his own house, and bring these men back with him, so he could account for them before God. On October 20 of the previous year, there was a fierce tank battle at the edge of town. The Soviet troops were passing through. The camp inmates were home in November. By the time we returned to town, they had learned what happened to their families; had heard and even read about the gas chambers. But they were still not sure that their wives had been gassed, too. Possibly the women were sent to work instead; after all, they were young and strong. But the men did not take into account the fact that the extermination-camp leaders wanted a smooth and quiet operation. The Germans knew well that the children would cry and make scenes if separated from their mothers. The naked children, allowed to stay with their mothers, would walk more obediently into the shower room. For this the Germans were willing to sacrifice a valuable labor force.

My sister and I were now the only two Jewish children in town. The hundred or so Jewish men who had lost their wives and children were nice to us, were glad we were alive, but I couldn't help feeling that our presence was a constant reminder to them of their misfortune. Uncle Imre used only two rooms of his house. He slept in the old bedroom. I was given the bed next to his, the one in which his wife used to sleep. The housekeeper and my sister slept in the other room. Uncle Imre did not sleep much at night. He was a tall, broad-shouldered man with large hands, who said little. In bed, he smoked a lot. His lighter, made of an old cartridge, kept flaring in the dark. Out of the corner of my eye I'd watch his face lit by his cigarette. Sometimes he smiled to himself; I imagined that he was thinking of his family then. Once he wept, the way men weep. Rising from deep in the chest with powerful pounding thrusts, the cry reaches the throat. He lay on his stomach, his face dug into the pillow, his shoulders heaving. He bit the pillow so I wouldn't hear him. I pretended to be asleep.

I was back in my old class at school, in the room I had been in when the school year came to such an abrupt end the previous April. The same teachers, the same pupils. Except that Zoltán was not sitting next to me; he had stayed in Budapest. There was no course now in national defense, from which I had been excluded. This time, I was a full-fledged, equal member of my class. Both teachers and pupils were uneasy dealing with me. They asked me where I would like to sit. Nobody was sitting next to little Bárczi. I asked to sit next to him. He was the one who less than a year ago had said that the Jews were going to get it. A frail, flippant boy, the class dunce, and poor. Our geography and physical-education teacher used to beat Bárczi regularly, slapping him on the face and pulling his hair in the opposite direction to make the slaps more effective.

I played with Bárczi, and we shared our sandwiches. "Where is your father?" my classmates asked. All I knew was that my parents had been deported. Some of my classmates' fathers fell in battle, some were taken prisoner; no one knew whether the prisoners were dead or alive. We heard that people there were starving, and many of the weak were dying. I was not the only orphan. Gradually we got used to one another again; we did not talk about our families. On the metal taps of our boots we skated together on frozen ponds, looted burned-out tanks, and collected cartridges. We found belts, helmets, and ammunition pouches with dumdum bullets. We drilled holes in a board, put the bullets into them, and hit the blasting caps with nail and hammer. The board was our gun, and we called this game Katyusha. There were plenty of bullets, and plenty of crows on the fields to fire at—there had been a good crop in 1944, so the crows had plenty to scratch for under the snow. It was a miracle that none of us was hurt.

But the year away from home, in Budapest, lay like a wall of silence between me and my Christian friends. They were still normal children; I was no longer the same. Something had been ruptured. Why Do I Love My Country? That was the title of our essay in March 1945. I was supposed to write that I loved my country. It wasn't so simple. My country had tried to kill me; it was like those cases of parents who murdered their children. And if it was not my country that tried to kill me, but only a few people in it, I still failed to understand how my country was different from the country of those who had planned and executed these horrible deeds. They, too, loved their country, their motherland, and talked about it all the time.

We had the same hot-tempered geography and physical-education teacher as before, a squat, fair-haired man who always seemed on the brink of explosion. The year before, he lectured us on the evils of Bolshevism. He was not doing that now, of course, but neither did he have anything to say against the Germans. They might come back, riding on the power of their secret weapons. This possibility our teacher had confidentially conveyed to one of his pet pupils. After the Russians took Vienna, but before the fall of Berlin, he applied for membership in the Hungarian Communist Party. The previous summer, the children were full of dreams about miracle weapons as they ran around the schoolyard, screeching and hooting, imitating German dive bombers. One of the boys was nicknamed Tiger, after the famous German tank. By the spring of 1945 the Germans were out of fashion. It was the cossacks in their red felt hats, trimmed with fur on the side and decorated with a golden cross on top, that caught the imagination of the children.

These cossacks would come into the house bringing bacon, eggs, and onions, and ask us to cook for them. They would eat everything they had brought, punctuating their feast with vodka: a head of red onion, a gulp of vodka, another head of red onion, another gulp of vodka. They would get drunk, break down and cry. Even so, my sister had to be smuggled out of the house through a side door. Duci Mozsár, a pretty, buxom girl, barely fifteen, was standing just outside the front gate of her house when a motorcycle with a sidecar came tearing up the street. The cossack in the sidecar reached out and grabbed her, plunked her down next to him, and the motorcycle vanished in the dust. They came back a year later; the motorcycle sped into town like a tornado, the cossack in the sidecar deposited Duci Mozsár and her baby, plus a suitcase, on the sidewalk, then disappeared in another cloud of dust. Another case: A whole rifle squad took turns on a peasant woman while two soldiers kept her husband at gunpoint on the porch. The cossacks were unpredictable. They would bring us something, but they would also take something away. One of them showed us a photo album he had found frozen in the mud. He took it with him, and has been looking at grandparents and grandchildren, not his, ever since.

The strongest man in town, the blacksmith, was elected president of the local branch of the county council. During the few weeks of the Hungarian Soviet Republic in 1919, he'd been president of the local directorate. Although grumpy and sour, in uncertain times he enjoyed everybody's confidence. Nor was he handsome; his face was covered with little scars, from stray sparks. He wore oily, loose linen pants and black laced boots; his hands were the size of plates, and his fingernails were always black. He went to the Soviet headquarters, in our former courthouse, to lodge a complaint with the colonel in charge, against one of the soldiers, who had been doing a little looting on his own. The soldier might take a goose from one backyard to the neighboring house and ask the woman there to cook it for him. While waiting for his meal, he might take an eiderdown and exchange it later for some whiskey. He loved to barter. He would take a hog from a rich peasant and give it to a poor one, meting out justice but not losing anything on the deal himself. While the blacksmith and I looked on—I had followed him to headquarters—the colonel made the culprit stand, his back to him, at the top of the stairs leading down to the coal cellar. The colonel, although he had a huge belly, got a running start and kicked the soldier with such force in the rear that the soldier went flying into the depths of the cellar. I did not personally witness the rest, only heard it told later. For a few days the soldier was given only water, and when he was good and hungry, the colonel asked him: "Are you sorry for what you did?" Oh, yes, was he ever! And that was the end of it; the soldier was allowed to eat.

The blacksmith got along well with the colonel but not with the higher authorities. Back in the fall of 1919 the police had beaten him nearly to death. Now, in 1945, he again proved obstinate; he resigned his presidency and returned to his workshop. That same year, this time as head of the local revolutionary council, it was the blacksmith who once again led the demonstration and carried the national flag. After the revolt was put down, and men of the old regime regained power, some drunken peasants, enjoying the chance to carry weapons, took the blacksmith away and beat him to a pulp. He died soon afterward.

My father and mother arrived in May, from a camp in Austria. They cleaned the house and reopened the store. It would never occur to my father not to pick up where he left off. First there were only four shelves in the store, then six, then twelve; gradually the store filled with merchandise. Father had his and other children in his house to feed.

I attended a Protestant boarding school in Debrecen. To me, Debrecen was a city, strange and without form. We made the journey on a hay wagon. Both my parents came with me. We took a trunk with my personal belongings, food, and, besides the money for tuition, we brought along what was called tuition-in-kind: lard, smoked meat, flour, beans, and eggs. The wagon ambled through wide Market Street and reached the main entrance of the boarding school. Venerable bronze busts. On the façade of the inner wing, the inscription in large letters read: ORANDO ET LABORANDO. The old wooden stairs leading to the library creaked. Cold stones in the hallways; iron beds in the vast dormitory on the third floor. After lights-out, the hazing of the new boy. Star-kicking: the lighting of slips of paper stuck between the toes. As the fire reaches the skin, the victim tries to get free of the heat by kicking hard. Strict rules of the house: silence between three and five in the afternoon, a study period to be spent around the common table. The bell goes off at six in the morning; running around the courtyard; in the sinks one can wash only to the waist; then hurrying to the dining hall in the basement, where for breakfast every day caraway-seed soup is served. We stand behind our chairs, murmuring prayers: "Sweet Jesus, be our guest, this is the food that you have blessed." I could have said the Jewish grace: "Blessed art Thou, O Lord, King of the Universe, who has brought forth bread from the earth." But I didn't. By then I wasn't praying to anybody, not to Jesus, and not to the King of the Universe. The ladle makes the rounds. First served is the chief-of-quarters, who must be obeyed unconditionally, and then the rest of us, according to age: upper grades, lower grades, then those under fourteen, the wretched first-year students. I am a first-year student. In our room, crude jokes about farting. My roommates: sons of well-to-do peasants, Protestant clergymen, cantors, and teachers.

My new best friend and I were strolling up and down the hall under the gaze of a statue of Petöfi, as he told me how he had to go through the Nyírség Forest to get home from the nearest train station, and how during last Christmas vacation he chased a whole pack of wolves, wielding a club. I wanted to believe him, but in those days I was skeptical. All in all, this regulated life was not for me. I moved out of the boarding school into town, lived with a family, was master of my own time. On bicycle, train, and farm wagons I went home to Újfalu as often as I could. But I was already becoming a city boy. The following year I went to study in Budapest, and the story of me and my hometown came to an end. If that story can ever come to an end.

The Garbage Speaks

A small Polish town, the journey's end for the Jewish children of Újfalu, had become the most important reference point of my thoughts. It was by chance that I did not end up there whereas, in the ordinary course of things, the other children did. I should have perished there, too, in Oświęcim, in Auschwitz, but our bad luck, my parents' untimely arrest, proved to be our good luck. Father and Mother were deported to Austria, thus avoiding the death camps, and were able to come home. My sister and I survived the war in Budapest. In the summer of 1945, then, the four of us resumed our lives in Újfalu, in our own house.

We were the only intact Jewish family in the village. My two orphaned older male cousins came to live with us, and my cousin Zsófi, too, a good-looking, strong girl. Mengele had ordered her to the right, to work, while her mother and little sister were ordered to the left, to death.

As a child I decided—and have kept to it ever since—that everything that denies Auschwitz is good, and everything that leads to it, or resembles it, or revives it in some other form to be used against other victims is bad.

My Jewish classmates, children, went up in flames there.

Of all possible crimes, the mass extermination of children must occupy a special place of infamy. And yet that crime of crimes was born of the most ordinary reality. The crematorium was not a demonic surrealist idea, but the last step of a gradual cultural process. The last step of the perversion of nationalism.

The gassing and burning of people came from ideas and books. The extermination took place first in people's heads. The planners and camp commanders, ordinary people, believed that what they were doing was correct and necessary. Such outrages will cease in human affairs only when people refuse to consider the possibility of the extermination of their fellow human beings. When they refuse to allow human life to be subjugated completely to the interest of the state. Because the collective mind of a nation-state will not exclude mass murder from its modus operandi. This is the Auschwitz syndrome. It is my duty to resist any logic, any line of thought that leads to mass murder.

The designer of the death camp, who after the war was hanged next to a gas chamber, had acted in the name of the state's logic. Logically he reduced to a bare minimum the lives of those to be gassed. Logically he arranged for their profitable exploitation. The notion of profit was comprehensive: Only the prisoner's smoke may leave this place; his skin, hair, bones, fat, and gold teeth will be made use of. In the designer's model state, there was no room for opposition or resistance, and no supervisor was held accountable for the lives of those he supervised. The Auschwitz syndrome: the enemy must be wiped off the face of the earth. And the enemy is anyone who has been declared an enemy.

At age eleven, I was an enemy. My spiritual and racial characteristics offended the protectors of the state's purity. I had to be
removed, much as one removes a piece of garbage.

For thirty-seven years I refrained from visiting Auschwitz, the
museum. The visit finally took place in February 1982, as an un-
planned side trip. We were taking some food to one of the suburbs
of Katowice, and also delivering a secret letter to a very reliable man.
The business of the letter was quite innocuous: our circle of friends
wanted to arrange a summer vacation at Lake Balaton for the children
of the Solidarity activists who were being kept in detention. The letter
was addressed to Michal, who said, "Let *them* be afraid, they have
reason to be afraid, the ones with the machine guns." But his wife,
Agnieszka, said that she was afraid. They could arouse suspicion just
by keeping the lights on too long. People had been taken away for
unguarded remarks.

The detainees are kept in well-designed, solid, one-story brick
buildings. When released, they do not talk—not to their neighbors,
not to their colleagues at work. In shops they say hello and good-
bye, and hurry home. If they talk about what happened during their
detention, they might be taken back there. When we went to look
for the village doctor we knew, we found his house locked. His
neighbor was very frightened: "They're gone, I don't know, the militia,
I don't know anything." Twice, on the road, we came across the sign
KONTROLPUNKT. Behind the signs, young soldiers warmed their hands
over a pot full of embers. My friend was asked to open the trunk of
his car. The soldiers were looking for weapons. He was also subjected
to a body search. In those days, Hungarians were the only foreigners
allowed in Poland. In such a national crisis, our foreign car with skis
on top must have seemed a strange sight.

An hour out of Katowice, the sign OŚWIĘCIM came into view. A
railroad station, factories, pipelines, housing developments, a death
camp.

I am standing inside the gas chamber. The gas produced by the
dissolving of small white pellets thrown in from above was to pour
out through a number of holes, then spread and kill. The prisoners
do not yet know that they are inside a gas chamber. They still believe

it is a shower room. Their fear is not much greater than the general fear in which they have been living. The pounding of their hearts is still bearable. But now the gas appears, eating up the air. Now they choke. The children, closer to the ground, suffocate first.

Everyone is gasping for air, mouths wide, inhaling the gas deeper. They want to get to the door, to the wall, which is gray, perfectly gray, like the undercoating of a cruel painter's canvas. But this is the wall you cannot go through. There is nowhere to turn. You are trampled on; falling to the floor, you try to avoid the slippery, sweating feet. Above, there is only the dimly lit ceiling. But then it seems as if out of that ceiling a terrible, divine countenance is staring down at the writhing innocents, a gas-spewing visage, gray as the wall. Now the gas is rising from below; everyone gropes upward. The shiny bald heads begin to droop. The hair of these heads was turned into cloth. I can see a roll of such cloth in the museum. Behind glass, a whole mountain of hair, blond and black, young and old. A few obstinate hairs stick out, not conforming to the weave.

Vera had long blond braids. She was a proper little girl, given easily to crying. It had taken her a long time to outgrow her childhood lisp. I can see expectation and a touch of sadness in her blue eyes because I left her to wrestle with her sister, corpulent, temperamental Zsófi. Zsófi was in Auschwitz and Birkenau, then liberated by the Americans in Bergen-Belsen. She returned home, became a chemist and the wife of a diplomat, has since retired, and is now a grandmother many times over. When she wears summer dresses, you can see the number tattooed on her arm.

Awkward little Vera. I always felt that the two of us had some unfinished business. I knew she loved me, and I loved her, too, but less. Holding hands, we would walk to the agricultural school, stand at the fence, and insult the turkey. We told him that peacocks were much more beautiful than turkeys. It filled his wattle with blood and, turning red, he screeched angrily.

At Vera's, we played hide-and-seek in the corncrib. With our white socks and sandals we climbed the heaps of corn and dug holes for ourselves so that the one who was It would not find us. Vera's father was a produce merchant, a touchy man who kept to himself.

215

Here, in the corncrib, Vera forgot my faithlessness, and we held hands in silence. It was this sort of game—hiding, crouching, huddling together—that suited Vera best. You couldn't play rough with her, twist her arm, or knock her down and pin her shoulders to the ground, because that would leave black-and-blue marks on her delicate skin, and because she cried so easily. When she smiled, a likable smile breaking through her apprehension and sadness, I would stand in front of her, pull her head toward me, and kiss the part in her hair.

She, too, went up in flames, and I am still here, more than forty years later, writing this.

But according to a French historian, Vera was not gassed, because there never were any gas chambers.

5.

In which Klára, too, gets to speak

T H E   M O V E M E N T S:

Klára: 1

Klára: 2

Klára: 3

Klára: 4

Klára: 1

Come, my darling, come to the Crown, to the presidential suite. I am waiting for you. I have been watching you for days. You seem so confused. You look out of your window, draw the curtains, and turn on the lights, then you open the curtains again. With my binoculars I watch you from behind the closed windows of my hotel room, where I let in only the chambermaid.

I haven't yet met anyone I know. I bribed the porter not to tell people I'm in the city. When I go out, I wear a blond wig and sunglasses, and speak only English. I didn't want you to find out that proceedings against you have been initiated. It is a political, moral, and romantic inquiry, and, yes, I am the chief prosecutor. You are to answer to me, because I am flesh of your flesh, your closest blood relative, cousin and ex-wife, an eternal guilty conscience as old as you are. I am your imperishable other self.

I am cleverer than you, but less fertile. I perceive more quickly the thoughts that in your head lumber like bears down the street of a provincial town. I am a nest-building woman who grasps the nature of space on the wing. I am cleverer than you, but know that true creation is the product of trudging, of grim, ponderous, manly determination, and not of the smoke rings I launch at the fireplace. Work makes one dull. You men consider women who engage seriously in scientific pursuits to be obtuse gnomes. But you are more obtuse than I. Lazier, I worked less, concentrated more on the essentials, which I found mostly in things having to do with the body. You, on the other hand, with the perseverance of the narrow-minded, do nothing but multiply words on paper. From my darkened room I watch you work by your lighted window. You are reassuring and steady, like this hotel that was once my father's, as you were once mine.

My father is long dead, but this establishment has preserved his spirit. It is not as flamboyant as it used to be, but the reliable service promises a rebirth. The coffee and the crescents, the possessed pianist, and the cut of the women's made-to-order coats, their matching shoes and handbags, the porter's free and easy linguistic virtuosity, the effortless use of credit cards, the quality of the Wiener schnitzel with horseradish—all these convince the experienced guest that the Kobra hotel, despite the changing management and changing government, is what it has always been.

I look in the mirror. Silvered black hair; gray lizardskin shoes; painfully familiar wide green eyes in a puzzled, wondering, scrutinizing expression; a touch of contempt at the corner of the mouth. I know this woman only too well. In my days as a dancer I inspected myself carefully, naked before the mirror. Before the mirror, wrapped in rags, I also practiced every morning. I was to dance the angel of death. I was right for the part, they said; it called for long legs. Klára is so grotesque, they said. Her whole body is an art-deco spiral, with cordlike muscles and a Floréal style; her eyelashes are like peacock feathers. Idiots!

It will not be me who leans back into the muscular arms of the male soloist, the one with the thighs of a stag, to be lifted and spun around. I am not the type to be picked up and moved from place to place. It will be on my own two feet that I rise above those dancing men. I am a sexless angel roaming freely through time and space, and the wings on my boyish white shoulders are symbolic. I unite the young lovers in a final, flawless movement. I raise my knee high, higher, practically to my chin, turn to one side, and in a sharply drawn horizontal line thrust my leg out, instep tautly arched, as if I were kicking you in the pit of your stomach.

An angel mediating between two worlds, but herself all alone—that's what I wanted to be. What I needed, to perform, were the terrifying extremes, not the tepid compromises. So I had to humble myself before my audience. I was successful, but no longer wished to dance in public, to be part of the show, not even its star. I longed to fold up and be motionless. Now I have a room with nothing superfluous in it. I still put up with a mirror. I dance on an empty stage, for an empty auditorium, without music.

And then, as you recall, I locked every door and covered every window with black paper; let Egyptian darkness reign in my apartment. I stopped eating. On the seventh day I had visions. Pacing in the dark, I wanted someone not just to ring the bell, but to break down the door. I saw myself: my nails twisted like a snail's house, my uncombed hair in clumps like wet rags. There was a paper knife on the desk; I stabbed the darkness with it. With my eyes shut, my legs apart, my feet planted firmly, my strength was multiplied a hundredfold in my fingers as I tightened my grip and choked the serpent of fear. Done with the fear of death, I am ready for murder.

I tore the black paper from the windows, walked out on the balcony, and watched the movement of the leaves on the poplar trees that line the street. I inhaled deeply the odor of burned leaves and listened to the sound of tennis balls at the courts nearby. I left my fortress, my head wrapped like a Muslim woman's, my feet shod in high heels, accentuating my still magnificent calves. In a tight English skirt, ready to pounce like a cat, I propelled myself forward, penetrating the city's danger-filled space.

And now I live in Manhattan, on Avenue A in the East Village. The neighborhood is strange, full of crazy, gaudy, frail little stores. The bookstore stays open till midnight. It even has a couple of your books. Early in the morning of my last Sunday in New York, in the St. Marks cinema, I saw a John Waters film. Divine, the transvestite star, was in it; dead now, the poor thing. Wearing a cat mask, the vicious three-hundred-pound hermaphrodite cries out in pain in the electric chair, his face gradually stiffening. Later that morning I joined a demonstration under the window of an evil landlord on the Upper East Side, who'd raised the rent of a nice corner café by four hundred percent. In that café smiling girls have served me my morning coffee and chocolate doughnuts. On weekends the city stretches lazily. It goes to bed late, it gets up late. Budapest could never be so harum-scarum, wide-eyed, bitchy, and gorgeous.

The headwaiter at the Crown recognized me. He kissed my hand and said he was glad to see me. I love to hear that people are glad to see me. Those few friends and acquaintances from here, who visited me in my apartment on the corner of Avenue A and Fourth Street didn't smile or ask questions, and they didn't listen. You could see in their eyes that they were preoccupied even as they were talking. Anything personal is alien to them. I laugh at their sense of hierarchy: they listen to the person who is considered important, turning their backs on the lesser lights. In the world of business, people are not as calculating as that. But let me look at you! Your face has grown wider; I can see a few bomb craters in it. Your gaze is more curious, alternating between power surge and power failure. I'd like a cappuccino and a grappa. Sorry, make that tea with apricot brandy.

Two weeks ago I was in Zurich, in a cowshed. The wooden structure and the trough were several hundred years old, but the feeder was controlled by computer. Later, on the lake shore, I fed seeds to the swans, hoping that somebody would pick me up. Somebody did. A building contractor. He said: "By eight tonight I have to be back with my family. I have a beautiful wife and three children. My family happiness lacks only one thing. You." You cannot resist such a line. I was right not to resist. The building contractor was the devil himself. He made every inch of my body sing.

A week later he took some time off, and we went to Dubrovnik. It was early fall. We walked around the ramparts of the old city, down the winding stairs to the large rocks on the beach. We sat down. The sea rumbled and swelled at our feet. I climbed up one of the rocks and taunted the sea: You can't reach this high no matter how hard you thrash. And with the next wave I was soaking wet. We had a nice room, a view of the sea. And when we went to a café in the town, I would watch the sea from there. We walked around the base of the ancient wall, drank slivovitz in the bars tucked into the narrow streets, and peeked into courtyards. In one, ripe oranges hung on a solitary tree.

The windows glimmered in the approaching dusk, and after more wandering along stone alleys we returned to the Gradska Kafana, which faced a marble promenade. Young girls, their dark hair loose, their features clean, were swaying and gliding like sailboats. With arms linked, they passed proudly in review, a soft, swift regiment, to and fro. The boys, leaning against a stone wall, watched them with blinking eyes. This wonderful silent inspection is repeated every evening. The boy who has made his choice studies the arc of one set of lips only, the curve of one neck only, but the gaze and the voice are not yet his. For that he must go to her and, with her permission, walk up and down by her side for all to see.

At seven, as if by magic, the promenade emptied. The building contractor and I imagined ourselves inside many homes, living many lives. We had only three days, three days to explore the quaint alleys and passageways, to watch the sea from the small, neglected graveyard of a monastery, to enjoy pure red wine, goat cheese, and fresh scallops, and to note the slow strokes of the oars as boats returned to the old port.

We had planned to go back together to Zurich, but at the airport I noticed there was a plane about to leave for Budapest. I kissed my lover with the beautiful wife and three children, and said, "You've been wonderful, darling." I had my ticket transferred to the flight to Budapest because at that very moment, in the check-in line, I knew that I had a date with you, here in the old Crown, on Resurrection Square.

Klára: 2

Do you remember that afternoon when we swore that we would never be tricked again? We were standing on the shore of the Danube. I showed you the place where I threw my coat when they told us to undress. I happened to be sent home; the rest were shot and pushed into the water. There, on the riverbank, when the Germans were still holding the city, you said that our parents had been too weak. You said that one must not be weak. You overlooked the one closest to you, foolish relative of mine. You cast your eyes far, but you didn't get far. Even though you left me. That was a terrible mistake. We went our separate ways. We could say that both ways have been good, but that would be too easy. Which of us is weak now, you or me?

Let me offer you a little wisdom, my dear, a pill to take with mineral water, and this day will seem to you your last.

Opposite us, on the sofa beyond the marble table, are Mama and Papa. We are all together, the flood has started, Noah's ark is launched. We can pull up the ladders and spread the sails. I hope old Jeremiah will join us. Even fifty or so years ago my father referred to him as old Jeremiah. Let our dear younger "sister," Melinda, come, too. We never miss an opportunity to needle her. And I would be glad to see our friend János Dragomán, that somnambulistic demon. The lives of all of us are pretty well entangled. My father, Arnold Kobra, and his best friend, Jeremiah Kadron, once loved the same woman, Zsuzsa Tárnok. On January 13, 1945, when I was eleven, in the lobby of that Swiss-protected building that faced St. Stephen's Park, and before your eyes, my darling David, my father was shot by an Arrow-Cross man.

I chose Jeremiah as my spiritual father, and so had two fathers, and of the two, one is still around. I haven't called Jeremiah, but have the feeling that he'll soon be here. But the father is always the doubtful parent. For example, the situation involving you and that other cousin of ours Zoltán. Between two cousins, I became pregnant and gave birth to our serpentine Regina. And of course you, lecherous rhinoceros, unashamedly appropriated her. But by marrying my beloved little girl you may have fallen into the heinous sin of incest. If not heinous, at least horrible; if not horrible, at least avoidable.

Zoltán is coming, too. You'll sit next to each other, not an easy thing to do for two partners in sin. And even if the dead seek no revenge, you still stand accused. I am not threatening you, but don't look so innocently happy. My father may have found a way to have himself shot by a third party, but you assisted in the act. He was no resister; you forced him to resist. They shot him; they spared you.

For my mother, every January 13 became a chasm that was hard to step over. She, too, will now join us, Zsuzsa Tárnok, who survived her husband by fifteen years and then on that January 13, from the balcony of her eighth-floor studio, jumped to her death. She was nineteen when she married the hotelier and manager of the Kobra Revue Theater, and gave birth to me when she was twenty. A widow at the age of thirty, she accepted Jeremiah's loving devotion to her and to me as an undeserved gift. Her last lover—he was hanged— lies in an unmarked grave.

In 1956 I followed Zoltán, leaving my mother. Leaving you, too. My mother both adored and loathed the obstinate, savage Kobra blood that coursed in my veins. And in yours, and in Zoltán's. I think she meant to bring me into this world as a son. She knew that I would be a temptation for both you and Zoltán, a temptation as a woman or as a man, because you find only blood relatives exciting.

I realized early in life that boys would prefer more feminine creatures to me. I had a bottom, I had breasts, but my mind was brutal and teasing. Boys were afraid of me, and so were men who liked their calm, self-satisfied security. I could be the cuddly cushion, the comfortable kitten, then I'd bite your hand. I loved to lick wounds.

Before and after you I had lovers, and would like to see them around our table, but considering the domestic character of this gathering, I will not invite them. The two women, mother and daugh- ter, are the foci. Two men at my mother's side, Arnold and Jeremiah, and two at mine, David and Zoltán. My so-called younger sister is becoming a woman. I wonder what romances she will add to the annals of love.

And there is my daughter, Regina. I do not want you to have her. You can have her only if you submit to her completely: if you become her pet; if you let her make all decisions, including yours; if you don't cheat on her, not even in your dreams. In a word, if you agree to be not you. What does a middle-aged woman with a grown-up daughter wish for? A grandchild to be fussed over. But if the baby issues from your loins, the loins of David, it will possess that cursed Kobra blood. The blood of suicides, impersonators, gamblers. People for whom fate itself is a game, and thus they never become involved in any scene; they're always looking to the next one. Do we need another character like that?

I suppose I've grown bored with myself and with the daring playing at life. But, even bored, I wish all of us a countless number of birthdays to come, many happy returns. My dear David, please forgive this allusion to your age, but you have eaten the better portion of your bread. This is why we are gathered here, to make a decision about you. More than halfway through life, where one can actually stop and look around, do you intend to get off the train, whose route you are beginning to be familiar with? Or, instead, will you play the hale and hearty graybeard for the remaining half-century? You'd like to outwit us, foolish suicides, wouldn't you?

But now you are gone from your seat, you are somewhere else, gasping for air. This continual shortness of breath is not good. As your former mistress and one who can appreciate your wildness, having been wild herself, I must admit that you don't look too well. Your future, dear, is cloudy.

Klára: 3

Before I leave for the second or perhaps the third time, let's admit, just between the two of us, that I was in a pretty wretched state when I left the first time; I was not myself at all. I spoke of suicide, detailed possible ways of doing it, and you, my cowardly, suspicious half-wit, thought I was only playing games. On the eve of my almost-serious suicide attempt you were at my home, but I knew—be honest—that you would rather have been elsewhere. There are more exciting things than attending the nadir of someone's depression.

In those days a handful of sleeping pills couldn't put me to sleep. I was afraid that if I lay down, I would choke to death. That my nose would start bleeding, and the blood would drip into my lungs. I'd wake up gasping, get out of bed, sit in the armchair, and look out the window. I asked you to take me to the hospital, then turned childish and insisted we get out of the taxi halfway there and go the rest of the way on foot. Coaxing, threatening, you had to fight for every step to the hospital, besides having to carry my sizable overnight bag. At the intersection I didn't dare step off the sidewalk, afraid a truck would run over me. I clung to a lamppost. And when finally you pried me from it, a truck actually came by and nearly ran me down.

That evening, you came bearing flowers and delicacies, as was your style. "Don't take me to the hospital now," I begged you. And no, I haven't read the books you brought me the other day. And please don't bring any more; I won't read them. I am interested only in my own strange thoughts, not in novels. Most novels are a waste of precious time. They soil our minds and tell us things that never happened, inanities.

And you, my darling, came because I called you. I knew you didn't want to answer the phone but that finally you would. You'd move toward it slowly, hoping it would stop ringing. Yes, you avoid me, you protect yourself, but I pry you away from your tranquillity. In good middle-class fashion, you offer me sober advice. Smug, you tell me that most of the things other people want, you don't. I could strangle you.

There was a time I took dancing seriously, so I can understand your withdrawing, away from confessions, away from being a witness, out of the world of sour obligations. Not long ago, I wrote something. You said it was icy, funny, and that it contained a certain refined disgust. That's what you said. After a week of self-immersion, I forgot about that spiral notebook. You are such a dense, well-meaning person. Your insight into human nature is poor, your sense of humor is weak. You are stupid enough to believe in the written word.

When you tell me how many people have called you, how many you've met, how many pages you've written, how many books you've read, how many facts you've jotted down from your newspapers— and not how many women you've been flirting with, prowling for in stairwells—when I see your gargantuan gorging on life, I sometimes think: He is only pretending, pretending to be that hungry.

I have enough money for the rent and food. This woman, Mariska, comes three times a week, cleans the house, cooks, does the shopping. I have no time to bother with such things. She pesters me to eat. Says I smoke too much. I've had six silk pajamas made. I'm a throwback, I belong in the thirties; Marlene Dietrich, Katalin Karády, and Mother are my idols. I can meditate in the lotus position.

You weren't in Budapest at the time of the fly sting. Well, a

227

cousin can't be present at every fly sting. It was on a Sunday outing. I was walking down from János Mountain toward Hüvösvölgy and stopped to eat a sandwich on a bench. After I drank my lemon tea spiked with rum and looked leisurely about me, I brandished my hiking stick, drew a dance movement in the air, thinking about teaching it to children. I had collected poems about the dance, was planning an anthology. I amused myself with the thought of making all the guests and employees of the Crown get up on their toes, as if the demon of dance had entered their feet. My waving stick must have annoyed the fly, and it stung me. The next day, my temple swelled. I went to see the doctor. He said to wait, but the swelling didn't go down; it grew worse. Wanting to know what was inside it, I lanced it with a heated razor blade; you can still see the scar. Fly larvae issued from the sore, in the pus that ran down my face. I washed the wound with alcohol, but still they kept pouring out. With my face covered with blood, I lay down in the bathtub, submerged my head, and kept it under for as long as I could.

In the Tatras I took long walks in mountain meadows, the grass waist high, the wind blowing the poison from my body. I stayed in a log cabin, drank lots of gin, and watched the snowy peaks in the August sun. What if I became a forest ranger? Or married a taciturn forester, for whom I'd cook hot chicken soup every evening? Come, sit beside me. It's all right; we don't have to talk. You can read, or watch something silly on TV, or play dominoes. I know you don't want me, that you're afraid to sleep with me. The healthy recoil from the one who carries death.

Opposite my studio there is another studio. I can see the steeple of Mátyás Church, the tower of the Bazilika, the red star on top of Parliament. My mother used to live here, and Regina will live here when I'm gone. Mariska, who was also my nanny, still looks after me. I have pasted up the photographs of seven women, one below the other, my great-great-grandmother on top, Regina at the bottom. A row of mothers, of beautiful Jewish middle-class women well dressed in changing fashions. But even on the face of my great-great-grandmother you can detect a distance, a slightly jeering smile. All seven women have big noses, beaks. Dangerous birds, all of them.

Clothes bother me. Either they are too tight and thick, and chafe and stick to me, or they are too flimsy and thin, and then I'm cold. Here I sit in my armchair, not writing, reading, or listening to music. For a whole year now. I used to talk for hours with my friend Ilonka, about liver cancer and her beautiful black hair that fell out because of the therapy. A Japanese violinist came to see her and suggested a massage; with his tiny feet he walked on Ilonka's large body. That didn't help, either, and we buried her. Now there is only Mariska to talk to, and she is not bright. I am probably boring company. In ever shrinking circles my thoughts center around myself. People get bored when a person talks too much about herself. But you do not bore me. I can tell you everything. Here is tea and wine, sweet and salted pastry, there is no need for you to jump up out of my father's favorite easy chair.

Klára: 4

Edit, my friend from Chicago, is here. You know what happened to her? She waited for her husband, Jonathan, to retire from his business, so he'd stop his philandering under the pretense of business trips and dinners. But as soon as he retired, he had a stroke. He recovered from the paralysis but was left with the intelligence of a three-year-old. He kept grabbing the tablecloth and pulling everything off the table. When his friends came to see him, he would pull the chairs out from under them. He would grab at the women's breasts. If Edit locked him in his room, he would cry and kick the door. He behaved himself only when she sat next to him, turned on some music, and patted his hand. So she left, came back to Hungary, and rented a room in the Nádor Hotel in her hometown, Pécs. She saw nobody, only used room service. She phoned me. I couldn't face the train, so I took a taxi to Pécs. When I got there, I didn't go to see Edit but took a room in the Pannonia Hotel instead.

The trip to Pécs is a story in itself. I stepped into the taxi and gave the address of the hotel. The driver was a handsome young man and he kept looking at me in the rearview mirror. I looked back at him in the mirror. When we got to the hotel, I asked him to come up to my room and take my clothes off. When we reached the city on the way home, I asked him to hop into a tobacconist's and get me a pack of cigarettes. While he was in the store, I slipped out of his taxi and hailed another one. I didn't want him to bring me home.

I used to be more critical of people. Now, I quietly write obituaries for my acquaintances, as if they were dead already. Because, in a sense, they are. And when my contemporaries actually do die, I approve. It is as if they have received the death for which they labored all their lives. Death always comes at the right time. And perhaps it is time for me, too, to depart, before my host gets fed up with me. In my relations with people I was impatient, but I was impatient with myself as well. I am able to look at myself as an appliance whose warranty has expired and which is not worth repairing anymore.

I concentrate best while standing on my head; the problem is, I can't stand on my head very long. Do you have any idea how awful it is when all you can think of are platitudes? But your sensitivity to platitudes is not developed. I suppose urban sophistication was late reaching your town. I am more finicky than you, and have better taste. Sometimes you write lines that would be better off in pop-song lyrics. But then, prolific output and kitsch go hand in hand.

You can eat many different kinds of food, and some, which you devour with such gusto, I can barely look at. Black pudding, for example. You can share a good laugh with the most awful people, while I stand aloof, a glaring wallflower.

I used to enjoy introducing you to clever people, and then, like a referee, keeping score of the blows. Later, when we were alone, I would tell you how many lame retorts you had coughed up to parry your opponent's strong arguments. As a coach keeps a heavyweight boxer in shape. I did the same with your writings, which you compulsively showed me. Klára would always tell you where it was inflated, where it was flat, and where it needed cutting—for which you got down on all fours and in gratitude kissed my foot.

You couldn't bear my gaze; I could always read your mind. Go ahead, dear, I thought, go and reap your married women. Have as many little affairs as your strength will allow, but don't you dare move in with anyone. And if there's a woman you plan to be seen with for any length of time, bring her first to me, for an audition. I preferred doctors' wives for you, those who wore mink coats and beeped three times under your window.

I check my front door more than twenty times a day. I open it, stare into the emptiness of the stairwell, and withdraw, frightened, when anyone approaches. The neighbors probably think I'm nosy. I should leave and do my gaping in the street. But when I set foot outside, people make remarks about my clothes.

The other day, I ventured down to the corner espresso. Ibike, the waitress, said she hadn't seen me for a long time. She hoped I wasn't working too hard. I looked tired, she said. I ordered coffee and a glass of club soda. "You know what it means to give up the ghost, Ibike?" I asked. She gave me such a stupid look that I threw the soda in her face. On the way home, a bearded man sidled up to me and whispered obscenities. "I'd sure like to stick it in you, Felicia!" Felicia? I turned on him like a hawk: "What would you stick, you miserable wretch? Your words?" He fled.

In my dream we were sitting in a taxi, you and I. We were going to my funeral. You told the driver to hurry; we didn't want to be late. We arrived at the mortician's arm in arm. People made way for us. You were wearing a black hat, black coat, and a white silk scarf, and you led me to a door that went from the mortuary to an adjacent room. You opened the door and motioned for me to enter, but you did not follow. Inside, two cheerful young men welcomed me. They were fumbling with an old crank-operated record player. I had on a surprisingly short skirt. We danced. There were mirrors along the walls, and the lighting was the color of blood oranges. My thighs still were beautiful. I hoped the curtain would go up, but it didn't. Then silence. My eyes fell on a ribbon draped over a wreath: Klára Kobra. "Shall we start?" I asked hesitantly. The boys nodded. They put Chopin's "Death Sonata" on their scratchy record player. I looked through a peephole in the mirror. There you were, sitting to the left of the catafalque, wearing your black hat. Sincere grief on your face.

What time are you leaving today? Ten? Eleven? I'll set the alarm clock so I won't have to look at you stealing glances at your watch, your eyes clouding over, the cloud a chintzy black drape that hangs between your departure and my solitude. For years, despite your visits, I've savored the pain of loneliness. I've enjoyed your successes, and am amused to see how blind, deaf, and dumb you have become. You are the sun now, and I am the moon eclipsing you. When I die, you will no longer cast a shadow.

6.

In which János Dragomán
swims away and takes
the train back

He Was Received

János Dragomán was driven out of this small country by a need for space; he left as a stray bird leaves a room. Yet he has not become a truly Western man, for, though he likes a swift mind, he hates to hurry. He admires the ability in others to apportion time, people who make purposeful haste, who fill even their leisure hours with activity, and always reach their destination on time. He admires athletes, too, but is no athlete himself, does not swim with a stopwatch, would rather walk than jog. He runs only when chased. For him, the whole cult of achievement is an absurd fad. Thus he is an outsider both in the East and in the West; he may be an outsider, too, in the club of outsiders. It took him twenty years to look upon his own youth the way you look upon your old suits hanging in a rediscovered closet.

He takes no pleasure in chafing against censorship. In Budapest he does not hole up or look over his shoulder. He tries to find life interesting and not succumb to the bad habit of judging others. But how does one avoid being restricted, watched, spied on? Here everything is socialist realism; here crossing a border is a dramatic event. János is an observer, and crosses borders with his eyes. Self-pity he counters with sarcasm.

In libraries he reads old newspapers; he visits the Tango, where his father once played the piano; he comes here to Leander Street, shuts himself up in my father's room, right above me, and spends long hours poring over manuscripts. When he first came here, he spoke in short, clipped sentences; now he is more talkative, his tone more melancholy. At dusk, his slow-burning eyes grow so wide that, to protect myself, I put *The Magic Flute* on the record player.

He comes down and goes out to the garden. He senses a change in the weather, complains of a headache. Maybe he has a tumor. He laments his passing, composes his will. Asks for tea with rum and accepts a few apricot-jam turnovers. What bothers him particularly is the first half hour after they bury him. The mourners leave by the cemetery gate, the body huddles in the coffin, fills it with a peculiar odor, although above it are flowers, bouquets and wreaths, on the newly piled mound of earth. What does he do now? Stick around, keep this poor immobile body company? My poor friend, *mon pauvre ami*, I will stay with you, but not for long. I'll have to leave; the cemetery is now covered with wet leaves. You do understand, don't you? And on quick spindly legs, the soul takes off, hurries after the mourners, desiring the warmth of their cheerful company. But it's not much fun sitting with them in a small restaurant, where red wine and beef stew appear on the checked tablecloth but no place has been set for János Dragomán. And there is talk of another funeral two days from now, one that is much more important than his. "I will never again have a clean body," János complains.

David Kobra arrives; the scene is set for a good conversation. János courts me best when Kobra is around. On this occasion, too, he reverts to his preoccupation: "When I die, *lieber* Kobra, arrange for my cremation. Before my death, however, I'd like to get a little closer to the state of holiness. A little transcendental investment may yield a nice return. I must therefore avoid looking at Melinda's legs, which aside from a few blue varicose veins are flawless. But my friend Kobra moves away from me; he disapproves. He may think that occasionally I devour young boys and girls, delighting in the curves and folds of new flesh. Not so. At supper, one after the other, the master revives young and old with flashes of his spirit. He pays tribute to the sparkling row of eyes and to that face in the candles' shadow at the far end of the table. Together they write slow movements on the parchment of time. My memory is fading, the dinner table grows brighter, the kind, dead faces look with encouragement. It is a weakness that I am in love with all of you. This was not meant to be my mission."

Willows and blackbirds in the garden; behind the flower beds, a bench, and an arbor in the corner; ash trees and poplars near the road. Life is good here on Leander Street, with many friends living nearby. The cellar and attic full of trunks, leather-bound books about the fleet of the combined forces of the Austro-Hungarian monarchy.

The portrait of our kaiser and king as the frontispiece, under a transparent protective page. You can also find Brussels lace and gala dresses designed with authentic Hungarian motifs; aquarelles from Florence; the yearbooks of the polo club.

The rooms are spacious, the ceilings high. Our bathroom was recently redone, but there was no money left for putting down a new parquet floor. Maybe next year. Here lives a historian, there a physicist, here a sculptor, there a poet. The children have lots of places to hide in the garden, which is not too disorderly. These gardens may grow tired, but they never lose heart. Beautiful women at the cusp of youth and middle age switch between English and French with ease. One has secondary-school children, another just had a baby. Plenty of liberal arts diplomas, psychology, art history, literature, sociology. Some women teach school, some tutor at home, some translate, edit, or do research in libraries and archives, or work at clinics or in planning offices. None are rich, none are poor.

Somebody rang the bell of the garden gate this morning. It was a beautiful tall girl, Iroquois crest on her head, eyelids painted black. A rat, wiggling its tiny nose, was perched on her shoulder. Absently, the girl took the rat's tail into her mouth and sucked on it. In English, but with a German accent, she asked me where she could find János. "Who is János?" I asked, and that was all she could get out of me. "Maybe he will be killed," the girl said calmly. "The problem is that he paid for it. Our company is very reliable." "What company?" "Murder Inc.," the girl said, and walked away with long, swaying strides, but not before we had sized each other up. I know János did not pay. He told me that he asked for a price, nothing more. Unless he lied to me. Could he have paid for an assassin to follow him around? It's not impossible. Perhaps he feels that it was beggarly of him to arrive with only two suitcases, that he needs to enrich us with the intricate plot of a crime novel? If there is anything János hates, it's boredom.

I didn't tell the girl that he comes here every day. But they will be able to find him. The heartless bastard, he turns even his death into a game. Most likely, she is one of his lovers. Why did she come? To inform on him? To protect him? Or was she in fact representing the company? She'll be back. Maybe she just wanted to see me. I send János from the garden back to my father's cave; let him poke about in manuscripts.

I can thank my father that I feel so cruelly at home in this house. All the others moved away to get married; their bones do not yet creak in tune with the timber framework of the house they live in. It was my children who gave me the feeling that everything we do makes sense. It is said that there's nothing God's eyes can't see. But I have my doubts about God seeing everything. Children, however, always do; they see and note everything. I'm weeding the flower beds. My son, István, is watering the plants. He gives plenty of water to János's little Christmas trees, which are growing from Lebanese seeds. István is on good terms with János, as he is with the puppy and the kitchen and with every friendly being. In our family he is the one who senses most keenly the psychological situation; his taste is the most fastidious. At thirteen, he is a bashful young gentleman. And I am an average middle-class woman who raises her children, looks after her husband, and does what she has to do. That job can be well done, just as love can be. When the text to be rendered is good, the translator pays tribute to the author after each sentence. Man is a letter properly written. And the purpose of life is to read the letter carefully.

Most things I keep from Antal, but I tell my diary. János, about whom I think constantly, is taking up more and more space in these pages. I summon him, dissect him, fondle him, insult him. The flood comes, the banks collapse, the walls crumble. If my husband read these delirious thoughts, the raptures and curses of this two-track mind of mine, I wouldn't be surprised if he brought down his bearlike paw so hard on me that I would be unable to write another word about János Dragomán, good or bad.

Melinda wears a white skirt, a black silk blouse, and her brown shoulders are exposed. She is not afraid of skin cancer or AIDS. She fears only god, with a small *g*. Tonight we gather on the balcony. I will say good-bye to the pale stranger. My heart will make no sound as it breaks in half. Winds are whipping the city. Summer rain lashes the trees and the roof; it rustles along the pebbled garden path; then suddenly plum-size hail is falling.

Come to my bedroom. In my white linen dressing gown, I await you. I will undress you. Your rugged, tumescent penis is in my hand, in my mouth, and now it roots in my vulva. Fitting into me this best part of you, with the smallest movements you bring all my being to attention. My fingers tease your testicles, I chew your ears, your deceitful eyes, I show off the recently discovered art of my throat, a music of squeals and yelps. How did you guess, pale stranger, that the place to concentrate on is the area around my left breast? Melinda's womb is open to János; she's stopped taking the pill. Let there be children from both men. And whoever leaves our triangle loses.

Every day I write something in my diary about my mother, my father, my daughter, son, husband, János, Kobra, Regina. These few people I consider worthy of attention; I view them from a particular angle. Antal, János, and Kobra are exactly sixteen years older than I am. They were all twenty-three in 1956; that's when they learned the most important lesson of their lives. The generation of '56. In his own way, Antal has done what it has been possible to do, and done it well. What Kobra is doing is so much his own it borders on the impossible. But since he is doing it, it must be possible after all. And János did not want to be for or against anything. He wanted nothing to do with whatever happened here after the uprising. He left, but not too early, in 1966, having been around for a good ten years of the Kádár era. Twenty years have passed since then. What have we done all this time?

Peace in the garden. Papa translates; I study. School, university, library, counseling. Papa takes walks, saws, reaps, drinks wine on the balcony. My husband, my lover, and my friend were all twenty-three years old in 1956; I was seven. When I was nine, I mourned Imre Nagy. My father knew him; he had been to our house. And I was there in 1968: May in Paris, August in Prague. In 1969, at age twenty, I married Antal, because he had stayed here, like a rock, like a pine tree. Parallel lives, all tied to Budapest, hover over the city like colorful, lost balloons. But they are not lost; they are held together, the ends of their strings in a merciless fist on the ground: their origin.

Pointing Fingers on
the Shore of the Canal

János gets off the bed and looks out the window of the Hotel
Esthella. There was a snowstorm, but the wind is chasing away the
clouds, the sun is coming out. Steel-blue and rust-brown rooftops.
Tourists in raincoats are walking along the stone banks of the canals
of Amsterdam in front of the narrow-breasted commercial buildings.
János celebrates his fifty-fourth birthday tonight. He should invite
somebody for dinner; at fifty-four, he is still alive, no pains yet. He
has gold teeth in his mouth, and gets up in the middle of the night
to go to the toilet, but he is still able to walk and maybe even to
procreate. As the snowstorm abates, he notices a woman across the
canal. From his bag, which also contains a compass and a hunting
knife, he takes a pair of binoculars. The woman was rearranging
things in her store window, but because the weather is unpredictable
and there are few potential customers, she is now reading a book.
Occasionally she looks up and no doubt notices János, who is watching
her through his binoculars from the second-story window of the Hotel
Esthella. He goes downstairs, has a dark beer at the corner, ambles
across the bridge, stands hesitantly for a while, then enters the store.
He shudders, but keeps a mask of pleasure on his face. The woman
is a comrade in misfortune, his age. He will not be able to make use
of her physical charms more than once.

With his paradoxes about Eastern Europe, János Dragomán has
lately become a star on the lecture circuit of American universities.
Being from Eastern Europe is also his own incurable affliction. If,
say, his great-great-grandfather had been a Dutch merchant, he would
have inherited only a quarter of his present problems. But God forbid
that his ancestors turn out to be Dutch Jews; that would make life
too sensible, consistent, and practical. There, in the Danube basin,

240

the coexistence of East and West has become an art form. Neither unity nor trinity ever really gained our sympathy; it is on duality that we get good and drunk.

János's students are afraid to get too involved in debates, lest they be considered impolite. And irony escapes them, even when they are Jews. What an American child learns from his parents is something uniform, logical, having continuity, whereas a Hungarian child is introduced to a world of which one can say, summing up: "Those poor bastards certainly had their share of trouble." Hungarians are tough players. They don't really respect authority, and are more tenacious in the struggle for existence than Westerners. The West domesticates and tames; the East, full of obstacles through which you have to claw your way, is not so tame. Here, for political reasons, perfectly well-meaning people have denied their own fathers, children, friends, and loves. Here, after failures and defeats, we always start from scratch. We do not continue the lives of our fathers.

The mind is sharpened when affronted by absurdity. The best thing to put before the humanist as an object of meditation is a mass grave. Little wonder that an East European feels his Western counterpart is not bright. Looking through Western eyes, on the other hand, we may conclude that absurdity, becoming the natural environment through constant assault, makes the human mind conform to it. We become accustomed to the military, to the conditions of a camp.

In New York, János has learned to write essays about cities, not nation-states. Cities have their own wisdom, their own criminal aesthetics, and political style. In New York, he finds he does not need to take part in the self-deception that accompanies all collective selves. His intellectual anarchism is appreciated; it earns laughter from the audience. He appreciates a city where he can make money by being impertinent.

János's list of residences is long and varied. Of course he wouldn't exchange it for Melinda's, who has lived mostly on Leander Street and in Ófalu. But Melinda wouldn't want to exchange hers, either. According to János, staying in one place is a sign of spiritual indolence. But to Kobra, roaming the world is a sign of spiritual confusion.

"You should come with me, just so you are not always here," János said to Kobra once. "Why this philistine clinging?" Kobra was lacking in intellectual courage, he said, he was an ignorant country bumpkin. "You managed to get away from your unpronounceable town to Budapest, and now you're out of wind, like a fat goose.

"Only the present moment counts," he went on, "and the hemp pipe. Only the fig tree and the almonds. Let me have another plum brandy. I brought Melinda a small mother-of-pearl box. For Antal, a jackknife with which to slice his ham and green peppers that go with the bread he cuts into uniform cubes like soldiers. For Kobra I brought a pebble. He of the seven-league-boot sentences. Our distinguished dissident writer and human-rights activist, I see, has a new young wife and new children. Again. He has this role down to perfection. An honorary member of the opposition. Lucky Kobra, the years are working for him; he is being mummified into a classic. It's very clear that he is faithful to Regina; he no longer goes on secret trips, and his conscience is as free of wrinkles as Baby Zsiga's behind. I am the heliotrope; Kobra, the potato. But tell me, friends, what sunflower wants to be a potato?

"This has always been the guiding principle of our conversations: I while away the time, and he talks about his work. It's strange to be here in my mother's apartment, surrounded by the old lady's belongings. I have gathered young people around me. I suppose I wouldn't mind stirring the city up a little before I leave again. And the crazy emigrant would like a little applause from his homeland. It's not easy to leave everything behind and dwell in strange lands for decades. The explorer deserves some recognition. But the people at home are not interested in his report. Perhaps I need your company more than you need mine. Come, noble friend, light up, pour; there'll be plenty of time for you to sit by your typewriter.

"Can you, learned friend, solve the following riddle? There must be at least a million thirty-eight-year-old women who are eating bread and jam at this very moment. Why is it that the bread-and-jam eating of this woman here seems to me to be the most beautiful? Why is it that I cannot get beyond this particular case? Why is it that I find such mystery even in the combing of her hair. And why have I been condemned—it's humiliating—to agree with Melinda's every observation?" And now Melinda chimes in: "It's because our weaknesses neatly complement each other."

Leisurely we make our way to the other side of the mountain, to a small Swabian restaurant. We start with beer, shortcakes, and lung soup, the kind served at wakes. We follow this with bean soup and minced cabbage, and order smoked shank of ham on the side. Antal told me he was leaving and wouldn't come back as long as János remained. He told me to send János away. Until I did, Antal would live in Ófalu. So the loose woman, having been seduced by a flamboyant scoundrel, returns to her husband and to her former provincial morality. We cut across rows of trees and snow-covered fields. Yesterday, at his apartment, I went around wearing one of his shirts, with nothing under it, and today, behold, I have become unapproachable. That's the power of words for you. We cannot meet, but he is still here in the city, driving me mad with jealousy.

János tells me that my mother also had two men on her leash. And she was very demanding; she had to see everything, hear everything, be deeply involved in everything. This way, she had a great deal to talk over with the human race. Witches such as she sit by the fireplace and foresee our fate. They pretend to be ignorant and silly, but in secret pull the strings. A pity I couldn't know his mother. I can feel her spirit growing in me more and more. Perhaps that is why I sit so much now in the Tango Bar.

There are other reasons, but they will not be spelled out just yet. I will mention only the name of the Tango's owner, Kamilla. She likes to buy dollars from János at the Greater Budapest rate of exchange, and involves him in various business deals. I'll get her yet, that nouveau-riche goose, who is always licking her full, voluptuous lips. Perfidiously, she asks nothing of János, she accepts him as he is, whereas I ask a great deal, and make him suffer even for being five minutes late. I torment him especially when he acts too conceited. He likes to sit at a sidewalk table, in the stinking, polluted air. He appreciates my garden and balcony, but loves the sidewalk, can spend hours looking at it glisten after the rain. "*Je suis un citadin*," he says, and leisurely continues poisoning himself with the air and the pungent cigarettes he puffs on.

He sits at the bar, off to the side, propped on his elbows. Occasionally he helps out with the drinks, to show how much at home he is in this place. He puns, he talks, talks endlessly; his listeners get lost in his verbal avalanche. When finally he tires, he falls silent and hangs his head, and refills the customers' glasses. The customers lower their heads, too; a real nodding contest. Kamilla kisses the back of János's neck—and I make a cutting remark. I am good at sticking pins in balloons.

On one of our trips, in a local gallery in Pécs, János and I are standing in front of a painting by Lajos Gulácsy, *The Dream of an Opium Eater*. Blue faces pull on a pink narghile; the undergrowth, a carpet of poppies. The lighting suggests the meeting of moonlight and dawn. Cavelike mouths gape before the view; a mulatto boy in a green cap blows soap bubbles; a pug-nosed, red-haired woman with an amulet around her neck stares at some point. From female loins a tree trunk or a fish branches, or mushrooms. Breathing evenly, János is blowing a bubble large enough to hold an entire city.

Kamilla has bought some film equipment. With her friends, who drink on credit at her place, she wants to make movies, combining avant-garde comedy with hard-core Budapest pornography. János should be the director. The Tango is not enough for Kamilla; she wants to be a porno star, too. After closing, she continues to party with her most confidential customers. Wearing a white wig, she dances barefoot on the tables. Looking at her legs and waist you can tell she has never given birth. She doesn't have to be careful for my sake, because she can't get pregnant. I'll get you yet, my fairy queen.

Around midday, after a leisurely cup of coffee, János makes a few phone calls, takes to the streets, loafs, chats with people, visits a couple of places, and winds up at the Tango. His conscience does not seem to bother him in the least. The balcony across the street is supported by bent-over Atlases with enormous quadriceps. An acacia tree in front of the bar is overrun by a parasite evergreen. On the sidewalk, a muddy heap of snow decorated with a discarded Christmas tree. Parked near the entrance, the three-wheeled chair of a cripple. These are the things János delights in. It is in this most densely built area of the city that you find the least vegetation, the most drinking establishments, and the highest crime rate. And he always comes late to my idyllic garden. While I wait for you, I am only waiting. And as I wait for him, I grow older and uglier.

The Tatar-faced Kamilla is meek, giggly, and always has plenty of time on her hands. With her, János comes and goes as he pleases. Sometimes he sits at the piano, and then people stop and listen. He is also allowed, in the late morning, to do the rumba on the dance floor with some off-duty slut. Across the street, in the Crown café, the plush, overstuffed chairs are occupied mostly by tourists in the summer, but by September the more refined local clientele reclaims them—perhaps only to defy the Tango, that dive across the street, from which János makes periodic forays into the Crown, gathering material for satire. In the Tango they make fun of what is serious in the Crown.

From the greener zone of the city he returns to Resurrection Square on his bicycle, carrying an umbrella. He keeps track of the still-existing umbrella repair shops, and the pipe maker, and knows the location of the last watchmaker's shop, which is full of the sounds of chimes. He frequents the workshop of a philosophically inclined typewriter mechanic because of the old Remington he bought recently. János likes to type his first drafts on the Remington and make his corrections with a steel-nibbed pen dipped in ink. He buys fruit from the funny bald man who writes rhymes on pieces of construction paper above his merchandise. Nor has János been able to exhaust the varieties of sauerkraut sold in this area. When he buys a cheese blintz at the corner, he receives a purring "Come again" that is full of promises. He can take his pick of several wine cellars in which honestly (moderately) watered wine is sold. In the former coal cellars of the neighborhood, more and more small restaurants are opening. Love thy neighbor? Talk to János. For him, every day is a holiday. On Resurrection Square he meets his old classmates, those who have strayed here and those who left but have come back to visit. If he wants to brush up on world events, all he has to do is go to the Crown or the Tango.

It was in the Crown that he told me about his affair in Amsterdam, which, unhappily, has something to do with my father and therefore with me as well. I relate to János as the upper classes do to the common people; once in a while I throw him a bone. "Tell me, Melinda," János asks, "who are you working for?" That will forever remain a secret. I tell him only this much: I am a secret agent come from afar, though I have lived here all my life. I am as calm and resigned as the guard of the inner sanctum who knows that there is nothing inside.

At the Hotel Esthella, in Room 213, the food was excellent, there was whiskey in the refrigerator, and János, holding his binoculars, was standing by the window once again. His notebook no longer interested him. Patting the switchblade in his pocket—he'd heard of tourists being stabbed on the banks of this canal and rolled into the dark water—he returned to the woman who was neither young nor pretty. The curtain in the store window was drawn. There was a familiar smell. Speaking no Dutch and not wanting to speak English, he called to the unknown woman in Hungarian. Though they had made furious love on her bed, illuminated by light beams bouncing off a crystal ball, he hadn't really spoken to her until now. In Hungarian he invited her to dinner. "Nearby, madam, is the Café Bern, at the new marketplace. Yesterday I tried their entrecôte, and it was not bad. But we could go to any of those small cafés that promise a reasonable ambience. We'll drink hot chocolate, have a brioche, each of us speaking in our mother tongue. We'll get along very well." The woman smiled. "I'm sure we will," she said in Hungarian, then turned off the light in the store window and picked up her coat. "How long have you been here?" she asked. "I arrived this morning," I said. "And in every city you pick your dinner partner on the first evening? Excuse me if I see right through you. We both have abandoned the humiliated and miserable people of Budapest. I sell my body, and you, I guess, sell your head. There are still customers for my body, but I am getting old. Here I am, in Holland, and I've managed to save a little."

János got home early in the morning. He was about to fall asleep when the phone rang: It was my father, Jeremiah. He said he wanted to say good-bye. "You're not planning to leave this vale of tears, are you?" János asked. No, not at all, but the old gentleman had a plan. He would even have plans in the twenty-first century. But János had better things to do than wait for our unfortunately located nation to thaw out and open up. Jeremiah spoke of some moral lesson, hinted at things that could be done locally. "You've all taken the burden of the nation on your shoulders, and you're welcome to it," János said. Shabby Atlases supporting a balcony about to crumble. And that Melinda! Conjuring tea parties around the state of resignation.

Crossing the Border, on the Way In

Most likely I am only a fragment. I cannot accomplish anything great. Bits and pieces, yes, even some books, but a major work, one that nearly kills you, a work to which you give your whole self, a magnum opus that is wiser than its author, never. Improvise mostly, without making any real effort. For me, elegance is more important than diligence. Everybody has something spectacular to boast of. In Budapest, people most frequently boast of having been in jail. But I cannot: What is there to boast of, that in my youth close-minded people closed steel doors on me? I haven't been tested yet, but when the big test comes, I wouldn't mind avoiding it. Perhaps my most impressive deed was leaving. Just as Kobra's most impressive deed was staying.

I am interested in monsters. When I left, I had the opportunity, as a reporter, to be present at places where there was shooting. I looked for the big villains, for the insane theories, suspending moral judgment, which has been the rule of conduct of our exclusive intellectual family. We owe much to Nietzsche for this strict aesthetic view, though we can do without his romantic bluster. That was his weakness. The phrase "ultimate answer" appeared on every page of our textbooks. And just what is this ultimate answer, somebody asked Kobra. The cemetery, he said. In men who have seen the world I recognize a common contempt for humanity. With two words Kobra could finish people off. For him people were either fools or stool pigeons. I once went to see one of our classmates, who, like us, used to write poetry. His father distilled his own brandy—clandestinely, of course. The elderly gentleman kept it in small, labeled bottles, and had his son's more distinguished visitors taste his product, which he served in tiny shot glasses. When I rang the bell, there was no answer. I knew that the boy's parents were in the country. Looking through the window, I saw him hanging from a rope, by the neck. He was still alive; I cut him down. Later, when the police questioned him, he informed on me. He wasn't an informer, but played the role of one, enjoying the undivided attention the police gave to his performance. When I got out of jail, I told the story to Kobra. "You know what you should have done instead of cutting him down? You should have pulled at his ankles and put an end to his suffering." That's what the great humanist said, with a smile.

I would cry over my own poems. I would sit on the kitchen stool, warming my hands at the gas range, and read them over and over. Oh, God, how beautiful, and my tears would flow. And Kobra's reaction to them? A humph. Some he considered not bad, but only a very few would he qualify as really not bad. Ah, the sixties! I was no longer interested in the way people behaved in crowd scenes during revolutionary rituals. Emerging from jail, I cared only for the most mundane, banal aspects of life, I wanted only to seize the moment. In my mother's apartment the walls are lined with records of those days: I took pictures of courtyards of old tenement houses, complete with the wooden stands for beating carpets; pictures of the countless useless objects scattered in front of doors and in every corner; pictures of chess players in the park facing each other over a stone table; of a teacher guiding her charges across an intersection; of masons tugging their ropes and pulleys; of street cleaners resting on their enormous brooms and eating sandwiches. I photographed the people of Budapest as they rode the escalators of department stores or stood on railroad platforms. A father pushing his child on a swing. These are eternal moments, the fundamental elements of human life.

That was the time of reform; moderation had become the byword; the population was increasing; and the uncouth mini-capitalists, the socialist nouveau riche, made their appearance. Western products were still a rarity, objects of an absurd adoration. And in the arts, too, you could become an avant guru if you were the first to import some novelty that had long been passé in the West. My friends were mutually proclaiming one another geniuses. Murkiness became not only legal but fashionable, like historic murkiness—taking into account, of course, the dangers that lurked in the revealing beams of light. I decided that with my criminal record of '56 I had no chance of gaining a university position. As long as this form of government remained in power in Hungary, I could not devote myself to my favorite occupation: receiving money to speak to interested youngsters about the books I liked. I could publish only a small portion of my writing, the least interesting portion, and that not often. My manuscripts came back full of editorial cuts and pedagogical comments in the margins. After one of these rejections, I took to the hills of Buda and in a beautiful clearing lay on my back under the May sun. Then I turned over on my stomach and wept, as if somebody had beaten me. In that field I decided that I wouldn't let myself be beaten anymore. I was grateful to that editor for humiliating me. No more crawling into mouse holes. I would go to America; I would teach literature in English. In secondary school I had amused myself by translating Hungarian poems into English. I understood Shelley better than I did English tourists in Budapest. In three or four years I should be able to learn English well enough to write it, too. Not so much to write literature as to write about it. In the United States, among so many different immigrants, there had to be a place for a wandering scholar like me.

I was determined never to relinquish my liberation of January 18, 1945. On that day I had become János Dragomán, not some entry on a questionnaire. In 1945 you could leave the ghetto, be a person, claim a name of your own. For a while, at least—because soon we were again put into a collective. I don't like to be classified according to some pseudoscientific concept. And I don't classify others. I hate, or love, only individuals. The leaders of the nation were no more intelligent than the words they uttered. And their followers: like gravitating to like, the unremarkable to the unremarkable, each ac-

cording to his kind. I was suspect from the start: One of these un-
remarkables would look at me, and before I had a chance to open
my mouth, he would hate my guts. The new bosses were proud of
the few abstract ideas they had managed to learn and retain with
great effort. Once they mastered these ideas, they kept repeating
them. Repetition is the mother of knowledge. Although it was supposed to be a system that they hated, they hated me, who was not a
system. I shouldn't call them, they would call me. At the end of the
forties, when questionnaires again became important and the barriers
at the border were closed, I became an antisocial, cynical prisoner.

It was a curious feeling to enter the country from Vienna and
stand in the train's corridor on the way to Budapest. I shared my
compartment with a half-Hungarian, half-Serbian couple. Traveling
east, the landscape grows sparser. As you leave Vienna, a few
factories—with their lines and colors of modern architecture—still
remind you of international capitalism, but soon the buildings become
neglected, grayer, and blend more and more with the soil. In the
distance, a row of trees; then the wooden-framed watchtowers come
into view, telling you that here something different begins, something
distrustful and strict. In Állampuszta, on the state prison farm, sitting
in front of the barracks after work, we used to see the faces of the
young men in the glassed-in watchtowers: Who is more bored, he or
I? How many times in a century does a guard climb down from his
tower and, leaving his weapon behind, go for a walk in the woods?
The young men with the machine guns, their job was to fire on whoever
didn't stop. A man, just by running despite being warned, can turn
another man into a murderer. Can turn a whole country into a murderer. Large, brown, plowed fields; clumps of mistletoe among tree
branches; crows landing in formation. János feeds brown shreds of
tobacco into his cherrywood pipe; he sees only the widening
emptiness.

As the train rolls slowly into Hegyeshalom between the watchtowers, you notice things you'd never see at borders in the West.
Parallel barbed-wire fences with strips of raked sand between them.
The kind of meticulous care that should be applied to the maintenance
of a home. At the station, armed soldiers at fifty-foot intervals on

either side of the train. Why? We're not allowed to get off. A sinking feeling in my stomach. The guards, all in their twenties, are joking with one another as they pass by the cars; one knees another in the behind. That's encouraging. But why aren't they letting us get off? They board the last car and enter the corridor where I'm standing. Suddenly their faces become stiff, official. "Good day. Hungarian People's Republic passport control." They look entirely different now, puffed up with a sense of duty. One guard walks along the cars outside; he squats at each wheel, looks carefully to make sure there isn't an outlaw concealed somewhere in there. He doesn't skip a single wheel. Here comes another guard; his ears are red. He says: "Compartment check!" He gets down on his knees and looks lingeringly under the seats, as if somebody were holed up there, trying to sneak into Hungary. What mythology has given birth to this ritual? Who wrote this scene?

A young woman arrives—although wearing a gray uniform, she is still a woman—and asks us if we wish to exchange currency. A curious alliance of banking services and military might. She takes a little too long to enter everything in her ledger, but I don't complain; it is interesting how the uniform is sent to greet the hard currency from abroad. I ask her if there is a dining car on the train; I'd like to buy lunch with my new Hungarian money. Yes, there is, but I can use it only when the passport control and customs inspection are over. An hour, perhaps. They are taking their time getting here, to the end of the train. I realize that the woman is telling me not to leave my compartment. The train is moving. Here come the border guards again. They ask for my passport, only for mine. They ask for information not included in my passport or on the visa application form. They take my passport with them, for identification purposes; they have been instructed to do so.

The customs people arrive. The little commander, handsome, red-haired, looks like a city slicker; behind him, two waddling subordinates twirl their mustaches to show their authority. "Your passport, please," says the redhead. "They took it," I tell him. "They took it? Well, which is your luggage? Would you kindly open that suitcase?" In the whole compartment he is interested only in my belongings.

251

He pulls papers from among my clothes, handles foreign-language books, examines every letter, reaches into my shaving kit. "What are you looking for?" "We're only looking. He who seeks, you know, will find." He takes his time with each item. Feels the toothpaste, unzips pockets, puts his fingers into the cuffs of my spare trousers. He does all this with unvarying indifference, as if despite the thoroughness it was only a formality. They don't want to take anything from me, only to make me understand that from now on I will be watched. They know I'm Kobra's friend. Occasionally we talk on the telephone.

Those who left the country are free to come back. The officials are polite, but let you know that you have arrived in a place where the rules are stricter. The guards could reappear at any time and tell you to follow them. The customs official does not make me open my other bag; he salutes and moves on. I look out the window. On the platform, an unfamiliar passenger is carrying—rather, dragging—two heavy suitcases. Are there no luggage carts here? The passenger is followed by a young guard with a machine gun. In his incomprehensible language he tries to explain something to the guard, but the guard, unapproachable, looks over the man's head. Why doesn't he help the man? From the opposite direction a higher-ranking guard arrives, relieves the first guard, but makes no move to assist the passenger with the heavy suitcases. If worse comes to worse, they'll make me get off this train and put me on the next one out, sending me back to the West, and good riddance! This time I may have to drop the idea of a visit home.

The night before last, in Vienna, there was a reception given in honor of Professor Dragomán. I ate little, hardly drank. Discipline, restrained smiles, don't say too much but come up with something elusively appropriate. I behaved, in short, like a civilized man. But hot spells come in waves: Let me, Lord, do my vanishing act. I got into a taxi, got out somewhere, aimlessly wandered the empty streets of downtown Vienna, looking at store windows, Persian rugs, china dolls. I drank in several bars. In one bar, some blond young men tried to pick a fight with me. Right hook to the chin, toe of left shoe into the pit of the stomach—or should I turn tail, instead? The good old days, when, in the Rosemary Espresso Bar, Antal and I put our backs against the wall, and an obstinate bunch of drunks kept running into our fists. We laid out all five of them, paid for the damages, then sauntered over to the Savoy to see what was happening there. It was different, of course, when Antal was at your side. These blond kids outnumbered me, so I left. Back in my hotel, in bed, I snuggled into that bright orb of womblike peace in which I sometimes found refuge. Everywhere in Vienna arrows point toward Budapest. All over the city, roads offer to take the motorized traveler to the neighboring capital. So I decided to go on an excursion to the place where I not only was born but also survived, a place of much trouble, such as this possible expulsion now, despite the fact that I did obtain an entry visa. A bad joke.

"They certainly gave you a going over! Where I come from, they don't look so close!" says my fellow passenger in Hungarian. Until now he has been talking to his wife in Serbian. And here come the young guards again, headed straight for me. They are all smiles as one of them returns my passport. They wish me a pleasant journey. Relieved, I stuff brown shreds of tobacco into my cherrywood pipe. Maybe this border is trying to be European, though it hasn't quite made it yet. What was that young man trying to say with his wink? I walk into the dining car. The customs men and border guards are there, drinking something, maybe beer, maybe Coca-Cola. The rest of the people are in their first-class compartments, behind drawn curtains, asleep with limbs asprawl, flushed, like little boys. The waiter is amiable, cracking jokes, conspiratorial; he tells me the soup is slop but highly recommends the fried chicken. Wonderful. Yes, please, with cucumber salad and a bottle of Villányi Nagyburgundi. Calmly I look over at my former searchers, and they, with youthful respect, nod to me. They're back to normal again. We are past official procedures, we are inside the country now, the chattering uniformed young men and the strange foreign gentleman.

As the train approaches Budapest, the scenery becomes lukewarm brown and everything slows down. An empty country; fewer buildings than in the West. On the other hand, the eye can see farther: plowed fields and trees. The fried chicken was indeed not bad, if a little fatty; the wine makes me feel heavy. I look at a town, a new lane lined with uniform, nondescript houses, and wonder why the young couples chose to build their houses here of all places, and no doubt with considerable effort. They will have to wait a good many years before the freshly planted trees in their gardens will give shade and bear fruit. And I look at my native land, the soil, the mud, the dust from which we come and to which we return. Death is also part of nature; the earth has no objection to being fertilized. I look at the large, serious fields, the makeshift buildings, the piles of brick covered with plastic sheets, the acacias and poplars, all so familiar.

On the train I decide that I will not tease the natives. Rather, I will annoy them by behaving. I will find everything to my liking, take everything as it is. I look out the window: crows, pigeons, bare shrubbery, slivers of light in the sky, enduring indifference. In the valley of lamentations I will camp, maintaining a mild cheerfulness. But why do I expect so much from aluminum pipes, mistletoe among bare branches, machines, sheds, cement-carrying freight trains, a railroad bridge, red storage drums, yellow streetcars. The train crosses the Danube; floating cranes, basketball courts, socialist-realist housing projects, laundry drying on the balconies.

In the glass-roofed terminal of Budapest East a young man and woman fly toward each other with open arms. How can love give two faces such light? The average person here is grayer, more downcast, slower moving than his counterpart in the West. With my luggage in the trunk, I lean back in the seat of the taxi: "To the Hilton, please." For the next two days this is what I need: neutral internationalism, American-style. In the Hilton I will still be surrounded by the tactful West, the same reliable service you find anywhere in the world. I will ask for a room overlooking the Danube. I don't look out of the taxi, I even close my eyes; there will be plenty of opportunity to look later, from my hotel window, and on my first outing, when I start from the Castle and walk down the hill and continue on foot all the way to my mother's apartment on Klauzál Square. And from the windows of her apartment I will be able to look at the square for hours, just as I used to, long ago.

The hotel and all of Trinity Square are geared for tourism—but there are local peculiarities. The way the bellhops act indicates that the coming together of foreigners and natives is still awkward. You sense a certain strain, an uneasiness. The woman behind the desk asks for my passport and says she will return it to me tomorrow. I cannot help but make a rebellious little speech: "Dear lady, after a twenty-year hiatus I am returning to the bosom of my native land. Why emasculate me in the very first hour of my visit by depriving me of my American citizenship for a whole nerve-racking day? Why separate me from my passport? Here, you see, I have filled out the registration form for the police. You do have eyes, you are an educated, multilingual woman, you can verify that the information on the form is identical to that contained in the passport. In a proper hotel this would suffice. That my passport is not forged was verified at the border. There it was indeed taken from me, and a photocopy was made. They kept the pink visa form, so they know that I am here. Why do you need my passport until tomorrow? And why do you insist, dear lady, that this procedure is perfectly normal, when you know it isn't? It seems normal only here, and only to some higher-ups, but it isn't, and the proof is that I detect a certain disharmony between your words and your opinion. You are angry because you know that the procedure isn't normal and still you have to take the passport from me. You even expect me to cooperate with you in this little ritual, to behave as if there were nothing wrong in my dark-blue American passport's being in the hands of the police on my first day here. As if this were not a blow to my integrity as a citizen. As if this twisted normality in itself were not a scandal on the part of an abusive administrative authority, a scandal repeated every ten minutes and therefore a scandal parading as routine. For a whole day the guest's identity is rescinded. If he politely says nothing, he has passed the first lesson in being tamed. And you, madam, are at once a tamed public servant and an official tamer of visitors, although to me both your face and figure are quite pretty."

"Thank you for the lecture, Professor Dragomán. It's been truly comprehensive. I will let you have a nice corner room overlooking the Danube. From it, you can see the Mátyás Church and something of the old City Hall, too." I am satisfied with the room. I drop down on the bed. I love hotel rooms. I'll eat in the hotel's restaurants, drink coffee in the cafés, swim in the hotel's swimming pool, and in the sauna purge myself of all evil. I'll buy three or four newspapers in the lobby, drop in at the bar, rest my eyes on a shapely body. I'll have my own castle. Checkout day after tomorrow.

The first few days, I walked around mostly in the outlying districts of the city, with a certain amount of euphoria, just feasting my eyes. I felt a resurgence of the old sensory hunger that took hold of me upon my release from jail. I knocked on doors and asked perfect strangers to let me photograph them in their own home. I roamed, heard sounds of hammering everywhere; of sawing, building, installing, and assembling things. This was real labor, people working for themselves. Everyone was doing something for the family nest, something different, unique, having its own personality. You could tell that the people living here did not plan to leave soon. Time resides in the objects made at home, by those who stay at home. They invest love, themselves, in what they already possess.

But why was the city's air so full of dust, lead, and acid, making the light gray? The local conversation was enervating. Oh, yes, we need more independence and less central control, we need more democracy. The same tune that was sung twenty years ago. A lot about people trying to get scholarships to go abroad, the countries they hoped to go to; and of course the usual who was doing what behind whose back. Somebody tapped me on the shoulder: "People are no good, Jani." I also heard about the most likely successors at "the royal court," about which dukes of intellect had attached themselves to the train of which pretender to the throne, and who was invited to their vacation homes. Sometimes I had the feeling that even the television screen was winking at me.

People like to exchange bad news. In company, a really bad piece of news is a delicacy. Anyone predicting a catastrophe is sure to be listened to. Serious patriots burdened with public problems. Listening to what my friends were saying, I look at the books on the shelves, the flowers in the vase, the shoes under the table, my friends' children and grandchildren, the armchair facing the TV. There were good books in the bookstores; the service in the stores was bearable; public transportation was all right; fruits, vegetables, and meat still tasted better here than in the West. With a day's delay I could buy the *International Herald Tribune*. A good place to retire, many advantages here. I was pleased that the butcher, the stationery store, and the flower shop I used to know were still at their same locations. And the measured, serious, dignified way of speech was not without its charm.

Only a Good Bed

"A change of scenery won't help," I said to myself in San Francisco or in Hong Kong one early morning, awakened by a pain near my heart. I needed to make peace with my life. Perhaps I could draw new strength from the secret powers of my motherland. So I came here as a palimpsest on which anything could be written. What happened happened; the past was finished and done with. Done with, perhaps, but it didn't go away. During my first days here I was taken aback: Even my friends seemed to have adopted a paternal, authoritarian tone. The flat and unctuous voice of officialdom. Whereas the man who believes that he's finally found the truth puts his words on the table the way a drunken player slams down his royal flush. From this I concluded that telling the truth was still not a simple and common practice here, that it was still the privilege of only a condemned minority.

And David Kobra was still on the blacklist, still a suspicious shadow, though he had burrowed his way into the body of socialist Hungary—yes, he the distinguished socialist-realist democrat. I wondered, since he was not stupid, what compelled him to lead this public life; I didn't believe it was only weakness. But then, neither did I understand this force inside me arguing that I should move from a place of greater freedom back to one of less freedom. Was it only because it was here that I first fell under the spell of women and their mystifications?

257

I was expelled from secondary school not because I rebelled against authority but because I slept with the principal's wife, a peach-faced biology teacher. After finally graduating, in those busy days of Stalinism, I was relocated to the country along with my grandparents. Since my parents did not have to leave the city, I could have protested. But that might have jeopardized my parents, and I didn't want to drag them down with me, and also I didn't want to desert my grandparents, so I made no fuss. The footloose city boy ambled along country lanes, chewing on a stalk of wheat. Later, I was ordered to join a forced-labor battalion. The soldiers in charge there, just for the fun of it, beat me several times. Not amused, I waylaid one soldier in a path in a cornfield and returned the favor. I told him that if the soldiers didn't stop beating us, we would rip their throats out with our teeth, and to demonstrate I lifted him up and took his throat between my teeth. Forced labor had given me muscle. I expected to be arrested, but wasn't.

After my discharge I worked as a hod carrier and then as a reader of water meters. Still later, I played the piano at the Purple Cat, was a consumer of poppy extracts. I was the most depraved existentialist. In '55, I called myself a socialist-dadaist and wrote a lot of poetry, usually at dawn and on the kitchen table. Living in the maid's room of my parents' apartment and not wanting to disturb them with noises of love, I nailed a mattress to the door. My bicycle I kept on top of the wardrobe. I wrote an essay entitled "Two Poles of Aesthetics: Kitsch and Blasphemy." In Jewish mysticism, I was interested in the concept of redemption through sin. At the state prison farm I had occupied my mind with logical structures, but now, after my confinement, I surrendered myself to the magic of reality's illusion. The simplest things—going to the movies with a girl, then a long walk, followed by a drink somewhere—were enthralling. For eleven years after my release, driven by this hunger and sensuality, I carried on an illicit affair with Budapest. But in 1966 I tired of this.

When I left in 1966, I was thirty-three. "I can't get in tune with the music of scholarship here," I said to myself. I needed a cooler, more caustic, and more internationally oriented approach to literary analysis. For this attitude I was labeled a cynic. Later, the same was said of me in New York. But in New York, being a cynic did not prevent you from being a college professor. At the time, I thought that a man ought to address himself only to the great problems of the world. But how could I talk about the world if I hadn't seen it? My dear Central European guardians of kitsch, do you remember Pilinszky's toothy, silvery laughter? He once said at our table (where I modestly hid myself behind László Nagy, Miklós Erdély, and Béla Kondor) that the only problems worth thinking about were the ones that were insoluble. For the solution of soluble problems you had the professional experts. Sometimes Tamás Lipták, the mathematician, would drop in on us. "Give me any problem," he said, "and I'll write an equation for it." Erdély thought that Lipták could conjure the red wine out of the bottle with his equations.

We talked a lot about the differences between inner and outer freedom. Kobra maintained that even in the most confined circumstances inner freedom was possible. The thinking man could carry on because there was always freedom of thought. I replied that a carefully fenced-off inner freedom would become something rather parochial. I did not believe in novels "written for the desk drawer." And I did not want to remain, for the rest of my life, a schoolboy ordered to stand in the corner when he was bad. The feeling of being locked up, a very physical feeling, sometimes made me throw violent tantrums, and other times made me depressed and silent. But many people do not mind being locked up. By the sixties, the average Hungarian citizen had become used to, and accepted as natural, that form of public celebration where the presidium, sitting at the table on the dais, did the talking and the audience politely did the applauding. No walking about, no noise, no disorderliness. The citizens neglect their city, their houses, their bodies; they have no respect for one another, for their work or their time, not even for themselves. They ask to be allowed to go abroad as schoolchildren ask to go to the toilet. Am I throwing myself on the mercy of public officials by having my permanent address in Budapest? This is my hometown— but there are other cities in the world.

Even when I left, I sensed that nationalism was gaining ground in this country. I am no nationalist. I find national characteristics interesting, much as I do differences between individuals, but nationalisms are not, because they are all alike. I have seen national socialisms, national communisms, and national capitalisms; each has a strong leader, only one political party, and in all of them opposing views are punished. Nationalist rhetoric everywhere undermines civil liberties. National truths have difficulty crossing linguistic borders. Creative centers, on the other hand, are more likely to develop in large cities where people come from all over the world, and where a few like-minded, talented people find one another. I like the technical and intellectual networks of the globe, the possibility that with the right passport and credit cards you can go anywhere. I don't want to spend the rest of my life fuming over the insolence of local authorities.

I began as an essayist. It doesn't matter if the subject is a masterpiece or a mouse. The mind swings between the palpable and the abstract. But with things the way they were in Budapest, I could not indulge in this impudent and witty genre of literature. You may write, but only in allusions and generalizations; nothing for irony to sink its teeth into. I killed time by having fun, by eating a lot and talking a lot. I didn't read, I only flipped through books. I preferred company to serious thinking; I liked being the center of attention. I became a Budapest personality, was afraid of drinking too much, of growing fat and diabetic.

When I was a child, people spoke about Our Father, Horthy; the older people said, Our Father, Franz Joseph. And then came Our Father, Rákosi. He was followed by Kádár, to whom, in rural areas, I heard people refer as Our Father, Kádár. That's when I left. It seems that people here, even when grown up, need a father to tell them what to do. I said to myself: "You are like the peasant who all his life complains about the lack of electricity. Well, move to a place that has electricity."

It was with a forged Yugoslav passport that I left my country. Pooling all my funds, that was all I could afford, not a passport to the West. I received my doctorate at Columbia University in 1969. In 1971 my first volume of essays was published, and in 1973 I became an instructor at New York University. I visited other parts of the country, but returned, for a higher salary, to NYU. I teach fairly good students fairly well. I have been successful enough not to hold grudges.

The streets of New York City are full of graceful, beautiful people and full of freaks. There is no nation on earth that does not have a sizable representation in this city. You don't need to budge; people will tell you what's going on back in the old country. In one bar you can tour the world. No matter how many times I take a taxi from the airport, I become ecstatic when I see the skyline of Manhattan. Nothing stands between me and others except my own limitations and theirs; no outside power of any sort is involved; nothing is dictated from above; the only restrictions are your home-grown stupidities. Common people have come from all over the world and done what they could not do back home. Each has fled a terrifying authority and come to huddle where he has nothing to fear but his fellows. The local crime, seen in that light, is tolerable.

When I go to Europe directly from New York, everything seems more sedate and ceremonious; prestige is more prestigious. In Western Europe, people dress elegantly; in New York they are informal, outrageous. New York is sensual, cheap, and down-to-earth. It's also shoddier. During my first years, having little money, I bought my clothes in secondhand shops while dreaming of new, clean, high-quality European outfits. But my favorite jacket I found displayed on the sidewalk. I tried it on: a perfect fit. I think I paid ten dollars for it.

You should not expose your private life to your students, whose primary goal is to get good grades, which will help them get good jobs. Sometimes it is the good students I dislike. They are like parakeets, eagerly regurgitating today what they hastily swallowed yesterday. But chewing your cud is also a way to digestion. They are much more human when they stop chattering. My students would be especially interested in the time of your student days, David, and in the novels you grew up on. Could you stand a little mutual analyzing, friends, as we take one another apart? Let us put Kobra on the dissecting table, although he is still eating and talking. Step out of your skin, as if it were a pair of pants. Our seminar appreciates a person under examination who does not become riled. It must be clearly understood that we spare no one. Nervous, you defer your plans, you make yourself inconspicuous, you reduce your dependence on material conditions to an absolute minimum. Faced with this state of affairs, my students begin to waver; they don't know what to think.

What else do you do in the Wild West but drown your sorrow in shopping? You pamper yourself, you call yourself pet names—overgrown baby that you are—and pump yourself full of desires that can be satisfied in shopping centers or finer and smaller establishments. You buy a heady after-shave, a soft cashmere sweater, a laser printer; there are lots of things to make a mortal happy. While I had my house, I bought all sorts of merchandise I didn't need. It's no great credit to our species that we celebrate by eating and drinking, filling our orifices with things or with each other. Clumsy, futile longings. "If most people are poor, why shouldn't I be poor?" Kobra once said to me while we were still in secondary school. Now, that's a rather strange form of perfectionism. Where every resignation is a victory. Suddenly you realize that what you needed yesterday, you don't need today. I, fallible János Dragomán, have not reached this stage. I'm so far from it, in fact, that I don't even believe in it. I grow anxious when I cannot acquire something I want to wear or put into my mouth. For me, the city is one long row of shop windows, and I want all kinds of consumer goods and people to offer themselves to me.

Human contact in the middle class in the West may be superficial, but with how many of my fellow creatures would I want to be on more intimate terms? That is why we hide in our country house or behind our answering machine. Isn't it preferable for conversations to be superficial? And why shouldn't we be clean and well dressed? What can be beautiful, after all, if not appearances? I like company and repartee, conventions and seminar discussions, press conferences and public debates; I like living speech. Shows, ceremonies, spectacles. I like to incite people against one another, to make sparks fly, to make something happen. Let each have his solo, as in a jazz band, where one musician stands up, comes downstage, and takes over, but the rest gather around him supportively. Here at home, I have my best times at big parties, in the small hours, when the bottles are empty, the ashtrays are full, and my arms ache from playing the piano. I can't go to bed before five in the morning. When you people, with whom I'd love to talk, are sleeping the sweet sleep of the just.

But I don't want to sleep, I want to be where people are; in nightclubs, where they all imagine themselves to be wilder and more mysterious than they are the next day at the office. The more artificially they act, the more interesting they are. The overriding instinct of man is to have a good time. The moment I'm not hungry, I want to be entertained. "And the crimes committed by the state, you don't find them entertaining?" says Kobra. My answer, dear maestro, is that for the last twenty years I've had about as much fun with that particular subject as I'd ever want to have. Unlike you people, who are so deeply rooted in the home soil, I have grown a set of floating roots, roots that dangle in the air over unknown landscapes. The wandering Jew celebrates exodus, not the conquest of his homeland.

I have no absolute principles to pit against the world; instead, I try to feel out, in my writing, what it is I like and dislike. Since Gutenberg, this form of private meditation has had a chance to become public. Most people are immature, and the leaders of the world are generally no more mature than the man in the street. But, luckily for the human race, when the ship is about to crash into the iceberg, a few more mature individuals appear. As for me, I make very little difference. All I've done is give the initial impetus to an idea or two. I am a peculiar bird, outside religious and political affiliation, living in a liberal academic community that can boast of a certain sense of humor. But my basic medium of communication is not the classroom; it is the printed word. Too bad that my dragomania is stronger than my graphomania. My verbal brilliance outshines my writing. I walk half the length of Manhattan Island, down to Battery Park, and rest my elbows on the railing above the water, under fluttering helicopters.

It was from my father, Döme Dragomán, that I learned to sing in different languages and to play the piano, and to make a living anywhere in the world. During my first years in New York I played in the bar of the Gramercy Park Hotel. And my mother, after my father's death, played the piano in the espresso-bars of Budapest. Her hair dyed, her scarecrow face heavily made up, and with eyes goggling, she would tease and call by pet names the young men around her. And she would pass them the drinks other customers had bought for her, the ageless Fani. My father died a year after I left. Fani and Döme were a great couple. My father would be seen in his bathrobe chasing my mother in Dob Street with a fur coat under his arm, because she had run out of the house in her nightgown and he was afraid she would catch a cold.

Usually I eat lunch at the Pipa, where the waitress is a wild, hefty wench who regales me with stories about orchids stuck in her womb. The boss is a second cousin of mine who flunked Chateaubriand in catering school, but then not only passed with his beef Stroganoff and stuffed cabbage à la Cluj, but received the board's honorable mention as well. He's a good cook, but I don't like it when he chases that wild amazon, in his fits of jealousy, with a cleaver. I have my beer and am now just looking around, waiting for my soup. On the whole, I approve of everything here in Budapest: the way people eat, the way they court one another, the way they fight. The best people come together to exchange insults, to find scapegoats. They are angry because they haven't got what's coming to them. "So what have you done these last twenty years?" I ask a former colleague of mine. "I've been disgusted" is his answer. My acquaintances all seem shriveled and squeezed dry; they are fussy and tiresome. Minds destined for higher things waste their best years analyzing a mistake.

Sometimes I meet Kobra at the Pipa. We eat, then go for a walk. Of course he was up at five, had a bath and a walk, did the shopping, brought home fresh milk and crescents, prepared the cocoa and poured it into Zsiga's cup and Döme's bottle. With his beautiful young spouse he had his morning chat over tea. At eight, Kobra looks at the school across the street. The pupils are in their seats, just as he is at his desk. He is neither sleepy nor depressed. He rings the bell for inspiration, and it, like the teacher now entering the classroom, appears with a slight bow. That is not my scene. I don't know how I put up with this pedestrian, dogged Kobra. I think I'll torture him a bit.

My poor friend, haven't you noticed that out in the big world positivism has become the latest fashion? The bitterness of the left is passé! Gardening and gastronomy, horror movies and videos, these are the in things today. Haven't you noticed that it's old hat now to air our dissenting views? You are now a conservative. Humanism? Autonomy? Professor Kobra still puts such words on paper. And people don't even laugh at him; they are kind to him, as to a provincial parish priest. Behold the cheerful product of a proper childhood and underground integrity. Well, my stylite and provincial blockhead, may I pour for you? No more nocturnal carousing for the master. He and his charming spouse keep a close tab on each other's daily schedules. But, you know, you could drop a few pounds if you came along with me to the Carpathian Mountains to check out the bears. Lord, please do not let each day begin and end the same way. (I realize that this is not what you people pray for.)

Young men and women come to me and tell me that they'd like to leave Hungary for good. Coldly, I advise them not to leave. They look at me strangely. A young woman arrives with her husband. Their apartment is too small, the money they make is too little, the child is noisy, they both drink; where could they get a scholarship and a nonroutine job abroad? They are fed up with the restrictions here, they are looking for excitement, freedom. I should give them addresses, advice, money, help. I do this, but then I'm embarrassed and confused. What are they getting themselves into? They don't really want to work hard, they don't really speak any foreign language—and they are not willing to make any allowances for their homeland. There is nothing you can do in this country. Abroad, they will all be famous artists, scholars, renowned thinkers, sought-after directors, charismatic stars, and not the gray little nobodies that they are here. But what if the West does not greet them with open arms, what if it is unfriendly and indifferent? Impossible. There must be a place where all you need to do to succeed is show up.

Hungarians abroad. The farther you are from your country, the smaller it appears to you. I'm having some people over to my apartment in America. A Hungarian acquaintance phones; he's just arrived. I invite him over, too. He explains to my guests that his loyalties are not with the government but with the opposition. However, the opposition he belongs to is not just the opposition; it is a very special variety of the opposition. To his American listeners this explanation means very little. In their eyes a Hungarian is a Hungarian. With a great hunger we sally forth into the wide world, and return to hide. Coming back, I was surprised to find that everything was normal size. The suburb was a real suburb, bread was real bread. In a blue enchanted evening I rode a yellow streetcar. All one really needs is a comfortable bed.

Laura

Twenty years ago, as János Dragomán swam from Kopar to Trieste, from Yugoslavia to Italy, from the East to the West, Laura sat on the shore and watched her husband going farther and farther away. She picked up a handful of sand and let it sift through her fingers, as in an hourglass. János had to cover seven kilometers in the sea, which despite perfectly clear skies was very choppy. Laura followed his receding head until it was the size of a cherry pit. Near the first hotel on the Trieste beach, three ancient stone walls with arched gateways run into the water. Laura saw the cherry pit reach the first arch, then pass under the second, but at the third the pit turned to the right. And János, beyond the third wall, felt hidden from Laura. The hotel's swimming instructor led János to his room, then went out to give a scheduled water-skiing lesson. The fugitive took off his wet pants and crawled into the instructor's bed. Later, János promised the instructor his camera and Omega wristwatch if the man drove over to the hotel in Kopar and asked Laura for her husband's clothes and papers.

After his swim to Trieste, János turned himself in to the Italian police. He was put into a camp, where he was bored. Every day young well-to-do women came by in their cars and called to the more attractive men. "No, not you, the one over there, the tall one with the long hair!" János wouldn't go near the fence. Then one day he did. Shyly, awkwardly, a woman said to him in French: "*Monsieur, je voudrais le plaisir de votre connaissance.*" János nodded. She went to the camp headquarters and signed an affidavit, assuming responsibility for the refugee's welfare and expenses until his status was settled. She gave her permanent address in Parma; she was staying in Trieste only temporarily, at the Hotel Stendhal. Her name was Gwendolyn, she was British, a leftist, and weighed one hundred seventy-six pounds. Her hands were large, and so were her feet; she was awkward and eccentric. She got János out of the camp and kept him well. She was bashful and believed herself to be unimaginative in bed. With János, she claimed, she experienced for the first time those feelings that she had only read about in books.

Each morning he walked around the frighteningly high castle of Parma, loafed in the marketplace, sat in a café, had grappa with his coffee, and wrote homesick letters to Laura. A letter every day. In a few months the bonded servant grew accustomed to his situation. With Gwendolyn he traveled from city to city; the Italian autumn was beautiful. Her body was slightly clammy and had a bad odor. She was a free-lance journalist, a film producer, and a feminist with a sense of self-irony. Lots of sweaters, flat shoes, powerful thighs, breasts not too large, angular shoulders, bundles of muscles. A woman of firm opinions and suppressed thoughts. Gwendolyn would break off in the middle of a sentence for fear of uttering a platitude. Of course, János cheated on her; he had brief, chance adventures. He would coax more pocket money out of her and spend it on whores. She often slipped him money in advance so he could pay the bills in restaurants and bars. He taught her the word *strici*, which means both pimp and gigolo. Gwendolyn would yell after him on the street: "*Strici!*" Hungarian tourists would turn around to look.

She worked on his horoscope. "Women will pave your way. Whatever your future holds, good or bad, you will go from one woman to the next. You are a gigolo by temperament. Have you ever been with a woman for money?" Yes, János had been. In his university days he serviced opera singers. He would hang around the dressing rooms of opulent coloraturas and dramatic contraltos, who availed themselves of him so that afterward their voices would ring richer and brighter. The abdominal cavities, when excited and then relaxed, proved to be more resilient resonators. That is how János acquired his camel's-hair winter coat, silk scarf, and sizable library, and was able to afford capricious side trips to small towns. He wore soft jackets, fine shirts, loosely knit sweaters, and at home liked to sit around in costume, in a hussar's pelisse or in a redingote. Clothes were more mood-evoking on him than on other people.

In the Paris apartment Gwendolyn rented, he continued to play the rascal and frighten others; he had had his share of fear at home and understood that he could get further by misbehaving than by behaving. "Dear Gwendolyn, how much you must suffer from me, this poor ham from Budapest!" His new acquaintances were weaklings, so he played the tough East European who will tour the West next time on top of a tank. He would get off the steel monster and, while the looting and general mayhem were going on, plop himself down in front of a TV in some children's room and watch, one after the other, every episode of the "Adventures of Lucky Luke." When the pillaging was over, he'd get up, salute, and rattle off in his tank. He also had a scenario about being an East European male prostitute sent here on a spy mission, an expert in the arts of karate and knife throwing. And indeed once, at a country inn, dealing with a repugnant character, János threw a number of serrated cheese knives into the wooden wall around his victim's head. Gwendolyn had a hard time explaining the origin of this Hungarian folk custom to the offended party.

János often phoned Kobra, and also wrote lengthy letters, in which he bragged about his bright tomorrows. But he heeded Kobra's stubbornly repeated advice to obtain a Ph.D. And a job. As an adjunct lecturer and then as a tenured faculty member, János could afford to do many things, such as teaching only in the fall semester, spending the rest of the academic year flying here, flying there, free as a bird. An exceptionally large number of pretty girls attended his classes. They expected to be entertained. He obliged them by acting out the style of people in different major cities of Europe. He told them stories about Venice and Ragusa, Granada and Amsterdam, Novgorod and Vilnius; nor did he neglect to describe the sleepy events on Klauzál Square.

Laura was back in her studio in Budapest when one day, suddenly, her entire field of vision was flooded with a milk-white cloud. She could not see anything at all. "You took the light of my eyes with you," she told János on the phone. But the doctor said it was inflammation of the optic nerve caused by some Vietnamese virus, no less curious an explanation than Laura's. "At least I won't see the aging of my body." Just as suddenly as it had come, Laura's vision returned. As for her body, which tanned so easily and which she rubbed with a variety of creams and lotions, it showed very little aging. She was still in her springtime.

When her vision returned, she bought a roll of paper, fed it into the typewriter, and began an endless letter to János. She knew the bastard was unfaithful to her just as surely as he breathed. A skirt chaser whose day was disaster if he failed to pick up a new woman. Who needed to be liked over and over again. Who worked to reach the point where his partner loosened up and her reluctance turned into clinging, but then the double bed became too narrow for him, and he longed to go for a walk alone in the dawn streets of Paris, when the butcher scrubs his block with a carving knife and one can sit in a café and order coffee and a buttered croissant. With the first light of day, János is wide awake and wanting to be out of his confinement.

Laura did not know that Gwendolyn was wise to this game and therefore was always careful to rent three-room apartments. Late at night Gwendolyn would leave the common bedroom to sleep apart, letting János wake up alone. Working during the day, she was at his disposal only after six. By then, words had accumulated inside him, and it was good to start chatting over a glass of cool white wine while sitting under a wild chestnut tree in that little garden in the Twentieth Arrondissement that used to be the courtyard of a former carriage repair shop. János loved looking at the blue sky through green foliage, lounging in a deck chair, having on the table beside him a bowl of fruit salad, an ice bucket with white wine, and one of his favorite pipes. If he had all his props, if his discourse was appreciated by the woman journalist who wanted to write a book about him, then the evening could begin.

269

In the early sixties, János and Laura were regulars here at the Tango. An elderly lady, probably an English teacher, liked to sit at the table next to theirs and eavesdrop. Laura, with her large mouth and deep voice, had a wonderful whisper. János also liked the fact that her breath was always fresh as a baby's, even after waking up. Her teeth were healthy, her pink gums, too, and she had a hard, meaty, tireless whip of a tongue that elaborately licked everything it came in contact with. Sometimes he felt jealous of the food as he watched Laura's tongue tap and surround each bite. While she ate, she smiled, a personal, wicked smile, as if she were making love with someone else right in front of his nose. "Spit it out!" he would say angrily. But she usually finished everything on her plate, to the last crumb.

Seven years went by. Then, in 1974, Laura followed János to America. In the second half of the seventies, her health deteriorated: alarming symptoms of multiple sclerosis, gradual paralysis, a motorized wheelchair, increasing helplessness, accusations. Although he saw to her every need, she grew more and more suspicious. They lived in Princeton; he would hurry home to her from Manhattan. He fed her, bathed her, entertained her, and whenever he left the house he jotted down the telephone numbers where he could be reached. Her calls preceded and followed him. The house was full of photographs and notes, which she cataloged and recataloged. Until everything burned down. All that he could rescue was his wife in her wheelchair.

He has a small round leather bag, which he never opens. It contains Laura's urn, one of her silk blouses, and a few pictures that he took when they lived in the twelfth-floor corner apartment at 172 East Fourth Street in New York. This was after the fire. From the twelfth floor, Laura could take the elevator up to the roof. Above her head, white seagulls were blown by the wind. She inhaled the barrel-like odor of the water tank, and rode up and down on the green outdoor carpet, as if running around in a meadow after the rain, except in a wheelchair, honking her horn.

Actually, Laura—inside the urn, inside the bag—could be buried now, here in Hungary. But she had asked János to take her ashes with him everywhere he went. Was she serious or only joking? He took her seriously. He has her urn, a tiny, hidden shrine, in a box lined with red velvet. He wonders: Should I bury her beside her father? Or, instead, take her to the Serbian cemetery in Ófalu, where she spent many long summers and said it was a happy place? There are beautiful headstones in the Serbian cemetery. From there, the entire valley and the lake can be seen. Three small church steeples, lots of blackberry, dogwood, and sloe bushes, and the quarry-stone remnants of a house. It must be wonderful to be buried in that windswept place. I would like to sit on that dilapidated stone bench. The dead sometimes stroll from their chambers and give garden parties. Shadows, too, need social life, Laura had said.

Our traveler is now on a diet; he consumes neither meat nor women. A silvery question mark appeared before him in the form of a long-legged Japanese model in a gallery on Spring Street. A sense of liberating joy coursed through him as he walked past her even though she was very attractive. I won't be the one to undo the long row of buttons on her back. The visitor is content with the Tango: the continuous hum, the swarm of bodies. He remembers the insane pursuit of a quarter century ago, here in the Tango and all over town, when he was released from jail. Every night a different woman. He remembers how, like a tomcat, he would accompany mothers on their way to fetch their children at school. He would wait for them, walk with them to their house, and the following morning he would be there again, waiting. And not in vain, either. He would walk with women on their way to work, strike up a conversation, say that he would be waiting that evening at such-and-such corner. Some he addressed immediately; with others he was more hesitant. He might follow a woman upstairs, almost to the door of her apartment, debating whether or not he really wanted this one, who carried a shopping bag full of food for her family's supper. Would it be worth the uncertainties and fear involved? But in front of the locked door he always made a date, and the following day the two of them would walk together and climb the stairs of some attic or crawl into some cave. The oddity of the place was part of the adventure.

In János's album there were also skinny violin students in knit

271

caps, lugging their violin cases and marveling at everything with the eagerness of virgins. And there were buxom section heads of the civil service, who stepped out of state-owned limousines, and after love-making they would clarify every obscure political question for him. Many partners would not have minded repeating the experience, but János was bound by his vow: never twice with the same woman. In promiscuity he discovered universal human love, and was ready to lie down in any bed.

In the house in Princeton, Laura was having a heroic dream; she was helping to put out a fire. With her powerful legs she ran up the stairs and climbed out onto the roof. She scooped up a baby and lowered herself to the eaves. Smoke billowed all around, and the baby squealed, choked, and laughed at the same time. With the baby in her arms, she let go of the roof and began to float above the fire. Both she and János were awakened by their own coughing. The ceiling was in flames.

In the East Village, Laura was fed up. She couldn't stand the mice, the cockroaches, and the scavenger birds that flapped at her windows. On Sundays, the Chinese family next door treated them-selves to a holiday feast of putrid shark, and the odor that crept in through the cracks in the door was unbearable. From the schoolyard next door Puerto Rican kids came up on the fire escape and peeped into her room. She'd lie on the couch, switching television channels, bored with all of them. She wasn't interested in the commercials, either, since she didn't go shopping. And she hated the detailed, dramatic weather reports with their handsome, pointer-wielding meteorologists.

She said to him: "It's time to get a divorce. Separate yourself from me and the past, get free of it all. Forget about academic success—you're no college professor. The toga looks good on you only because all costumes suit you. You'd look smart in a caftan, hussar's pelisse, or kimono. Find yourself another profession, do something else. As for me, you know I don't scoop out the bottom of jam jars. Some like the last part best, but I'm too proud for that." On the surface of her small pocket mirror, using a razor blade, she lined up white grains into neat columns, and through an ivory cigarette holder sniffed up the small columns, one after the other, into her nostrils.

She also couldn't stand the old woman who came in to ask if they wanted to buy some furniture because she was a little short of cash. The old woman used to cart home the furniture she found on the sidewalks in rich neighborhoods, but nowadays she was afraid to go out on the street. She had been mugged, knocked down in the snow and her bag taken, a nice snakeskin bag she had inherited from her older sister. Laura could not bear this woman with her junk and her memories. "I hate junk. I am a piece of junk myself, broken down and beyond repair. You feed me, take me to the toilet, and keep me, and kiss me, out of pity. And I sit here listening to the mice, to the scream of the fire engines, and watch dark columns of smoke rise from the distant stacks of the power station. My sweet, I release you. You don't have to listen to me anymore."

Laura, black bird, smaller than a crow, longer than a raven, glides from the forest with low winnows of her wings. Black T-shirt, black skirt and blouse, black tights. She is mourning herself in advance, knowing that János does not have what it takes to mourn.

During her last week, she spoke of her aunt Lenke from Balatonszemes. About this time of day, in the early afternoon, having finished with the dishes, Aunt Lenke usually sat on the veranda knitting and listening to the radio. Laura did not get back to Balatonszemes; she made it only as far as the window. Shattering the glass with an ashtray, she drew her wrist across the sharp edges and had bled to death by the time János returned from his walk. She was all white in her wheelchair, her head slumped to the side and a large pool of blood under her left hand. Finally she had risen from this disobedient body that had made her suffer so much humiliation.

For many an evening afterward, János got drunk and had fights with Laura. He writhed like a fish on a white marble counter, leaping, slipping in the blood of other fish, knowing that the cleaver would fall any minute on the back of his skull. He would be gutted and quartered while still alive.

273

Work Diary

Dear Melinda, I really don't understand your husband. Has Antal lost his mind? He lives for his hobbies, in Ófalu and on five continents, so why can't he tolerate a tactful friend of the family like me around his stay-at-home wife? But no, he won't have it. Suddenly he's had enough of me, wants me to disappear, or else he'll kill me. The children have moved in with him and they choose him over the intruder. And you follow the children. I guess it's time for me to go. I can't say that this has been a successful experiment. Good Lord, leaving again. And the idea of death is as bitter as ever. One buries one's friends with swinish suddenness. Here in the Erzsébetváros section of town, a bitter sorrow is taking possession of me. I'm tired of commiserating. The gallows humor of unrealized people irritates, no longer entertains. In two minutes I become a clipped-wing bird. I have nothing to do with brave ideals and daring visions. I am suspicious of those few who are doing something decent. With my fainthearted philosophy of resignation I do myself more harm than others can ever do to me.

Besides Jeremiah's papers I am swamped by notes and diaries of my own, dating from the years before my defection. The shelves are full of files. Some people are haunted by the past; others happily forget everything, and nobody reminds them. But for me, forgetting is betrayal. In my house in Princeton, too, I collected documents of the past; I lined my room with them. And there were old Persian rugs and classical novels from my mother. My room became like a guilty conscience. And then it all burned up.

And now Melinda speaks. I always stuck by my husband, was interested in what he had to say, and he understood what I said to him. Not that we talked much. We discussed mostly practical things. In the evening, left to ourselves, we went down to Leander Street and made the rounds. I chose to live with Antal because he wanted me the most, and at his side I've been able to be myself. His success, too, has an erotic appeal. And it hasn't corrupted him. Antal, a reformed Calvinist, does his duty; the success is secondary. Duty is clear, well defined; success is ambiguous, more a temptation than a reward. This cuckolded husband of mine is the kind of man people sit next to in waiting rooms, parks, and restaurants. Wherever I look into the space that my past has become, I see Antal. Adjusting to him has not been difficult. We invite each other to our respective rooms, we knock politely on each other's doors; we protect the tranquillity of our private dawdling. I don't want to choose between them, to leave either one of them. I'd like to have them both around, not necessarily here in Leander Street, but within a range I can cover by car. I like to live with men the way I lived with my father. In brown-covered spiral notebooks, I track the layers of my father's conscience. I also follow its disintegration, complete with forgetfulness and repetitions, a process similar to a city slowly falling into ruin. But in the old man's mind new constructions were always under way, one section of the city would shine again, another would be born.

János has the floor again. With your permission I'll take another deep pull. That's the order of things in the cafés in Casablanca: first the coffee and kef on a small tray at the center of the table. In clay pipes, men pull deeply on the kef. They grow calm, sip their coffee, and only then turn cautiously to the true topic of the conversation. My means of flying is the glider; Odysseus and Don Juan are my kinsmen, and my emblem is the random walk, which is the English name of a Hungarian mathematician's theory.

The fire, by obliterating my possessions and all traces of my existence, told me that we were put on this earth not to work but to find the best way of killing time. I decided to squander the insurance money, to go on a spending spree—but that was so conventional. Then I became sentimental, altruistic. To the point where I considered a life devoted to starving children in some famine-stricken land. The idea got its hooks into me. But I also wanted to indulge my incorrigible selfishness—so I would start my humanitarian work after a brief respite in Hungary. In Budapest, I have managed to blow the hundred thousand dollars I got from the insurance people. What? I should have invested this piddling amount sensibly? But all my sensible enterprises had gone up in smoke.

For a while I considered putting together an illustrated walking tour of Budapest for Western tourists. Then I thought better of it. Why should I? So tourists could follow me around in droves? So I would have no rest here, either? I'd written hedonist guides before, secret offerings to brothels of various cities. Believe me, I know the score.

You, Melinda, if my arithmetic is correct, were conceived in 1948, the year of the forcible introduction of Communism. You are almost the product of this regime. You are growing old with it. In the so-called terrible fifties, you played in the garden of Ófalu; your father worked as a forester; you had enough to eat. Ever since you started watching TV, you've seen Kádár on the screen. You, a true daughter of the Kádár era, are one of the foci of my home ellipse; David Kobra is the other. Two foci, independent of each other. Luckily, you haven't slept with each other. Kobra, of course—what else would you expect?—keeps boring me with his plans to enlarge the house in Ófalu. There is a guest room, both in his house and in yours, at my disposal. You both do what you can to make the room remind me of my childhood. Alarming empathy! The woman of my soul, like a good wife, keeps an eye on my schedule. To make every day begin and end the same way?

I fill up the tank of my car; I'm moving on, this reporter is off to Eritrea or Bangladesh, in pursuit of sensational scoops. I don't care who's going to be the new member of the party's political council; I am more interested in the ways people can be helped in times of hunger and flood. Here, you have too much pork and too many selfish, overweight people interested neither in truth nor in God. It's no different here from the civilized and free West. Few of us can die nobly—maybe only the Chinese. But I am not Chinese.

I allow myself to overshoot the mark. It's a weakness that I am in love with my woman; my mission takes me back to the Wailing Wall. I stick no rolled-up wishes into the cracks of the stones; I don't bow and scrape. I put my palms on the wall and support it for a long time. I let myself be parched by the sun. Everything there has a validity, denseness, and sharp shadow. Then I return to East Europe to acquire a dose of stubborn influenza. I feel the urge to come here, the gravitation of the mind to the spectacles of genesis.

So spoke János Dragomán. My mind wandered, and there he was, my beloved, sitting before me, and suddenly he began to phosphoresce, to turn into a character in my novel. I see infinite rows of mirrors, but every reflection is different. What is at the center of a man? A mystical orb of light, or only the inexhaustibility of repetition?

After breakfast, under the shower, I asked him what he thought of my figure. I won't repeat what he said. It wasn't nice. I sent him up to my father's room, wanting to go for a walk by myself. I'll go down the hill to do the shopping, my black satchel over my shoulder. Snowy gardens, one- and two-story villas, a flock of crows at the corner. Inches of snow on the new Ping-Pong table in the playground. Along the top of a swept-off stone wall a black Hungarian shepherd follows me silently. We know each other. I talk to him; he agrees with me.

At the turn of the millennium I'll be fifty-one; my son, István, twenty-six; my daughter, Ninon, twenty-three. For some reason I think it will be exciting to be young in Budapest in the year 2000. When my children were born, I tended to think of them as messages. Every child, of course, drops straight from heaven; each is a book that the parents try to decipher. Until they get tired of trying.

A lot of things have happened in the last few months. Visits by filmmaker colleagues of Antal, and by Kobra's fellow writers from all over the world. The calendar has been full. Regina and I did a lot of cooking. The men have been drinking and smoking more than usual and sleeping less. Conversations in several languages; these gatherings mentioned in the world press; much futility.

Lying on my back, I try to think of what to do about Tinti Lakatos, who doesn't like to go to school. To the races, yes, because there he usually wins, while in school he is a loser. He takes a taxi home from the racetrack and flings handfuls of five and ten forint pieces in front of each school he passes. These characters around me have become more like family. We grow bored with one another, insult one another to the quick, are deeply interested in one another. If you pick at random any one among us and weigh his or her soul, you will find a person who is worn out, wry, gloomy, and occasionally giddy.

A person with no propensity for ecstasy is dangerous. Here is my bed and table; on the right is my work, on the left the zone of confidential hospitality: a small table and three armchairs. The simplest thing to do, should a guest arrive, is to bring a pitcher of wine from the cellar. We seat the guest in the large overstuffed chair and settle ourselves into the small ones by the stove; from there only the treetops can be seen through the window.

When the guest leaves and the children are in bed, I like to scurry back to my desk. This work is not like translation. I concentrate on the divisions into sentences, paragraphs, chapters. After each sentence I feel a breeze of doubt. Who could see deeper into the well of my stupidity than I? I calm myself by being the aloof Chorus, who makes her remarks, then turns the stage over to the players. I am a window between two rooms: My acquaintances are in one, my chimeras are in the other.

There is room for at least a dozen people around our old green dining table. Chic, dignity, vulgar anecdotes, and gallows humor—everything is tolerated here. Except for the moaning of a bad conscience. This is a motley group. Nobody represents anything other than himself or herself. In a properly wiretapped kitchen and dining room, we are uninhibited. I beg the appropriate authorities to tape every word of this brainstorming orgy. They owe it to the collective memory of the homeland to keep an accurate record. Clever women make up the heart of our circle; male arrogance can hardly get a word in edgewise. It is not the death of the nation but the abundance of offspring that matters here. After midnight, the fervor flags; wearily we descend into the swamp of cultural politics. The bell rings. A journalist from Hamburg or Los Angeles. He has a tape recorder; takes out his list of questions. But we don't like being asked questions. We don't go around asking other people questions, do we? Especially questions that are not nice. We could play collective silence, but we prefer instead to tease each other, like children. I stare at the moon

278

above the poplars, and at the hollyhocks and oleanders around me. They stare back.

World test, that's what I used to play with the children at the educational counseling center. Picture a large table with blue indentations: That's the sea. A bucket of sand is the island. On the shelves around the walls are all sorts of plants and animals, puppets and furniture, everything in miniature. Each child puts together his own world. He may build a cave, put a small boy inside, and place a tiger or a crocodile at the opening, while at the center of the island he sends his parents or siblings for a walk. The ideal novel has loose pages, which can be taken out, their order changed according to the reader's will.

Dramaturgically, triangles are satisfying. And in addition to the jealousies and anxieties, there is the homosexual temptation between the males. I have no problem saying "the three of us." I give myself to the other two. A love triangle is the most banal frame for a story, yet it's so handy. We, the characters of the novel, tell one another what has happened to us. And at our age there is plenty to tell. I think I fell in love with János because I could talk to him in a way I had never been able to talk to anyone. And here we have a metaphysical duel between a walnut tree and a migrating bird, my two men. One runs away, then comes shuffling back from the mental hospital; the other suffers a mild stroke and needs constant care and supervision. One is depressed; the other is paralyzed. They prop each other up; for a short while they are inseparable.

In one of his maniacal moods, János makes a mad dash to the border, a valid passport in his pocket. Will they catch him? Won't they? Will Antal be cured one day? Will he fly the coop? Or will these two men, growing more and more decrepit, accompany me for as long as they can? Sometimes János goes on binges, gets into fights. He wants to leave but can't. He pulls taut the string of his bow, but it keeps snapping back. Antal recovers, goes back to work. He sculpts on the hillside, is the owner of a vineyard, withdraws to Balatonfalu. János pays another visit to the Lake of Gennesaret, and that's when the ironic incident with the little Arab boy takes place.

Here comes the story, the great family novel that lasts a lifetime.

We are doing the same thing children do on the floor of their room, using dolls and figurines. I close the door behind me, and now we chatter away for a few hundred more pages, until the text breaks loose. This is not a novelistic novel, because guests keep arriving; there are more and more of us. So many, in fact, that not everyone knows everyone else, and—behold—we experience in these pages what we do in life: We don't know what will happen next. Because one thing is just as possible as another. Not the arc but the intersection is our structural pattern. We intersect at this garden, this table, this evening. Tonight every player sees things more clearly. Shadows roam the garden, pondering, meditating, dredging their memories. They listen to one another, then excuse themselves and walk on.

7.

In homage to Regina

Wild Grapes on
the Brick Wall

Even with his back, David Kobra can sense whether or not Regina has had a good night's sleep, whether her dreams were pleasant or disturbing, or if she has a headache or stomachache. Whenever she is in a confined space, a pressure builds up in her chest; he fetches a glass of water, opens a window. Why does our beloved pull back from the fence? She must have seen a dangerous dog in the garden. We must leave this taxi immediately; the driver has sprayed it with deodorizer, or else he is speeding, not an uncommon phenomenon among Budapest taxi drivers. Kobra tests the wine, swishing a small sip around in his mouth—not too dry, not too sweet—yes, Regina will like this smoky taste. When somebody gets carried away with his topic, Kobra glances at Regina: Is she becoming restless? He has learned which of the day's stories can be turned into an anecdote that will not burden, only entertain. He searches his mind for something that will make her laughter resound in those long *e* sounds. On their walks by the cemetery, he anticipates which poppy or cherry will catch her eye, and rushes to pick it and hand it to her reverently. Their stroll is a slow floating on the stream of summer; an olive tree or a broken faun-faced bust glides into view; the hours take their time. Regina is amazed at how much there is to see in the side streets of Ófalu.

Slanting light on the poplar trees. It's not yet six. Kobra awakens to the noise of thrushes. Regina, too, raises her head for a moment, acknowledges that the thrushes are warbling, then goes back to sleep. Yesterday she thought she was pregnant. Her breasts felt tight; she had a brief dizzy spell in the swimming pool and thought her heart skipped a couple of beats; and she saw flashes when she closed her eyes. She took a tranquilizer, then steeled herself and cooked supper: veal Marengo. She likes to cook dishes that are pale in color, pink, yellowish green, gentle tastes soothingly delectable. It's probably because of her presentiment of pregnancy that she now spends more time, on the streets, looking at the wise little creatures who observe the world from their baby carriages. She sniffs the cow smell of mothers. She wants to repaint the house, rearrange all the furniture. Lovemaking is filled with soft rejoicing when a child is allowed to emerge from it.

Regina is cultivating the garden, planting flowers in the flower boxes on the balcony. Kobra groans under the sacks of black soil. In the maternity ward, he'll look at the baby through the glass partition, not sure whether it is beautiful or not so beautiful. He is permitted to hold it; the small head fits into his left palm; the tiny mouth yawns, grimaces. With the tip of a finger Kobra touches the crooked little jewel of a leg, each perfect toe. Does the baby have everything? Everything, even the little root. It's eager to nurse, too. The mother giggles proudly; generosity makes her beautiful as she lays on her belly the little creature that had been inside her. There is a need for a decent young man in the family—but what the husband is now saying goes only as far as the garden of the wife's mind; it does not reach the house itself. In that house there is a new tenant now, a brand-new love and constant preoccupation. Kobra's job is to provide all necessary services, and spend his free time being enchanted by both mother and child. Out of the rain, he steps into the kitchen, where a pot of chicken soup simmers, flavored with vegetables grown in their own garden. From the baby's room happy squeals are heard.

In the afternoon, children come to Regina. She teaches English, French, and German to rascally little boys and angelic little girls; plump children, skinny children. To the music of songs they jump and dance in the area between the tile stove and the bay window, which is framed by wild grapes. Her legs tucked under her, a serious look on her face, she sits in the large armchair. Teaching ten hours a week, she earns enough for groceries, and has time for her dissertation. Green index cards with quotations in many languages fill small wooden boxes. Regina uses just the right amount of sarcasm, so her professor will not fall asleep as the student displays her exhaustive knowledge. A silk blouse and a pair of pants draped over the armchair; in the corner, a pair of shoes; books and magazines all around; hairbrush, perfume, tape recorder, photographs, drawings. Regina is careful with money. In her drawer there is always a reserve; in the pantry, always an emergency supply of food. If Kobra's pocket is empty, she treats him to supper. When shopping, she is unceremoniously frugal, never buying more than is necessary. Yet she has several pairs of glasses. The right frame for the right outfit. She does not like to walk in dark streets. She is afraid of elevators and escalators, and does not like to get on the train by herself. Before going on a visit or to somebody's house for dinner, she comes down with a cold at the last moment, but the symptoms disappear just before, grow worse during, and, thank God, vanish after she phones and says she cannot make it. When, in company, Kobra waxes verbose and everyone hangs on his words, she looks for an empty room to lie down in. Or simply says: "You stay. I'll go home by myself." And he gets up, and they go home together. She loves to get letters, to see Kobra's mailbox fill up, but becomes exasperated if there's hardly anything in hers. When she was eight, she expected to die because she swallowed a fish bone. In school she thought her classmates hated her because she was ugly; she thought of herself as a smudge, an inkblot. In the movies, when something horrible happens on the screen, she closes her eyes, lowers her head, and keeps asking if she can look up again.

The afternoons roll by slowly outside the bay window; the poplars tremble in the summer heat. Everything is idyllic, and then a word or two, and—how it happens, neither of them understands, but they've had a fight. Kobra storms out of the house; Regina throws coffee cups after him and screams, "If you don't come back this minute, you'll never set foot in this house again!" He stalks off furiously. With swift feet, she overtakes him, grabs him from behind, tears off his shirt: "Now you can go, like that!" Fifteen minutes later, they are laughing and kissing in the nearby park. All is beautiful again. They order champagne in an espresso shop. One glass, and Regina loses her inhibitions; her eyes sparkle like a child's. On the way home, she is astounded by the lush foliage overhanging the sidewalk, which gleams in the holy yellow light of the street lamps. Softly the wild grapes roll down the brick walls.

They are resting quietly in the blue bed, Kobra on his back.

Regina's head on his shoulder. Amazing, how angry they can both get. In the pool, she easily outswims him, and when she makes her way to the showers, most men turn to look at her. In the dressing room, she enjoys the chatter of the old women. Who's cooking what for dinner. Who just died. Poor Manci has cancer. With comic revulsion, Regina describes the female bellies, wrinkled and grooved with folds of fat; someday she will write a novel about that steamy cave. The throwing of the coffee cups and the ripping of his shirt were good, something they'd never tried before. As a rule Kobra leaves, goes to his own apartment; Regina paces her room, hissing, "At last I'm free of that bastard!" At his apartment, Kobra collapses in an armchair. The phone rings. He lets it ring. It keeps on ringing, merciless. He picks it up. It's Regina, of course. "I can't sleep. Come back and tuck me in. Can you be here in ten minutes?" "Not even if I take a taxi," he says. "All right, then eleven minutes. Or else!" "Or else what?" She is washing dishes in the kitchen. Friends ring the bell. "Come in!" She tells stories: unexpected, surrealistic details. The night's rest is far away, the legitimacy of snoring. Maybe we should go to Ófalu.

Kobra is not at all in love with Regina. Love is the invention of money-hungry novelists for their female readers. What follows the great gushing? Fights, errands, worries, growing soft in the brain. Go ahead, take a trip around the world; David Kobra will manage on his own. He'll go down to Ófalu and shake Regina out of his system. He feels a pressure around his sternum. Perhaps he should fast. I can love this woman only when the Atlantic Ocean is between us. The guests have left. He lectures her on why a grown person should not look for truth in the society of others. (Tonight Regina was the star of the show.) "Where should one look, then?" she inquires. A person should look within himself. It does not matter where he is. "As long as he is not here," she says. "Among my friends you were an iceberg sitting in the corner." There comes a time when a person gets fed up with words and prefers to take his hat and— "You don't even have a hat," she shouts. "Your head will freeze off in this awful cold." "I've heard that for the last fifty years," he grumbles. "All the careful hat wearers are bald now." Regina makes the bed. David watches the bending figure: harpy, shrew, fury, supersensitive little mewling character. Most writers, he thinks, write falsely about love because they are afraid of their wives. Behind every writer stands an Argus-eyed marital censor.

Fully dressed, David Kobra sits in the armchair facing the bed; a slowly rising east wind brings the scent of lilacs through the window. Regina has opened a travel bag, begins to pack: notes, translations, cassettes of ethnographic fieldwork, family histories, her doctoral dissertation. "Go on, keep moldering here, old man," she says or thinks. "Your drinking companions appreciate your humor more than I do. Tomorrow you'll be only a memory. I'll cross the border before midnight. The only problem is, I've had a little to drink, and I hate it when the police make a person take the breath test. Perhaps I should get a good night's sleep first. No reason to run off. And you can get into bed, too, you scoundrel. You really must resign yourself to being a henpecked husband. As your reward, I will continually surprise you, changing myself, before your eyes, into something altogether different. No more fainting spells, skipped heartbeats, blackmailing frowns. I'll be a woman of the world by your side, but flexible, willing to listen to you extol the virtues of staying a stick-in-the-mud. All I ask is that every morning you bring me cocoa and crescents. You have my permission to putter with your typewriter in the adjacent room, like an animal in a cave. But only until early afternoon. Then you belong to us, to our growing family. Your friends can come, but only when we are present. If you want us to stay together, subject yourself to my authority. I know that if I want a child and a father, I have to be faithful. However, I also know that you love me, not for my goodness but for my elusiveness. If I were to say that I'm staying here forever, within five minutes you'd be miserable; sorrow would sit on your face."

In the small baroque bar, she likes to listen to the old pianist sing old songs. She fingers the lace tablecloth while sipping her Tokay. "And I bet you could go on and on about the people here, about what they were doing in the year of my birth," Regina says icily. "I could," Kobra admits. "But my stories bore you." She consoles him: "One need not waste many words on a woman. You always provide me with new things. Your imagination makes the most ordinary, provincial subjects unusual, exotic. Sometimes, when I'm with you, I am flooded with a feeling of unreality, as if I, too, were a colorful character in a novel. And that short, bird-faced, grinning drummer, perhaps he is only a character, a literary shadow. We are having lunch under the weight of eternity."

Most likely, Kobra will find himself alone in the end. While Regina was with him, he wanted only her. It was easy to be faithful; he had found his true mate. But now her face looks back at him only from the crowns of trees. He snuggles into his mythology of safety as into a sleeping bag. "Isn't the problem of freedom more interesting than the problem of the lack of freedom?" she asked. He did not answer. And will not answer her, not anymore. He has grown comfortable in this trapped space, where the figures of the clock tower make their rounds every hour on the hour. He likes the dust, the shabbiness, the cunning resignation. He protects the petty, does not believe in the heroic. Let drunken figures prowl under tumbledown scaffolding. "I'm leaving," she announces, "not because of our nation's bad luck or because we are like East versus West in our love. I'm leaving because I'm afraid. I see myself lying on the rug in your study, frozen in my own blood. Or sometimes I see you get up, walk to the window, and die. You don't tell me what's ailing you, but I feel the cold sweat on your brow. You can rest, now. You will have all the quiet you need. Accompany me to the airport, take the bus back to the city, go for a long walk, then trundle home. Enjoy the luxury of not having to call anybody. In the slow snowfall, silence is more silent."

He knows that she'll be back, that next summer the two of them will be working side by side in the garden in Ófalu. On the table, peonies from the garden; a red rosebush running up the fence; a cherry branch swaying in the wind; the strong fragrance of jasmine from the bush at the entrance to the cellar. Her bathing suit drying in the sun. Last night they swam in the lake; the water was like velvet, frogs croaked, a police car flashed its lights. She whistles softly, like a titmouse; inhales, exhales through her nostrils with the evenness of a baby's breathing. Then starts, gets up, stands naked in the garden, looking herself over, inspecting the nettle stings, mosquito bites, the blue bruise caused by Kobra's ardor.

Not too far from the threshold, she squats, avoiding the freshly cut but not yet gathered grass. She urinates. She will bathe later in the morning; they went swimming yesterday. If the sun is strong, she heats water on the electric heater, sets the bathing bowl on the tombstone table, carefully dips her hand in, her wrists, and with raised palms splashes water on herself, laughing. She washes her face thoroughly; her breasts she soaps from below upward; finally she puts the bowl on the grass and sits in it, keeping her long legs far apart. A mood has come over her, something different from the nervousness that usually precedes her period. There is no blood now, will be none; she is pregnant. Her movements are sluggish; she doesn't feel like exercising. Should she make the effort? Could this languor be the anticipation of Christmas? The Christmas Day on which the child will arrive? Secret preparations; the verdict has been pronounced; we are servants of the life force that has chosen us as its vessel. She will carry out the task assigned her, to give birth, following the instructions page by page. A man is also needed here. Protect the belly of this woman; listen to the kicking inside; bring choice delicacies for this belly. For all these duties Regina has appointed Kobra. In the garden, their elbows on the table, they look at the full moon and listen to the crickets and the dogs. All is well with the world.

Regina Speaks of Family Matters

You probably don't remember—you were drunk—but I once asked you what Grandmother Zsuzsa's body was like. I wanted you finally to come clean. Her, too? With her, too? With whom haven't you? But a gentleman, apparently, remains a gentleman even when drunk; you stuck to your old story: the eroticism only of a child's admiring looks. According to you (but you always exaggerated, Mama said), my grandmother was an aerialist, able to stand on one foot, like a stork, on the parapet of the balcony, balancing herself with her arms. She was a swan among people bearing stars. A swan, too, in the ghetto hospital, where her mother, my great-grandmother, lay dying, a bullet having entered the right side of her skull and come out at the back of her head just below the left ear. My grandmother, before her admiring guests, would do wonderful cartwheels on the long blue rug between the door and her bed.

If I had not left home—for you—my stepfather and I would probably have had my poor mother committed. To work others into a suicidal state, that's your method. You're an expert; in your books you compile the horrors of the world. When one leaves you, one looks back to make sure that you are not following. You eat your lunch, drink plenty of wine, and take an hour's nap on the bed from which so many of my relatives have departed this world. Mother told me of that day in November 1956 when in a state of inebriation and not altogether with her consent you made love to her. Soon after that, she went to London and married Zoltán. Nine months later, I came into the world, a desperate rationalist who would like to know who her father is. The answer was a mystery to my mother, to Zoltán, and it must be to you, too. She says I resemble both of you, just as the three of you resembled one another. She would have loved the two of you even if you had not been her cousins. You both possessed the same cruelty of mind, she said, a cruelty of which I also have a share. A family conspiracy. It takes a monster to know a monster.

Did you know that after Zoltán's death she worked at a high-class brothel in Geneva? In the morning she'd drop me off at the *école maternelle*. In the afternoon she was the good mother again. We did not become rich that way, but we managed. She sewed her own clothes, and would dance just for me. Her guests loved to talk to her. One entrepreneur spoke at length about his business, and when her advice to him turned out to be valuable, he kept coming back, like one possessed. But Klára never gave a man more than one hour a week. This was agony for the entrepreneur, who had to cram both pleasure and business into that single hour.

When we returned, Mother did not like me to sit on your lap. She preferred your visiting when I was not at home. On your lap, I'd move to arouse you, and Mother would grab me as you'd grab a lecherous cat, by the scruff of the neck, and fling me off. When she was blooming, I'd become ill to get your attention. I liked to call you aside when she was making everybody laugh. "Come into my room. I feel so anxious." I learned this trick very quickly. "Be careful, or I'll feel anxious in a minute," I once threatened her. When I lured you into my room, I would say, "See how my heart is beating?" and put your hand on my breasts. I had no breasts to speak of at the time, but I knew that I soon would. On my eleventh birthday, I remember, I caught my mother looking at me as she sat in her rocking chair. Eyes full of hate. But all she said was: "You are beautiful, my little kitten." I think I had better leave you, David, before you and my daughter-to-be-born put me on ice.

So I, too, instead of having a half-dozen friends in Mexico City and Lagos, have become a stubborn Kobra stick-in-the-mud in this dilapidated city. Here I am, waiting for you in my mother's room, and you, grown older, do come to join me in my bed. My bed or my mother's bed? I don't know; you have entangled me in this Kobra mythology, in your international thriller to which I am now tied by stories of anger and forgiveness. As if we had agreed upon a common madness, I guard the ghosts of the family. Please say that it isn't true, that my mother, Klára, was only your invention. And that you don't exist, either, even though I am straddling you, howling and squealing while I ride.

You lie to everyone. You have a brow-knitting aversion to everything that soars. You find a blocked and crooked mind more interesting than one that is unimpeded and straight. You like slovenly neglect, indolent disorder, the crud that settles in the bathtub, the floor that creaks. You delight in the vulgar; misfortune enchants you. In people you are drawn to failures. You believe that this city is sick, but that's precisely what you love about it. Even your caresses are a paradox of disciplined, stifled needs. I know you more intimately than in the bedroom; I see your hesitations, tautologies, banalities. I pity your provincial, loin-girding generalizations. In your mythology the flowers of evil are covered by the October frost; in mine, omissions are on the rampage. In your eyes, man is a tragic experiment; in mine, a comic mediocrity. You have become slightly old-fashioned, my darling. In the good intentions of languorous good health you would not find your place. You've grown heavy. You are in a slow, bubbling simmer, like a turtle in the swamps. I look at you, as I look at you in the bathroom, and your body is no longer that of a twenty-year-old. I look at you loyally, as you would look at yourself, indulgently, cruelly. If I were to read your palm, what could I tell you? A garrulous gentleman from the Crown café who tells antireligious jokes. Yes, we know him, we've had enough of him. "The last prophet," said one of your disillusioned admirers with a sneer. A prophet? *Mein lieber Gott*, more an advertiser of mud baths. The city is all right, he says, not because of the system, but because, well, because it is all right. Now, there's an idea of genius for you.

Come to my place for lunch. Work only in the morning; no need to loaf all afternoon. I'd better brush the collar of your coat; you have dandruff. And last night, why did you go berserk, why couldn't you sleep quietly? What possessed you to clutch your table, as if all the world, including me, were slipping away? And then, when you finally slept, I asked you who Regina was. "Dragon," you mumbled, "monkey, succubus." I am withering away at the side of an aging man. Who could be richer, too. Who could take me to balls, if there were any. Where is my long evening gown? Where is the white limousine? You bought me a used bicycle, which was stolen. But do look into my soothing eyes: lake at the bottom, wind above. What are you afraid of, darling? Who is threatening you?

The Bear and the Raspberry

Kobra is content that Regina's here, breathing by his side. He has made a vow that for him it's Regina and no one else. This axiom may last as long as he lasts. Death, and a few other things, cannot

292

be shared. A corpse, a widow. Oh, works of fiction; in them, he who takes what belongs to another, who learns the taste of a strange woman's mouth, must pay at the end of the novel.

Child, house, wife everlasting; you seek security at the side of a woman. You, the stronger, protect your property. The man who wants to win your spouse will have to fight for her. Let him name his weapons: fists or knives? On the other hand, the Old Testament does not say, Thou shalt not share thy wife with thy neighbor. In the battle for the possession of the woman, Kobra sees almost everything and forgives nothing. If you sleep with somebody else, so will I. We have our duel, and on the veranda of happiness we work up an appetite for separation. Regina is safely here, but Kobra is unsure: Maybe she'll pull away from him, take an unforeseen turn in the wrong direction. In her presence he is busy filling in the coloring book of his jealousy. He cannot see below the surface of the calm lake. Wherever I am not, others are. Carnivorous beings, we are sad that we can't completely devour each other. I could tie you up. I could even strangle you. In lovemaking, like the pit in the fruit, lurks the possibility of rape and murder. Perhaps rapist-murderers are only security seekers gone overboard.

You go away, and I miss you. Yes, I am capable of missing you. I have a drink, look around; noonday bells. I begin to understand the blessing of emptiness. It's not so bad to be bothered by people. My guests from Ófalu I accompany to the bus, make sure they depart, wave to them, then wash my hands and face. Tea, grapes, an idle sky, no watch on my wrist. I lock up your playacting in the room of memories and return to sit at the tombstone table.

Of books, too, I can be jealous. The kind that take your thoughts far away from here, to distant cities where you wandered without me, to a seashore village where the moon was very bright, and to a quaint old apartment where you kissed someone under the piano. I have devoted myself to you for a long time now; have met my friends less frequently, have gone to the country less. Not wishing to be away from you. My mind revolved around your femininity in ever-decreasing circles. I've felt a clinging anxiety, like an illness. "You're in it," I kept telling myself. "See it through to the end."

The seducer seduces by offering more than others do. More, but for a shorter time. He likes divorces; he luxuriates in the poetic moments of parting. But when he finds his match, he is capable of settling down for a while. Some men never grow up; they go from their mother to their wife-mother, trying to please, hiding behind her skirt. As for David Kobra, he has seen splendid mornings even when waking in his bed alone. "It was a wonderful night." "If you feel you gave more than I did, just because I started snoring in the middle of one of your stories, then tell yourself that it's better to give than to receive." In the contest between two lovers, the loser is the one who begs the other to stay. On the other hand, with time, you can grow accustomed to being abandoned.

From Regina's indictment: "You made all your women believe that you wanted only them, then you became frightened and left them in the lurch. Each bed you slipped into, you kept your eyes on the door, planning your retreat. Why haven't you run from me? How long will this great fidelity last? I suppose if I were a man, I'd be a lady-killer, too. Women are delicious. Take that red-nailed waitress with the multitiered coiffure and the stiff lace cap on her head, her pretty breasts poking in your direction as she leans over the table to put the pear brandy before you. If I were a man, I'd seduce her on the spot. As one picks up a ham sandwich.

"If I were one of your readers, I'd be cheating on you constantly. Variety is the spice of life; everyone should have adventures; that is what the author is saying. The serpent-corrupter. Is it possible that there are no innocents, only frightened people with suppressed desires? Once you told me how good it felt to prop yourself up on your elbows in a strange apartment, to enjoy the morning light. In your new woman's bed, while she busied herself with breakfast. The view from her balcony. Then the rest of the day spent with her, loafing around town. On your way home you bought flowers and a bottle of red wine. You said, and I remember every word, 'There is nothing more erotic than an unfamiliar bookcase.' You like to be surprised. What will you find in Santa's socks, or under the bushes on Easter Sunday? I have a feeling that as a boy you tore the wrapping off your presents impatiently.

"If you had been smarter, if you had fathered a baby, you'd give the carriage a shove, the baby would squeal happily, you'd run after it, give it another shove, and neither the passenger nor the servant could get enough of the game. A dark suit and overcoat would have looked good on you as you stood by the carriage. Love has its own time, and so does foolishness." With his excellent night vision Kobra knew, even before she said it, that she would leave now. The daughter avenging her mother. Behold, David Kobra was hers. She became pregnant. But there was no child. The experiment is over. Everybody returns to his or her place.

Regina came for only two weeks. She made fun of the city's threadbare intimacy, of its slow warmth. She was interested in seeing the world, not in Kobra's stifling chronicles. She stayed two years. And will stay longer. But this, Kobra does not yet know. Sometimes she had the urge to escape, but promised herself that eventually she would leave. Here, everything belonged to Kobra. Her dissertation, too, if she wrote it here, would belong to him. "I am not your pet or possession. On your home court I cannot rise above you, and that is the only way that we two can make a couple. With children, though, I could break you. Then you would be outnumbered. It is insufferable that I think the way you do, use your words, your gestures. And that I have even, for your sake, come to this narrow and musty coziness."

It's already midnight, and the phone hasn't rung. Where can Regina be? Kobra sits in his grandfather's armchair until dawn. He does not look good in the early-morning light. He walks to her house. The windows are dark. He goes upstairs, rings the bell. No answer. He puts his key in the lock; it turns, but the door doesn't open; it's bolted from the inside. He breaks down the door. Sleepily, she comes to meet him in the hallway. "What is it? What do you want?" Kobra walks past her, toward the bedroom. "Don't go in there. Oliver is here." He slaps her in the face, harder than he intended. Her hand flies to her cheek. "Oh," she whimpers. "I don't ever want to see you again," he says, and like a thundercloud takes his leave. An hour later she rings his bell. He doesn't let her in. She shouts through the door, "You beast, can't you hear me crying?" He doesn't answer. "Even if you slap me every day, I'll still love you, only you." He doesn't answer. She is out on the street again, cheerfully swinging her pocketbook, obviously pleased with herself. The next day, she knocks on the door and presents him with nine beautiful roses. She is beautiful, too, giggles a lot, and leaves, saying, "Call me tonight." From the window he pours the contents of the vase on her head. Bull's-eye. She is soaked. She turns around, runs upstairs, rings the bell. He opens the door and receives a huge slap across his face. "I don't ever want to see you again," she says, and runs and locks herself in the bathroom. He sits in an armchair, pretending to read. She comes out of the bathroom and quietly curls up on the floor beside him. "Yesterday you were getting too strong for me. Oliver told me I was lovely." "You are lovely," Kobra says from the depths. "When you slapped me, Oliver was shaking in his boots. I told him he'd better go, because you might come back. He was glad to leave. I can see you're not reading." "I'm starved. How about making me some fried eggs?" Together in the kitchen, grievances aired, they cry and hug. "Only you!"

The days pass. It's midnight again. Regina is late. Kobra forces himself to read the lines his eyes have only been skimming. Voices; the closing of the front entrance; light in the stairwell. Outside, in the square, the sound of receding steps; Kobra does not look out the window. The door of the apartment opens; Kobra goes to meet Regina.

"We shouldn't be having these conversations," Kobra sighs at dawn. "In old-fashioned, till-death-do-us-part marriages, both husband and wife go about their own business. They pass the bread, the salt, or the lamb to each other. Their eyes say the few things they want to communicate to each other. They enjoy delicious silences together. And look at us, we don't ever shut up." He rises on his elbows, and as he does he receives a final touch on his chest; it is only Regina's fingers saying good night. Her body is now curled up, her mouth emitting those leave-taking grunts that inform him that until eight in the morning her physical self is off-limits. She'll have many dreams, and remember them all, and tomorrow morning ponder their meaning. In them, Kobra is following her with evil intent. Or perhaps he is leaving her.

Eye Telegram
to Silent Brick Wall

How many years has it been since Regina saw her so-called stepfather? She translated a few of his books, she wrote about him, even made some money doing that. In the meantime she is writing her dissertation on extended families of relatives, friends, and neighbors in a large city of a socialist country. Sometimes the web of intertwined lives oppresses her, and she wants to escape from Kobra and return to the sensible, civilized, comprehensible world. She whispers in his ear: "Come, let's roam the world together for a couple of years. Let's be two international con men. You can lecture on Kafka in a traveling circus in Oklahoma. I gave up my Brazilian Indians and Tasmanian natives on your account. For the last two years I haven't sent a single line to the newspaper I'm supposed to be working for. I no longer am the flying tourist-observer. And you know how much I like to move from place to place, and sniff things. Now I sit at your table, unable to tell which of us is in the other's clutches."

Once, Kobra woke with a heavy feeling in his chest and saw that Regina was on the telephone talking to somebody in English. She replaced the receiver and said that she was leaving the next day. He was not shocked. "Go, then. Go, little girl, the airport is waiting for you. Wearily I'll wave after your climbing plane. I'll go home, have a cognac, and clear my desk of unopened letters. I am as dry as instant coffee, as empty as a raided closet. With a push of a button you will lower the back of your seat, stretch out, and not even look at the receding city below you. Go, because if you don't go, I'll tie you up with a string of writer's words under the moldy, fungus-ridden beams of the balcony's carved roof. What, you're back already? You never left, my only one? Put your slender fingers into my hand. It's good to walk after the rain. To sit in the Winter Garden. And then —what else is there?—to go home. I open every door for the woman, arrange the lighting around her, soothing music for her ears, a drink within her reach. The aroma of a promising dinner wafts in. She should understand that her place is here."

There was a time when Kobra went from city to city, country to country, woman to woman. It was with women that he learned about freedom. At first he believed that you should love forever the woman you held in your arms. Then he learned that one embrace does not necessarily lead to another. That there is no such contract. Only this, simply: I am in your power, and you are in mine. Vows were really no more than compliments. Kobra stopped feeling guilty. Wallowing in flesh, he disconnected his mind. He heard his mouth utter the sounds: You, you, you! Then, showering, calling a taxi, checking the time. Two people; he goes his way, she goes hers.

Come, all of you, come into the garden. Come by car, bus, or on foot. Knock on the gate, bring flowers. Let's place the gifts around nicely, arrange the table and the evening. Plate under the ham, saucers under the cups, thin glasses for the red wine. It's after dark. Where are you, my only one? How depressed I used to feel when finally, rusty-limbed, I left the street corner where I had waited for you in vain. The buses kept arriving to no avail. Though filled to capacity, for me they were empty, lacking you. But our love was the finest of them all. Other lovers have been unfaithful to each other; we never were. When will I see you again? Never. I abandoned everyone, and everyone abandoned me, and yet remained with me. At dawn they stand around my bed, together spinning the thread, together cutting it in half. We are words, but in whose book? How many wretched solitudes, how many fortuitous meetings of future mates? What an enormous forest of infidelity I have crossed!

I look over the fence into a strange garden. Eye telegram to silent brick wall. In any couple, one person is stronger, the other more dependent. Like celestial bodies, the lighter one orbits the heavier one. Orbits, and wants revenge, for having to orbit. The opportunity arrives with precise dramaturgical timing: the moment the strong one weakens. This has nothing to do with morality.

The pull between mine and thine cannot be resolved. Each of us would like to be surrounded by a house and a garden; a space of our own, set up and arranged to our liking. It's good to have my own coat, books, pocketknife, fountain pen, corner to read in, route for walks, favorite bar. Kobra observes others as they raise their houses not far from the graves of their parents. And the fact that men are increasingly drawn to marriage and monogamy, repelled by the thought of being touched just by anybody. The wanderer clings to the place he left. A city becomes associated with one woman. When a love begins moving, it increases in weight, in momentum. "So be it," Kobra says. When Regina speaks, he hears her every word, suddenly deaf to the chatter of others.

As we stroll across the desert and stop at this corner bar, where several people have been stabbed—would you like plum brandy or marc?—I must tell you that you were the most beautiful woman at the party. From now on I'd like to fill my time and space with you. Any place where you are not is for me a place of banishment. May I come in and talk to you for a moment? The curves, arches, smoothness, and smell of Regina are just right for Kobra. An Arab sage said that it is a great happiness when your beloved is kind to all five senses. Hearing her hum, walking with her, visiting her, resting a hand between her thighs. His fingers travel her body. Murmuring, going mad inside, simultaneous arrival at pleasure. The gentleman begs permission to plant a kiss on the lady's sole. Since the sole is very ticklish, the request is denied.

Away from bodies—with glasses on his nose, book in his hand—Kobra moves to the edge of the bed. Now he is an intellect longing for distance. Would you kindly retract your feet to your side of the bed, madam? By what right does another person (a descendant of apes) touch me with her feet any time she likes? This is my territory. Or the scholar may be interrupted by the request for a peach. And later for a wet towel. Look what you've done to my bed. I lie on my back; you put your head on my shoulder; I smooth your hair off your forehead; you drool on the pillow. Your soft lips close on your way to dreamland, but suddenly you stick out your tongue and send a smile back from the shores of sleep. Then, with this small farewell, you sink to the bottom of the lake.

Regina's eyes open. The dark irises appear concave in the lamplight. Should I cut my hair? Was it nicer when it was short? If I have it cut, I won't look like a mouse? You were only lying, I see, when you said you liked it short. Now I don't know whether to have it cut or not. It's good, you know, that we live separately. Easier to fight that way. Breaking up means only that you won't sleep at my place. If by morning we haven't had a fight, you walk home, sit at your desk, putter around. Later, after dark, you go for a long stroll in the city, until you turn in to a narrow street where only one window is still filled with light. Always tactful, you give your whistle signal before you use the key. I hide my diary and wait for you. On the wall of the balcony, the wild vines rustle in the growing breeze. We embrace in the hallway.

Together we watch the verdigris roofs, the red-capped drivers, the heads of hackney horses stuck in their oat bags. The horses stop their munching as we take our seats beneath the leather top of the hansom. After the ride, we sit at the Crown. Anxiously I wait for the white-bearded porter to come, put his hand to his visor, and hand me a bunch of flowers. The handwriting on the attached envelope is always the same, yours.

I move my painted, slightly quivering lips closer to you. See that woman over there? She is wearing the same hooped skirt I wore when I threw my strawberry ice cream at you—remember?—because you were putting a red candy into the mouth of that bitch Elfride, asking her to stick out her big cow tongue. How many women have you deceived to date? You must have been the same in your previous incarnations. Sweet-talking a jeweler's widow, removing her under-things, then losing interest, looking out the window.

His head resting in his hands, Kobra sits on the shore of the lake. His warnings to the world were ignored by the superpowers. The town's bad boy resigns himself to being the village idiot. There are advantages to this demotion. He roams the town to exhaustion, to the point of giddiness. And then together, he and I bake apples, drink mulled wine, and with booted feet follow the blue markers on hiking trails over the mountains still spotty with patches of snow. He throws snowballs at me, of course, finding my dark greatcoat an amusing target. With his back straight, he sits in the large armchair, one hand holding a cup, the other on the lion-clawed armrest. Hands that long to bathe a baby.

Like a slinking thief he slips through the velvet drapes, turns out the light, and locks behind him the house surrounded by yellow leaves. Gingerly he turns the key. The wind shakes a late-ripening pear on a rain-soaked branch; almonds crackle under foot. Out of the garden at last, before winter settles in and, shivering, a pale-blue shadow, he has to light the Christmas tree. As he reaches the gate, David Kobra realizes that the serpent and the cave are not inseparable. We are getting away at the last possible moment, clearing out of this butcher shop where he has been pulled at and eaten by a slow-working madness.

Regina, as a gangly, long-legged little girl, used to sit mournfully on the swing, barely moving. Shall I tell you about my first sexual encounter? We were both twelve years old. Through a green door we went into a storeroom, squeezed behind some crates, and settled down in a pile of wood shavings. I had heard from one of my classmates that to begin you had to knead a man's organ with a gentle but firm hand. So I kneaded. At first, one boy was frightened; then he moved his head from side to side and dug his hands into his hair. But I didn't stop, because I also wanted to see him bite his lips. And he did bite his lips. A few days later, I met the boy and his mother on the street. I offered my hand to be kissed; the boy obliged. To the mother I said, "And how are you, my dear?" Without waiting for an answer, I strutted off with the fur-coated swaying of fashion models. As a girl I dreamed of going to school in a chauffeur-driven British limousine. Wearing snakeskin shoes and a blue fox around my neck, I'd walk into the classroom, and everybody would gasp when they realized who I was.

In my dream, I was wearing a veil. I had a date with you in an autumn cemetery. You said we should copulate in the mausoleum. "Why there?" I asked. Because the mausoleum was swarming with souls, you answered. It would be more sacrilegious than copulating on a grave. Not to mention the fact that in there we wouldn't get wet. Weary drops of rain fell from the large thujas; tiny pools gathered on the dead leaves. In the rays of the setting sun, almost horizontal under the rain clouds, the gravel path reddened. Inside, in front of a cabinet filled with urns, I pulled off my panties, stuffed them into my bag, and waited, took off my skirt, too, and waited. I turned around. You weren't there.

Courtship

The sofa is comfortable, the tea fragrant, the rum warming. Welcome, dear lady. Which of us, do you think, is more unreal? Come, have a seat at this tombstone table. Let this coarsely chiseled pink slab of marble with teacups separate us. Or should we go, instead, to the nightclub at the Crown Hotel? The piano player with the signet ring is playing a song about how man is woman's greatest enemy and woman man's. Today I'd rather be the audience than the actor. Romantic mysticism has fenced me in; even without being touched, I know I am surrounded by bodies. Your lightness has its specific weight, my darling; I have no weightier challenge than you. The currents between us flow strongest when the light of already-a-memory falls upon the darkness of not-yet-a-memory. A statue of light on the velvet sofa; with clouded eyes you catalog the soft figurines of memory.

Remember? We were walking in Père Lachaise cemetery. To get out of the rain, we took cover in one of the mausoleums. I had a flask of plum brandy in my pocket, but felt it disrespectful to take it out there. Wet cats scurried among the graves; hungry, fierce-eyed cats. A crow perched on the black metal sign offering directions in the cemetery. I leaned my back against the stone wall of a stone crypt, like a resident spider. The spider sits in the early-autumn sunshine, motionless, not rushing after its prey. Spiders take their time.

How long have we been sitting like this, just the two of us? My one and only, we swim around all day, side by side, like wild ducks. We fight, sputter, then once again I enjoy the peace of the garden with you. We gave the house a second coat of paint, and bought this

302

secondhand sofa, on which a young man shot himself in the head
because his wife left him. You put a red cover on it. I wanted to be
out of every relationship that meant living together. I used to be vain
and curious, always longing for strange women. For a while now I
have been faithful. And now we are preparing for a party. You put
on your makeup. In front of the mirror, you show that merely by
rearranging your hair you can be an English governess, a Japanese
terrorist, or a mysterious woman out of an old American detective
film. Dancing in the middle of the room, you are the cynosure of all
eyes. Boys with birdlike bodies and sparkling eyes gape at you with
astonishment, as at a dazzling mother. In the center of a spiral galaxy
in a science-fiction universe, you sit on an organ-shaped throne of
light and show off your sexy legs.

Kobra's hands cannot get enough of Regina's body. It is the body
he's been looking for all his life. Her lap, her loins, the cockscomb-
red lobes of her vulva, the clitoris sticking out its nose expectantly.
Her thighs clasp his neck; the dense frizzle of her pubic hair tickles
him; and the avid tightness and artful movements of her vagina are
just right for him. He curls his fingers around her bosom. If there
was a department store for breasts, he would pick exactly this size
and fullness. For him, the slopes of her shoulders and the nape of
her neck are scented pastures. Turned toward the wall, she is fast
asleep. The wind blows into the room, making her nipples shrivel.
Her long fingers rest forgivingly on the coverlet. He watches her
dreaming face, tries to peer into the narrow slit she has left open
between her lids. The whites of the eyes are those of the angels when
they behold their Lord. With voluptuous yearning he scans the fresco
of the ceiling toward the center of the dome, searching for the re-
deeming sheep, the hanged man.

There is no punishable sexual crime that Kobra hasn't committed.
When he rapes an underage virgin, he sucks her hollow, as one sucks
a chicken leg. You will not frighten him with words like *cannibal,
satyr, vampire*. Incest and necrophilia are no more to him than down-
ing a shot of cherry brandy. How many wonderful ideas there are in
the criminal code; one more tempting than the next! With his morning
tea and soft-boiled eggs he will have a little sodomy. No matter how

303

many abominations this sex fiend tries, there are still more days in the week than acts of sacrilege.

We are building up and demolishing each other's vanities. Danger lurks in our stories; we share our present, but not our pasts; you may see the pasts as sheer infidelities, if you like. You look at my brow and read the sentence I haven't yet uttered. You sit here facing me, even when you do not sit here facing me.

Wherever he may be, Kobra longs to be back in Regina's arms. At her side, he equates the pleasurable with the moral. The elderly gentleman sits cross-legged on the bed, chatting away and drinking wine, laughing and drunkenly doing forward and backward rolls. Nothing happens. Time passes. Kobra does not move from the garden, does not set foot on the overgrown, sloping, graveled street. Regina has brought mushrooms and honey.

8.

Of the vicissitudes of Melinda and János's love

Hablibabli

The last time János Dragomán felt comfortable in a place, he was in the café of Ahmed Husseini on the Via Dolorosa, pulling on a narghile nicknamed hablibabli. Powerful sunshine; then, at eleven in the morning, hailstones the size of quail eggs. The Jewish holy men pulled nylon bags over their hats; the Arab holy men clutched the hoods of their djellabas. Holy men in a comic race. With smiles to indicate pleasant surprise, English, Swedish, Dutch, and German pilgrims—all blond and all curious—took his picture as he shared the hablibabli with Husseini. János had a date with a former classmate of his, a Jewish boy from Budapest, who in Louvain became a Jesuit priest and professor of philosophy. With the permission of the authorities the priest had organized a home for Jewish, Muslim, and Christian children to be raised together; which would prove, it was hoped, that enmity between the three religions was not inevitable. The children received their respective educations and got along well together, the differences in religion posing no barrier. But without exception they all became nonbelievers. Wonderful, János thought, slapping his knee joyfully. The priest said that his former charges were looking for a religion of their own, and personally he did not object to that. "Hasn't it ever occurred to you that all these religions are simply nonsense?" János asked him. "You've written a book about mystic poetry and you say that?" the priest replied.

When his friend left, János asked for kef: Lebanese, pink and sublime. The proprietor said: "Relax, friend, relax. On this rug a man can sit a long time. At noon we will have falafel, pita, vegetables, and in the afternoon sip tea with na'nah. That is the custom, and customs should not be changed. It is also the custom to take risks only for a friend, and to enter into illegal transactions only with men one can trust." In this café, many narghiles waited on the shelf, their brass turned green by time. And if the charcoal needed replenishing, fifteen-year-old Ali, eyes modestly lowered, was there to help. Why live in a house? A place like this, several hundred years old, was just fine. János considered staying in the Old City of Jerusalem and, as a Hungarian-American Jew, taking up residence in Ahmed Husseini's boardinghouse, which had only a few rooms. He preferred the more leisurely Arabs to the rushing Jews. And it was more fun chatting with Muslims than with Christians. There he was, a city loafer, sitting in an Arab café in Jerusalem because he could not find a decent Eastern European Jewish café. How can one wait for the Messiah without a decent café? Where do you think the Messiah would go first, where would he start his preaching? In such a café, obviously.

Blabbering his way around the world, János now entertains beautiful, serious Nordic girls near the Damascus Gate; charms others with his irresistible lines at the Jaffa Gate; and, even at the Wailing Wall, inserts into the large cracks between the stones no rolled-up requests addressed to God, nor bows and rocks back and forth on his heels, but says, "Perhaps tomorrow we can meet at Ahmed's place." But the lunatic time is over: He does not take a new woman each day to his apartment, does not require fresh prey every twenty-four hours. He has grown cautious. Actually, it's good that there are no bars here. He had such a hangover yesterday, after drinking kosher plum brandy, even though it was twelve years old. Sometimes his left hand goes numb, or his left foot hurts. Did not his mother warn him in several letters: "Be careful, son, you know that in your father's family everyone died of heart attacks"? And she added, "But you can take some comfort in the fact that on your mother's side suicide was more common."

With self-conscious postures but alert eyes, three uniformed Jewish boys, submachine guns in hand, stand on the stone steps of the Damascus Gate. They are taking no chances. They puff on their cigarettes, exchange a few words, fall back into silence. The hablibabli mood, too, has its military side. Here, merchants speak several languages, smile at their guests and customers, are unarmed, but they will buy, hide, and sell weapons should the opportunity arise. Merchants are not fighters, just as oranges are not dates. They do not like their alleys to be taken over by armed men. Still, occasionally a bullet or a knife will find a Jew or a stray British tourist.

"It is difficult to obtain marijuana," says the Arab proprietor. "Because of your people. They are deaf to the beneficial effects of hemp. They want to protect their sons, knowing that the weed impairs the ability to fight. They caught one dealer in hashish, and must have given him a good beating, because he told them the names of three hundred other dealers, each of whom received a sentence of three to four years in your prisons. If I count correctly, that comes to about a thousand years." "I have no prisons," János said. "Are you not a Jew?" "Yes." "Do you not agree that there should be a Jewish state here?" "Yes." "Then those prisons are yours, too. And the dealer of hashish who betrayed the others, what do you think he got from you people? You put him in a uniform. He is a policeman now, walking up and down here, lording it over us, spying on us, and shaking in his boots among us. You pay him so that we have somebody of our own to spit upon. No one with any sense would bet much on that man's life. And you also understand, don't you, what I risk by befriending a guest like you, since you are one of those who in their narrow-minded strictness would deprive their sons of the beneficial effects of hemp?"

Along Ethiopia Street, János made his way to Mea Shearim, with its tortuous streets. Century-old, two-story, makeshift houses; tin façades, collapsed roofs. Old and young Jews in wide-brimmed black hats, extremely pale faces, long earlocks because the Torah says you should not trim the corners of your beard. So the earlocks grow indefinitely. Some curl up their earlocks, some wrap them around their ears. János contemplates the different schools of thought on the subject of earlocks. Here is a bookstore where zizith are sold. All the men wear black. The women's garb is not as uniform; it may even be pink. In the shop windows, holy books and kitsch. A men's tailor; bales of fabrics; numerous yeshivas advertising themselves. Torah for beginners. The competition of doctrines keeps this quarter busy. People here live on donations: distant Jews pay so that the Jews of Jerusalem can spend their time studying the Torah and the Talmud, which they do in singsong, in debating tones, their bodies swaying. If you can't sleep, go to one of these places and study; you'll always find someone there. Young men who torture themselves by hardly sleeping stand facing each other in pairs and study. They spend their lives clarifying the distinctions between what is permitted and what is not. A small diamond business may be compatible with piety; you may even sneak off to an Arab whore in the Old City; but the Sabbath remains sacrosanct. In one synagogue, on benches and pillows down two long tables, Jews are rocking and studying. The master, his especially wide hat pushed back on his head, is gesticulating. His pupils range from the very young to the very old; you can study at any age. Tea break; a young man closes his book and kisses it. Women can sit only in the rear, behind a partition; they cannot participate in the studies. János is not crazy about this male-centered religion that shuts women out.

Holding hands in public is not allowed. A handsome couple is coming down the street; they are not touching each other. The man, with beard and earlocks, is wearing the customary knee pants, caftan, and strehml. His wife is like an actress out of the last century; her hips are opulent, for her age perhaps too opulent. On a second-story balcony, little boys, all with earlocks, run around, making noise, jostling one another; the railing keeps them from falling off. One boy sticks his tongue out at János. Passersby look at him askance. These are Hungarian Orthodox Jews. Two rabbis are conversing at the end of the balcony; they are the boys' teachers. Sweet, fatty smells and the odor of fish, just as in the old Jewish quarter of any small town in Eastern Europe. One could work one's way into this life, too, as into the life of a monastery, where they say the uniformity of appearance hides a great internal diversity, anarchy, even. You and I could not live like this, yet these Jews are more real than those secular Israelis who build their houses and have barbecues in their yards on Saturday. Like materialistic people anywhere in the world. Whereas in Mea Shearim, the passionate circular arguments are groping toward truths. For these people nothing is sufficiently holy. The truth is always deeper. Try rocking back and forth for eight hours, and you will stay on the heels of the truth, though it keeps eluding you. The separation of body and spirit is not for these people. The man who sways, chants, reads, and closes his eyes has deep sadness on his face, for God cannot be pleased or ever satisfied. That is why Jews of different persuasions are also dissatisfied with one another.

On Saturday, a black-clad father takes his children to stop traffic. He dresses them in costumes, extinguishes their will to care for anything other than studying the Talmud all their lives, here in Mea Shearim, where you can still hear Hungarian spoken because the holy tongue is not to be used for profane matters. A few leave, a few join this group, but the community remains intact. Whoever winds up here will become a monk with a family. He will search the Law and its commentaries for an answer to anything and everything. Not a bad idea for János to move in here and put on a costume. In prison, too, he appreciated the security of a regulated existence.

He is sitting beside his uncle in the car. "Look at that wild animal," Pali says quietly. The "wild animal," holding the hand of one of his three children, is blocking the road and shaking his fist at the car. It is Saturday; János is accompanying Pali to the military cemetery. "Doesn't religion attract you?" János asks. Pali answers: "As the years pass, one gets a potbelly and becomes sentimental. I'd like to avoid both weaknesses." Pali's small daughter was gassed in Auschwitz. After he was liberated, he found his wife in one of the camps. They came to Jerusalem, where they had two more children. The son fell in the Yom Kippur War of 1973; the daughter has children of her own. "I don't want these fanatics to force my grandchild into something that his parents don't approve of." Pali and János quietly tend to the grave; there is not much to do. A bus arrives full of American tourists; the guide is loud. "What tactlessness," Pali bursts out.

Just before dusk, János picks up the phone, jots down a name and date. There, he has profaned the Sabbath. In the evening, with the holy day over, and under the full moon, dark descends on the city. Youth takes over the promenades of Jerusalem. Beautiful girls with their hair down to their waists are taking a walk, making noise, their red tongues working on enormous scoops of ice cream. They laugh freely; enough of the family for one day! These Sabbaths are a burden to them. On Ben Yehuda Avenue, János met a twenty-three-year-old Wagner scholar. She had flashing eyes, hair that hit her behind, fantastic breasts, a wet mouth, and a face that could keep three men riveted simultaneously. Possessing all these treasures, the girl said that she was writing her doctoral dissertation on Wagner, titled *Unfortunate Eros*. "And Fortunate Eros?" he asked her. "Who would that be?" She laughed and said, "Myself, of course. You probably don't know that this street is the marketplace of lasting relationships. It is the street of young people, and it leads to the wedding canopy." They exchanged cards, and János said he was sure that they would run into each other at some very prestigious international seminar on aesthetics.

He went back to his room and sat on the balcony, from which he could see the entire Old City, the Valley of Hinnom, and the pink mountains beyond the Judean desert and the Dead Sea. Among cemeteries and domes painted white by the moon, he listened to the rustling branches of an orange tree and thought, "This is all well and good, but in Paris at this hour I would still be sitting in the Select, with plenty of intellectual company. I would be swimming not in the Lake of Gennesaret but in metaphors and bibliographical footnotes. But here the holy men and historians of religion go to bed with the chickens and rise with the roosters. No, for a notorious café addict like me, whom nothing attracts less than a wedding canopy, this is definitely not the place."

He is displeased with himself, wanting to be both saint and hedonist. The ungraspable floats before him as he swims; he can never catch up with it. It is in moments like these that he sees his imperfections. He doesn't like Jewish sharpness; he feels more at home rounding things off Budapest style. He prefers race to religion, ethnography to metaphysics. And tradition and customs he can do without. Still, as he grows older, he enjoys discovering the Jew in himself; always looking for his one true self, always finding two. Two warring selves that exist simultaneously in different times. Self-justification, self-hatred. Every search for God takes two paths, and the other self is always on the wrong path.

Our lives, say the religious ones, depend on whether we think right and act right. A train hits a school bus; forty-one children die. The Minister of the Interior orders an investigation. It turns out that in the school forty-one mezuzahs contain defective scrolls. A misspelling incurred the Lord's wrath, declares the Minister of the Interior. But János Dragomán believes that every—nearly every—punishment from God is unjust. And what an insane God it must be who kills children for a misspelling made by others. This stiff-necked, priestly people has little or no concern for the pleasant things of life. Confusion, depth, beard-twisting cogitation, greater depth, inaccessible depth.

He now sits in a different café, near the Jaffa Gate. Icy rain, white pavement, the caftaned men carrying umbrellas; their shoes pointed, their earlocks wet. It's pouring now but the sun is shining, too. Elderly female tourists in white linen hats—they are English—are amused by the weather. They have guidebooks about the Holy Land, the Land of the Bible. Wearing a crimson red kerchief, a young Arab woman enters the café. János is drinking the juice of three freshly squeezed oranges. The love of three oranges. A broad-shouldered, lean young Jew from the Old City passes—dark suit, white shirt, hat with upturned brim. His eyes are drawn to the Arab woman; for a moment their eyes lock; then both lower their eyes. János has selected a pipe and tobacco pouch; he will bargain for them, will be a tourist even in hell. Past fifty, one's future dwindles, one's past expands. Be grateful that you're still alive. And he is grateful. Sunshine and clouds, fluctuating moods. It looks as if he will cross the Holy Land, too, off his list of life-solving utopias. Should my right arm wither? No, he won't forget this city. He's leaving soon, but he'll be back, eventually. A decision that he does not quite understand.

To Melinda

He is on his way to Melinda. A plum tree, laden with its dark-blue fruit, stands by the sidewalk. Fallen wild chestnuts; the pointed cones of ash trees; lush rosebushes. Melinda is setting the table on the balcony; she's waiting for János, who had quite a bit to drink earlier this afternoon, and that may have affected his sense of time. For a moment she goes upstairs into her father's room. From there, too, she can see the garden and keep an eye on the gate. On her way down, she finds the TV flickering in the living room, and sees János reaching for a book in the bookcase, stretching higher, higher, until he falls backward onto the floor. Heart attack, ambulance, death, undertakers. She rubs her forehead and goes to turn off the TV set. Odd; she doesn't remember turning it on. Even odder; it is not on after all. She goes downstairs, runs to the garden gate, and looks out into the street.

Here I am, Melinda of Leander Street. People who otherwise do not see one another gather in our hospitable house. On our table there is always something to eat and drink. I sit in the middle like a spider slowly weaving little flies into its endless tapestry. At the back of our garden there is a small cave, the walnut tree and the millstone table are in front of it. I hear the creaking of the gate; I withdraw to the edge of the picture. Both my men will come back to me, but only after some punishment or calamity. My father will come back, too, to die here. But in the end, I will be left alone in this house.

János, I know, is afraid of this house on this chestnut-strewn street. Lately he spends less time up on the third floor with Father's manuscripts and letters. I know that he is fascinated by the material—he may be writing a book about Father—but is still hesitant to give himself completely to the project. But he and my father are tired keepers of the past's rubbish. Father nailed János to this safe full of papers, and threw in his daughter for good measure. It is disappointing that János did not refuse the offer. Most men, in his place, would have made the same choice.

He comes here by streetcar and subway. He likes to ride the subway, but shudders to think how deep beneath Budapest it runs. When he left the country, the subway was still being built. On the escalator, he looks at the people flowing by in the opposite direction, and they look back at him. Mutual glances. With which one would you like to have a conversation? Whose face is lit up by an inward smile? Whose is made of putty, whose of brick? Coarse faces, definitely not for magazine ads. The average passenger dresses properly; nothing conspicuous about him; he talks little, is frugal with his smiles. He has lowered the shutters of his face. Many read; some jostle one another amiably. There are no panhandlers, no threatening hooligans; pickpockets are rare, with a policeman at every station. The foreigner reveals himself not so much by his clothes as by his eyes. He looks around, is not apathetic. But if he stays here long enough, he will blend into the brownish gray of the surroundings.

János takes a good look at a young woman: powerful muscles on a solid frame. She knows what she knows: that she will have a home, a husband, and a child. The only hitch would be if she has the child too soon, or not at all. But no; this girl will have everything, and at the right time, too. He closes his eyes. The other passengers are pressing close to him. He dreams, nodding off on a slow and crowded train as it rolls out from under the ground, rumbles through the Great Hungarian Plain, where the flat landscape's few objects can easily be counted. The smell of bread, lard, fetid meat, and shoes. Where are you all going? Only as far as Denver, they say, and nod. "Me?" said János. "I'm going to a small town called Báránd." The train stops, the doors thunder open, and he is shoved and carried along by the throng toward the escalator. If he were being followed, he would jump back into the train at the last moment, but he already has word that there are followers waiting for him at the next station. It doesn't matter; let them follow him. As when he is at Kobra's place and the company there is made up of people of the opposition. János submits to the human current, and the escalator carries him up from the depths.

He roams the streets at a time of feverish inflationary shopping. Impatient crowds pitched against weary salespeople. So many on the move in this city, and what do they all want? Where are these nimble old women running to? Have they gone mad? His eyes take comfort in the fact that the pissoir is still green, the streetcars yellow, the buses blue, and that shabby old cars with racks on their tops are busily hauling things here and there. He turns down a side street. He knows that sooner or later he'll wind up at Melinda's place, but he's putting it off. In one of the cafés he looks at a TV screen: A

315

government leader promises that the nation will do everything it can; the new position of the Party and the government is good, though there is still room for improvement. All very reassuring, like water running from the kitchen faucet. He enters a courtyard that houses several boutiques. Displays of spinning lights; bored salesgirls in the garment caverns. Why has he come here? In the Lukács Baths pool this morning, he became dizzy, disoriented, swam to the side instead of straight. "What's got into you, János?" they asked. He was embarrassed. The pool spun around him; how to swim ashore? A joke, with the punch line "sclerosis"?

He drops into a cellar bar for a glass of old burgundy. The burgundy is ladled out of large porcelain containers with copper measuring cups. Under one of the arches of the brick ceiling, he leans on a counter, drinks. In a corner, somebody waves to him. The man approaches, won't let go of János's hand, has bad breath. "Would you mind getting us another round?" János says, giving the man some money. While the man goes for the wine, János slips out of the bar. He crosses the square, stepping on dead leaves. At the stone tables, the eternal pensioners and convalescents are playing cards. Teams of mismatched ages are kicking around a white ball. On the playground, the wooden train is, as always, full of romantic teenage girls in deep discussion. And the slide has, as always, one indefatigable little girl in white tights who quickly climbs the ladder, slides down, lands with a jolt, shakes herself, and climbs up again. On the horizontal bar, János does a few chin-ups. Suddenly he feels something strange, a stoppage or interruption, as when an air bubble and not blood passes through the tube during a transfusion. He lets go of the bar and falls to the gravel. Propping himself up, squatting, he waits. Wet pebbles are sticking to his palms. "You'll get up in a minute," he reassures himself, and is reminded of a joke about a drunk lying on the sidewalk in front of a bar, saying to himself: "If I can get up, I'll go back in and have another drink. If I can't, I'll go home."

He sits on a bench and thinks as bugs swarm under the yellow street lamp. He drags himself to the nearest espresso-bar. In every street he finds memories; even the ugly ones are welcome, as if he were emerging from a long amnesia. This is the table where I refrained from punching that fellow with the gold tooth. This is where I composed the longest love letter of my life, which I never sent, but in different circumstances made good use of its better passages. And, yes, it's this time of the year, late autumn, that pears, mushrooms, and pickles are available at old Mrs. Grünberg's. And walnuts, honey, and poppy seeds and almonds in large glass jars. It was on the third floor of this house that I rang the bell, a bunch of flowers in my hand, and sat in the living room and hoped that nobody would talk to me. But the daughter of the house came over and danced with me. I talked so much that the girl's mother told me to go home and said I was the last guest to leave. And over there, at the corner, I once rented a room on the fourth floor to have a place to take women.

He wanders the dirtier, narrower, more neglected streets of Pest, taking video pictures in dim courtyards. He steps into a bar, but forgets to turn off his camera. Back on the street after a glass of wine, he realizes that the camera has been living its own life, recording things he never saw. Then finally he arrives, is on the balcony. "Hello, Melinda!" he says. "That green sweater looks lovely on you." "You're on time," I say, which isn't true. He never is. "And you're beautiful!" he rhapsodizes. "Instead of complimenting me, sir, go and play the piano." We fall silent. He looks at the quivering of my lips. A message different from the one my mouth utters.

A familiar voice in my head says that my father will show up this evening. It was a year ago today that he left here forever. Shortly after he left, he sent me a dozen postcards, all mailed on the same day and written in his own hand, but each from a different city. Unable to believe that the old man, through some strange but prolific mitosis, was annoying his fellow humans in a dozen different bodies on this small planet, I concluded that he must have involved several of his acquaintances in his little prank. People of that generation know how to do April Fools' jokes right. The humor of our generation, of today's men—the less said about it, the better.

János, for example, tells me a tasteless anecdote. He had a woman, Estella, green eyes and green slippers, who made a point of coming home late every day. And every night he beat her until her skin was as discolored as an old tablecloth. Then he stopped beating her and tattooed decorative plants, whole vegetable gardens, on her body. In one of the more exclusive bars, on a narrow platform along the rear wall, Estella would walk back and forth wearing nothing but her high heels. The men sat on barstools, ogling. "Can we smell the flowers?" they would ask. But then János's designs began to take up too much of Estella's body. The men didn't like that. They didn't want to feast their eyes on a zebra! And it wasn't just vegetables now, but fish and even planets. An art critic congratulated János: "Postsurrealist," he said. But the customers objected: "This is not a museum, damn it, it's only a bar." I recorded the history of the art on Estella's body. Our love was reaching a sensitive point: there was no more room on her body and no more money in my pocket. Estella finally had to leave. Perhaps, János said, she found work in a circus.

He thought of throwing a party to beat all parties. He'd rent the entire Fürdő Hotel in Ófalu. The luckier guests would get the rooms facing the lake, but even those who had to look at the monastery and the mental hospital on the hill would have nothing to complain about. In the Fürdő Hotel there is a bed for every guest of the hotel, and for one guest not only a bed but also the hotel's manager, Franciska. And at the moment, if I'm not mistaken, that one guest is my husband, Antal. So perhaps this is the beginning of that great farewell party János has been wanting to throw. A grand exit, a memorable blowout. The man moves on, the woman stays where she is.

The nocturnal dialog of our genitalia has been made more lively by the possibility that out of these confluent secretions a child may be born. On the bright steps of a hillside chapel, János raves about this possible child. "He should resemble me." That I can promise him. But then, as we walk downhill, out of the morning light, I feel him leave me, a cloud intervenes. Perhaps, in that one moment on the hill, when our light shone brightest, there was even a church wedding, one that only I knew about. From the mountains, shadows come and surround me, their heads roar behind my shoulders, they crawl up on my thighs, spread around my neck like a silver-fox collar. The master of masquerades takes my arm. International dark butterfly, he sees death in everything, but particularly in repetition, which is

318

my element. He wants to hide from death; hence his different disguises.

János is skinny and dresses in layers against the cold. He wears several undershirts, shirts, and sweaters, and wraps fringed silk scarves around his neck. He dyes his hair silver, and paints his mouth red. Clothes are important to him; they affect his moods. He is constantly putting something on or taking something off. He combs his hair in a different way, sits cross-legged on the floor, undulating like a snake. Then he switches to an armchair. Then tries standing in the corner of the room by a tall lamp. What kind of impression is he making? While Kobra listens patiently to everyone and with a few words can put things in their proper perspective, János fidgets, constantly changes his interlocutors. He is sensitive; a blunt remark can dishearten him so much that he will go into the garden, or even home, without a word. Right now he whines that he is so hungry, he feels faint. He pulls the sandwich tray closer, picks something off every sandwich, a slice of hard-boiled egg, an anchovy. He wants to make me angry, to see me trying to control the twitching of my face. The fool.

At an unsavory bar, where several people have been stabbed, we order mixed-fruit brandy. I steel myself and down mine. János puts his hand on my hand. "What's your rush?" he says. Leaning against the bar, a tanned youth; nail-studded belt, leather jacket; in a leather scabbard, a curved knife that could easily slit a man's throat. The young man says to János, "Let's Indian wrestle." Two profiles facing each other; two right hands in a mutual grip, motionless. Intense effort; arms as stiff as posts. Each waits for the other to tire. Eyes look into eyes; the duel of the faces is more important than that of the muscles. In his left hand each man holds a glass of red wine. Elegance is the main thing. "That's enough, gentlemen," I say. "Please shake hands." I can't believe my eyes: They do as I ask.

"I'm afraid you are a psychopath, darling. You fall in love with a city, then walk out on it, as you do with women and with books. Carrying only a light bag, you can turn your back on these pieces of furniture that possess the magnetic power of shared memories. Stay in my house. I will tie you up with a silk thread. I will cure your

319

claustrophobia with an infusion of claustromania. Tarry awhile in this introverted, slow part of the world; settle down in our common bankruptcy. Reduce—at your age, you should—the radius of your rambling."

János calls: He's at home and waiting for me. I try to extricate myself from my family chores, to slip out to him. He is more and more comfortable in that apartment. It's all set up now, he says; he has everything he needs. He does his reading in an armchair, under a strong lamp. From his balcony he can look at children in the playground, the trees, the moon. To exercise his wit, he talks a lot on the telephone. He has subscribed to numerous periodicals, and mail is being forwarded to him. His acquaintances from abroad are beginning to visit him, asking him to show them the mysteries of Budapest. What he says and where he goes is considered to be important, as if he were a celebrity. Young people hardly give him any peace. I'm afraid their smoking sessions may get him in trouble with the authorities. For his part, he rolls out the carpet of trust and invites each guest to sit at the other end.

He devotes time, too, to Jeremiah's manuscripts. He sees in them the layers of a major work. Now chronologically arranged, the material takes up more space than the *Encyclopaedia Britannica*. János comes here to Leander Street every day. In his apartment, on his mother's old desk, which has been emptied and cleared, he has set out his own yellow writing pads, but hasn't used very many of them; inspiration does not often push the nib of his fountain pen across the paper. Also, from time to time he has tendonitis in his right hand. He doesn't mind taking a break, is only too happy when something occurs to him that he hasn't told me yet and I am willing to listen. He then puts his drink and pipes in front of him; he has something to do for the next hour.

He is on his way to Melinda, approaching Leander Street. He crosses the wet park. On the yellow bench, as always, the same old lady sits with her fat, gray-haired, blind dog. The dog, lounging on a small rug, occasionally swallows a piece of honey cake. But here come miscreants: a lecherous old man with a lecherous mongrel, which has the nerve to sniff the behind of her venerable matron of a dog. "Satyr!" the old lady snorts. Her girlfriend, the spindly-legged, doubled-over widow of a former Supreme Court justice, settles down next to her. The old lady greets János kindly, and he exchanges a few pleasant words with her. A man walks by, the head of some government office. He will shoot himself in the head next year. Another man walks by; he, too, is the head of a government office, but he will be stabbed in the heart with a kitchen knife, instead. The papers will hush it up, calling it a suicide. And here comes the prince of the country's writers, out for a walk with a young colleague. The prince is telling his listener that the young generation ought to save itself for a higher purpose. Until that purpose is achieved, of course, there will be hard times. János remembers what he read earlier that day in the Royal Castle Library. Thirty-three Turkish carts piled high with severed heads, heads flung in by their mustaches or long hair. The heads of royalty and peasants, of the wise and the foolish. János hums to himself with relief. He is glad his house burned down.

The Reality of Time

The longer you live on this earth, the more real you become. Old people are more real than young people, because the old have arrived and the young are setting out. And the longer you love, the more enduring your love becomes. It takes time, also, to build a house, bring an enterprise to fruition, establish a tradition. I must spend a long time in a house before my heart desires to return to it. It takes time to develop virtues and vices. Character, taste, quality, and beauty all take time. A civilization not willing to spend the time will not be truly real. It will be only packaging, a nice wrapping. A stage set that can be struck at a moment's notice.

True art is not minimalist, but maximalist. It does not strive for the greatest effect at the lowest cost; it spends, rather, as much effort on a work as that work deserves. Minimalism saps the joie de vivre

321

from things. The cake tastes good at first, but when you realize it's store-bought, the taste is gone. If you can buy everything ready-made—a car, a house, furniture, a whole wardrobe—if you can order anything by catalog, why shouldn't you be able also to acquire your mate, child, education, and friends ready-made? And why can't I be ready-made? Already delivered? How much, please, is the least expensive version of history, wrapped in plastic, delivered to your home? And I'd like my mother's memoirs, in an inexpensive edition, of course. Let God make house calls—if he and the networks are willing—via television. The priest has a stylish haircut and his gestures are those of a pop singer. He has a half-hour time slot to jump and sing so I won't fall asleep.

János says that for an academic career in the United States, being from Budapest is not a bad thing at all. He has predecessors in many fields: mathematicians, physicists, philologists, social scientists. It's no worse to come from Budapest than from Prague, Warsaw, Odessa, or Vilnius. They like it if there's a sense of history behind you, and if you learned European culture not from a book but imbibed it with your mother's milk. And, indeed, János is European through and through. It's what he has always craved, with all his five senses. The art, the music, the poetry taught him to see, hear, think, jest. But he also wanted to make this bundle of accumulated culture completely portable and transform himself into an American. And he did fairly well. Different universities from different cities in the States competed for him, each upping the ante a little. Thus, for a while, János was at a different place each year, mostly working hard at charming the members of the local faculty. He cooked Hungarian dishes for his guests, increased their meager knowledge of Central Europe, Hungary, and particularly the Budapest intelligentsia. But with this constant drifting, where have we really been, whom did we really meet? All that we are left with are a few mannerisms, a cellophane wrapper in our hands, a smile, a turn of the head, where each gesture has an expiration date.

And then János came back to Budapest for a short visit, to be among us, people whose speech is familiar, people with whom conversation is a shared action. With us he took walks in the mountains, spent long hours in cafés. János is tied to us because we say unexpected things, are blessed and/or cursed with delight in the spoken word, because our game is telling stories. Our get-togethers are a way of keeping track of each other as we all stumble toward death, which today I consider to be our greatest treasure.

János claims that the man who has reconciled himself to himself is not too happy to be confronted with new questions. He is incapable of letting extravagant emotions loose on the stage; he is dogged, moderate, unalterable, fully formed. No extremes clash within him; he does not experiment; rather, he protects himself, worries about his possessions, everything he has managed to acquire. He wants to believe that he, his world, his nation, and his city are the best and the richest, that he is shouldering all the world's responsibilities. When you want to place your own community above all the others, he can engage only in quantitative ostentation. If you are aware of qualitative values, on the other hand, he must accept the idea of coequality. The existence of other dazzling virtues in a mysteriously complicated spatial structure. The stars in the sky are not in competition with one another.

Poets are not truly in competition, either. And neither are beautiful women, not really. With all their jealousies, they become each other, they are beautiful together. A good world is one that is like a novel. So it must be small rather than large. Good friends are those who meet often and always at the same place. A culture should have great inner articulation, be full of mature, inimitable qualities. Then we can afford to be led by our sense of beauty, and love or not love. As we grow older, we become increasingly more predisposed to the aura of others; we linger in the warmth of those we have come to know well.

From the best known through the lesser known we reach out into the unknown. The dot of light spreads for a while, fills the whole screen, then shrinks, grows faint, and vanishes; it is the dialog of durability with fluidity. Are we still capable—spinning in the same whirlpool—of surprising each other?

I wouldn't go so far as to say that János learned nothing from his travels. I, on the other hand, could not relinquish my demand for permanence, durability. During the last few years, I translated a number of modern classics: enduring works that grew richer with time, more mysterious after each reading. With the years, they ripen like good brandy. But even a table or armchair ought to last. So should a coat, and shoes. Then a person can travel anywhere. With only three well-made suits, you'll always look good, not like a department-store dummy. Your own clothes, in time, mold themselves to your shape. True, everything must fit into two large travel bags.

This is the city to which you return, a city of burials, a necropolis. You can do your shopping on foot, without encasing your body in General Motors armor. On the streetcar, you press against other living bodies. You have freedom of movement; you can cross the street to meet or to avoid someone; you can change your mind unexpectedly in mid-stride. You can take as many side streets as you like to reach your destination. Suppose you want to see whether that acquaintance of yours, whom you wouldn't visit in his home but don't mind sitting with at a table in the Tango, is at the corner espresso-bar. Budapest has many streets and many sidewalks, and down them anticipation and memory pull you in every direction. The unexplored parts of the city also call; we haven't been to this bar, we haven't turned this corner, we didn't know that on this street, lined with poplars, new yellow benches have been installed.

In that faraway country, János knew the solitude of long silent evenings, the calendar free to accept dinner invitations. He taught only four days a week, and also had long months of vacation. Laura was still in Budapest then. He lived with a butterfly. She cooked for him, attended his classes, took rides with him into the mountains. But then she flew away; she left to join an amateur theater group in Houston. There, the butterfly moved in with a designer.

János would walk into the classroom with a cup of coffee in his hand, wearing a jacket, a little under the influence. No papers, no index cards, no outline, only improvisation, spur-of-the-moment creativity, rolling with the conversational punches. Around noon, he left the class, exhausted, and with one of his colleagues would have a sandwich in the cafeteria. He'd go to a downtown bookstore and browse, have a cappuccino in a German pastry shop, then a whiskey in one of the red-brick lounges, then make his way home, greeting many people as he went.

Two of his female colleagues lived only a block away from him. One an instructor of classical Greek, the other a ceramics teacher, who was also a swimming champion. He could have asked either to come over to his place. But he didn't. Why? Perhaps he felt a little like a European cat among Australian birds. Since there are no predators in Australia, the birds are not afraid of other animals. They wait as the cat approaches; they trustingly place their necks between his teeth. What nice weather we're having, they note. The cat then lets go of the prey and sighs a sigh of ennui.

There were months when János hardly drank. He got up early and went to bed early. He worked out with a dumbbell and swallowed vitamin pills. He got a suntan. He built a snowman for the grandchild of a neighbor. Everything was pleasant and comfortable. Then he threw a farewell party, picked up his two travel bags—straps across the top, wheels on the bottom—and with a smile flew out of the city. A butterfly himself.

The Tango

From the street, János Dragomán looks through a window: two gray heads at a table; house plants; part of a framed mirror. Next, a hairdresser's window: bridal hair-pagodas, hot and cold permanent waves, archaic curlers. On the street, stinking, mud-spattered cars are parked. The sidewalks are dirty. Indoor plants in every window, even on top of wardrobes. A little boy climbs a bronze griffin. "Lacika, come on, let's go home." Lacika's mother wears a beige knit see-through dress, no bra, large pink earrings. Her nails are bright red. She knocks on a ground-floor window, receives a three-knock reply from within. A potbellied, stick-wielding scavenger pokes in garbage cans. Young girls in shorts sit on the iron railing of the playground, licking their ice creams. On a balcony: petunias, a parked scooter, and a woman in a white bathrobe raising her elbows high as she puts her hair in a bun. An acacia tree, half of it alive, half of it dead. A plump young mother in a purple sweatsuit and high heels, smoking a cigarette: "Sylvie! Come home! You can watch 'Tom and Jerry' at home, Sylvie! It starts in five minutes!" Sylvie is doing cartwheels. A woman on crutches, her legs bandaged, sinks down on one of the park benches. A fat, bespectacled boy wants to pat a dog, but the dog is barking; the boy waits patiently.

In an hour, János has a date with Melinda at the Tango. A rumbling yellow street-sweeper passes. Straw-hatted old women, their arms linked, are out for a stroll. A blue-and-white police car with a large spotlight on top. Wild grapes running up a column. On the balcony the column supports a pillowcase on a clothesline. A streetcar stop: the jingling of bells, the squealing of brakes. Across the street a bearded art student walks, carrying a heavy portfolio. A German shepherd, always kept on a balcony, barks. The legs of old women, the tight lips of old men; ruined faces, ruined bodies. Depression can make everything ugly, futile. What are you clamoring for?

Yesterday, Melinda and he spent the entire afternoon roaming the city. They jumped over the old cannon barrels on the ground near the War Museum; they kissed on the parapet of the Royal Castle. Over mulled wine Melinda suggested they exchange dirty jokes. They crossed a line of trees, pretending they had seven-league boots to carry them over every obstacle. Only a stone's throw in front of them, two old ladies made their way cautiously uphill. The hill, small houses, clusters of roofs and courtyards. János didn't let go of the warm hand in his. In one of the bars, they watched a married couple play pool. Cue stick in one hand, beer in the other, the man and the woman argued, chased each other around the pool table. In their Sunday best. They had started with brandy, celebrating their anniversary. The woman did most of the chasing. The game over, their cheeks were flushed as they ate their chowder and hot cherry peppers.

János's hot breath on Melinda's neck, below her bun. A yelp and goose pimples. He watches her eat a large Jonathan apple. He says, "All over the world, millions of thirty-eight-year-old women are eating apples, and I am stuck with you. Wretch that I am, I have reached the point where I love the way you put on your makeup, the way you comb your hair. I even agree—oh, shame!—with your opinions." She breaks all the toothpicks on the table, says that if he is enjoying the pleasures of the city, he ought to surrender to its morality, too. They might sit in silence in a church, side by side. Lamb of God, you who take the world's sins upon yourself, have mercy on our souls. The choreography of those receiving Holy Communion: In a column, by twos, they advance to the sacred wafer, then part and in single file, to the left and to the right, return to their places. Eyes full of ascension.

János is sitting at the Tango. In twenty years Micika has acquired a few wrinkles, but as a waitress she is better than ever. With the loose limbs of a dancer she carries her tray. Coffee, cognac, seltzer. A large mirror in a gilded frame hangs on the wall of the Tango's inner room. János cannot figure out how, sitting where he is, at a seemingly impossible angle, he can see himself in the mirror. German tourists sit down at one another's tables, drink beer, stretch and yawn. The waitress puts on a hit song in the jukebox. János orders another coffee, another cognac. Arm in arm, middle-aged twin sisters enter, followed by a used-car salesman with a large mustache. He scolds the women. From their conversation we learn that he is their older brother.

A taxi pulls into the square, a driver coming in; his relief is already waiting for him. The two men can't have been working long together; they seem to be just getting acquainted as they sit and chat awhile. The newly arrived driver is talking about a former colleague, now retired, who called him up, saying that he was looking for some-one to live with him as a nurse-companion. The union representative also called the driver, the one telling the story, to tell him about the situation. The retired driver's wife started drinking heavily. She lost a lot of weight, hardly ate. Whenever the driver came home, she was in bed. Then she sued for divorce, claiming she couldn't stand her husband's body odor. "A man has no chance in court, my friend, no chance at all. And the judge was a woman and in the middle of divorce proceedings herself. She awarded both children and the apartment to the wife." On top of everything, the old man now has problems with his equilibrium. Sometimes he falls down. The driver, on permanent night shift, helps out in the afternoon, does some of the cooking, washing, and cleaning for the old man.

János is moderate with the cognac. Nowadays he gets a headache if he has more than three glasses. And he gets heartburn from spicy food. Sometimes he feels pressure in his chest. One of his teeth is loose; it's one that supports a bridge. And that small mole on his side, it worries him. But not now; now we drink a third cognac, which is full of nourishment, and take a good look at yonder wench of ample proportions, the coffee-colored Gypsy whore giggling at the bar, firing her jokes in all directions. Her mouth is bright red, and she waves her bag and swings her bottom as she steps over to him and coos, "Can the gentleman be seduced?" "Not just now." "But I'm in the mood now. I may be big, maestro, I may eat goose legs and chocolate cake and not go on diets, but I still make a good living." With a sweeping professional eye she surveys the place to see if there are other prospects besides János, but does not seem to find anyone worthy enough. Uncle Sanyi has no money, not a cent. Uncle Sanyi: "All alone, I listen to the murmuring sea. . . ." Goose Legs: "Well, keep listening." A young man smiles sweetly in her direction. "Stop grinning. Just show me what you have. Not behind your fly; in your pocket." And again to János: "Don't keep looking at me like that, free of charge, because I'll get hot. You're not the one hustling here, honey, I am. And don't make me wait too long. If you'd like to see me later and I'm not here, just tell the girls, or the pianist with the gimp, that you're looking for Fruzina, Fruzi." This woman has confidence in her charms. She'll sit on your bed, like an enormous cooked goose in the middle of a table. "I have a long black slip that buttons in the back. Go home, maestro. I'll ring your bell in half an hour, I know where you live. I'll wear that black slip, I'll let you unbutton it. By the time you get through with all the buttons, you'll be in the mood. If Fruzi tells you you'll be in the mood, you can bet your life on it. When you see me naked, your parachute will open." "I'll take a rain check," János says.

The two middle-aged sisters come over to his table; their brother has left. They've been quarreling; they want him to decide. The younger called the older a whore. The older says the younger has no right to sling mud at her. "May I inquire, ladies, what is the age difference between you?" "Almost ten minutes. My sister here, sir, is constantly upbraiding me because I still need a man. Well, it's true, but not every day. Once a week I still need a man." "A man! She sleeps with her own son-in-law!" "Is it my fault if my husband won't touch me?" János asks the two witches what they'll have, snaps his fingers. Micika is on her way with two glasses of wine.

A man with a large mustache is brooding over his loss in the lottery. A little girl stands next to her scar-faced mother, bored. She turns her attention to a woman in a fur coat who keeps adjusting her false teeth. A bearded man puts his hand on the mother's hand. A short man comes over, says something annoying. "Go away, little asshole," says the bearded one. The short man stands his ground. These two know a few things about each other. "And who do you think you are? You think you can still dance like an acrobat? You were kicked out of the show a long time ago." "Go away, little mosquito, or I'll flatten you!" János and the little girl exchange a look; they both have been watching the fur-coated lady with the false teeth, who has a tic. Every five seconds she sticks out her tongue, punctuating the unfolding dramas around her.

These chairs were here before János left the country, but the wallpaper is new. Unpainted pipes wind around the walls. The lottery expert calls, "Bring me a rum!" He left his family, Micika whispers to János, pawned even the mattresses from under them. Beside the lottery expert sits a soccer fan, who follows his favorite team everywhere. You can ruin your family with soccer, too. He used to be such a good husband; he even cleaned the house, shaking out the dust rag on the balcony, a polka-dot kerchief on his head. But on Saturdays he became a maniac. The scar-faced woman says to her lover, "There is a crisis. Please understand, there is a crisis between us." The bearded lover muses, "To the dog you give the expensive sausages, to me the cheap ones." Uncle Sanyi, sipping his raspberry juice, asks Uncle Józsi, who is drinking beer, "You remember Dezső, the butcher? What a shrew he has for a wife! Even in the rain and

329

snow he walks the streets, afraid to go home." The two old men get up and go to urinate.

Melinda sweeps in. The waitress changes the record in the juke-box. "Let's Twist Again," a song a quarter of a century old. János used to dance to it with Laura. He danced with Melinda at one of the crowded Saturday-night parties this last summer. Dancing, they looked at Antal, who was standing by himself, and he looked back at them. Giving them his blessing? A half hour later Melinda found Antal in another room of the apartment. He was not dancing, he was sitting in an armchair, and in a chair opposite him sat a young girl. He got up, leaned back against the window frame, and like a silent cat she went and played with his necktie. Melinda took all this in. He wrinkled his nose a little, like someone making fun of the situation, but then in front of everybody he put a hand on the girl's hip, as if to demonstrate that whatever he put his hand on belonged to him. But Melinda stepped in, called Antal away. They were alone for a while, but then the girl appeared again, bringing a saxophone, which she handed to Antal. And he began to play purring notes to inform his wife that he would be leaving the party with this girl, because she knew when to bring a man his saxophone.

In Ófalu he plays his saxophone under wild fruit trees in the old cemetery. Below him, a brook in which women stand barefoot while they do their wash. Antal takes a dip in a natural pool fed by the brook, then goes to the garden of the hotel, from which Franciska calls him into the kitchen. She opens the oven, bends over to have a look inside—knowing that he will appreciate not only the stuffed flank of pork but also her large magnificent body. With the self-confidence of the woman of the house, she sways as she walks, making her keys rattle. She curtains the balcony of her top-floor apartment and sunbathes there naked. From the hill of the cemetery where Antal plays his saxophone, he can see into her balcony. The silent, half-witted cowherd, who early each day with his bugle calls the cows of Ófalu out of their sheds to the blue pasture, listens to Antal's music, to Antal playing for his woman. Franciska, on her back, pulls up one of her knees. But Antal waits; he is in no hurry. Just as he doesn't open his mail right away. Melinda wants to go after him, to

Ófalu, to keep him out of Franciska's bed, to bring him back. But she doesn't know what excuse to give. "I had a bad cold, a sore throat. For breakfast today I ate only a little müesli with yogurt, but when the Number 5 bus crossed Elizabeth Bridge, the sight of the Danube made me feel immediately better."

János and Melinda together in the rickety elevator. They thought of having lunch at the Gay Catfish, but then decided to be alone, just the two of them, in Suicide Fani's bed. Melinda, over her shoulder: "What do you want from me, you devil? Why don't you go back to your America? If I were to give you a boy, he'd turn out to be all beak and claws, like his father." János replies: "You arrange everything so well around yourself, I'd like you to arrange me, too. I'd like to rest in your shade, to look at the sky through the leaves of your olive tree." In her company his manhood still soars, like Gothic art. In sweet, stolen hours they grind each other to exhaustion. At other times, they are prey to intense hurts, insults, omissions.

A couple of old ladies in the building are protective of Melinda's and János's affair. The one-eyed, eye-patched watchmaker also greets Melinda in a specially friendly way. This watchmaker has a tomcat whose duels with other cats leave a bloody trail. Amalia, next door to János, complains about the cat to the watchmaker, but he laughs at her. Kálmán, Amalia's young friend, hints at some physical retaliation. That's all the watchmaker needs; he's already rolling up his sleeves. "Come on, come on, you cream cheese. I'll spread you all over the street." Kálmán walks away, not wanting to dirty his hands with the watchmaker's ugly face. On the indoor balcony, elbows propped on the railing, head propped on hands—an unmoving statue—stands a wilted man: a former member of the Arrow-Cross Party. During the hard years of socialism, he distinguished himself as a prison guard of the security police, and is now a volunteer policeman. His mustache quivers whenever he sees somebody ring János's bell. Spy and informer, he remains at his post in front of his apartment all day long, leaning on his elbows, hoping that something will happen that he can report to the authorities. During the afternoon rush hour, however, this vigil is interrupted, and János's door goes unobserved for a while, because the good neighbor has to put on an arm band, go to the corner, and direct traffic. He stops the cars when the light is red, hurries them on when the light is green, and they obey him, they all wait for him to point or raise his hands. The only thing that bothers the old man is that at the next corner a fat boy, with his tongue hanging out like one retarded, is doing exactly the same thing.

At the Corner
of Tompkins Square

Through the north window of my study in New York, I can see the East River and the jutting edge above the Lower East Side. To the northwest, I have a view of the Empire State Building, its tower lit up each evening, sometimes with different colors. From my west window I can see south to the World Trade Center. This is the world's first mythological skyscraper ensemble. The proper way to look at this city is from above and at an angle. What you see, then, is a structure made of roofs, towers, unevenly ending vertical prisms. When I work until sunrise, I see the towers go from ink black to a glowing purple against a blue background. Every daybreak is a holiday. Then comes evening. You throw yourself into it, into the reflection of the reddish-yellow lights on brick-red walls. New York is, actually, the color of flesh.

Filth, neglect; the makeshift, obsolete remnants of an iron age. The variety of physical and emotional deformation is all part of the city's magic. And the danger. This is not a good place for the weak and the sick; this is a cruel city. It tells you that you are a nobody, or that you are really somebody. It tells you to accept yourself. Tells you that your success is yours, and your defeat is also yours. Here people are not overly cautious; they open up, they confide to you their life stories. They are serious, friendly, benevolent, slightly insecure, intelligent, but not particularly good at irony.

For a long time I was homesick for Hungary. Where the air is just humid enough, not too humid, and the seasons alternate evenly, mildly. I imagined myself in the woods of Buda or on the lake shore in Ófalu. I would stay away from politics and give literature the time it deserved. Nor would I deny myself the earthly joys. I would spend my declining years in idyllic rumination. Such thoughts were especially strong in the swelter of August. I needed a place to escape to. Perhaps there was one, perhaps there wasn't. My face twitched; sweat poured from my forehead; my right shoulder ached whenever I lifted my arm; I could hardly breathe on the street. The noise of air conditioners drove me mad. The air-conditioning gave me a cold. I was weak; my vision was blurred when I tried to read; I had to lie down. Behind my closed lids I saw Klauzál Square. But then a few images of neighboring Tompkins Square flickered, and then the two squares merged: they almost seemed to rhyme with each other. But you must always have a target for your misanthropy. The need is obstinate within us; it will not let us enjoy our new surroundings. Nothing is as good as it was in our childhood. The climate here is no good, nor is the food; the stores are full of junk. This is capitalism in its most unbaked form. The ostentation of little people. I fought New York for a long time.

I go for a walk. There is always something to look at. Facing the triumphal arch on Washington Square, a black man delivers a speech to a nonexistent audience. When writing, it's enough to reach the next sentence; when walking, it's enough to reach the next corner. Here in the Village, I've been freer of the emotional push and pull of my country than I was when I lived in it, was submerged in it. I begin to see what is good about my country. The apartment I have in the Village is the first one with a mezuzah on the doorpost, the first since my childhood. The mezuzah is painted the same color as the front door, which is equipped with large brass locks.

Everything done or made by human beings may be judged in terms of its aesthetic value. Even mass murder—the orchestra and the carefully mowed lawn welcoming the new arrivals in Auschwitz —has its aesthetics. But it is only in the West that you can afford to be a free aesthetician. Here in the Danube region you are, willy-nilly, a moralist. Still, the strictest of moralists also wants beauty. I've heard that there is a military aesthetics, and an aesthetics, too, of international banking. In our youth, my friend Kobra was unwilling to accept this. I understood his emotion-driven arguments, yet didn't care for the moral icing he was putting on his cake. The life of sinners makes for better literature than the lives of saints.

The memories of my youth in Budapest are rather sketchy. The whole thing is locked in a frame. Now and then a character may step from the frame. But while I flit about in New York, David Kobra pulls page after completed page out of his typewriter. A stubborn creature, he turns the mill wheel around and around. This city is, perhaps, not a mousehole for me but a mousetrap. Could this sort of thinking be the result of growing old? Meanwhile, Kobra, with the simplemindedness of a resolute person, smiles at my perplexity. In this old Budapest apartment in this old building on this old square and on this old balcony, I surrender to senility, I contemplate my wayward past. Could this be the right place for dying?

János can be at home at any point on the globe, but he cannot find the right place anywhere. The truth is, the right place is tied to the right woman. Where your wife is, where she is happy, that is where you belong. But unfortunately I haven't yet reached that level of intimacy. Things are not made any simpler by the fact that the husband of the woman I love, who is also my friend, appears to have no intention of divorcing her. After three days both the fish and the guest begin to smell.

Of you, my dear Kobra, I ask only that, when the time comes, you scatter my ashes into the Danube from the Chain Bridge. Because this morning I did precisely that with Laura's urn. I was the person closest to Laura, and you are the person closest to me, so this will be your job. Why the Danube, you ask? The Danube is both the fluid and aesthetic heart of Budapest. The city is most beautiful there. Széchenyi, that nineteenth-century baron, engineer, and statesman, built a sensuous bridge between East and West; the Chain Bridge, for me, is the center of Central Europe. That is where I want my discreet and belated funeral. You should be the only one present. The undertaker will give you the urn. Put the porcelain vessel under your arm, and take a streetcar—not a taxi, for God's sake!—to the Chain Bridge. I'd rather be poured into water than into dirt or mud. Everything that's left of your friend will be in that package. Throw me in with both hands, then watch how I lie in my watery gray-green grave. You'll be able to see me even with your eyes closed. From that day on, think of me whenever you cross the Chain Bridge. Think of János Dragomán the provocateur. He throws up the red ball, and it does not fall back down.

True, my master, all this is taking place at ground level, at a very great distance from Vesper, the evening star. If I look out the window of my dilapidated New York apartment, I see sights very different from those of Leander Street, where five minutes can go by without the sight of another human being. Tompkins Square, like Klauzál Square, is a place more for the common people than for the upper crust. On Sundays, especially in the winter, when it's freezing, soup is distributed to the homeless, mostly black, as they stand in line, stamping their feet, tin cups and bowls in their hands. And the unemployed in Budapest, are they still considered vagrants, hooligans, a public menace? Are the unemployed still required to have certificates from a mental hospital declaring them insane? And what if a man simply doesn't feel like getting up in the morning? Because his job is boring. Do they still lock up people like that? The Tompkins Square homeless would not stand for such a thing. Their union would file a complaint. On Klauzál Square, true, there is no need for a mounted policeman to guard my safety. On the other hand, I could not demonstrate there against the battle cruiser in the harbor carrying nuclear missiles. In Hungary it would be unheard-of for a citizen with a bullhorn to rail against his own navy. Aside from the fact that Hungary has no navy, no harbors, no battle cruisers.

Actually, very few people are interested in the yelling that goes on in Tompkins Square. We might also mention that four or five police cars, to be on the safe side and prevent anything's getting out of hand, are continually patrolling the neighborhood, and one radio call could summon forty or fifty cars in no time at all. People are looking at a leaflet. Oh, well, the American Communist Party. The leaflets are being handed out by a kindly old man, a few young girls, and a

boy who is also setting up a loudspeaker. Klauzál Square is quite
different. I don't have to open my window, or even my eyes, to see
what happened there on Christmas Day, 1944.

Here on Klauzál Square, I am the oldest tenant. When I was
born, this was a four-room apartment. After the war, co-tenants were
assigned to us by the government; in the sixties my mother managed
to get rid of them by dividing the apartment. Which meant she had
to say good-bye to the bathroom. That's why we had a shower stall
put in, illegally, in the kitchen. When the apartment still had four
rooms, and Klauzál Square had become the heart of the ghetto, at
the end of 1944, one of two arm-banded, booted young men shot to
death a young Jewish woman in our living room because she refused
to go with them for sex. And they shot an old man who got up and
said in a choking voice, "You see what you've done?" "Will you shut
up, Jews?" That's what the young man said after he shot the old man.
I remember his little smile, which indicated that he thought this brief
lesson in manners witty. There was silence in the room. It's possible
that the young man was a born teacher, the kind who wants to hear
a pin drop, and until he does he will not look at his pupils, but,
instead, pace menacingly up and down, staring at his feet. Then the
other young man pointed at my mother. In the silence, everybody
looked at her. "May I ask you not to shoot me in front of my son?"
We stood side by side, holding hands, looking at the two young men.
The one who'd done the shooting said, "Let her be, if she doesn't
want to. Don't force the Jew to eat pig." That's right, don't.

There are many kinds of people, many kinds of madmen, living
on Tompkins Square, but a thing like that could not and would not
have happened there. On Tompkins Square, one group of people does
not say that another group of people has to be killed. That type of
rhetoric will find no takers. What can and may happen around there
is that just as you are about to open the inner door of your building,
just as the key reaches the lock, you feel two knife points, from the
right and the left, pushing through your leather jacket in the area of
your shoulder blades. That's how I was once robbed of my change,
my wallet, and even my faithful old cap. Luckily, my favorite fountain
pen, in its own special pocket inside my jacket, went unnoticed. All
in all, I feel safer in Tompkins Park, where all these different races

come together and organize street parties on Sunday mornings, where to the music of each group the others dance in their own way. Let me have the whole bottle, so I won't have to bother you for it glass by glass.

János played two jazz pieces for Kobra in a seashore inn. The audience slowly surrounded the piano, conversations stopped, as he improvised. They both had a number of Irish coffees—who knows why?—maybe because of the afternoon sunshine. And they both decided, at the same moment, that it would be better to go and lie on the beach. They woke up to the rumbling of the tide. There was an old wooden pier nearby. They ran out on it and jumped into the ocean, even though it was getting cold. They swam hard, when suddenly—again, at the same moment—they both grew frightened. The sea was getting rough; they couldn't see land. It took them forever to swim back. Shivering with cold and out of breath, they finally made it to the grassy shore. Irresistible laughter, building slowly, took hold of them; as it increased in intensity, it became more and more like crying. Laughing, they squatted, elbows on their knees, facing each other. Then ceremoniously they forgave themselves and each other for everything.

János claims that it is only at the edge of a mass grave that he is willing to say "we." He feels himself one with those shot and pushed into the pit. But otherwise no. Why should he feel himself one with these characters on the street? Why with these and not with those? European streets are so much alike when seen from the America of countless family houses. From the America that loves to function well and does. The European streets, in classical revival style from the turn of the century, from Lisbon to Budapest, are all so similar. Similar characters sit in similar cafés on similar streets. Their animosities, to János, are no more than folklore. A cosmopolitan or an emigrant, they are really the same thing. Neither takes local politics to heart. At the corner of Tompkins Square, János's fate does not depend on which candidate is elected president. Politics is not above him; rather, it is next to him, inside the TV set. Whatever the administration, it does not force him into uncomfortable roles or keep him from doing what he likes to do.

In the autumn of 1956, I stayed here in Budapest. I believed that

337

while they controlled my body, they could not control my mind. But of course they did control my mind. When friends were released from prison (with the exception of one or two who were put into unmarked graves, according to the custom of an earlier regime) and the breeze of political thaw began to blow, I thought that I could become inconspicuous. I was tired of being interrogated. That my writings were regularly rejected for political reasons I viewed as a phenomenon typical of underdeveloped nations, like high infant mortality. I expressed this opinion at a gathering of the Writers' Union. I also happened to mention it to a British journalist I met by chance. Shortly afterward, I said the same thing in a café in the presence of my regular companions, among whom were a couple of informers. As a response to my remarks, I was denied publication altogether. I realized then that the overwhelming majority of my friends were able to accept the political regulation of their lives. Comparing the ways in which my friends expressed themselves before and after my imprisonment, I also realized that they were adjusting their thoughts to their behavior. In the sixties, the memories of hangings and imprisonments were still vivid in our minds; we were still reeling from the sound of Russian tanks rolling into our country. Organized opposition did not yet exist. Of course, we had friends. I took up a kind of sober civil-rights position. If I could afford it, I said, why shouldn't I be able to travel, to leave my place of residence any time I liked? Why shouldn't I be able to publish my ideas, whatever they might be? And by what right was I subjected to listening devices? A swift car took me to the infamous Swiftcar Street jail, where I was kept for months. Although the courts dropped the charges of sedition, a colonel told me to lie low if I didn't want to be their guest again. I wasn't a free citizen, in other words. But neither was I a mole, to dig myself into mother earth.

Here in Budapest, I'm told, the way to be is unhappy and mildly disgusted with everything. That's the message you get from our books and movies. Here the tragic approach to life is considered the human approach. Existence is a mousetrap, a dead end, a crisis with no solution. My students in America, in Joseph K.'s shoes, would have skipped town first thing and not waited to be condemned. They don't understand why K. kept trying to prove his innocence to a phantom court. They would all have made fast tracks to America. "Something doesn't work?" asks the American. There must have been an error; the thing has to be approached differently. "Something doesn't work?" asks the Central European. "Well, what do you expect, that's our fate."

Impressionism and cubism, Marxism and psychoanalysis, surrealism and structuralism are phenomena that have nothing to do with national or governmental groupings. They have to do with two dozen people who meet in various great cities. The prophet's wrath directed at Babylon. (In Babylon, even the harlots serve Babylon.) I am a big-town man; I love where I am; in New York you can roller-skate or sing in the street. I make my living by thinking—by words written or spoken—about what interests me. Some of my books can actually be found in bookstores. When I call someone, I don't worry about my phone's being tapped. When I look out the window there is always an airplane in the sky.

On the street, black plastic garbage bags. Blacks are ripping up an old carpet. A black woman, her mouth very red, is telling an endless story to a bag lady. It's cold. In several layers of clothes, the fat owner of a secondhand store sits in front of his establishment, reading the paper. On a bench near a nightclub, a young black man looks around, shoves his white cap farther back on his head; he is smoking grass; he is relaxed. In the forecourt of the university, casually dressed New Yorkers. Holding hands, students stroll in pairs, talking, explaining things to each other. It's getting dark. Reddish-yellow, velvety mood lighting for the entire city. In the neighboring lot, Puerto Rican kids break dancing, their waists thrusting out in wide arches from necks and heels. A wrought-iron black fence; on the stoops, prostitutes. I say hello to Chinese and Ukrainians, Poles and Mexicans, Germans and Jews, whites and blacks and yellows and browns. Joggers, some in pink outfits, with earphones on their heads, some in loud jackets; a mustached man in a visored cap, his large dog running at his side.

In my apartment I have both mice and cockroaches. I stumble out of the corner supermarket, hardly able to bear the smell of disinfectant. The junk food is not cheap but it's colorful. In a bar, lonely people watch a TV screen: gigantic figures with padded shoulders crouch and run. Animated Jewish families with children; plump Latin Americans with even more children. One of the houses is trussed up by metal scaffolding, resting on steel piles. An orange peel on the sidewalk. A little girl plays conductor in her kitchen, using a large wooden spoon as a baton. In this parking lot, people get mugged; in that Chinese restaurant, the food is good. Thick, red cast-iron fire hydrants, and at every step, patches of tar and asphalt.

America. Stars thrive on scandal, secrets revealed. You are considered a bad player if you don't advertise yourself. Silver-screen polytheism, like the gods of Olympus. It is a democratic religion. Any undertaking is valid if it makes money. Why not swim with the current, go with the flow? Why tie yourself into knots? Is there a higher proof of your existence than being sought after? Than having a horde of people want to buy you and take you home with them? Thousands if not millions want to go to bed with you. Tear you apart, eat you alive. That is bliss. Ideally, the star no longer exists. He is completely bought up, down to his last enigma. That is fulfillment.

Adultery Domesticated

János Dragomán once survived an explosion; the walls collapsed, but not on him. In a car accident, he was not sitting on the side of the crash. A tile, falling from the roof of a five-story building, missed him because he turned to look at a woman. As he stepped off a curb, a truck almost ran him down, but his girlfriend of one day yanked him back on the sidewalk. Another time, he received a strange envelope, suspected it was a letter bomb. At first he just put it aside, laughing at himself, but then he looked at the envelope again, smiled, and called the police. In New York, he once picked up his phone and heard a Hungarian voice whisper, "You don't have long to live."

His border crossings are always full of unpleasantness; customs officials always search him and usually do find, by accident, some hashish on him. This happened in Turkey. He was taken to an island and locked up. He swam to freedom, was picked up by a Greek fishing boat, but they returned him to the jail, since he had been involved with drugs. He was freed at last, and in the first New York bar he went to, wandering in by chance, he had to hit the floor because of a sudden exchange of gunfire.

He always paid attention to omens, and there were always omens. "You'll bring me trouble," said Cheryl, his girlfriend. Like the time the police broke in on him in a Paris studio and found him with a girl, unquestionably a minor. Academicians intervened on his behalf; even the president of the republic was informed of the case. János finally was allowed to leave France, but they gave him to understand that he would not be a welcome guest there again. He went on a conciliatory honeymoon with Cheryl. They were robbed. They got caught in a hurricane. Sobbing, Cheryl said good-bye. "Darling, you're a walking disaster." After she left, he sat in Bradley's Bar on Fifth Avenue and without loosening his tie polished off thirteen Jack Daniel's while mumbling to himself, "The silly goose. She wants guarantees, insurance."

He asked Murder, Inc. for an estimate. What would it cost to have John Dragoman, the well-known critic, bumped off? The price was flatteringly high. For thirty-five thousand dollars he could have himself put on ice. The money, he had. It would be interesting to see if he could shake his hit man. Kill his hired killer. But this form of suicide was like masturbation. Why should he pay, anyway, for his own murder? Whenever he heard that so-and-so was his enemy, he struck while the iron was hot, dialed the person, and began to insult him, cunningly, irremediably. To provide this enemy with a little motivation. Thirty-five thousand dollars could be spent so many more entertaining ways. Why not have a ball in Hungary?

János's mother was buried during his absence. At the time, he was on a walking tour of the Galilee. Swimming in the Lake of Gennesaret—in the middle of the lake, so no marksman could take potshots at him from the Golan Heights—he felt a wonderful serenity.

341

The dark-blue sparkling water, the translucent lake bottom, the mountain peaks painted red by the sun. A dreamlike state. Now everything would work. Now everybody would be content with two fish and two loaves of bread. Now the spirit would be more powerful than the flesh. He thought of the Last Supper. If you make your pupils sad by departing, you should at least leave behind you some good tidings. That young man does not know that his murder will be a turning point in world history, but he knows that what is happening on the Mount of Olives is also known on the Temple's plaza. The public has been prepared, the floodlights have been hooked up. The son surrenders his life to the paternal law with the same firmness with which the paternal law takes it. Through his goggles János looks at the layers of sand and light in the blue heat under the sea.

He was invited to a seminar in Jerusalem, on narrative literature; to Paris, to lecture on European identity from an American point of view; to Amsterdam, to deliver a speech entitled "Metropolis and Culture." The fashionable author going places. On one of these quick trips, Laura's urn snapped open in his suitcase. Some of his wife's ashes spilled. In ever-increasing numbers, Hungarians were going to New York, and they all looked up János. Young authors sent him their manuscripts. At home, he began to be mentioned in various publications. They were proud of him. A young man called from Budapest, asked if he would be willing to grant an interview to Hungarian Radio. "You rush from continent to continent, but it's all surface," Laura would have said.

At the hotel, Kobra was waiting for János with the news of his mother's death, her funeral, the key to her apartment. "She said you should come home and live here. Let him sleep in my bed, she said." Why shouldn't he sleep in his mother's bed for a few weeks? She died in the most beautiful nightgown, her head on an embroidered damask pillow. Securing her chin in advance with a muslin scarf. But her eyes were open when they found her. János was shown a photograph of her taken by the local doctor, who was the first person called by Amalia. (Amalia also had a key to the apartment.) The doctor took out his Polaroid and, as Fani's image slowly came to life—or, rather, to death—on the extracted photosensitive paper, with a respectful dip of the head said, "Neither of us, my dear, can top this in morbidity." The doctor and János's mother used to compete with each other as to who could tell the most morbid story. Going up the stairs, János met a middle-aged woman with whom he had played as a child, but she didn't recognize him, and he said nothing to her. He unlocked and opened the door, walked around the apartment, opened the windows, sat down on his mother's wide bed covered with a camel's-hair bedspread. Here, too, the photograph of his piano-playing father, who looks lost. The apartment is too full of things. He invited the girls to come and browse among his mother's silk blouses and underthings. Even during the Rákosi years, Döme was able to bring Fani fine things from Paris.

Melinda asked János why he hadn't come to visit Hungary before. "I could have, and probably wouldn't have had any problems. But if I kept coming home, I wouldn't have been an emigrant, only a Hungarian citizen living abroad. Now I have a chance to emigrate to Budapest, too. I could retire from New York University and, on the pension they'd give me, live well here in my mother's apartment. Go swimming early in the morning, work at home for a few hours, have lunch, take a long circuitous walk that leads to Jeremiah's tower. From which, coming down one flight, I'd be glad to accept your invitation to tea. I could settle back here, not have to move a finger for money, be a good-for-nothing, garrulous barfly, a vagabond, an Oblomov of Budapest."

Another shot of rum to go with the tea. A dash of Hindu-English Assam. A heaping spoon of Russian tea. A spiced tea with a smoky Chinese flavor. In the kitchen of his apartment on Klauzál Square, János chooses from among several teas or combines them. In his suitcases he always carries boxes of tea and a small earthenware teapot. His concoctions are dark and heady. But they could benefit from a little moderation, I say to him. He replies by observing that when the teacher points to the moon, the imbecile looks at the finger. He means that he is the imbecile; he means that he is looking at me. Yes, I've noticed. The doorbell, just in time. It is the local doctor. "Your mother, Professor, was a beautiful woman, and her sense of humor was indomitable, to the very end." Luckily, the doctor

343

doesn't stay long. As I lie down on the camel's-hair bedspread, János disconnects the phone.

He has a photograph of his mother taken during her last days. Large eyes, shiny face. In the courtyard, she would take children by the hand, lead them out to the square, and dance with them. Once a week, her masseur supplemented his massage with a sexual service. For this, too, he was paid. Mincing no words, in her letters she told János why she needed an increase in her monthly allowance. If, instead of this regular arrangement, she were to go out to satisfy her needs, it would cost a lot more.

In his closet there is an amazing selection of liquor; every available space is taken up by bottles. Maybe we won't be here next year. Maybe we'll be standing in line in front of a detention camp with packages for our husbands, and I'll be carrying two packages. János asks me, "Would you like some soup? A rump roast, a leg of lamb? Or should I make you a tenderloin steak?" There's only one person whose cooking I like as much as my own. Yours, you bastard. You wine and dine me, wicked seducer. Making full use of the fresh-food market and the kosher liquor store on the square, not to mention the cheese turnovers and floating islands at Andi's. You know how to fatten a person for the kill. Normally, a female form of treachery.

Your mind, I know, wanders incessantly behind your closed lids. Antal is even worse. His attention leaves me for his film studio. All men are absentminded. Here, with you, it's a little different; there is still some panting and rattling in our relationship. So many things—anger, pleasure, dying—make one rattle. But at a cocktail party, rattling is not allowed. Just as blood cannot be washed out of a towel, so the smell of blood cannot be removed from the air of a stairwell. Blood spots persist on a parquet floor.

No one has ever been killed in our house on Leander Street, and no one has committed suicide there. Only natural death leisurely claiming its victims. So far, in our house everyone has had a long life. Still, people leave, running, as people do, from their salvation. János said to Antal: "I don't want to take Melinda from you. I'm no poacher, no cattle thief. All I want, with your permission, is to be a pleasant, gracefully aging friend of the family. Don't be so conventional. Let Melinda slip up to my apartment once in a while; we're depriving you of nothing." I'm slipping right now. When János is in town, my legs take me to him. I ride the old elevator up in the building where he is the oldest tenant. He takes his time opening the door. People are watching me. I am not popular among the female tenants. Once I ran from him, and he chased me, barefoot and in his pajamas. And they cursed me: What had I done to the poor man? Finally he lets me in, his arms full of celebration. An hour later, such peace courses through me that this light rain following the thunder and lightning seems to be a rain of magic.

I could never see polygamy, and said so whenever the men brought up the subject. Polyandry, on the other hand, has always had a fascination for me. I don't see why the ménage à trois shouldn't work. It would ease Antal's guilt about spending so little time at home. He would have a replacement. These big successful men think that their absence is the occasion for sorrow and pining. It isn't. And the children love János. And they don't like it when I lie to them. They are much more sensitive to lies than Antal. Also, I could yell at János instead of yelling at Antal, and no matter what tantrums I threw, he would know how to make me laugh. He would come with me to the market, carry my basket, peel the carrots and the potatoes, and hold forth expertly on his appreciation of my physical charms while I did the cooking. He would praise all my dishes instead of wolfing them down and mumbling, with his mouth full, "Good, very good." When it comes to compliments, Antal is not very imaginative. Soon we'll have been married eighteen years. He could work in peace down in Ófalu, and whenever he needed a woman could bike over to Franciska. It's a fact that in bed his approaches have become less frequent. And he farts, too, in bed, in my presence.

When it comes to sheer muscle, Antal could lay out János with a single blow. True, he does speak appreciatively of that left hook with which János once flattened him while they were still in school. János corrects him: "I put everything I had into it, right on the chin. And Antal? His head shook a little, a strange light appeared in his eyes, and he took a step toward me, laid his hand on my shoulder, and said, 'Good punch.' " János sometimes pounds his fists jokingly on my husband's chest: "What a beast! What an animal!" So many of us in Budapest are on intimate terms with one another, entangled in various ties of friendship, love, business, and politics. We are a kind of clan or extended family. A relative here is one you have slept with, or shared a lover with. Through Antal alone, I must have a thousand sisters.

Yes, I know, my dear, you're ready to pull up stakes. The whole thing is getting too tight for you. In your dreams you see eight-lane highways and feel the heat that hits you as you step out of your air-conditioned Oldsmobile. The call of Battery Park, the Statue of Liberty, Manhattan. But right now, in my house on Leander Street, in my living room, you are reading Eduard Mörke's *Mozart's Trip to Prague*. Sipping, as you read, from a glass of pear brandy set out for you within easy reach. There's even a hassock for your feet. The woman of the house leaves her guest in peace; she does not need to be entertained. A small portion of her men's conversation will suffice; she'd rather busy herself with something else. Antal wants to make a movie based on our story. It would take place in a house just like this. He's looked at several houses with gardens, but the owners want a lot of money from the film company. Have the actors play here, in his own house? No, says Antal.

My husband is more able than helpless; he knows how to protect himself; he is hard to chew, hard to swallow. All of us here, together, have always been hard to chew and swallow. Always getting stuck in somebody's throat. Now the emperor, now the tsar chokes on us, unable to swallow yet unwilling to spit us out. Antal knows that everything about him is known and that everything therefore can be taken from him. But maybe this is no longer the situation. Politicians and artists are keeping their eyes on each other. Politically, Antal retracts his claws; he likes to serve his own culinary creations to the luminaries and antiluminaries who sit at our table. Around that large green table there is room for clipped-wing heroes, conservative reformers, radical reformers, and patriots complaining of moral decline and the futility of it all.

Melinda's Circles

From the depths of the swimming pool, I can hear my family's monologues. I paddle smoothly from wall to wall. No matter in which direction I swim, my children are still attached to me, attached with a cord that can't be broken. Why did I bring them into this world? So that they could be. I was here, too, in the Lukács pool, when I imagined my son, István, for the first time. He was quietly pounding my belly from the inside, wanting to get out. And then suddenly he emerged, all eleven pounds of him. "This one is a bishop!" the midwife yelled. In the last month my belly was enormous, though the rest of me was thin. A strange, watermelon belly. People couldn't keep their eyes off it. During the last weeks, I sighed a lot: This is too much for me, enough, please come out! Then he came, almost tearing my body in half. I heard a dog bark outside, a streetcar clatter past, saw trees against an overcast sky. The pale-green tiles of the wall. That was the most important moment in my life. A moment of oblivion and awareness. Not all the placenta followed the child out; it clung to the wall of the womb; I kept bleeding. Two doctors worked feverishly, giving me injections, plasma. I felt very far away but was not concerned. They tell me that I nearly bled to death. In the old days, women did. When they handed me the swaddled baby, I recognized the features of my husband, of my father, and a little of myself, too. A sublimely serene face. The baby was not wrinkled, red, or tortured; peace radiated from him.

Few joys can match that of taking your baby in your arms, putting your breast into his mouth. István sucked hard, like a pump. The two of us became one, a well-working machine. For the first time in my life, I was a strategist, making schedules, anticipating difficulties. What was bad for me was bad for the baby, so everything had to be good for me. Was it pleasant to look at an old walnut tree in the garden? Then I looked at it, and positioned my son's crib so he and the tree could make friends. Then, of course, came the problems: an infected nipple, insomnia, and loneliness, because just then Antal had to go to India as a cameraman. To my surprise, my mother offered her services and worked around me like a cheerful nun. She was intoxicated with her first grandchild. To this day, she understands him, and he her, better than anyone else in the family. After two months, when I woke in the middle of the night, I would know, from the sound of the crying, that my son had an arm caught in the railing of his crib, or that he wanted to be on his stomach, or that he was hungry, or that he wasn't hungry but wouldn't mind a little pampering.

After his return from India, Antal spent a lot of time running to the pharmacy. Doctors became demigods. One doctor detected a murmur in István's heart; the second one heard nothing; the third one yes; the fourth one no. Antal needed more doctors; the sight of our healthy giant baby did not reassure him. He slept alone; my body now was off-limits to him. When I nursed, he would avert his eyes. He occasionally looked in on the feeding, bathing, and changing of the baby. If I left the house and he stayed home with István, he washed the feces off his bottom with such an air of martyrdom that I seemed to detect, when I came back, a gloat in our son's eyes. When we went visiting or just walked down Leander Street, the whole family moved in procession: in front, I with some friends; behind me, Antal with István on his chest, the little prince inside the kangaroo carrier making happy faces; in his wake, a train of escorts, my mother and father, aunts, and a few children from the neighborhood. István napped on the balcony to good music and the rustling of the leaves. Everybody wanted to hold him; everybody smiled at him.

Antal plays elevator with him: way up, way down, way up, way down. I close my eyes and predict that our son will live in one-story houses all his life and with his analyst try to figure out why he is so afraid of skyscrapers and planes. Still, I can see that the child loves flying into the air; he doesn't even blink when he plunges down. Hop, hop, soldier boy, two on a horse, oh, what joy! I used to love this riding game on my father's knees; István loves it, too. We get so carried away by the rhythm and the silliness and the foolish cooing that the minutes become pearls strung on an invisible thread.

348

At my job with the educational counseling center I was terribly upset when I encountered the first cases of schizophrenia and incest. But the hundredth case? You acquire a certain cynicism in this profession. You know that Mr. So-and-so, for all his good intentions today, will end up, again, at the bar tomorrow and not at his job. The flesh is so predictably weak. The bulk of human material is brittle, not tenacious. You peel off layers, looking for the reality, but none of the layers are real. Being well adjusted is not real, because it differs little from death, which is not real. A child, however, is very real.

Standing in front of an apartment, I ask myself who lives behind this door. The more familiar I am with the general pattern, the more intriguing I find the cases out of the ordinary. Entering the apartment, I am loaded down with the misfortunes of a family. On the way out, in the stairwell, I begin to shove aside what I have just heard, to create some room in my mind and prepare it for the next assault. Five minutes later, in the neighboring street, another story unfolds. On the way home, on the streetcar, I try not to think of my whimpering clients. I watch my fellow passengers. How alike from a distance, how enigmatic close up. We are simple, we are complex. Not too clever, not too disciplined. Our lives are thrown into confusion by breakdowns in self-control, and punishment is not always visited upon the one who deserves it.

Perhaps the reason I've been able to do my job at the center well for the last fourteen years is that there's something of the whore in my nature. I can become involved with other people's lives four or five times a day, yet I have the resiliency to remain uninvolved. It is very dangerous to help people. The professional helper avoids becoming sucked into the insanity of altruism, the call of sainthood. You can be a saint only if you have no idea that you're a saint, and others have no idea, even after you're gone. What, then, can one human being do for another? No one is loved enough; everyone is neglected; everyone has cause to complain. We are all discontented, troubled children.

I know that my house is better than those of my clients; I know that our income is higher. Still, I think there is little difference between us. We all eat, drink, and fornicate *à la hongroise*. And there is nothing bad about that. What is bad is to waste life, to make it anemic, stupid, and gray. Most people think the opposite: that a daring life is bad. And so stifle themselves.

After a ten-day vacation I am running breathlessly to see János, taking the steps by twos. In the foyer we cling to each other, and perhaps forget to lock the front door. In my absence he busied himself with reading, cooking, playing the piano, but mostly with waiting, waiting for me. I cannot wait a minute longer. Wriggling, I tear my underpants off my chestnut hips, step out of all my clothes, pin his shoulders to the floor, and let him put me on his spit. I ride him; I am a belly dancer above him. And he watches me. I yield completely to the illness that ties me to this aging male body.

That afternoon, Antal also came to see János. The door, usually locked, opened easily as he turned the knob. Antal entered silently, hearing our loud lovemaking. He stood there a moment, then just as silently backed out of the room. Did he feel, on the stairs, like coming back and killing us both? He didn't do it. He walked away. "Yes, she was clearly having a good time," he thought. "Why should she listen only to my voice all her life? And János, wandering János, has also found a harbor to rest in." Antal made the rounds of several bars, but no matter how much he drank, he could not forget what he had seen and heard. "Now what?" he asked stupidly, the way only he can. Later that afternoon, on my way from János's bed to the bathroom, I smelled my husband's after-shave lotion. My heart in my mouth, I tried the front door: God, unlocked.

Antal has moved to Ófalu. He does some gardening: planting, hoeing. He eats our homegrown raspberries, drinks our wine, and spends time in the bars with drivers who moonlight as masons. He took the large walnut stump to the sawmill and had three tabletops cut from it: two for us, one for Franciska. He is alone a lot. Every afternoon he bikes down to the garden of a restaurant on Zsák Street. He hasn't called me for a week. He's dug in his heels. If there was a phone in the house there, I'd call him; but even though on Zsák Street there's a red phone booth from which one can make long-distance calls, and I know he has the money, he won't call. He'd rather sulk, the angel. Staring at the lake, he polishes off two glasses of slivovitz. Then he is joined by the veterinarian, whose wife, Bobe, has left him. Together they sit and look at the fire under the caldron, at the swelling moon, their glasses empty.

You don't understand, Antal, why I'm hurting you. Now that your sense of security is shaken, you have lost interest in Franciska. Around the age of forty, dear, every healthy woman allows herself a little emotional turmoil. In a marriage, if it has lasted long enough, there is always something to avenge. Whether her spouse is unfaithful or is constantly at her heels, she finds reasons for retaliation. The husband who keeps avoiding her and the husband who is always clinging to her—she hits both over the head. Every woman should seek her happiness and not feel too sorry for her man. Men should be loved, not pitied.

I see one of my many futures so vividly it is as if it has already happened. One evening, on Leander Street—Antal has returned from Ófalu—he stares at me on the balcony as if seeing me for the first time. Then keels over, frothing at the mouth. Epilepsy? A cerebral embolism? A stroke? When he comes to, the eyes of a child are looking at me. The doctor, arriving, finds an abstracted little boy sitting in the armchair. Antal does not remember anything. He follows me around like a puppy, often crouching at my feet. I tickle him; he laughs. I have to keep an eye on him, so he won't overeat. He likes to carry packages, peel potatoes, grind meat. He amuses himself by knocking my shoes together. We go to Ófalu. He tries hoeing, but hoes the vegetables out of the ground. I give him a brush, but when he whitewashes the walls, he makes a mess of things. All that he is capable of is shaking the apple tree and gathering the fallen apples in a big bowl. When I ask him anything above the comprehension of a four- or five-year-old, he says, with a sad look, "I don't know." In bed, he lies next to me, holds on to me. I must confess that in his new humbled state he gives me more pleasure than ever before. His smile has the brilliance of the blue sky. Occasionally he hides at the bottom of my closet and giggles when I find him.

9.

On the adolescence of middle-aged men

Early Experiences

János is telling how Klára, Laura, Kobra, Antal, and he used to wait for one another every day around noon to do something together. If the weather was good, we'd go to the Danube. Laura had a keelboat and Antal a skiff. The keelboat was our cruiser, the skiff our destroyer, and the five of us were the navy. Antal, of course, was the admiral, and Laura the vice admiral. The two capitalists. Ah, the shameful power of wealth! In the boat, Kobra would stare at Klára's back; he, too, had an obsession with ownership, an instinctive sort of capitalism. By that time, he was no longer falling down and rolling in appreciation of my jokes. A fateful love was raging between those two, preventing them from noticing others. We turned a blind eye on Kobra and Klára. The only interesting thing about their weakness was its perverted character: It was almost incest, because they were first cousins, Kobras both. Both venom-tongued, and for that reason both as polite as mandarins. Two serpents, bodies entangled, necks stiff, facing each other.

Mixing love and friendship, Laura and I felt, was in bad taste. Friendship ought to be magnanimous, not possessive. It was loftier than love because it was selfless. In love, you could kill out of jealousy, but friendship never led to murder. Laura and I were the eighteenth-century freethinkers, advocates of the Enlightenment; Klára and Kobra were the romantics. They demanded that each be able to read the other's thoughts. Klára would lose her temper: "How can he be such a blockhead?" And there was something atavistic in the tie between them. They had a story about having slept together, completely naked, at the age of five, and a governess's spanking them both in the morning. Also, they were together toward the close of the war, two starving eleven-year-old comrades.

Laura and I were more sociable. We went to the movies together, to parties together, though at parties each of us was a free agent who could flirt with whomever he or she fancied. If I did not feel like going home, I slept over at Laura's. Her father was always glad to have someone to tell about the chaotic situation in his nationalized factory. Antal at the time was involved with a raven-haired waitress. He would meet her at closing time. After a night on the town, they would go to his house, because his father allowed such things. Antal kept his adult life separate from the one he shared with us, his younger and less experienced friends.

On Lupa Island, Laura's family had a vacation house, built on stilts, that somehow escaped nationalization. We would sail there, settle down on the terrace, and drink milk with rum. We took food with us but never enough. As for eating, I don't want to point a finger, but Antal could put away a whole roasted goose with all the trimmings. Laura was more exuberant with her food, Klára more nervous. Laura loved it when people used her stomach as a table. That's where the green-pepper-and-cheese sandwiches would be piled. "I'd rather have the calories on me than in me," Laura would say. Always careful about her figure. But when she did eat, she ate with incredible gusto, happily filling her wide-boned, muscular, appetizing body. And she always had hidden reserves to be conjured out of the dark, if nothing else a bag of sticky raspberry candy. And if she didn't have raspberry candy, she would say, "Come to my house." And that would open a new chapter in the interrupted stream of our novel.

In my adolescence, I dreaded the thought of marriage. No slave state could oppress me as thoroughly as a wife. Marriage was like patriotism; no wonder politicians were all for it. On the other hand, when you thought about it, what could be more wonderful than to walk into the late afternoon of Greater Budapest and pick up a woman? Or to buy yourself a woman for the night, a fresh new miracle served hot with all the trimmings that go with living flesh? Let us now tactfully follow the route of young János Dragomán. He comes to a yellow intersection, turns right, enters the first building. A neoclassical apartment house with a wide courtyard; wild grapes on a green fence; the smell of fried meat and stewed cabbage. On the pale-pink marble stairs, a frayed reddish runner. The brass handle is high on the heavy door; the bell hums invitingly. This young man should be solving the world's problems in a long philosophical poem, but he is here instead, standing in front of this door. In a short while he'll be face to face with Madame Calypso.

Madame Calypso is the greatest public mother-in-law of all time. She looks hard at your face, exchanges a few words with you, and knows exactly which woman to give you—like a wise old-time waiter who sizes up a person in a glance and brings him either cabbage soup or something spicier. The more daring guests, of course, want not only her girls but Madame Calypso herself. János is getting cold feet, but before he can turn and run back down the stairs, the maid, wearing a black hat and veil, opens the door. She leads him into the hallway. He'll have to wait a little. She presses a button, and a wall parts. On a small stage bathed in mauve light, an extremely large woman with flaming red hair appears before him. Green paint under the eyes; orange-yellow lipstick; ultramarine nightgown. "Your first time, isn't it, little prince? And I suppose you want a discount and sympathy? I know all about initiation, my dear. I have just the one for you. Do sit down and let's drink a toast to our friendship. I hope you will visit us again. I hope that our artistic institution can please the new generation, too. I will now put a black cloak over your head and remove it only when it's time. Remember, little prince, you are not taking an examination. There are no problems to solve and no grade is given. Relax."

He hears a rustling. Even through the cloak he can sense the light's turning red. A piano plays. The cloak is removed. He sees the piano player, a bald man with a white cane and dark glasses, who is only pretending to be blind. A tiny bell rings, and Dragina glides into the room. A strange coincidence of names, Dragomán, Dragina. She puckers her lips; her eyes are smiling, her hair is straw blond, her whole body still tanned from last summer. She wears a light lemon-colored robe and nothing under it. Her pubic hair, too, is straw blond. "You want me?" she asks. János nods. "Follow me!" she says. When he nods obediently, his wavy brown hair falls across his forehead. In the hallway she looks back at him; with a jerk of his head he flicks the hair back into place. A twittering of canaries.

Dragina puts her arm around János's neck. "My little seducer. Here is my room. You may lock the door. Take a few deep breaths, walk around the room a few times. You can look out the window, too." Stretching her long legs, she settles down on a hassock. "For your information, I am of Scandinavian-Polish descent, noble and proud. Now you can look at me. Yes, this room is mine only. The other girls can't come in here. Tell me, love, how much money you have on you." "A hundred forints." "In what denominations?" "Twenties." "And what did you hear about the price?" "Fifty?" "And how much did you plan to pay?" "Sixty." "A generous gentleman. Some people bargain, you know. Sometimes I pick a man even though I know his character is bad. Once, a man died right on top of me, and he wasn't that old, either. And once, a filthy creature offered to pay me anything if I took a taxi with him to the cemetery at Farkasrét and let him screw me on top of a grave. His mother's? Of course. How did you know? Do you read about that in your schoolbooks? I'm talking like this because I know it's your first time with a woman and I want you to loosen up a little. I imagine your heart is in your throat, poor thing. I'll take all five twenties. I want you to be left with nothing. You'll borrow or do without, but you will think of me.

"Before you lie down next to me," she says, "take a good look at the hill between my legs. You see it? It's yours. Approach it wisely. Let's not deprive ourselves of pleasure. Approach, withdraw, approach. Take your time. Now, just fit it in nicely. Good. And now get into a rhythm, tear me up, my precious. Let our throats fill with wild noises." And she demonstrates a wild noise. A shudder courses through the jungle.

Dragina had small pointed breasts. Her body was slender and unaccountably fragrant. On her left arm I saw a tattooed number, Auschwitz. She was nineteen, I was fifteen. When she came back from the camps, she had no one. She met Madame Calypso. Sometimes she would wake with her own screaming; in her dreams she was being whipped. I sold my books to see her. Eventually she married, and in 1956, with her children, settled in New Zealand. She jogs and swims every morning, and sails in her own private little bay.

In the Margin
of an Old Periodical

A few years ago—it was not long after the fire—Laura and I were returning to New York from a prolonged Eurasian tour. Lectures and conferences. Even in the taxi, we were enchanted by the city's gigantic reality and glittering make-believe. We unpacked and threw the suitcases into the walk-in closet. I took a short rest, tried out my new acquisition, a cedarwood pipe. Our old elevator groaned familiarly as it took us downstairs. We headed for the East Village, whose streets are far from rich and luxurious, and where tourists are occasionally mugged. But the people are friendly, and a wheelchair can easily be navigated over the small inclines built into the sidewalks at every corner. We bought ham and aspic from our Ukrainian butcher, oranges and vegetables from our Korean grocer, and bread from our hook-nosed Italian baker. They were all pleased to see us, asked where we had been, where we had spent our vacation.

This city makes Europeans anxious, because it includes not only Europe but also the whole world. Europeans dislike the nonwhite world; that's why they turn up their noses at New York. The big city is self-satisfied, arrogant; smaller cities console themselves with their greater refinement and intelligence. Many people would like to move here, but don't; they prefer to rail against New York. Good literature comes out of this situation. The Jewish prophets, in provincial Jerusalem, railing against metropolitan Babylon.

In that early autumn, at the beginning of the eighties, intellectuals were under pressure: The right was vocal, the liberals quiet. I could still publish and teach what I believed and not worry whether the mayor or the president approved of it. Thanks to the Constitution. But for me the atmosphere was not pleasant: silly conservative gloating, personal attacks, intellectuals settling accounts. A number of

Jewish writers appeared on the militant right; European critical relativism was not doing its job. But we, conference-hopping tourists at numerous locations around the globe, issued neatly worded declarations about the freedom of the writer.

When I walk alone down Avenue A, young men, hanging around, hiss at me between their teeth: Smoke, smoke. Or: Sensi, sensi. Don't buy Taiwanese sensimilia from these men; most likely it's some weed from Central Park. A small black boy offers a huge tape recorder for sale. He has it wrapped in burlap and is holding it under his arm. Everybody he stops assumes that the merchandise is stolen, but what the hell, what difference does it make? The police patrol could be tripled to keep an eye on children like this one, but the local voters wouldn't go for that. Professor Dragomán, who has acquired a reputation as a psychic because some of his predictions happened to come true, is now on his way to visit a real psychic in her Tarot-reading workshop. She sits in a window reading a book as she waits for her customers. In the back room of the establishment, you may choose among Southeast Asian and Central American grasses. I enjoy the throng at the corner of Sixth Avenue and Eighth Street. A block party is going on; different bands take turns playing; a woman on stilts coaxes children to dance with her. The local council representative is happy to announce that so many different people live in harmony in this community, and he rattles off a long list of nationalities. He is particularly pleased that for this party a band has come all the way from Houston Street. If the truth be known, I had tears in my eyes.

Cheap novels on the sidewalk, also Wittgenstein and Schopenhauer. And behold, a red-and-yellow booklet with a Hungarian title: *Társadalmi Szemle: A Magyar Dolgozók Pártjának Elméleti Folyóirata* (The Theoretical Journal of the Hungarian Workers' Party). It's the December 1949 issue, with Stalin's picture on the cover. Progressive mankind was then celebrating Stalin's seventieth birthday. The vendor is an aloof black youth who usually has good philosophy books wrapped in cellophane on his carpet; he sells them for exactly half their list price, not a penny less, and no bargaining. His speech is clipped, haughty. "Do you know what this is?" I ask him, after giving him a dollar for the Theoretical Journal. "No, but I knew someone would buy it." "How?" "Every item finds its buyer," says the black youth, and turns away from me.

December 1949. Along with others, the grateful Hungarian people had sent a trainload of gifts to the great Stalin. Countless miniature engines and ships; children's drawings depicting our carefree, beautiful, happy lives. All arranged in an exhibit for us to see before it was put on the train. In the windows of butcher shops, the image of the Great General sculptured out of hardened lard. The sculptors were paid by receiving as much lard as their creations weighed; they tended toward monumentality. Here and now, I am not afraid of this yellowed booklet in my hand. Back then, fear crept into our hearts as autumn creeps into Paris in Ady's famous poem. I no longer am required to listen, every afternoon until six or even later, to the "Stalin Cantata" played by the brass band of the State Security force. "Stalin is our battle, Stalin our peace, and with Stalin's name the world will be a better place!" The melody, repeated hundreds of times, was indelibly pounded into my head. One day we learned that our next-door neighbor, a state under secretary, had been hanged. In this way we learned the style of the State Security force. A style I would always hear echoed in the playing of their bombardons and kettledrums. The under secretary, a stout, short, self-respecting man, was the son-in-law of the republic's president. His wife was also stout, short, and self-respecting. And yet suddenly the under secretary was hanged. How could anyone feel safe after that? From my window, I could see the tuba. Above the band, red drapery with golden letters hanging on all the houses in the square. A robust choir joined the band in the "Stalin Cantata."

Every morning, on the way to school, I met David Kobra at round, busy Körönd Square. He was then living in what can only be described as a den of iniquity. But you can ask him about that. He lived with his aunt Éva, a redhead who worked as a dressmaker, had to put up with a senile husband, and knew a great deal about life. Kobra and I continued to school together. At Körönd Square (formerly Hitler Square), ageless plane trees shed their leaves. And the equally ageless Zoltán Kodály, white-bearded, stepped from one of the luxury apartment buildings. Whenever he appeared on the balcony of the Music Academy, the audience would turn around and applaud. Encountering him on Andrássy Road (now Stalin Road), we bowed, and the master bowed back. We made for the Oktogon (now November 7 Square, formerly Mussolini Square), and a couple of blocks past the Oktogon had to leave the sidewalk, because of the massive decorative steel chain that hung along the curb. The heavy links were looped over stone pillars topped with flowers. The favorite flower of the State Security force was the geranium, the flower of simple hearts. Guards, wearing parkas and carrying submachine guns, were posted in every doorway and at the corner of the block. Nobody stepped over those chains, and certainly nobody wanted to get too close to those walls.

The hub of the two square blocks chained off was the former headquarters of the Arrow-Cross Party, at 60 Andrássy Road. Today it houses an export-import company, but there is no plaque on the wall to inform us of the building's history. It was interesting to see each morning how this building—also the headquarters of the police of the People's Republic—kept swallowing up other buildings. First the adjacent buildings, then the formerly upper-class apartment buildings nearby. The moment it was done with one building, it seemed to develop an appetite for the next. Tenants were evacuated, relocated, and busy workers quickly altered the space within to accommodate the needs of the authorities. A flower box in every window. On the inside windows, bars.

Before we continue the description of this exciting political era, a word about Kobra. A country boy who couldn't have been more naïve, from a town with an unpronounceable name. This was in the fall of 1947. Kobra was so rustic he knew nothing about homosexuality. In the classroom, he didn't know what to make of it when we teased him by pretending to be queer. But Menyus Csillag was the genuine article. He would put his hands on Kobra's legs, because our friend had arrived from his godforsaken village actually wearing shorts. I could see that Kobra did not care for Menyus's caresses, but he submitted to them politely, not wanting to offend Menyus. Perhaps he thought that in Budapest such pawing was an expression of friendship. The next day, during recess, I told our country virgin that Menyus was a queer, and his father was, too, except that the old man also did it with women, hence the birth of Menyus. If Kobra had no such inclinations, he should slap Menyus, as a chaste girl slaps a masher; otherwise the school would put him forever in the category of faggots.

I took the boy under my wing. We would go swimming in the morning, in an indoor pool or at Lukács, or walk across the bridge to Margaret Island, to Palatinus Baths. Needless to say, we were always late for school. We did lap after lap, welcoming the new day, the golden September light. Kobra finally received some money from his father in the country to buy himself a suit with long pants. I took him to the tailor Mr. Gulicska, who had become our sartorial arbiter. Mr. Gulicska worked alone in a small shop, making suits from fabric his customers brought to him. He never joined the union. "I will leave this shop of mine," he said, "only for the tailor shop in prison." Kobra praised the tailor's small daughters, saying how pretty and smart they were. Mr. Gulicska nodded. "No wonder, Mr. Kobra, they are custom-made." On his knees, measuring Kobra's trousers, Mr. Gulicska asked the all-important question: "On which side do you like your tool?" "Which tool?" Kobra replied, wondering if he meant the multiblade Scout knife Kobra always carried with him. The tailor pretended to cough and looked away. I introduced Kobra to ethereal Blake, Coleridge, and Shelley. "It's ridiculous that you don't speak English. You will learn. A hundred words a day, that's nine hundred words in three months, and then you'll be able to read anything." He did not even know what the Bhagavad-Gita was. *Mon petit compagnard*, your education has been sadly neglected.

Kobra was in awe of every one of his classmates. In awe of me because I played the piano. In awe of Antal Tombor because he played the saxophone. In awe of a third because he was a champion swimmer in the butterfly stroke; of a fourth because he was a fiery revolutionary; of a fifth because he whispered that he was a counterrevolutionary; and of a sixth because he could belch Gershwin's entire "Rhapsody in Blue." The books that opened before Kobra were like a beautiful woman who unbuttons her white summer dress to reveal a tanned belly. The novice hurled himself into the world of

Dostoevski and Proust; he was Raskolnikov, he was the aging, jealous Swann. Real jealousy he learned from his girlfriend, Bori Székely. What happened was this. To tease him, I had asked how serious he was about Bori. He seemed uncertain. I was very serious about her, I said. Would he give her up for me? My intentions regarding Bori were serious indeed, albeit short-range, that is, for us to write our names in a hotel guest register as a couple. Kobra consoled himself with poetry, with Csokonai and Apollinaire. When we took him with us to the Royal Revue or the Plantage Bar (where Sanyi Madár, the tallest and most elegant boy in our class, could get us in, because his mother was a partner in the business), Kobra behaved stupidly. He hardly said a word to Bori. I had no choice but to entertain her myself. To her pearly laughter he was conspicuously indifferent. By this time he wore glasses, had learned to drink wine, and claimed he could taste the flavor of metaphors in his mouth. With Sanyi Madár's help we were able to have our raspberry juice spiked with rum and allowed to watch Sziszi Henciday dance. Bori kept laughing because of the way Sziszi wiggled her backside. I could see that for Kobra, Sziszi was like a red tornado. He was enthralled.

To the young man from the country our capital was a jungle full of wonderful and witty characters. My father, for example—a bohemian who rubbed elbows with journalists and poets, at home in gambling dens and at the races, familiar with all the conventions of night life, and prevented only by his modesty from making your head spin with his stories. An elegant bald man with a dyed, neatly trimmed beard. His shirts were ironed smooth as mirrors. He wore a wide-brimmed hat, smoked a short English pipe, and turned up the collar of his coat. The most splendid specimens of my father's generation belonged to a dying race.

In our own generation, the more unconventional ones left school, left the country, and some left the world of the living. Most of the rest were swallowed up by politics; they became Party functionaries, or soldiers, or prisoners. One institution or another claimed them. The borders closed; there were fewer things to read; private lending libraries were shut, and in the public libraries many books were weeded out and banned. Jazz disappeared from the radio. In our classroom, discussion and debate ceased. The essays of Zhdanov about Soviet art and literature, a book in a pale-blue binding, were sold all over Budapest.

An early winter evening. We're walking home after hours of loafing around. On Stalin Road, in that complex of buildings that is the mighty fist of the dictatorship of the proletariat, the lights are on in all the windows. Perhaps, in there, somebody has just been presented with a choice: sign on the dotted line, or else. A door in the block of buildings opens, and a man steps out to the sidewalk. He is hunched over; his coat is threadbare. Across the street, a woman is waiting, not daring to approach him. He walks to her and hesitantly, slowly, leans on her. "My God, your teeth!" A whimpering sound comes from the man. "They knocked me to the floor, they stepped on me, they kicked me. Like a dog." We move on. "Why like a dog? Who steps on a dog?" said Kobra, disagreeing with the simile.

Amalia

As János goes up the stairs, his neighbor Amalia comes down the stairs. She is on her way to church and then to do her shopping. She is nearer seventy than sixty but still walks with a bounce in her step and sways her hips. And János still finds her beautiful. She was the second woman he saw naked and was permitted to embrace. That was forty years ago. In those days, Amalia was the talk of the building; of the children in the courtyard, the women on the balconies, and the men around the card tables outside in the square. Even in the kosher wine cellar of the Jewish community they spoke of Amalia. Her blond hair in a large bun; her full lips and full breasts; her solid body. Before he dashed his brains out on the concrete below, Amalia's husband, hurling himself from the fourth floor, found time to yell, "I love you, Amalia!" Of course he loved her. Who didn't? The brass plate on her door was always sparkling; her pantry was always full of apricot jam. She was all summer laughter. Her next husband had a freshly ironed shirt waiting for him every morning, and a piece of fried meat with his customary tea. Amalia's bedroom was fragrant with the lavender she kept among her linen.

Now past his fourteenth birthday, János followed Amalia on her morning rounds, keeping a respectful distance. He was on the hunt. One morning, at the market, standing behind her, he opened his mouth and in a voice that sounded strange even to him said, "I'll carry that basket for you." There was a bottle of milk, cherries, a live hen, and eggs in the basket. When they reached her kitchen door, János, once again, with the daring of one who prepares himself for a mortal leap, said what was in his heart: "I'll help you with the cherries." His joy bordered on delirium when he was admitted. He was allowed to sit on a low stool by a white enamel bowl, in which the shiny, bleeding, pitted bodies of sour cherries were soon piling up. Meanwhile divine Amalia took a kitchen knife, whose blade had become quite thin through repeated sharpenings, and so adroitly slit the throat of the hen that it did not even have time to screech. As she cleaned the bird, she found a number of eggs inside it. That made her happy; they would taste wonderful in the soup, she said. János asked the lady of the house if he could kiss her. Amalia laughed, thought for a moment, then said, "All right, you may kiss me." She had only to put the knife down. He had never felt anybody's tongue in his mouth before. It was a soft, slow-turning tongue. He felt her heavy breasts, her belly against him, and his pants grew wet. "Come," Amalia said, and drew him into her room, where there was a sofa, a large radio, and a conjugal double bed. The bed was piled high with pillows, quilts, eiderdowns. Covered with pink plush, it seemed like a tall strawberry shortcake with the kind of whipped cream that made your teeth stick together. János would have loved to fall on it, but he didn't dare. Amalia turned on the radio. First, the song "My Room Is Filled with Tears." Then a report on the flooding. It was the season of heavy summer rains. From Paks to Mohács, the Danube was rising. Beyond the wardrobe, in the corner, behind a finely embroidered curtain, a shower stall and a bidet, installed by Amalia's first husband. One of her girlfriends claimed that Amalia shaved and scented her private parts. She had once seen her doing it. In those days, rubbing your whole body with a milk-based cream was considered a lewd act. Amalia also had her unique perfume, a kind János never again encountered. It was prepared by Amalia herself, from flowers and who knows what else.

And now she faced János, her dress open in the front. She kept the boy at arm's length, searched for something in his eyes. Whenever Amalia hurried by the men of the building, whether they were young or old, she panted slightly, smiling at her own haste. Once, on the street, a man grabbed her bottom. With the back of her hand she hit him with such swiftness and force that he called to the police for help. People always greeted Amalia with a feeling of happy surprise, even when they had been talking behind her back, saying bad things about her. In the early summer, already in her light, red silk dress, she would walk past us, her arms and calves the color of fresh rolls, gliding by as if on a magic carpet. At the butcher's she got the best pork chops; at the dairy, her sour cream awaited in her own special china cup. If movers had ever showed up at her apartment, the whole building would have been brokenhearted.

Chappy's jazz band was playing on the radio when their bodies parted. Amalia cleaned János with the wet corner of a towel she had prepared earlier, because he was a little bloody. Then she covered herself with a housedress and peered out the window. In another corner of the room stood a sewing machine. Amalia was a seamstress; her husband, a taxi driver. And taxi drivers, with their flexible schedules, could come home at the most unexpected moments. The sofa was covered with a red spread. The alarm clock, too, was red, as was the armchair slipcover. Only the curtain wasn't red; a red curtain would have been too much. It was lemon yellow. Amalia loved the color red. Her mother was Turkish. Her father had brought his young bride from Bosnia, where he served with the army. Turkish women are accommodating; their husbands, blessed. After a brief discussion Amalia and János felt the need to unite again. This way, that way, all possible ways. She breathed hard, made a strange groan, and said the word *good* very slowly through her teeth. Exhausted, they lay beside each other. More cleaning off, more peering out the window.

The radio inveighed against the church. Amalia, at the window again, turned quickly and almost threw János out of the apartment. "Go! Now!" He went downstairs and out to the square. Just then, swinging his flat cap in his hand, the taxi driver was turning the corner.

The taxi driver was unable to impregnate Amalia, who wanted children. Along came a bus driver, and fortune smiled on him. Amalia gave birth to a girl. For many years the daily routine remained unchanged. The bus driver came home in the early afternoon, shoved Amalia into bed, and afterward snacked on meatballs, which he washed down with a glass of wine. Grabbing his fishing gear, he would go fetch their daughter from school, and together they'd make themselves comfortable on the bank of the Danube, north of the blown-up Elizabeth Bridge, where schoolgirls sat with their books, and lovers were busy kissing. This was where he liked to sit with his daughter and his worms. While he set up his rod and reel, the little girl would sing what she had learned that day in the school choir. Her father thought she was destined to be an opera singer. But at home, Amalia would beg her, "Dear, would you please stop that caterwauling?"

One afternoon, the bus driver came home to find that his little girl had been shot by a boy who lived on the fourth floor, while they were playing with the revolver that belonged to the boy's father, an army officer. Amalia had been in the kitchen baking jam turnovers for the children, whom she heard whispering in the living room. Perhaps they were a little in love with each other. Then there was a loud bang. The children had been playing execution. The boy made the girl kneel and shot her in the back of the head. No, she would never get up again, and she would never be an opera singer. The boy thought he had removed all the bullets from the cylinders, but one had been left in. The officer was sent to jail and the boy to a correction home, and the mother moved away. Amalia and her husband remained, now childless. The bus driver kept taking his fishing rod to the Danube, but would come home with his bucket empty, staggering rather than walking. Instead of fishing, he'd drink from a bottle of wine and tell anybody who'd listen about his little girl. There he was often joined by an old man whose wife had put their one and only grandchild out to nap on their balcony, and the child got too cold and died. The old man also brought a bottle to the river. A mole on the bus driver's neck became infected and painful. It was removed at a hospital, and a week later a telegram summoned him to the cancer ward. Not long after, Amalia was wearing black.

Fani and the Rest

Did I ever tell you about my grandparents? Grandma Elza and Grandpa Vilmos? They lived on Körönd, on the third floor, above Stück's pastry shop. From their apartment they could see Zoltán Kodály standing in his window doing his breathing exercises. In those days one could still do breathing exercises in Budapest; the air was clean. Grandpa must have been about five feet four, Grandma about six feet. Leaning slightly forward, with her narrow, thin, birdlike face, she would tower over us at the table. But Grandpa, despite his size, sat at the head of the table with great dignity. He wore a bow tie all day long. At every meal he'd tie a damask napkin around his neck in such a way that he seemed to have four ears. A powerful voice issued from that silver little head, from that mouth with shuttling dentures. The voice of a respected retired wine wholesaler. There was no confusion in his life, no doubt or deception. He would pronounce judgment on the punch: bearable, awful. He liked to drink seltzer with a glass of wine on the side, from which he took small sips, as of a fine liqueur.

When the dishes were cleared, he asked me about my day, about what I was reading. Flaubert, he said, was better than Stendhal. I had my doubts about that. *Madame Bovary*, he said, was the pinnacle of literature. Poetry and precision. In the center of Grandpa's austere bookcase were many plaques, and on either side of the plaques, the classics, with gold-lettered spines. The Germans to the right, the French and English to the left. He would not go to bed without reading a memorable passage from one of the great authors. Széchenyi was his idol. The title greatest Hungarian, note, he gave, not to a military leader, but to our country's greatest citizen. An intellectual on a grand scale, Grandpa said. He had Széchenyi's diary in German. "Look at this, this is real drama. The man worked to create a middle class in Hungary, and believed he was responsible for the bloodbath that followed. What Hungarian politician since then has thought of himself as an Antichrist? He left his family; he wore the mask of a madman; he humbled himself. Why are there no novels about this man, who was a count, a diplomat, a planner, a builder, a lover, a writer, and one who feared God?" Grandpa regretted only that on the question of the emancipation of the Jews Széchenyi was not particularly liberal.

My grandparents lived near the Museum of Fine Arts. They could walk to the museum every Sunday morning and stand for ten minutes before a painting. Then they would stroll arm in arm along the park promenade, and with the disparity in their height it looked as if he were hanging on to her. Grandma Elza would hold forth on the painting they had studied that morning, and her husband, his head cocked slightly to the side, would listen carefully to what she said, now nodding, now clicking his tongue to show his agreement.

The lighting was poor at my grandparents' place. The smell of old furniture; old pictures in thick frames on the wall; chinaware and ivory figurines on the shelves. A cold apartment. Yet, at the age of fifteen, I moved in with them, having enough of my parents' dramas, of my mother's fits. I preferred to listen to Grandpa Vilmos, who said that man was the only work of art that was capable of correcting itself.

About once a month, my mother would move out, carrying luggage, which included Zizike, the canary, in its beautiful brass cage, and a mustard-colored lampshade. She always had trouble fitting all that into the taxi, and would yell at the driver. My father, sitting at the piano, would say over his shoulder, "Nusi will fill in for you tonight." Which never failed to infuriate her. On her way out, she might pull a decorative plate off the wall, throw it to the floor, and jump on it. Whenever this happened, my father would go to the nearby china shop, buy an exact duplicate of the plate, and hang it in the same place. Once, when she returned, carrying the birdcage and the lampshade, the rebirth of the hideous plate so annoyed her that she smashed it a second time, turned, and marched back out. Where did she go? To a small vacation house in Csilleberc, which my father, with good foresight and at a bargain price, had bought in the thirties. It had a large terrace, a large bed, plenty of clothing, perfumes, and cosmetics, and lamps that all had shades. I think that my mother dragged that lampshade around purely for effect.

After one of her stormy departures, I sold her party shoes and, playing poker, promptly lost the money I got for them. "What makes you think, impertinent creature," she said to me, "that I don't go to parties anymore? I want you to know that I'm going to the opera ball. Yes, I have an invitation. If your father again refuses to accompany me, well, the baron will be happy to take his place. Your mother is a lady, and a lady needs an escort. A man to show her off properly. A handsome man. And the baron is quite handsome."

The baron, with his half-inch gray crew cut, evenly tanned skull, and strong cheekbones, was always hanging around my mother. Always cheerful and glaringly healthy. He had nothing to his name except a pair of buckskin golf pants, a pair of hiking boots, a tweed jacket, and a hunting bag in which you could find everything you might need for camping out, from a sewing needle to the Bible. "Be prepared!" he'd say, always quoting the Boy Scout slogan. "What do you want from my mother, Baron? She is not even beautiful." "My dear Janos, meeting your mother more than offsets the loss I suffered when my two-thousand-acre estate was expropriated." My father hid his jealousy, adopted a phlegmatic attitude; he put up with the baron, possibly even liked him. "Your mother may cheat on me, but at least she's among the living."

A guardian angel had saved both my parents, not to mention me. Father returned from Bor, one of the three hundred survivors out of three thousand. He jumped into an open manhole, escaped, but was caught again by the Gestapo. Later, with a coal bucket in his hand, he walked out of the camp, right through the main gate. He came home to Mother on Klauzal Square. "Lucky, in a manner of speaking," he said of himself. In November 1944, our part of town became the ghetto. Father didn't have to move; he could sleep in his own bed. When there was shooting in the street, he would play his piano, softly calling to us as we huddled under the keyboard. "Curl up nicely down there, little kitty cats." Once in a while we had to go out into the street to help break up the frozen snow with pickaxes for drinking water. And the dead had to be buried.

After the war, Father was tired and didn't have the energy to accompany my indomitable mother on her long and eventful shopping trips. Suppose, for instance, she slapped a disrespectful clothier in the face. Sometimes she left the house for the sole purpose of finding someone to fight with. She loved to mete out justice. On the street, she would yell at men for letting their wives carry heavy shopping bags. If she saw a mother hitting her child, my mother would in turn hit the child's mother. After these excursions, the baron would be waiting for her across the street. Father preferred to stay at home, in his own room, and read about whales or the Amazon. Sometimes he would stand by the window, in the dark, looking out on the square.

"Baron, we're leaving this place!" Mother would announce. The baron helped her pack. By now he knew what had to be packed and where her suitcase and vanity case were kept. The two men shook hands and said good-bye. Father seemed unconcerned. Mother usually came back in a day or two. She always rang the bell seven times, to let us know it was she. "Three times wouldn't be enough?" Father asked her once. She would be standing at the door with the baron behind her, a few inches shorter than her six feet. Standing impatiently, shifting her weight from one foot to the other, her long legs in sexy net stockings. She would pat Father on the shoulder. "All right, my dear man, if you behave yourself, you'll get me back." Sometimes, slightly drunk, she would sob on his shoulder, "Oh, for the love of God, why did you have to pick me, you unlucky fool?" And Father would stroke her head and say, "Fani, my sweet, I am a lucky man."

In the spring of 1947 my mother became a Zionist. She was ready to break rocks on a kibbutz, irrigate the land, pick oranges, drive a tractor, cook in a caldron in a communal kitchen, and in the evenings work in the theater or teach jazz ballet. Perhaps she'd even perform

372

and sing herself. A milker of cows by day, the queen of the stage at
night. But it was hard to imagine my father on a kibbutz. "Döme,
you're a decadent petit bourgeois! Hopeless. How can I develop my
potential while living with you in this hole?" She turned to me, as
to an ally. "Your father has put down roots here on Klauzál Square,
between the chess tables and the jungle gym. Birds nest in his hair,
and little girls use his beard as a jump rope." Father only blinked
and smiled. For him a good evening meant the Tango: chatting with
people and crooning at his piano.

So Mother decided that we would go to the Land of Israel. On
the surface, the plan seemed feasible. Father agreed; he was Jewish
and circumcised. I agreed, but was not circumcised. The baron
agreed, too; but, not only wasn't he circumcised, he wasn't even
Jewish. "Tódor will be the ideal kibbutznik!" my mother said enthusiastically. "He's resourceful, knowledgeable, strong, and understanding." The baron considered conversion. For an agnostic mind,
Judaism was not too objectionable. "Just one of the stations on the
long road of a man's continuous observation of life." He had actually
thought of converting before, as a protest against the unfair treatment
of the Jews during the war. But instead of converting, he became the
commander of a Jewish labor battalion, and brought all his men home
alive. As a reward, the authorities offered him one hundred acres of
his former estate. All he had to do was testify against another officer,
say that the man had antihumanitarian and antidemocratic tendencies.
The baron refused, and lost his hundred acres. He liked to listen to
Father play the piano at the Tango, sip his cognac, and think. Every
fifteen minutes or so, he would come up with a sentence and jot it
down, using a thin pencil, in his leather-bound notebook. When he
had enough cognac in him, he would read to me from his notebook.
(Despite my tender age, I was often at the Tango late at night.) For
example: "If God exists, better to be a Jew than a Christian." But
the baron, I suspected, didn't need God's existence to be Jewish.

The cause of our exodus—or, rather, *aliyah*—was the great
Shlomo. He was the head of a Zionist club that dealt with immigration.
Falling under the sway of Shlomo's radical spirit, Mother would have
emigrated not just to Israel, but to the North Pole. So I had to go to

a hospital and be circumcised. A rabbi officiated, and Shlomo was the godfather; if I had been a baby, he would have held me in his arms during the proceedings. "A circumcised member is easier to keep clean," said the great Shlomo. I was not anesthetized, and the operation hurt. It came to pass, however, in that year of changes, 1948, that Shlomo, too, underwent a change. He was ready to lead us, his small group, through the Czech woods into Bavaria, in the American occupation zone, to continue from there to Haifa. He was ready to risk capture and possible torture. But then, to everyone's surprise, the light of Marxist-Leninist ethics was turned on so brightly in his brain that he immediately embraced "the Communist theory of values," as he put it, and became a "modest worker" in the Party. Modest, because he had found one even more perfect than himself. Yes, you've guessed it; it was none other than Josif Vissarionovich Stalin, the man who, rather than being led by ethics himself, determined what was ethical.

Mother left us and went with the great Shlomo to a hotel on Lake Balaton. It turned out there that Shlomo was short of funds. That was one thing Mother could not tolerate in a man. The baron always had money—Father would slip him a few bills before their departure. "Here you are, Tódor—to avoid unnecessary embarrassment." In addition to this, it was in that hotel on Lake Balaton—on that curious road to Damascus, as it were—that Shlomo's enlightenment occurred. He may also have been shocked by my mother's petit-bourgeois mentality and formalism. Suffice it to say that he exchanged his small-time religion for big-time world revolution. "The holy land is right here, beneath our feet. Here is where socialism and one's country must be built. What is a small nation's religious nationalism compared to international communism?"

Father and the baron spent two weeks drinking beer in a funereal mood. At the Tango, Father sang heartrending songs of separation and parting. Then, on a Friday night, he lit the candles and brought home a hot dinner from a nearby restaurant. The baron was surprised: How did my father know? He knew, although not all of the attending details. Mother arrived, tanned and wearing a poppy-red dress. Seven rings of the bell. I opened the door, Father and the baron behind me. The three of us must have presented a sorry sight. During Mother's absence I hadn't gone to school and, not wanting to be laughed at, kept my little operation a secret. The wound was healing slowly. I still had to walk bent over, holding my hand protectively in front of me. When my mother saw me, she laughed. "Like a woman just after delivery. Why those tiny, mincing steps?" Before we knew it, she was sitting at the head of the table. She was full of combative world-historical optimism. She told us that Zionism, in terms of dialectical materialism, was passé, totally obsolete. "Really, my dear?" Father said. "And what is Shlomo's view on this matter?" "Essentially there is no difference in our views," Mother said cautiously. "Does this mean we're not going?" asked the baron, hope in his voice. He had kept putting off his circumcision. Mother did not even remember where we were planning to go. I packed my belongings. "I'm going to Grandpa's," I said. Father nodded; the baron nodded.

Double Aria about the Year of Change(s)

"We should get out of here," János said to Kobra in the fall of 1949, after the beginning of the school year and the Rajk trials. Rumor had it that the border was being mined. We had learned this lesson in the war: Flee the place where they lock you in. Kobra, who in the meantime had begun to study English, French, and Russian, answered by quoting the famous line "Here you must live and die." A true patriot does not abandon his homeland. But the propeller plan should not be thrown out; we may need it someday. According to this plan, we would become living submarines in the Danube: propellers attached to our bellies, below us, and a length of rubber tubing in our mouths. The tubing would be camouflaged on the surface of the river by twigs fastened to a piece of floating corkwood. We'd sail to Mohács first, from there travel under water, and surface somewhere in Yugoslavia. Kobra had already carved Tito's name in his bench at school. True, he did it low, close to the floor; it was hardly noticeable. If Tito, whom both Radio Moscow and the BBC had praised to the skies during the war, was the most confounded heretic, that was enough for Kobra to like him. In all of Europe, it was the Yugoslavs who had put up the strongest, most tenacious, and most successful resistance to the Nazis. They were the least infected by cowardice. From Yugoslavia the boys would proceed to all five continents.

To survey the site, they actually sailed to Mohács. They slept in a tent and floated in Laura's keelboat, letting the Danube rock them on its wide back. They enjoyed themselves. They swam in quiet tributaries and dove off a blown-up dam into water that was green, deep, and wonderfully perilous. They were sixteen. Then, in Mohács, they heard that there was a wire net spread under the water, lifted only for boats that passed through legally. So much for that idea.

Ten years later, in the company of friends, they were talking about this propeller plan. Everybody had a good laugh. Kobra and János could still not agree on whether it would have been better to put the propeller on their stomachs or behind, over their buttocks. In front, and underneath, it could damage your family jewels; in back, on top, it would not be hidden from view. The plan still had some flaws. The informer sitting at the corner of their table was all ears. Dezsö had to be all ears, because from early childhood he had been hard of hearing. János liked to tease him. "How strange, Dezsö, to be an informer and half-deaf. There is something heroic about it. If you like, I'll dictate a nice little statement for you, slowly. I'm sure you could use it. I just got out of jail. And why shouldn't I help you out? After all, we were classmates. You buzzed around us even then. You, my dear Dezsö, are our favorite informer. So then, to continue, Dezsö, by leaving jail I came out of the inner circle into the outer circle. I wouldn't say there is no difference between the two, I wouldn't say that at all, because in there, for example, I couldn't ask the waitress for a vodka. You keep an eye on things. But we do, too, you know. I must tell you, Dezsö, that your prose is too bland, too pedantic. Your reports should be better written. The historians of the future will depend a great deal on the informers of today."

Not long after this, criminal proceedings were initiated against János. He was arrested, and many of his friends were called in for questioning. He was kept in detention for months. Although the state prosecutor filed charges, the judge assigned to the case—a woman —threw them out. The main evidence was János's statement, made in the presence of other people, that "when borders are closed, everyone is a prisoner." Interesting, that such a platitude could become the basis of a criminal charge. None of János's friends, summoned to testify, was willing to confirm that János had indeed made this statement. They couldn't remember. And the police didn't want to compromise Dezső by calling him to the witness stand. They were left with a half-witted whore, whom they managed to frighten sufficiently to sign an affidavit to the effect that, yes, she had heard János Dragomán make the incriminating statement. Cecilia was threatened; they would arrest her for soliciting if she didn't cooperate. At the trial she became even more confused than usual; she could not remember, for example, who else was present that evening at the Metropol café. But she clearly recalled that János's favorite song was the "Internationale." He was always humming the first line to himself, "Arise, ye slaves who know starvation . . ." The defense attorney was a former State Security officer who had remained an informer even after he left the service and became a lawyer. Having therefore been on both sides, as were many people below and above him, he had no difficulty countering the prosecution's charges. He obtained János's release, not by proving that the prosecution failed to provide sufficient evidence, but by proving that no crime had been committed in the first place. This was a common argument in 1963, when the majority of political prisoners were released.

Back in 1949, it was abundantly clear to us that the time of relative freedom following the collapse of Germany was coming to an end. No more arguing with the teachers or bleating behind their backs. No more no-holds-barred debates about Victor Hugo and Mallarmé. Farewell to the little school democracy we had enjoyed up to then. In our secondary school we had a student government of several parties, two newspapers, and an independent school court that dealt

377

not with legal but with moral issues. We had student representatives, with veto power, at faculty meetings. After the war, we cut our teachers down to size, curbed their often unfair, autocratic rule over us. We no longer stood for corporal punishment. A teacher had to prove himself; he was worth as much as he knew. Youth, hungry for knowledge, wanted exceptional human beings to look up to, but found only sad and pitiful men with large families to support. Awkward men, shabby from the tips of their shoes to their neckties, with nicotine-stained fingers and large pocket watches in their vests. Our chemistry teacher would scream at Kobra: "Look, young man, look at the sleeves of my jacket! What do you see? Yes, they are frayed. Look at my shirt! It, too, is frayed. On my salary as a chemistry and biology teacher I cannot afford to buy a new jacket or a new shirt. I give my all to these chemistry lessons, and you are reading poetry on the sly." Blushing profusely, Kobra looked at the teacher with empathy and contrition. To this day he remembers the chemistry teacher's sleeves and his own shame.

That was the time when Kobra and János, joined by Antal, began to visit Jeremiah. They knew Melinda when she was still in her crib. All three could make her laugh, but especially János; it was impossible not to laugh at the clownish faces he made. When Melinda started to fuss, it was usually Antal who picked her up and put her on his knees. There was always a teapot on the table, and fruit from Jeremiah's garden. And walnuts and almonds in a large wooden bowl. The boys talked about their day at school. Kobra refused to recognize the Soviet novel as the highest achievement of world literature. For making that statement in school he was promptly expelled from the student union. János put his own student-union card on the teacher's desk, as a gesture of solidarity with Kobra. "I feel much lighter," he said to Kobra, and thanked him for having given him the opportunity.

We enjoyed listening to our principal, because he had been a right-wing anti-Bolshevist, who then became a liberal democrat, and then, without missing a beat, a Marxist-Leninist. The more changes of the coat, the more successful the man. On festive occasions, standing on the dais, always with the same tics and blinking eyes, he would survey his pupils as they filled the gym to capacity and with the strong stale smell of feet. The speeches he gave were unimportant themselves, because, no matter what the subject, he was really always saying the same thing: I am the principal. By then Antal was making short films, Kobra was writing short stories, and János was passing judgment on everything.

Laci, the incorruptible Communist journalist, disappeared from our apartment house. He had been too friendly with our Yugoslav comrades. A university student next door also disappeared. When he came back from Siberia, seven years later, bald and with only a few teeth left in his mouth, he still had no idea what conspiracy against the state he was supposed to have supported. Huddled on the benches near the door of our classroom, sixteen-year-old party functionaries whispered among themselves. They looked at Kobra and his friends with the contempt they thought such dubious characters deserved. The atmosphere in the neighborhood around the school also grew increasingly gloomy. Cafés, hotels, cinemas, brothels, and antiquarian bookstores were closed. In the side streets, many shops were turned into apartments; there was no need to provide a selection to the shopper or variety to the eye. Socialist realism was spreading. A totally new aesthetics. Some of our classmates, decent and sensible boys, suddenly went berserk with the new style, the new ideology, as if in the grip of a strange fever.

The three of us, meanwhile, loved to argue with one another. One of us would mention an author, sing his praises, swear by him, and sweep the idols of the other two right off the table. Of course the other two would not take this lying down. "There's nothing more enjoyable," János said, "than knocking down the idols of your best friends and stamping on them." Kobra and János loved to stamp on each other's wool hats and grind them on the oily floorboards. Jumping up and down and dancing on each other's hats was how they emphasized their points. But with the political students—Bálint and company—we never got along. They would fawn and play up to us, and at the same time scheme behind our backs. They told everybody that we were not Marxists, but decadents and formalists. Kobra was labeled a bourgeois objectivist, János a bourgeois subjectivist, and Antal a right-wing *narodnik* Bukharinist. Since we knew that Bukharin was executed, this last label was worrisome.

Kobra said he was not anti-Marxist, but, rather, post-Marxist, because he was able to read what happened after Marx's death. "Well, what happened?" the listener asks the storyteller. "What comes after Marx?" That is precisely what Kobra found so interesting. Bálint only smiled sarcastically. Kobra wanted to be past Marx as you want to be past childhood diseases. He liked Marx's concepts—the world seemed more manageable with them—and admired Marx the author, perhaps because he was refreshingly impudent. The great beast of prey breaking through the thicket. Kobra read the first volume of *Das Kapital* twice, the volume that was well written, and then put it up on his shelf among the other great authors who, in their multitude, were the gods of his polytheism. The boys all agreed that Montaigne, Erasmus, Spinoza, and Voltaire were good. Out of respect they included Kant in their list of favorites, but did not read him much; he was too difficult.

When I was sixteen, the first day of school got off to a strange start. I walked into the classroom; everybody was sitting except János and Antal, who were standing by a window. The ones sitting were somberly intense as they sang songs of the Workers' Movement. They all watched the new arrival, to see what he would do. Will he sit with us, comrades, and join the singing? One class, one community, one heart, one soul. If not, then let him stand by the window with that rotten bourgeois elegant bearing of his and pretend to converse nonchalantly with those two. He'll live to regret it. I took my place next to János and Antal, and I knew that now all three of us were wearing yellow stars.

By 1949 you could no longer see cakes, crystal chandeliers, velvet curtains, or marble tables through the large windows of the pastry shop at the corner of Andrássy Road and Izabella Street. The windows were replaced by thick glass bricks. The pastry shop became the clubhouse of the State Security force. It must be cozy in there, we thought. It was in this pastry shop that our friends learned how to accuse themselves at their own trials. Cakes and cream puffs were the reward when the prisoner showed progress in reciting by heart the answers to be given, when the time came, to the prosecutor. Those in the pastry shop were already past the preparatory phase of torture, which took place in the basement. In the basement there was an underground stream bridged by wooden planks, on which the prisoners were made to stand. Standing there was not easy. The prisoner was forced to look into the murky, gurgling stream that ran below him, to contemplate how the water could take his body with it to oblivion. Here he learned that anything could happen to him. And the body gave instruction to the soul. Men accused themselves, condemned themselves to death. Nothing mattered anymore, when the prisoner was finally left alone, when on all fours he crawled into his cell like an exhausted animal.

And if you signed your name the next morning, you'd get a bath, you'd be allowed to sleep. All that remained to do was see the thing through to the end, to cooperate, to play your part in the show. The elevator would transport you from the depths into paradise, a paradise bedecked with gilded angels, chandeliers, and garlands, enveloped in the fragrance of whipped cream and vanilla. The father of one of our classmates, a cameraman, told his wife (who told her son, who told us) that all the trials were filmed. That out of the footage of all the trials, the final version was cut and edited. Is it possible that they actually made films? But where are those films?

In the afternoons, millions of sparrows perched on the linden and plane trees and turned all of Stalin Road into one huge stream of chirping and twittering. "The walls drip with fear. Aren't you afraid that I'll denounce you?" János asked Kobra. "Why would you do that?" "Why didn't you answer 'No, I'm not afraid'? You didn't say that because you *are* afraid. Because you are a chess player. A chess player rules out nothing." We were looking at the houses. They were permanent, they lived through and survived all regimes. A storeroom turns into the torture chamber of the national socialists, then of the international socialists, then goes back to being a storeroom. In the former playrooms of bourgeois children, prisoners were also being tortured, the soles of their feet beaten with rubber hoses. The walls were indifferent. No, they were not; they saw, they heard, they dripped with fear. The dusk, too, has something to hide, and in the innocence of the birds there is treachery. Under every construction taking place it is possible to add more floors under the ground, cellars under cellars. And there, shut off from everyone, it is you, really, who will be the torturer of yourself. Just how much resistance will you put up to protect your friend? How much pain will you take for

381

him? In the cellar, you will be told that your friend, just between us, is beating his head against a wall, carrying things too far, that he doesn't take reality into consideration, that he had ostracized himself while knowing full well that a man is more useful inside the system. By voting against him at the Party assembly, by spying on him, you are actually helping him. An honorable man puts his principles first, before his personal life. Honor demands that you denounce your friend.

Look at Bálint, in his seat at the back of the class, boasting about having gone to the border as a volunteer, in a State Security car, to help nab schoolmates, Zionists and members of the congregation of the Blessed Virgin Mary who were trying to flee the country. Bálint smiles, aware of the irony of different religions acting in concert. He is an intelligent boy, pleasantly sarcastic, but behind his pleasant sarcasm there is power, for he is already a local Party secretary. He still goes to school with us, but during recess huddles with those of his kind and in low tones discusses the Movement. Seven years later, he will agree with the process of de-Stalinization. He'll be a promising natural scientist full of wisdom and skepticism. He will have completed his studies in Moscow, will have seen something of the world. His eyes will be opened; he will believe in the democratic renaissance of Communism. But in 1949, it is Bálint who delivers the keynote address on Stalin's birthday. He speaks of the golden eagle, of a will like rock, dauntless, merciless, relentless. Bálint, like Stalin, is a man of few words. He tries not to be swayed by fear, pity, or memories of friendship.

I was expelled from the student union. One of my crimes was that "ideologically I sided with György Lukács's right-wing, bourgeois humanism and objectivism." I had claimed that Tolstoy and Dostoevski were greater than the Soviet writers. Also, in my essay on the government's three-year plan I wrote about a tired laborer, and allowed myself a few ironic thoughts concerning the enthusiastic shibboleths of the press. Having returned all the graded essays but mine, our teacher of Hungarian literature kept avoiding my eyes. After class he said, "My dear David, I had to show your essay to the principal. My back is wide, I can carry a lot, but not this. I cannot take the responsibility for your paper." He was telling me that the matter was now out of his hands, and that it was my fault, for having taken things too far. Lowering his voice, he said, "You have outgrown this school, David. If I were you, I'd seriously think about continuing my education privately."

I was called before a disciplinary committee. The physics teacher, who was the Party secretary of the school, chaired the committee. I used to sleep during his classes. He had such an awkward sense of humor that I tended to believe what was whispered about him, which is that in 1944 he was a member of the Arrow-Cross Party. The prosecutor was a student, later my friend. He was intelligent, well read, and, as they used to say in those days, "a fierce Communist." "We are angry with you, not at you," he said. He raised high the notebook that contained my essay, then dropped it on the floor. "This essay is the platform of the enemy," he said. "This is how low you have let yourself sink." In a way it was flattering that they attributed so much importance to my humble little school exercise. The committee, headed by the principal, filed into our classroom, and the principal read out loud the decision to expel me from the student union. And that, although I was being expelled only from the student union and not from the school, the latter possibility might become a reality if I persisted in spreading my poisonous ideology. After I had placed my card on the teacher's desk and left the room—I was no longer entitled to share the space with the assembled members—János got up, too, quietly put his card on the desk, and followed me out into the corridor.

The Strong Man

I always hated school. I hated the hurry, the fear of being late. The smell of school. Having to say hello left and right before eight in the morning. The prize pupil of the class turns to say, "Hello, David. A new week, new possibilities." My answer: "You want me to strangle you?" He just laughs. I hated nothing more than to listen to other people's chatter in the morning, when my mind was still fresh and active. I wanted to read. In school, my fellow humans are apes. I have to sit for five hours among forty apes, look at their shoes, their hair, and hear their inane reports. The beginning of the roll: Agamek, an idiot; Bakó, an idiot. And so on. For my eyes, the old brown slate roof of the house across the street is a pasture of relief. Winter sparrows on the lightning rod; icicles on the eaves. With the spring thaw, the snow, yellowish and hardened, would slip down the roof, the light reflected in its network of grooves. How dare this strange man rebuke me: "Mr. Kobra, would you please return your gaze to education? And kindly keep your sarcastic remarks to yourself." And I answer: "Good teacher, spare me. I'm *Mimosa pudica*, sensitive plant."

On the façade of our school, at the far end of the square, four Muses muse. Their gold has turned brown, as has the wall of decorative brick. Inside, it is dark. The floors are covered with oil to keep the dust down. The wooden windowsills are grayish green, covered with carved initials. The sooty light of winter filters through the dirty panes. I like to sit in the back and look out these windows. I don't want anybody behind me, fiddling with my back or spying on me, seeing what I'm reading. Sitting in the back, by the window, is the closest thing to not being there at all. Antal is in front of me, providing a good barrier, and János, next to me; he jabs me in the ribs if I've been asked a question. "Sir, I'm sorry, but I can put up with school only if I'm allowed to sit in the last row. Please forget your seating plan. Either I stay here in the back, or I jump out the window."

Not that the teachers are all bad. Some, in fact, are good, even excellent. But these bells are humiliating: now class starts, now it's over, and you have only a ten-minute break to talk. For the other fifty minutes of the hour they can tell you what to do, call you to account, and punish you. A regular concentration camp. If you don't revolutionize your school, it will resemble a penal colony. We are, János said, the petrels of the permanent revolution of the individual. Pupils are tamed animals. The two of us were always dressed in black, and we chose our own model: Bakunin. Marx has the whole system; Bakunin has János and Kobra. Ah, we'd say, we were Anarchy's Hydra; two heads with one body. János's aristocratic individualism was thrusting me more and more in the direction of Tolstoyan neopopulism, and a taste for physical labor. János was not tempted in the least. Stalin City was his contemptuous name for the town of Dunapentele, which was being transformed into a major industrial center through volunteer labor. Let it be built, let it bloom, without me.

Kobra spent a lot of time at the Academy Library, going through a series of books called *Hungarian Literary Rarities*. He was also making money translating *Pravda* articles dealing with culture. The translation department of the Hungarian Soviet Society paid him ten forints a page. The price of a good whore was fifty forints. He could easily translate five pages in a single afternoon. One afternoon devoted to translation, one to the libido.

What did I see in the city park one day but my precious János pushing a baby carriage and cooing at the baby of the doctor's wife, who happened to be the Dragománs' co-tenant. I found János, several times, to be quite an emotional creature. For example, he would ask to be allowed into a kindergarten to play with the children. He could also play, any time he wanted, on infamous Conti Street, on the steel beds of trunk-sized women.

On sunny mornings we would park ourselves in the long main room of a brothel, where whores would be sitting on benches on either side, knitting. János entertained them by imitating well-known actors. When Antal joined us, his herculean muscles provided a manly balance to János's tomfoolery. "You boys can come for free," the whores would say, but they meant János mainly.

Both János and I applied for private-student status. Since neither of us suffered from any serious illness, our requests were denied. From then on, with inexhaustible invention, János would list, in writing and in his father's name, the family reasons for his many absences. But the truth is, he preferred hating school from within its walls. He would answer the teacher's questions either in screams or in whispers, but otherwise brilliantly. He would close his eyes and imagine the boys as old men and the teachers as young boys. To jolt things up a bit; to change the context; to make the situation less boring. He would entangle his interlocutor in one harebrained digression after another, amusing himself but keeping a straight face all the while. You took him seriously at your peril. A harmless clown, some said.

When it comes to showing off, teachers can hold their own. They're all performers, each playing himself. Let's call on Arpád Bolensky, lecturer of mathematics. You may begin, Professor.

"All right, Mr. Kása, you may sit down. Mr. Kása is stupid, gentlemen, fatally stupid. He will remain stupid all his life. That is why nothing fazes him. Mr. Kása does not mind our lesson in mathematics as long as he can go on taking bites out of his goose-liver sandwich. His intellect focuses on the secretion of his stomach. His appetite is not spoiled by non-Euclidean geometry. Mr. Kása, with his goose-liver sandwich, expensive shoes, and fine clothes, lives better than poor Arpád Bolensky, teacher of mathematics, physics, Greek, and philosophy, summa cum laude, who in two world wars had his skin perforated several times by bullets because he was too cowardly to desert. And now this miserable teacher with an ugly and sickly wife at home and only a photograph of his daughter in his wallet—she was killed by a bomb—has to stand here and inhale the odor of Mr. Kása's goose-liver sandwich. But I want my students to know that my life is not without its pleasures. I am now reading *The Brothers Karamazov* for the seventh time, gentlemen. I spoil myself with a cup of coffee after my modest supper. I scratch the head of my dog as I read. My eighteen-year-old cat takes her place on the back of my armchair. I occasionally give in to the temptation of a bribe, but am careful that it is done publicly, for all to see, as is happening now. Ahem! No matter how stupid he is, I will let Mr. Kása pass, so that our school may be rid of him at last. On one condition. I assume that his carnivorous family tosses a number of bones into the garbage. I hereby call upon him, in front of witnesses, to put aside—or have his family's cook put aside—those bones and deliver them every Monday, before class, to my house, for my dog, who in our household has not the luxury of such a tasty item in his bowl. Behold, Mr. Kása, the price of graduation. Gentlemen, as I look at you, I am compelled to reduce the dignity the word *man* conjures up. I can do nothing else while standing here before you.

For what can a poor teacher of mathematics do, who is pierced, nay, perforated with bullet holes, and who hands over his salary, to the last penny, in an envelope, to his ugly, sickly, but still good-hearted wife?"

Let us develop the scene further. Let us summon our teacher from the dead and invite him to do a little haunting among us. Come, teacher. Sing the song of yourself, play the role of yourself. You are entitled to one return visit. He approaches our table, walks cane in hand; this Sacred Lamp of Knowledge, this apostate and prodigal son, is seeking his Father, the Eternal. Wide-brimmed hat, unbuttoned white shirt, no tie. Rosy cheeks, thick brows, a strange visage. He has come a great distance and has much to say. He has come to preside over our cabalistic hocus-pocus mystery play on Resurrection Square.

"All right, who said that?" Suddenly he stops, turns halfway around, as if to shoot from the hip with his left hand. "What did you say, Kobra? If you have any balls, Mr. Kobra, you will repeat what you just said. Aha. *Lux perpetua luceat tibi!* So the eternal light should shine for me? I should drop dead; is what you mean? Gentlemen, Mr. Kobra has given voice to the age-old wish of students regarding their teachers. Very well, impudent cur, you will stay after class for ink soup and paper dumplings.

"It is a human being you see before you, ladies and gentlemen. This teacher of mathematics, for whom Mr. Kobra, the blackguard, wishes eternal light, is a wretched man, wretched to the uttermost core of his heart. See my wounds. Here, on my chest. I'll remove my shirt so you can see it. And here, on my side, is another wound, and here, in my loins, and on my wrist, and on my ankle. Gentlemen, you have in common one advantage over me, namely, that you have survived me. Don't laugh, Kása. Your turn will come, and soon. A problem now for you all, for your feeble little brains! A problem to make even the geniuses among you quail. Get out your pencils, gentlemen. And no daydreaming about whores while you're working. I'll do that for you. The whores are mine, all the best ones! I, Arpád Bolensky, mathematics teacher, am the king of the whorehouse, and not this snot-nose freshman, Kobra, whom I send to the pharmacy

387

for *canis merga*. In that salon where strawberry lights smooth out all wrinkles, the ladies buzz around me, ignoring the sour Dragomán, whom I can compare only to Thersites. They laugh, they double up with laughter, as I deliver one wonderful joke after another. Note: They do not put cherry bombs under my chair. They do not put sneezing powder in my roll book. Or smear garlic into the collar of my overcoat. And I assure you it would not occur to any of them to bleat while I lecture. In that whorehouse, no one eats hot bread during the first period so that during the second, which is mine, he can blast stinking farts under my nose. No old-age home awaits me there. There, people can tell the difference between gold and sand. When I look at you, my dear students, I see forty bags of sand! But even if you are sand, you must sit still and listen. Quiet, there, in the corner!

"I will do selections from my program. I have been performing for quite a long time. Alas, my tuxedo has grown shiny with wear. The wings of my bow tie droop. My prostate, however, I am happy to report, is under control. The crotches of my pants are not yellowed by the laggard few drops that always remain in the hose that slumbers like an old dog. I can still afford the gold bridges in my mouth; I can still have my chin lifted. We are still keeping pace; the master is ageless, an indestructible wild boar, a thoroughbred stallion. Make way, make way for the *princeps maximus!* One of my stage names is Christo, the strongman.

"I performed one number that was not bad at all. *Pro primo*. I come on stage and slap my left biceps with a length of iron rod. The rod bends. There you are, gentlemen, all you strong johnnies and musclemen, come up on stage! Try to bend it back, straighten it out. Don't be bashful! No volunteers? Some men do come up. A sneer of contempt on my lips: for all their straining, they can do nothing with the rod.

"*Pro secundo*. An iron bar with a seat at either end attached by a chain. Well, gentlemen, who among you weighs the most? All you blubber boys, sacks of salt, Gargantuas with king-size behinds, come up here and take these seats. Two ungainly mountains of flesh clamber up on stage, sit down—and I lift the bar high into the air. I could do it with one arm, but a display of such strength might frighten them. One remains alone in mourning as well as in glory, whose wages are nothing but envy.

"And now we come to *pro tertio*, the climax. Two men carry in two gigantic steel blades, cutting edge up, fastened to a stand like a sawhorse. A flourish from the band, and Araukána, my twenty-five-year-old partner, prances in, a magnetic, fatally attractive Andalusian mare. She hugs me, and at the touch of her breasts I fall into a trance. My body is now taut, stiff as a board. In this state I am placed on the two razor-sharp blades. One under my ankles, the other under my neck. I lie across them as straight as a rod, a sweet smile on my face, as if I were resting on the softest couch.

"Then two muscle-bound giants stride onstage. Compared to them, our bodies are like graceful violin bows. On a crude cart these two gentlemen roll in an enormous rock. With all their might, their faces turning red, they huff and puff and lift the rock and put it—where, you'll never guess—on my stomach. The audience is stunned. The marrow is frozen in their spines. And your teacher lies unflinching under that stupendous weight. His body doesn't sag the least bit. It's as if a balloon had been placed on top of him.

"A woman screams. 'It'll cut off his head!' She means the blade under my neck. Araukána smiles mysteriously. And then, with enormous sledgehammers, the two giants begin to pound the rock on top of me from both sides. And note: Any member of the audience at any time can inspect the blades, can try to move the rock or lift the hammers, to verify that these are not the props of a magician. Everything is nerve-rackingly real. I am being pounded by two wicked Hephaestuses, scar-faced, their chests covered with pitch-black hair.

"Do you see that? He's taking it! Lord of Heaven, he's taking it! And with such aplomb. He rests on the blades as a bridge rests on its piers. Why doesn't the blade cut into Arpád Bolensky's neck? Why doesn't his spine snap? Why doesn't our teacher fall into a chopped-up, mutilated mass of bleeding flesh? Don't worry; nothing of the kind will happen. But probably that's just what you'd like to see, eh, ignoramuses? You'd like to be eyewitnesses, wouldn't you? Watch your teacher's dismemberment close up? Drooling for some

action, for a little gore. But the two hefty assistants lift Christo unharmed off the blades. The only signs of his ordeal are two pink
lines, one at the nape of his neck, one across his ankles.

"They put me on my feet. Araukána takes off her silver-crimson
cloak and wraps me with it. I come out of my trance. I offer the
whites of my eyes to the light. I stand on tiptoe, hold Araukána's
lizard fingers high in the air, and I bow toward you, ladies and
gentlemen. Attendants run in and dress me. Top hat and cane. With
a white-gloved hand I twirl my cane and look the audience straight
in the eye. They are mine now, completely. For three minutes we
are all silent. No clearing of throats, no rustling of candy wrappers.
Now is the perfect time for the message. The lesson to be learned
from what just took place. Our credit is good. We have
demonstrated—haven't we?—the miracle of mind over matter. With
a little help from the supernatural. Here the teacher stands, his own
Lazarus. And then what happens? Nothing happens. I wave my hand
in resignation.

"Ladies and gentlemen, the truth is, I live alone. Araukána belongs to one of my giant assistants, if not to both of them. Only on
the stage does she embrace me. I have sired a dozen children, all
with such brave genes that they have every one of them gone out to
dare the world; in other words, they have dispersed globally. On this
square, which despite renovation and the new lights is still seedy,
like myself, I am the only one left of my large family. And for what?
To sweep the ancestral crypt. To be a tent pole, a scarecrow. 'Are
you still there, old man, babbling away in the Crown?' my sons and
daughters ask when occasionally they bother to call. 'Still spouting,
are you, showing off, feeding your old lines to your second-rate
public? The world has passed you by, Papa; you're out of it.' 'What
are you doing here, Mr. Christo? Weren't you told not to come here
anymore? Tell your tall tales at home, to the four walls. Here, at the
Crown and its Ecstasy Bar we keep our stories short. We offer bright
lights and happy music against the nasty hours of the night.' "

Yoga

These walnut, cherry, pear, and fig trees are my grandfather's trees. They were planted by Jeremiah's father, János, born in 1830. In 1848 he volunteered as a revolutionary; in 1897, at the age of sixty-seven, he sired my father. The son, too, waited patiently to sire. He was fifty-one when, one lighthearted night, he and Mother assured my existence, providing the garden with an heir. There is no other house here on the mountain that since the middle of the last century has kept the same family in its womb. On this lot, the dwelling and the dwellers have intimately influenced each other. My father felt a strong obligation to the house; that's why he always returned to it; that's why he's left it to me to continue to take care of it. Yet I cannot understand why he had to put János Dragomán, like a detonator fuse, into this house—unless he liked the thought of a romantic novel blooming here, as the elm trees bloom in the garden, the edges of their leaves already brown.

My father left me this four-acre piece of real estate. The other day, a lawyer showed up. Adjusting his Italian silk tie, he said, "Madam, tomorrow we can put twenty million forints on your table, for this house and the garden." "We?" "I represent a group of investors." The house they would tear down, of course, but the lot was invaluable. That is, worth twenty million to them. The lawyer indicated that I was free to bargain—possibly I could get as much as twenty-five million—because his associates (an entrepreneur, a famous artist, and a political personage) had their hearts set on this location, this view. A postmodern house would be built here, for three families. A three-leaf-clover design. At the center of the property, a tower for meditation. On the roof, a rim of evergreens to protect against inquisitive eyes outside. The garden there, a penthouse garden, would have outdoor carpeting, all green plastic, like Astroturf. Magnificent parties would be held in it. The pond, too, would be redone, its bottom covered with bright sky-blue tiles, and so on. In other words, on this spot, in the spirit of the times, an architectural masterpiece that would have no equal in all of Hungary. And if I was unwilling to leave at any price, the three-leaf clover could be turned into a four-leaf clover, and I would become the fourth partner/owner, acquiring a group of wonderful associates in the bargain. The senior politician, the entrepreneur, and the opera star—who, by the way, had brought much honor to our country with her appearances abroad—would all love to make my acquaintance and the acquaintance of my family, which included, the lawyer believed, some well-known personalities of the opposition.

He must have detected a gleam in my eyes, because he grew more and more animated. He must have thought that I liked his offer, that perhaps I was attracted to him. The successful entrepreneur, he admitted, was none other than himself, successful because anyone in real estate, unless he's a complete idiot, is successful. I could picture myself seeing this man's face every morning in the tower of meditation, where he would be doing his breathing exercises. I asked him if he was into TM. He was flabbergasted: How did I know? He had also taken courses in relaxation. He hit the table with his right hand. "Tension!" With his left hand he stroked the table. "Release!" I smiled at him, then threw a beautiful red apple, wine-flavored, at his head. Then another, and followed that with walnuts. Ripe pears at his serge suit. Furious, he shouted that he'd send me the cleaning bill, and I would see, just wait, how his politician friend repaid me for the apples. Did I need an enemy? Well, I had one now. We'd meet again; I could be sure of that. There were some oranges left in the fruit basket. Having a good arm and taking careful aim from the balcony, I hit the man again. "You just wait. I'll get you yet, you wildcat!" No, I'm not giving up the house. It can be bombed, but I'll tear apart anyone who tries to take it from me or from my children.

And my father will come back, too, tired of his round-the-world foolishness, to be buried here in his own garden. He will lie in this ground, beside my grandfather, and I will lie beside them. It does make a difference where one lies. I sleep in the bed in which my mother conceived me and dream that my son and daughter, both gray-haired, are sitting in the garden as man and wife. With muffled thuds the large Vilmos pears fall to the grass. I cut the grass with a sickle;

I would not defile it with a lawn mower. This house lives its own quiet life. Its tenants and ceremonies do not change. We expand cautiously; we try not to destroy anything. In our eyes, the new is suspect, boorish. Let us keep all our beautiful tools, books, coats, and dishes alive.

János likes to drive at night and cross borders at the crack of dawn. Early one morning, after a farewell party, he got into his car and headed for Vienna. Near Mosonmagyaróvár he pulled off the road, got out of his car, and continued on foot to the border. He tried to climb the barbed-wire fence. Was caught. Refused to talk. Was searched. He had a valid passport and visa: an American citizen of Hungarian origin, the visa properly extended, the stamps on it authentic. The guards didn't understand; they kept questioning him, but he would not answer. He was taken to the nearest mental hospital, the one in Ófalu. Somebody there got in touch with the U.S. embassy, and at the embassy somebody called Kobra, and Kobra called me.

János squats in a corner of the lobby of the hospital, whose doors are always wide open. Treatment is based on work therapy. Suddenly he straightens up and walks diagonally across the lobby, stepping only on the black tiles. Then retraces his steps, squats again, and looks through the glass into a garden. He has spent almost a year here. Quietly, for months on end, he watches the mistletoe on the plane trees, the crows, the ambulances bringing in new patients. Elbows on knees, fingers clasped before his mouth, he sits lightly on his heels. Whenever he enters a room—his eyes on the floor, hurrying by with dance-like steps—the other patients make way for him. If, out of ignorance or by mistake, someone stands in his way, János matter-of-factly shoves the person aside. He also does breathing exercises.

Who is coming up the driveway? Is it the short dark-haired psychologist or the tall blond one? When the glass door is opened, János obediently steps aside. He doesn't speak to anyone, but is attentive when spoken to. Dr. Samu, the bespectacled psychiatrist, his face turned to the sun, consults with Kinga, the short psychologist, and Bori, the tall psychologist. "Professor Dragomán, would you like to share a cigarillo with us?" Dr. Samu asks. "Dr. Kinga here is of the opinion that you are dissembling, that you came here only to do yoga. Not at the expense of the Hungarian government, I might add, but at the expense of an American insurance company, which pays good

American dollars to the People's Republic in return for our modest hospitality. Considering your financial situation, not to mention the republic's hunger for American dollars, you can stay here as long as you wish. Please feel free to order a little shock treatment or a therapeutic straitjacket whenever you like. Whatever strikes your fancy. In exchange for your dollars, we can provide your excellency with any form of torture. But if you tire of such masochism, Professor, perhaps you'd like to join us for bridge tonight, after the patients have gone to bed. Pleasant conversation, food, drinks, background music, and a few objets d'art to admire."

Dr. Kinga's voice is soothing. "Mr. Dragomán! I know that you are in no position to accept Dr. Samu's invitation. I must tell you that I do not approve of the harassing, ironic tone of my colleague. You do not speak because you cannot. Let me be your interpreter. Let me guess at what it is you wish to tell us. Look at me. If the answer is yes, close your left eye once. Would you like to join us this evening?" After some time, János slowly closes his left eye.

That was how things stood. When Dr. Kinga called to report on your progress, I thanked her, and the next day was at the Ófalu hospital, squatting beside my love. Into your hand I put the striped pebble you once gave me as a cabalistic talisman. (I rub it with my thumb whenever I'm nervous.) You dropped it. I picked it up, put it back in your hand. It fell again. We repeated this exactly seven hundred seventy-seven times. Later you laughed when I mentioned the number. Of course you were counting, and of course you knew that I knew you were counting. You were testing me, had devised a cabalistic test for the two of us. I passed the test. The next task was for you to give me back the pebble, without my having to scoop it from your hand. Three hundred and thirty-three, I said to myself hopefully. This went all right, too. You gave me back the pebble. From then on, it was child's play. You began to talk, and you returned to us. Obstinate Calvinist and stubborn Jew, you will both, Antal, János, be sitting in the living room, and my grandfather will be there, too, and my grandmother, and all my friends and rivals and conspirators. A room of grown-ups and one infant, in whom the redeemer is slumbering. Everybody I love will be there, in my house. For there is no more tyrannical will on earth, my dears, than the will of love.